GRIDIRON

Philip Kerr was born in Edinburgh in 1956, and lives in London. He is the author of *March Violets*, *The Pale Criminal*, *A German Requiem*, *A Philosophical Investigation*, and *Dead Meat*, which was shown on television as *Grushko*. He has also edited two anthologies.

BY PHILIP KERR

March Violets
The Pale Criminal
A German Requiem
A Philosophical Investigation
Dead Meat
Gridiron

Praise for Philip Kerr

A PHILOSOPHICAL INVESTIGATION

'Brilliant and scary'
Guardian

'Breathtakingly clever . . . awesomely ambitious
. . . like *Bladerunner* rewritten by Borges'
Time Out

'Kerr's is the sort of crime writing in which ideas
really dazzle and move the reader . . . clever, tightly
plotted, well-written and full of good jokes'
Times Literary Supplement

'A truly intellectual thriller that makes the brain
cells as well as the hairs on the back of the neck
tingle'
GQ

'With an observant eye for detail, Kerr reveals a
fine-tuned ability to make his fiction credible by
combining the futuristic with the familiar'
New Statesman & Society

'This remarkable novel [has] a freshness that's
cold as ice'
Sunday Times

'A stunning novel'
Ruth Rendell

Philip Kerr

GRIDIRON

VINTAGE

Published by Vintage 1996

2 4 6 8 10 9 7 5 3 1

Copyright © Philip Kerr 1995

The right of Philip Kerr to be identified as the author of this work has been asserted by him in accordance with the Copyright, Designs and Patents Act, 1988

First published in Great Britain by
Chatto & Windus Ltd, 1995

Vintage
Random House, 20 Vauxhall Bridge Road, London SW1V 2SA

Random House Australia (Pty) Limited
20 Alfred Street, Milsons Point, Sydney
New South Wales 2061, Australia

Random House New Zealand Limited
18 Poland Road, Glenfield,
Auckland 10, New Zealand

Random House South Africa (Pty) Limited
PO Box 337, Bergvlei, South Africa

Random House UK Limited Reg. No. 954009

A CIP catalogue record for this book
is available from the British Library

ISBN 0099594315

Papers used by Random House UK Limited are natural, recyclable products made from wood grown in sustainable forests. The manufacturing processes conform to the environmental regulations of the country of origin.

Typeset by Deltatype Ltd, Ellesmere Port

Printed and bound in Great Britain by
Cox & Wyman, Reading, Berkshire

For Jane, as always, and for William Finlay

'Did I solicit thee from darkness to promote me?'

John Milton

'. . . that glass of ice water in the face, that bracing slap across the mouth, that reprimand for the fat on one's bourgeois soul, known as modern architecture.'

Tom Wolfe

Prologue

'We are in pursuit of a new idea, a new vernacular, something to stand alongside the space capsules, computers and throwaway packages of an atomic electronic age . . .'

Warren Chalk

The American glanced at the setting sun in the sky above the new Shenzen Football Stadium and prayed that the execution would be over by the time the denuded centre spot was in shadow. Anxious to be getting shots, he focused his camera on a group of self-important men, some of them dressed in Mao jackets, but others wearing plain dark suits, who were taking their seats a dozen or so rows away from him.

'Who are those guys?' he asked.

His fixer and translator stood on the toes of her high-heeled shoes and followed the line of his long lens across the heads of the crowd beneath them.

'I think, Party,' she said. 'But some businessmen also.'

'Are you sure we've got permission to do this?' he murmured.

'Yes, I'm sure,' said the girl. 'I bribed the head of PSB in Shenzen. They won't bother us today, Nick. You can believe it.'

PSB was the People's Republic of Communist China's Public Security Bureau.

'Baby, you're a star.'

The Chinese girl smiled and bowed her head.

By now the stadium was nearly full. The mood of the several thousand strong crowd was expectant but good humoured, as if it really expected to see a football match. At the arrival of the four condemned men, each of them held tightly by two PSB guards, there was an excited murmur. As was usual, the heads of those who were condemned to be shot had been shaved and their arms bound just above the elbows. The crimes they had committed were listed on cardboard placards that hung around their necks.

The four men were forced to kneel at the centre spot. The face of one man filled the viewfinder of the camera and the American was struck by its dull expression, as if its owner cared little whether he died or not. He guessed they had been drugged. He pressed the shutter button and moved on to the face of the next man. His expression was the same.

As the PSB man aimed his AK47 assault rifle at the back of his first victim's head, the American checked the position of the shadow on the pitch. He tried not to smile but found that the urge was irresistible. These were going to be great photographs.

The Los Angeles Police Department had never cared much for public assemblies of the city's populations: Hispanics, Native Americans, Blacks, Okies, hippies, gays, students, and strikers had all felt the batons and stun guns of LA's finest on one occasion or another. But this was the first time that any of the twenty-five helmeted officers on duty outside the half-built office block on the building site that was to become the new Hope Street Piazza could remember the city's Chinese community gathering to voice its protest about something.

Not that Los Angeles had a very large concentration of Chinese when compared to San Francisco. Chinatown itself, in the city's North Broadway area, right on the doorstep of LA's Police Academy, was no more than twenty thousand people. Most of the city's fast-growing Chinese population lived in suburbs like Monterey Park and Alhambra.

4

It was not a very large demonstration either: just a hundred or so students, protesting against the Yu Corporation and its apparent complicity in the repressive rule of the People's Republic of China. The Corporation's eponymous chairman and chief executive, Yue-Kong Yu, had recently been pictured in the pages of the *Los Angeles Times*, attending the execution of some dissident Chinese students in Shenzen. But because this was LA after all, and even small crowds could get quickly out of hand, an Aerospatiale helicopter from the LAPD airforce kept a discreet electronic eye on the proceedings and provided regular digitized communication bulletins for the central dispatch computer that was located in a missile-proof bunker five floors beneath City Hall.

The demonstrators were peaceful enough. Even when the motorcade of stretch limousines bearing Yue-Kong Yu and his entourage arrived at the site, they did little more than chant and jerk their placards up and down. Shielded by police and half a dozen private security men, Mr Yu moved smoothly up a flight of steps and through his new building's front door, a Neolithic stone dolmen brought from the British Isles, without even looking at the angry young men and women.

In the nearly finished atrium, Mr Yu turned and looked back at the door, obliquely positioned for better *feng shui*. He had bought the three ancient standing stones – one placed on top of the other two as a lintel – because of their similarity to the Yu Corporation logo, itself based on the Chinese character symbolizing good luck. He nodded appreciatively. He knew that his architect had not wanted the stones in such a modern building. But once Mr Yu made up his mind he was not easily dissuaded. For all the architect's opposition he had done well, Mr Yu thought. It was a most auspicious-looking doorway. And a fine-looking atrium. The best he had seen. Better than the Yoshimoto

Building in Osaka. Better than the Shinn Nikko building in Tokyo. Better even than the Marriott Marquis in Atlanta.

When the last of his guests had followed Mr Yu inside, the sergeant in charge of policing the demonstration waved one of its number towards him, having decided that the young man's loudhailer marked him as the group's ringleader.

Cheng Peng Fei, a visa student in business administration at UCLA, stepped quickly forward. The only son of two Hong Kong lawyers, he was not the type to make a policemen tell him something twice. He had a flat, almost concave disc of a face.

'You're going to have to move your people over to the other side of the site,' drawled the police sergeant. 'Seems like they want to drop a tree branch from the top level, and we wouldn't want any of you getting injured, now would we?' The sergeant smiled. A Vietnam vet, he regarded all orientals with deep suspicion and hostility.

'Why?' said Cheng Peng Fei.

'Because I say so, that's why,' snapped the sergeant.

'No, I mean why do they want to throw a tree branch from the top?'

'What am I, a fuckin' anthropologist? How the hell should I know? Just move it across the other side, mister, or I'll book you for obstruction.'

The topping-out ceremony was traditionally performed when the topmost stone was fixed to a building, an act signalled by a branch of evergreen being thrown to the ground and burnt, and a toast drunk to celebrate completion of the structural envelope. But as those who were waiting on the rooftop knew, the real topping-out ceremony had taken place some ten months before, when Mr Yu had been unable to attend. The envelope was already more than half-filled, but Mr Yu, making a rare visit to Los Angeles to sign a deal to supply the United States Air Force at Edwards Air Force Base with

6

six Yu-5 Supercomputers (each one of them capable of performing 10^{12} operations a second), was keen to see how his new smart building was progressing. Mr Yu's son, Jardine, who was managing director of the Yu Corporation in America, had wanted to mark the occasion of his father's visit, and so a second topping-out ceremony was arranged, with a cosmetic 'last' roof slate placed on top of the twenty-five storey building by Arlene Sheridan, a Hollywood actress rather advanced in years whom the seventy-two-year-old CEO had long admired.

The rooftop event was attended with an unusual degree of formality: a sit-down lunch of ripened fruit, Chinese hens stuffed with lucky red charms, a golden pig, and Tsingtao beer were provided for fifty guests, including a senator, a congressman, the deputy mayor of Los Angles, a federal judge, a USAF general, a studio head, representatives of the Downtown Strategic Plan Advisory Committee, selected members of the press (with the notable exception of the *Los Angeles Times*), the architect, Ray Richardson, and the chief engineer, David Arnon. No workmen were actually invited, unless you counted Helen Hussey, the site agent, and Warren Aikman, the clerk of works. A Taoist priest had been flown in from Hong Kong at the request of Jenny Bao, the Yu Corporation's *feng shui* consultant in LA, who was also present.

An urbane, effusive little man, Mr Yu greeted his guests with a left-handed handshake, his right arm having been withered since birth. For those who were meeting him for the first time, it was hard to reconcile his vast wealth (*Forbes* magazine had estimated his personal fortune at $5 billion) with the knowledge that he was on excellent terms with the Communist leaders in Peking. But Mr Yu was nothing if not pragmatic.

After the introductions, it fell to Ray Richardson to introduce the building and the ceremony. The fifty-five-year-old self-styled 'architechnologist' at the microphone would have passed for ten or fifteen years younger. He wore a cream linen suit, a soft blue shirt and a quiet tie with a hand-painted look, all of which might have marked him as a European, most probably an Italian. He was in fact Scottish, but with the kind of accent that demonstrated long exposure to the southern California sun. Those who knew Ray Richardson well said that the accent was the only thing about him that showed any evidence of warmth.

He unfolded several typewritten sheets, smiled experimentally and, finding the noonday sun too strong for his cool grey eyes, produced a pair of tortoiseshell Ray-bans and drew up the shades on his tiny soul.

'YK, Senator Schwarz, Congressman Kelly, Mr Deputy Mayor, ladies and gentlemen: the history of architecture is not, as you might think, an aesthetic one, but a technical one.'

Mitchell Bryan, sitting with the rest of the design and construction team, groaned inwardly as he realized he would have to endure yet another of his senior partner's breast-beating speeches. He looked at David Arnon and flickered his eyelids meaningfully, having first checked that Richardson's Native American wife Joan could not observe this small act of resistance. Mitch need hardly have bothered. Joan was watching Richardson with the rapt, close attention normally reserved for a religious figure. David Arnon stifled a yawn and settled back in his chair, trying to imagine what Arlene Sheridan, seated on the next table, would look like without her clothes.

'The history of all hitherto existing architecture is the history of technological advance. For example: the Roman invention of cement made possible the construction of the dome of the Pantheon – the widest dome in the world until the nineteenth century. In Joseph Paxton's day, the new structural possibilities of iron, and

8

advances in plate-glass manufacture, made it possible to build the Crystal Palace in London, in 1851. Thirty years later, Siemen's invention of the electric elevator enabled the construction of the first multi-storey structure in turn-of-the-century Chicago. Exactly a century after that, architecture was drawing on developments that had been made in the aeronautics industry: buildings that made the most of new materials to reduce their mass, like Norman Foster's Hong Kong and Shanghai Bank.

'Ladies and gentlemen, I have to tell you that the modern architectural scene presents us with the greatest adventure of all: architecture that uses the advanced technology of space exploration and the computer age. The building as a machine in which invisible micro- and nano-technology have replaced industrial mechanical systems. A building that is more like a robot than a shelter. A structure with its own electronic nervous system that is every bit as responsive as the muscles flexing in the body of an Olympic athlete.

'No doubt there are some of you present here today who will have already heard of so-called smart or intelligent buildings. The concept of the intelligent building has been around for a while and yet there remains little consensus of what makes a building intelligent. For me the distinguishing feature of the truly integrated intelligent building is that all the computer systems within the building, including those associated with the building's operations and those related to the building user's business, are connected together to form a single network using a data-bus, a screened cable containing a twisted pair of conductors. Like those minibuses that travel in a loop around the downtown area. Using the data-bus a central computer sends signals to various electronic sub-systems –security, data, energy – in the form of the time-multiplexed, high frequency, 24-volt digital data commands.

'So, for instance, the central computer will interrogate a variety of linear, point and volumetric sensors within the building, and watch out for a fire. Only if the computer is unable to extinguish the fire itself will it telephone the local fire department and request human assistance.'

For a moment Richardson looked away from his script as a sudden gust of wind carried the voice of Cheng Peng Fei up from the building site below:

'The Yu Corporation supports the fascist government of China!'

'You know,' Richardson grinned, 'just before I got here I was speaking to someone about this building. She asked me if we would demonstrate what it was capable of. I said no, we wouldn't.' He extended his hand towards the sound of the protesters. 'But hey, what do you know? I was wrong. There is a demonstration after all. The only shame is that I can't end this one at the touch of a button.'

Richardson's audience laughed politely.

'As it happens, the most important aspect of this building's intelligence can't be demonstrated so easily. Because what makes this building really smart is not its ability to anticipate the pattern of use so that energy can be expended with the utmost parsimony. Nor is it the computer-controlled base isolators that will enable the structure to withstand earthquakes measuring up to 8.5 on the Richter Scale.

'No, what makes this the smartest building in LA, possibly in the whole United States, ladies and gentlemen, is its inherent ability to cope with not just the demands of today's information technology, but tomorrow's as well.

'When many American companies are already struggling to remain competitive with Europe and the East Asian Pacific Rim countries, it's an uncomfortable fact that there are a great many office buildings in

America, some of them built as recently as 1970, that are prematurely obsolete: the cost of bringing them up to date to meet the demand of IT exceeds the cost of tearing them down and starting again.

'I believe that this building represents a new generation of office accommodation, one that will provide our country with the only means of ensuring that we remain competitive tomorrow; the kind of building that will guarantee that this great country is best placed to take full advantage of what President Dole has called the Global Information Infrastructure. Because, make no mistake about this, this is the key to economic growth. Information Infrastructure will be to the US economy of the next ten years what transport infrastructure was to the economy of the mid-twentieth century. Which is why I believe that you will soon be seeing many more buildings like this one.

'Of course, only time will tell whether or not I am right and if the Yu Corporation will continue to be a completely satisfied occupant well into the next century. What is certain is that the world now faces the same kind of challenge that faced Chicago one hundred years ago, when the storage, merchandizing and managerial demands of the railway and steam-power trade required the utilization of the new office technology of telephones and typewriters, and a new kind of building to put them in as land prices soared. The Chicago frame building, or the skyscraper as we know it better today, produced a new kind of city. In the same way that between 1900 and 1920 Manhattan transformed itself into the landscape of mesas and ziggurats with which we are familiar today, I believe that we now stand on the threshold of an urban metamorphosis wherein our cities become intelligent participants in the whole global economic process.

'And so to this morning's topping-out ceremony. Traditionally we mark this occasion by throwing a branch of evergreen from the top storey. I'm often asked about the origins of this custom but the simple answer is that nobody really knows for sure what they are. I was once told by a professor of Ancient History that the ceremony probably dates from the time of the Egyptians, when human sacrifices were associated with the completion of a building; and the evergreen is a substitute for an era when the architect was rewarded for his services by being enclosed alive within the brickwork of his own building, or hurled from the top. I dare say there are some clients who still feel that way about their architects, but I think I am safe in saying that YK is not one of them.'

Richardson glanced in Mr Yu's direction and saw that the ageing billionaire was beaming politely.

'At least, I hope he isn't. Perhaps, ladies and gentlemen, I had better just throw out the branch before he changes his mind.'

The audience laughed politely once more.

'And, by the way; I think it says a lot about Mr Yu's son Jardine that he was sufficiently concerned about the safety of those demonstrators down below that he asked for them to be moved away from the front of the building until this ceremony was concluded. Thank you very much.'

The guests laughed again and as Richardson was now advancing to the edge of the roof bearing the branch of evergreen, they started to applaud. Many of them followed him to watch as he threw the branch to the piazza three hundred and fifty feet below.

Mitch checked that Joan was among them and then, catching David Arnon's eye again, he pushed two fingers into his mouth, as if he was trying to make himself vomit.

David Arnon grinned and leaned towards him.

'You know, Mitch,' he said, 'as a Jew I hate to say this, but maybe those Egyptians weren't so bad after all.'

Book One

'Architecture is voodoo.'
Buckminster Fuller

The Richardsons left L'Orangerie, one of LA's most exclusive restaurants, in their chauffeur-driven, bullet-proof Bentley and turned west off La Cienaga on to Sunset.

'We'll be staying at the apartment tonight, Declan,' Ray Richardson told the driver. 'And I'll be in the studio all morning. I won't need you again until we drive to the airport at two.'

'Are you taking the Gulfstream, sir?' Declan's Irish accent was as thick as his neck, for he was also Richardson's bodyguard, as anyone seeing his Blackcat nightsight glasses, or the Ruger P90 automatic on the Bentley's front seat, might have guessed.

'No, I'm on a scheduled flight. To Berlin.'

'We'd better leave a little bit earlier than usual then, sir. The traffic was very bad on the San Diego Freeway today.'

'Thanks, Declan. Let's say one-thirty then.'

'Yes, sir.'

It was past midnight but there were still lights burning in the architechnologist's studio. Declan switched the diode on his Blackcat lenses from red to green to cope with the change in light conditions. You never knew what might come out of left field in the darkness. Not unless you were wearing a pair of wide-angle Blackcats.

'It looks as if they're still working,' said Richardson's wife, Joan.

'They better be,' growled Richardson. 'There was

plenty to do when I left. Every time I tell one of those krauts to do something I get a hundred different reasons why it can't be done.'

Designed by Richardson himself and built at a cost of $21 million, the triangular-shaped glass structure that housed his studio occupied a site amid giant billboards and sun-bleached Hollywood glitz, resembling the prow of an expensive and ultra-modern motor yacht. Pointing east towards Hollywood, with opaque glass panels screening the northern elevation from the road, the Richardson building did not conform to any coherently Angeleno architectural approach – always assuming that the eclecticism that characterized most of LA's buildings could be called a style at all. Like Richardson's other buildings in LA, it seemed almost out of place. More European than American. Or something that had just landed from another world.

The design and architectural critics said that Richardson belonged to a Rationalist tradition, and certainly his buildings had machine metaphors aplenty. There were even echoes of the Constructivist fantasies of architects like Gropius, Le Corbusier and Stirling. But at the same time his work went beyond the merely utilitarian. It declared its allegiance to high technology and can-do capitalism.

'Germans,' muttered Richardson and shook his head with contempt.

'Yes, dear,' cooed Joan. 'But as soon as we've opened the Berlin office we can get rid of them.'

The Bentley pulled off the main road and drove round the back of the building to the underground parking lot.

There were seven storeys, six of them above ground. The practice's offices and double-height studio occupied the lower part of the building, with twelve private apartments on levels three to seven. The magnificently appointed penthouse was where the Richardsons stayed when they were working late or starting early, which they often did. Ray Richardson was nothing if not single-minded about his profession. But otherwise they lived in their spectacular house in Rustic Canyon. Also designed by Richardson, this ten-bedroom house enjoyed the rare distinction of having been praised for its beauty and elegance by no less a savage critic of modern architecture than Tom Wolfe, in the pages of *Vanity Fair*, and was home to the couple's extensive collection of contemporary art.

'We'd better stick our heads round the door and see what's being done in my name,' said Richardson. 'Just in case there are any fuck-ups.'

The couple swept up the dramatic granite-clad staircase like royalty, acknowledging the armed security guards on duty with stiff nods of the head. They paused at the edge of the huge, luminous studio, almost as if they expected to be announced. With only a vase of irises on the receptionist's desk to relieve the monochrome of this modern Angeleno Bauhaus, the Richardsons were suddenly the most colourful thing in it.

Ninety metres long, with seventeen twelve-metre work benches set at right angles to the southern-facing glass wall that commanded a panoramic view of the city, Richardson and Associates was one of the most modern architects' studios anywhere in the world. And one of the busiest, too. Even now there were architects, designers, engineers, model-makers, computer experts and their various support teams working late in open-plan harmony. Many of them had been there for thirty-six hours without a break, and those who were relative newcomers to the studio paid little attention to the arrival of the sleekly suited principal and his wife. But those who knew Ray Richardson better looked up from their computer screens and take-out pizzas and realized that harmony was about to turn into fundamental discord.

Joan Richardson glanced around and shook her head

in admiration at the sterling service that was being given to her husband. In her adoring brown Navajo eyes it seemed only his due. She was used to putting her husband first.

'Just look at this, darling,' she gushed. 'The creative energy. It's simply breathtaking. Twelve-thirty and they're still working. There's so much going on, it's like a beehive.'

Joan took off her wrap and hung it over her arm. She was wearing a cream linen sarong-style skirt with a matching shirt and tabard, a multi-layered outfit that did a great deal to disguise her large behind. Joan was a good-looking woman, with a face not unlike one of Gauguin's Tahitian lovelies, but she was also a large one.

'Fabulous. Just fabulous. It makes you feel so proud to be a part of all this . . . all this energy.'

Ray Richardson grunted. His eyes searched the hard-edged, black, white and grey surfaces of the studio for Allen Grabel, who was working on both of the largest and most prestigious projects currently occupying the firm. With the Yu Corporation building nearing completion, it was the Kunstzentrum that was immediately preoccupying the firm's senior designer, not least because his principal was about to fly to Germany to present the detailed drawings to the Berlin city authorities.

The Kunstzentrum was an arts centre, Berlin's response to the Paris Beaubourg, designed to revitalize the Alexanderplatz, a huge, wind-swept pedestrianized plaza which had once been one of the German capital's main shopping meccas.

The two projects kept Grabel so busy there were times when he had to stop and remind himself which one he was working on. Spending a minimum twelve hours a day in the office – often as many as sixteen – he had no private life to speak of. He knew he was not a bad-looking guy. He might have had a girlfriend if he could ever take the time to try and meet someone, but with no one at home he spent more and more time at the office. He was aware Richardson took advantage of this. He knew he should have gone on holiday after the major design work on the Yu Corporation building had been completed. On his salary he could have gone anywhere he wanted. He just never found the right window in his increasingly busy work schedule. Sometimes Grabel felt he was on the edge of a nervous breakdown. At the very least he was drinking way too much.

Richardson found the tall, curly-haired New Yorker staring into the screen of his Intergraph terminal through a pair of glasses that were as grimy as his shirt-collar. He was re-shaping the curves and polylines of an architectural layout.

The Intergraph software system for computer-assisted design was the cornerstone of the Richardson practice, not just in Los Angeles but throughout the world. With offices in Hong Kong, Tokyo, London, New York and Toronto, as well as new ones planned for Berlin, Frankfurt, Dallas and Buenos Aires, Richardson was Intergraph's largest customer after NASA. The system, and others like it, had revolutionized architecture, providing 'drag and drop' handle-based editing that allowed a designer to quickly move, rotate, stretch and align any number of two- and three-dimensional entities.

Richardson removed his Armani jacket, moved a chair closer towards Grabel and sat down beside him. Wordlessly he tugged the colour AO-size plot across the desk and compared it with the 2-D image on the monitor while he ate the last slice of Grabel's takeout pizza.

Already tired, Grabel's spirits sagged. Sometimes he looked at how CAD transformed an input pattern into a work of architecture and wondered if he might not as easily have created a piece of music. But such philosophical musing disappeared out of the window whenever Ray Richardson arrived on the scene; and whatever pleasure and satisfaction he took in his job seemed as ephemeral as one of his own computer drawings.

'I think we're just about there now, Ray,' he said wearily. But Richardson had already accessed the Smart Draw icon on the floating toolbar with a right-button mouse click that would allow him to judge the design for himself.

'You think?' Richardson smiled coldly. 'Jesus Christ, don't you know?' He put his hand up in the air like a kid answering a question in class and shouted: 'Someone get me a cup of coffee.'

Grabel shrugged and sighed simultaneously, too tired to argue.

'Well, what's that supposed to mean? That shrug? Come on, Allen. What the fuck is going on here? And where the hell is Kris Parkes?'

Parkes was project manager on the Kunstzentrum project: although not the most senior member of the team, it was his job to run the regular in-house coordination meetings and to articulate what the project team was thinking.

Grabel told himself that right now the project team was probably thinking the same as he was: that they wished they were at home, watching TV in bed. Like Kris Parkes probably was.

'He went home,' said Grabel.

'The project manager went home?'

Richardson's coffee arrived, brought by Mary Sammis, one of the project model-makers. He tasted it, winced and handed it back.

'This is stewed,' he said.

'He was out on his feet,' Grabel explained. 'I told him to go home.'

'Get me another. And this time bring a saucer. When I

20

ask for a cup of coffee I don't expect to have to ask for that as well.'

'Right away.'

Shaking his head, Richardson muttered, 'What kind of place is this anyway?' And then, remembering something, he called out: 'Oh, Mary? How's the model coming along?'

'We're still working on it, Ray.'

He shook his head grimly. 'Don't let me down, love. I'm flying to Germany tomorrow afternoon.' He looked at his Breitling wristwatch. 'In twelve hours, to be precise. That model has to be boxed and ready to go with all the customs paperwork. Understand?'

'You'll have it, Ray, I promise.'

'You don't have to make promises to me. It's not for me. This is not about me, Mary. If it was just me it would be different. But I happen to think that the very least we can do for a new office, with thirty people on board who are going to spend the next two years of their lives working on nothing but this project, is to show them a model of what it's going to look like. Wouldn't you agree, Mary?'

'Yes, sir, I would.'

'And don't call me sir, Mary. This isn't the army.'

Richardson picked up Grabel's telephone and punched out a number. Taking advantage of these few seconds of grace Mary walked quickly away.

'Ray, who are you calling?' said Grabel, giving a little twitch. His nervous tick only started when he was dog-tired, or needed a drink. 'Didn't you hear what I just said? I said it was me who told him to go home.'

'I heard you.'

'Ray?'

'Where's my bloody coffee?' Richardson shouted over his shoulder.

'You're not calling Parkes, are you?'

Richardson just looked at Grabel, his grey eyebrows raised with quiet contempt.

'You bastard,' he murmured, suddenly hating Richardson with an intensity he found alarming. 'I wish to God you were dead, you mother . . .'

'Kris? It's Ray. Did I wake you up? I did? That's too bad. Let me ask you something, Kris. Have you any idea what this building is going to be worth in fees to this firm? No, just answer the question. That's right, nearly $4 million. Four million dollars. Now, there are a lot of us in here working late on this one, Kris. Only you're not here and you're supposed to be the goddamn project manager. Well, don't you think that sets a bad example? You don't.' He listened for a moment and then started to shake his head. 'Well, frankly I don't care how long it is since you've been home. And I couldn't care less if your kids think you're just some guy their mother picked up in the supermarket. Your place is here, with your team. Are you going to drag your ass down here, or do I have to look for a new manager on this job? You are? Good.'

Richardson replaced the receiver and glanced around for his wife. She was stooped over a glass case near the stairs, examining a model of the Yu Corporation head-quarters which, in real life, was now nearing completion on the Hope Street Piazza. 'I'm going to be a while here, honey,' he called. 'I'll see you upstairs, OK?'

'OK, dear.' Joan smiled and looked around the studio. 'Good-night everybody,' she said and left.

There were a few people who smiled back. But most of them were too tired, even for polite smiles. Besides, they knew that Joan was every bit as monstrous as her husband. Worse. At least he was talented. One or two of the more senior designers still remembered the time when, in a fit of bad temper, she had thrown a fax machine through a plate-glass window.

Ray Richardson returned his attention to the monitor and, clicking the mouse again, changed the picture to a 3-D image. The drawing revealed a giant semi-circle about two hundred metres in diameter, gently disked like the city of Bath's Royal Crescent and surmounted by what resembled the wingspan of an enormous bird. There were some architectural critics, most of them in Europe, who had suggested that the wings were the wings of an eagle, and a Nazi eagle at that. For this reason they had already described Richardson's design as 'Post-Nazism'.

Richardson moved the mouse forward across its pad, bringing the 3-D image closer. Now it could be seen that the building was not one crescent but two, enclosing a curving colonnade separating shops and office buildings and the exhibition halls. These were the contract drawings, representing a statement of agreed information from the various consultants who would be involved in constructing the Kunstzentrum, and they were due to be passed on to the quantity surveyor when Richardson visited Berlin. Entering the colonnade, Richardson zoomed up to the ceiling and clicking the mouse twice, exploding a detailed diagram of one of the shape-memory steel tube supports for the photochromic glass panels.

'What's this?' he frowned. 'Look, Allen, you haven't done what I wanted. I thought I asked you to draw up both options.'

'But we agreed that this is the ideal option.'

'I wanted the other one, just in case.'

'Just in case of what? I don't understand. Either this is the best option or it's not.' Grabel started to twitch again.

'In case I change my mind, that's what.' Richardson performed a cruel but accurate imitation of Grabel's nervous twitch. Grabel took off his glasses, buried his unshaven face in his trembling hands and sighed deeply, stretching his cheeks towards his ears. For a moment he looked heavenwards, as if seeking guidance from the Almighty. When none arrived he stood up, shaking his head slowly and put on his jacket.

'God, I hate you sometimes,' he said. 'No, that's not true, I hate you all the time. You are a stray dog's rectal cancer, you know that? One day someone is going to do the world a big favour and murder you. I'd do it myself only I'm afraid of all the fan mail I might receive. You want it drawn? Then do it yourself, you selfish bastard. I've had it up to here with you.'

'What did you say?'

'You heard me, asshole.' Grabel turned and started to walk towards the stairs.

'Where the hell are you going?'

'Home.'

Richardson stood up and nodded bitterly.

'You walk out now, you don't come back. D'you hear me?'

'I quit,' Grabel said, and kept on walking. 'I wouldn't come back here if you were dying of loneliness.'

Richardson exploded. 'You don't walk out on me,' he screamed. 'You're fired. I'm firing you, you piece of twitching shit. All these people are my witnessess. You hear me, Twitch? Your ass is fired!'

Without looking back Grabel held up a middle finger and disappeared down the stairs. Someone laughed and Richardson looked around angrily, his fists clenched, ready to fire anyone who stepped out of line.

'What's so goddamned funny?' he snarled. 'And where's my fucking coffee?'

Still seething, Grabel walked the short distance along the strip to the St James's Club Hotel where, as usual, he had a few drinks in the art-deco piano bar while he waited for a taxi. Vodka with Cointreau and cranberry juice. It was what he had been drinking six months earlier when the police had arrested him for driving under the influence. That and a couple of toots of cocaine. He had only taken the cocaine to help him make the drive home. He might not have been drunk at all if he hadn't been working so hard.

He felt better about walking out on his job than he had felt about losing his licence. If only Richardson had not called him Twitch. He knew it was what people sometimes called him, but no one had ever used it to his face before. Only Richardson was a big enough shit to have done that.

There was a cocktail waitress who worked in the hotel, a resting actress called Mary, who was sometimes friendly to him. It was as near as Allen Grabel got to having a social life.

'I just quit my job,' he told her proudly. 'Just told my partner to shove it.'

'Well,' she shrugged, 'good for you.'

'I've been meaning to do it for a long time, I guess. Never had the nerve before. I just told him to stick it. I guess it was either that or blow his friggin' brains out.'

'Something tells me you made the right choice,' she said.

'I dunno, y'know? Really I don't. But boy, was he mad.'

'Sounds like you made quite a performance out of it. The whole dramatic gesture.'

'And how. Boy, was he mad at me.'

'I wish I could quit my job,' she said wistfully.

'Hey, it'll happen for you, Mary. I know it will.'

He ordered another drink and found it disappeared even more quickly than the first. By the time Mary told him that his taxi had arrived he had drunk four or five, although he was so exhilarated by what had happened the alcohol hardly seemed to have affected him. He peeled a couple of bills off his money clip and tipped the girl generously. There was no need, since he had been sitting at the bar, only he felt sorry for her. Not everyone could afford to quit their job, he told himself.

After he had gone Mary breathed a sigh of relief. He was not a bad person. But the twitch gave her the creeps. And she hated drunks. Even friendly ones.

Outside the front door Grabel ordered the cab driver to take him to Pasadena. They were only a few blocks away from downtown, heading south-east on the Hollywood Freeway, about to make the north turn towards Pasadena, when he suddenly remembered something.

'Shit,' he said loudly.

'Is there a problem?'

'Kind of, yeah. I left my door-key at the office.'

'Want to go back for it?'

'Pull off here, will you, while I try to figure out what to do?'

After such a dramatic exit he could hardly return. Ray Richardson would assume he was returning with his tail between his legs to ask for his job back. He would just love holding him up to ridicule. Maybe call him Twitch again. That would be too much to bear. The trouble with making a grand gesture was that it was easy to forget your props.

'So where's it to be, my friend?'

Grabel looked out of the window and found himself staring up at a familiar-looking silhouette. They were on Hope Street, approaching the piazza and the Yu Corporation building. Suddenly he knew exactly where he would spend the night.

'Here. Drop me here,' he said.

'You sure?' said the taxi driver. 'It's kind of rough around here at night, man.'

'Perfectly sure,' said Grabel. He wondered why he had not thought of it before.

Mitchell Bryan was beginning to think that his wife, Alison, was actually getting worse. Over breakfast she had informed him, with an insane look in her eye, how she had read that there were certain South African tribes who believed that the product of a miscarriage could threaten or kill not just the father but the whole country, even the sky itself: it was enough to cause the burning winds to blow, to parch the country with heat and drive the rains away. Laconically, Mitch had replied, 'Well, I guess we got off lightly then,' and headed straight for the car, even though it was still only seven-thirty.

He did not think Alison had ever really recovered from losing their baby. She was more withdrawn than she had ever been before, neurotic even, and kept away from babies like other people avoided the South Central area of LA. There were times when Mitch could not help forcing the endoscope of his memory into the maw of their relationship and asking himself whether or not a child would have kept them together. Because twelve months almost to the day after Alison's miscarriage Mitch stopped making excuses for her eccentric behaviour and started an affair. He hated himself for doing it, knowing that Alison still needed a lot of care and understanding. At the same time he was aware that he no longer loved her quite enough to give it. He felt that what she possibly needed most was to see a psychiatrist.

Right now what Mitch needed was to be in bed with a woman called Jenny Bao, the project's *feng shui* consultant. Usually he drove straight to the office or the Yu Corporation building, but sometimes he found himself making an early-morning call on Jenny at her West Los Angeles home, from which she also ran her business. On this particular morning Mitch chose the now familiar route off the Santa Monica Freeway on to La Brea Avenue and, just a few blocks south of Wilshire Boulevard, entered the quiet, leafy neighbourhood made up of well-built Spanish and ranch-style houses where Jenny lived. He drew up outside a pleasant grey bungalow with a raised floor and veranda, and an immaculate lawn. Next door was a house with a For Sale board that advertised it as a 'Talking Home'.

Mitch turned the engine off and amused himself for a moment by listening to the ninety-second description of the property on the designated wavelength he could receive on his car radio via a computerized transmitter inside the house. He was surprised that they were asking so much, and that Jenny could have afforded such an expensive neighbourhood. There must be more money in *feng shui* than he had imagined.

Feng shui, the ancient Chinese art of 'wind and water' land magic, involved locating sites and building structures so that they harmonized with and benefited from the surrounding physical environment. The Chinese believed that this method of divination enabled them to attract desirable cosmological influences, ensuring that they would have good luck, good health, prosperity and a long life. No building on the East Asian Pacific Rim, however large or small, was ever planned or constructed without regard to *feng shui* precepts.

Mitch had had considerable experience of dealing with *feng shui* consultants, and not just the one he was sleeping with. When designing the Island Nirvana Hotel in Hong Kong, Ray Richardson had planned on cladding the building in a reflective glass exterior until his client's *feng shui* master had told him that glare was a source of *sha qi*, the harmful breath of the dragon. On another occasion the firm had been obliged to alter its award-winning design for the Sumida Television Company in Tokyo because the shape resembled the short-lived butterfly.

He got out of the car and went up the path. Jenny was still in her silk dressing-gown when she answered the door.

'Mitch, what a pleasant surprise,' she said and let him in. 'I was going to give you a call this morning.'

He was already slipping the gown off her shoulders and pushing her into the bedroom.

'Mmm,' she said. 'What did you have, steroids with your Cheerios this morning?'

Half Chinese, Jenny Bao reminded him of a big cat. Green eyes, high cheekbones, and a small delicate nose he had decided was probably cosmetic. She had a bow mouth that was more Odysseus than Cupid and it was set between the parentheses of two perfect laugh lines. She loved to laugh. She carried herself well too, with the long, leggy, self- conscious stroll of the cat-walk. She had not always looked so good. When Mitch had first met her she had been maybe ten or fifteen pounds overweight. He knew how much time she had needed to spend in her local gymnasium to be in such fabulous shape now.

Underneath the robe she was wearing a garter belt, stockings and panties.

'Did the dragon tell you I was coming?' he grinned, pointing at the antique *feng shui* compass that was mounted on the wall above the bed's headboard. The compass was a circular disc marked with about thirty or forty concentric circles of Chinese characters, and Mitch knew it was called a *luopan*, and that she used it to assess the good and bad qualities of the dragon in a building.

'Of course,' she said, lying back on the bed. 'The dragon tells me everything.'

His tremulous thumbs gathered the elastic waist of her panties and plucked them down over the twin golden domes of her behind and back up over the suspended sentences and Sobranie filter-tips of her stocking tops as, obligingly, she brought her knees up to her chest. She straightened her feet and the little stealth bomber of black lace and silk was his.

Quickly he threw off his own clothes and rolled on top of her. Detaching mind from over-eager gnomon and its exquisitely appointed, shadowy task, he began to make love to her.

When they had finished they lay under the sheet and watched TV. After a while Mitch glanced at the gold Rolex Submariner watch on his wrist.

'I ought to be going,' he said.

Jenny Bao pulled a face and kissed him.

'What were you going to call me about?' he asked.

'Oh yes,' she said, and told him why she had wanted to speak to him.

As soon as Mitch sat down at his desk in the studio he saw Tony Levine coming towards him and stifled a groan. Levine was too pushy for Mitch's taste. There was something hungry-looking about him, a generally wolfish effect that was enhanced by the gap teeth shown through his near-permanent smile, and eyebrows that were joined in the middle. Then there was his laugh. When Levine laughed you could hear it all over the building. It was almost as if he were trying to draw attention to himself, and that made Mitch feel uncomfortable. But there was no sign of a smile on Levine's face now.

'Allen Grabel resigned,' said Levine.

'What? You're kidding!'

'Last night.'

'Shit.'

'He was working late on this Kunstzentrum thing when Richardson showed up and started throwing his Limey weight around.'

'So what's new?'

'I mean, really tyrannical. Like he was ready to burn the place down. Like he was fucking Frank Lloyd Wright, y'know?'

Levine uttered a dumb-sounding guffaw and

smoothed a small pony-tail of dark hair. For Mitch the pony-tail was another reason to dislike him, not least because Levine insisted on calling his hair arrangement a chignon.

'Yeah, well, the ego's about the same size. He thinks he's a genius. That means he has an infinite capacity for making himself a pain in the ass.'

'So what do we do, Mitch? Get another designer on the job? I mean the job's nearly finished, right?'

Levine was the Yu project manager.

'I'd better give Allen a call,' said Mitch. 'There are a couple of problems I'll need his output on, and I'd like to keep Richardson away from what still needs to be done if it's at all possible.'

'Too late,' said Levine. 'He's already been through Grabel's diary. He's coming to this morning's project meeting.'

'Shit. I thought he was going to Germany.'

'After. What problems?'

'That's all we need. You know, Allen would just have sorted things out. But Richardson is bound to make an issue out of it.'

'Out of what? Will you *please* tell me what the problem is?'

'*Feng shui.*'

'That? Jesus, Mitch, I thought we sorted that fuckin' shit.'

'We did, but only on the drawings. Jenny Bao has been round the building and she's worried about a number of things. Mainly she's worried about the tree. The way it's planted.'

'That fuckin' tree's been a headache right from the beginning.'

'You're not wrong there, Tony. She's also worried about the fourth floor.'

'What's the hell's wrong with it?'

'Apparently it's unlucky.'

31

'What?' Levine guffawed again. 'Why the fourth floor and not the thirteenth?'

'Because it's not thirteen that's unlucky for the Chinese, it's the number four. The word for four is also the word for death, she tells me.'

'My birthday comes on the 4th of August,' said Levine. 'Too bad for me, eh?' He cackled loudly. 'This Kung Fu shit is just too fuckin' much.' Levine emitted an even louder bray of laughter.

Mitch shrugged. 'Well, I say give the client what he wants, Tony. The client wants space acupuncture, he gets space acupuncture. That way we get to present our bill as soon as possible.'

'I thought the client was in with the Commies. Aren't the Commies atheists and down on all that superstitious nonsense about spirits and good luck?'

'That reminds me,' said Mitch. 'Something else we have to discuss this morning. Remember those demonstrators? The ones who turned up when we had that cosmetic topping-out ceremony? Well, they're back.'

There were four teams working on the Yu Corporation project — designers, structural engineers, mechanical engineers and the building management systems (BMS) engineers — and it was Mitch's job to make sure that they all built the same building. Frequently a firm of architects was only responsible for the design of the building and relied on outside engineers as consultants. But being such a huge practice, employing some four hundred people, Richardsons had its own in-house mechanical and BMS engineers. An experienced architect himself, it was down to Mitch as technical co-ordinator to translate the designer's lofty ideas into practical instructions and to make sure that when changes were made everyone was aware of their impact.

Mitch located Allen Grabel's telephone number on his computer card file, but when he called him up he got the answering machine.

'Allen? This is Mitch, calling you at ten o'clock. I just heard about what happened last night, and well – I want to find out if you really meant it. And even if you did mean it, I wanted to see if you could be persuaded to change your mind. We can't afford to lose someone with your talent. I know Richardson can be an asshole. But he's still a pretty talented guy and sometimes talent can be difficult to be around. So, er . . . maybe you could give me a call when you receive this message.'

Mitch glanced at his watch. There was just enough time to familiarize himself with what the computer held on file about *feng shui* in the hope that he might find a solution to the problem Jenny Bao had thrown at him; and seeing Kay Killen walking along the studio gallery he waved to her. As drawings manager Kay's function revolved around the computer and the Intergraph design system, which made her the guardian of the database for the whole job and indispensable to Mitch for any number of reasons.

'Kay,' he said, 'could I have your help for a minute, please?'

'So what's the problem this time?' grumbled Richardson when Mitch brought up the subjects of Jenny Bao's concern at the project meeting. 'You know, I sometimes think these Kung Fu assholes dream these fucking things up to justify their fees.'

'Well, that sounds a familiar story,' murmured Marty Birnbaum, the management partner, adjusting his bow-tie with fastidious care.

For Mitch, whose father, a journalist on a small town newspaper, had worn a bow-tie all his life, bow-ties were the meretricious accoutrements of all frauds and liars, and it was yet another reason to dislike the overweight and, he thought, supercilious Birnbaum.

They were all seated around Richardson's democratically round white wood table: Mitchell Bryan; Ray Richardson; Joan Richardson; Tony Levine; Marty Birnbaum; Willis Ellery, the mechanical engineer; Aidan Kenny, the BMS engineer; David Arnon, from Elmo Sergo Ltd, the structural engineers; Helen Hussey, the site agent; and Kay Killen. Mitch sat next to Kay, whose long legs were pointed towards him.

'It's the tree,' explained Mitch. 'Or, rather, where it's planted.'

Everyone groaned.

'Jesus Christ, Mitch,' said David Arnon, 'this may be the smartest building I've ever built, but it's also the dumbest fucking client. He employs one of the world's leading architects and then gets his fucking Chinese witch doctor to scrutinize just about everything he does.'

Mitch did not protest. He knew that Ray Richardson already had his suspicions about him and Jenny, and he had no wish to draw attention to himself by defending her.

'Has this stupid bitch any idea of what it took to get the tree through the roof of that building? It's not exactly the kind of thing you can just pick up and move somewhere else.'

'Take it easy, David,' said Mitch. 'We have to work with this stupid bitch as you call her.'

Arnon slapped his thigh and stood up. Mitch knew that he did it to create an effect, because at six foot five Arnon was the tallest, and possibly the most handsome, man in the room. He was a long wiry streak of a man, with narrow, impossibly horizontal shoulders that seemed to have been tied on to his tent-pole of a body, and a box-shaped head with a closely cut tan-coloured beard. He looked like a former basketball player, which was exactly what he was. Arnon had played Guard as a junior for Duke University, and had been Atlantic Coast player of the year as a senior, until a knee injury had forced him to quit the game for good.

'Take it easy?' said Arnon. 'You're not the one . . . Whose shitty idea was it to stick a lousy tree that size in there anyway?'

'Actually, it was my shitty idea,' said Joan Richardson.

Arnon shrugged an apology in her direction and sat down again.

Mitch smiled to himself, half-enjoying the effect his announcement had produced. He could easily understand David Arnon's concern. It was not every day that a client wanted you to plant a three-hundred-foot-high dicotyledon from the Brazilian rain forest in the middle of his new building's atrium. Arnon had needed the biggest crane in California to lower the outsized evergreen, apparently a South American record, through the roof of the building, a task that had brought the Hollywood Freeway to a halt and closed Hope Street for a whole weekend.

'Relax, will you?' said Mitch. 'She's talking about the way it's planted, not where.'

'That makes a difference?' said Arnon.

'Jenny Bao –'

'Bow wow wow,' growled Arnon. 'Fucking dog woman.'

'– told me that it was bad *feng shui* to plant a large tree on an island in a pond, since the tree in the rectangular pond becomes a Chinese character meaning confinement and trouble.' He handed round some photocopies of a drawing which Jenny had made of the Chinese *kun* character:

35

Richardson regarded the sign with contempt.

'You know,' he said, 'I seem to remember her telling me about how it was good practice to make a rectangular pond because it resembles some other character meaning a mouth and symbolizing – what was it now? – oh yes, people and prosperity. Kay, I want you to look that up in the computer call report. Maybe we can screw this bitch for good.'

Mitch shook his head.

'You're talking about the *kou* character. But with the *mu* sign for a tree in the middle, the *kou* sign becomes a *kun*. You see what I mean? Jenny was kind of adamant about that, Ray. She won't sign off the *feng shui* certificate until we've changed it.'

'Change it? How?' said Levine.

'Well, I've had some thoughts on this,' said Mitch. 'We could build another pond, a round pond, inside the square one. That way the circle represents heaven and the square earth.'

'I don't believe we're having this conversation,' said Richardson. 'The smartest building in LA and we're talking voodoo stuff. Next thing we know we're going to have to sacrifice a cockerel and pour its blood on the front door.'

He sighed and ran a hand through his closely cropped grey hair.

'I'm sorry, Mitch. What the hell, I think your idea sounds like a good one.'

'Actually, I already put the idea to her and she seems to quite like it.'

'Well done, pal,' said Richardson. 'Get it drawn up, will you? You hear that everyone? Mitch is the kind of guy we want round here. He gets things done. Next item.'

'We're not finished here yet, I'm afraid,' said Mitch. 'Jenny Bao also has a problem with the fourth floor. Four is the Chinese word for death. Something like that, anyway.'

'Maybe she's right,' said Richardson. 'Because four is the number of bullets I'm going to fire into that bitch's fucking head. Then I'm going to tear off each of her limbs and stick them up her four inch –'

'Fucking A,' whooped Aidan Kenny.

Levine guffawed loudly.

'Couldn't you just leave a space where the fourth floor used to be?' smiled Helen Hussey. 'You know, miss it out altogether. Just let the fifth floor float on top of the third?'

'Do you have a solution, Mitch?' asked Joan.

'I'm afraid not this time.'

'How about this?' said Aidan Kenny. 'The fourth floor is where we have the computer suite. That's the main computer room, the electronic-mail centre, the document image processing room, the tape-drive room, the multimedia library with a secure store, and the control bridge as well as the various service corridors. So why don't we just call it something like the data centre? Then it goes like this: Second Floor, Third Floor, Data Centre, Fifth Floor, Ladies' Underwear, Soft Furnishings . . .'

'That's not a bad idea, Aid,' said Richardson. 'What do you think, Mitch? Will Mme Blavatsky buy it?'

'I think so.'

'Willis? You're making a face. Do you have an objection?'

As the project's mechanical engineer it was Willis Ellery's job to plan the Yu Corporation building's complex system of piping, cables, elevator shafts and ductwork. He was a thick-set man, with white-blond hair and a moustache stained fawn at the edge of his upper lip from the many cigars he smoked outside the office. He cleared his throat and gave a little nod of the head, as if trying to butt his way into the conversation. Despite his obvious-looking strength he was the mildest mannered of men.

'Well, yes, I think maybe I do. What are we going to do about the elevators?' he said. 'The indicator panels in the cars all have number fours.'

Richardson shrugged impatiently.

'Get on to Otis, Willis, get them to make you some new ones. It ought to be easy enough to make an indicator panel with a letter D instead of a four.' He pointed to Kay Killen, who was call-reporting the meeting on her laptop. 'Make sure you memo all this to the client, Kay. The cost of making all these voodoo changes is going to be down to him, not us.'

'Er . . . well . . . might take a little time to organize that,' said Ellery.

Richardson looked at Aidan Kenny with what passed for a twinkle in his eye.

'Aid? You're the one who has to spend most of his life on the fourth floor at the Yu Corp. What do you think? Are you willing to take the risk? Do you feel lucky, punk?'

'I'm Irish, not Chinese,' laughed Kenny. 'Four's never been a problem for me. My dad used to say that the fortunate possessor of a four-leaf clover would have good luck in gambling, and that witchcraft would have no power over him.'

'All the same,' said Mitch, 'perhaps it would be better if you didn't mention it to Cheech and Chong.'

'Who the hell are they?' said Richardson.

'Bob Beech and Hideki Yojo,' Kenny explained. 'From the Yu Corporation. They've been installing their supercomputer and helping me to set up the building management systems. Actually they're my chaperones. They're there to make sure I don't screw around with their hardware.'

'Do you think their being there might count as a completion offering beneficial occupation?' joked David Arnon, knowing that under the existing articles of agreement, this would have allowed his company, Elmo Sergo, to quit the site.

Mitch smiled, knowing how badly Arnon wanted to finish the job and, more particularly, to get away from Ray Richardson.

38

'That reminds me, Mitch,' said Richardson. 'Have you put a date in my diary for the practical completion inspection yet?'

This was the stage in the completion of a building contract when the architect accepted the building as complete and ready for occupation.

'Not yet, Ray, no. We're still running checks on services and equipment prior to obtaining the temporary certificate of occupation.'

'Don't leave it too long. You know how my diary fills up.'

'Hey, I forgot to mention it,' said Kenny, 'but, talking about dates and diaries, today is Big Bang. Our computer links up with the computers at every one of our projects in America.'

'Aidan's quite correct to remind us,' said Ray Richardson. 'Our Big Bang's important. Soon most of our site inspections will be done on closed-circuit TV via the computer modem. That should save a lot of you bastards from having to get your $300 shoes dirty.'

'We may even have that available to us for the next project meeting,' said Kenny. 'Most of the BMS is already working.'

'Good work, Aid.'

'What about security?' inquired Tony Levine. 'Mitch says that some of those demonstrators came back.'

'How come?' asked Richardson. 'It's six months since they were last there.'

'There's not half as many as last time. Only a handful,' said Mitch. 'Students mostly. My guess is it's because the semester at UCLA just ended.'

'You know, if it becomes a problem, Mitch, you should give Morgan Phillips a ring at City Hall. Get him to do something about it. He owes me one.'

Mitch shrugged. 'I don't think it's going to be a problem,' he said. 'We've got security men to handle things. Not to mention the computer.'

'If you say so. OK, everyone,' said Richardson, 'that's it.'

The meeting was over.

'Hey, Mitch,' said Kenny. 'You going downtown?'

'Any minute now.'

'Give me a lift to the Gridiron, will you? My car's in the repair shop.'

Mitch winced and glanced at Ray Richardson.

It had been the *LA Times*'s architecture critic, Sam Hall Kaplan, who had first dubbed the Yu Corporation building 'the Gridiron', because of the resemblance between its framework of parallel cross-braces and supports and an American football field. Mitch knew the nickname irritated Richardson.

'Aidan Kenny,' said Richardson sharply, 'I do not want to hear anyone calling the Yu Corporation building the Gridiron. It is the Yu building, or the Yu Corporation building, or even Number One Hope Street Piazza, and that is all. No one here should denigrate a Richardson building in such a way. Is that clear?'

Aware that it was no longer just Aidan Kenny who was listening, Ray Richardson raised his voice. 'That goes for everyone. Nobody refers to the Yu building as the Gridiron. This practice has won ninety-eight awards for outstanding architectural design and we're proud of our buildings. I may base my style of architecture in technology – I don't see how you can avoid that. But you can take it for granted that I believe the buildings are also beautiful. Beauty and technology are not as incompatible as some people would like us to believe. And anyone who thinks differently has no right to be working here. Don't mistake me on this. I'll fire anyone I hear using the word Gridiron. And the same applies to nicknames anyone might have for the Kunstzentrum in Berlin, the Yoyogi Park building in Tokyo, the Bunshaft Museum in Houston, the

Thatcher building in London, or any other fucking building that we have anything to do with. I hope I've made myself clear.'

Aidan Kenny was still commenting on this reprimand as Mitch drove them east along Santa Monica Boulevard. Mitch was pleased to see that he had not taken it to heart. Kenny even seemed to regard the experience as amusing.

'The Yoyogi Park building,' he said. 'What do they call that one, then? Sorry, how do they denigrate that one? Hell of a word that – denigrate. I had to look it up. It means bad-mouth.'

'There was a piece about it in *Architectural Digest*,' Mitch explained. 'The *Japan Times* commissioned a Gallup poll about what people in Tokyo thought about it. Apparently they call it the ski jump.'

'The ski jump.' Kenny chuckled. 'I like that. It is kind of like a ski jump, isn't it? Ouch. I bet he loved that. And the Bunshaft?'

'That's a new one on me. Maybe he's seen something I haven't.'

'What gets up that sonofabitch? Maybe it's Joan. Maybe she straps one on and shoves it up his ass. She's man enough: that's what I call an Iron Lady. She could play defence for the Steelers.'

'Richardson's not the worst architect in LA, I'll say that for him. Not by a long way. Morphosis would win that prize, with Frank Gehry a close second. Ray may behave like a paranoid schizophrenic but at least his buildings don't look that way. Do you think some of those guys think that there's some kind of redemption in making buildings look as ugly as possible?'

'Hey, come on, Mitch,' chuckled Kenny. 'You know that "ugly" is not a word that has any meaning in architecture. There's avant-garde, there's very avant-garde and there's security-guard. You want your building to look fashionable these days, you make it look like a fucking state penitentiary.'

'That's good coming from the man who drives a Cadillac Protector.'

'You know how many Protectors were sold in LA last year? Eighty thousand. Mark my words, in a couple of years we'll all be driving them. You included. Joan Richardson drives one.'

'Why doesn't Ray? There are lots more people who want *him* dead, surely.'

'You don't think his Bentley isn't armour-plated?' Kenny shook his head. 'You can't sell a car like that in LA without armour. But frankly I prefer the Protector. It has a back-up engine, in case the first one breaks down. Not even a Bentley has that.'

'So why aren't you driving it? You've only just took delivery.'

'Nothing serious. It's just the on-board computer.'

'What's the matter with it?'

'I don't know. My eight-year-old, Michael, keeps screwing with it. He thinks it controls the car's weapons system or something, and zaps the other cars with it.'

'If only,' said Mitch, braking hard to avoid colliding with the wayward tan Ford in front, 'it were that easy.' He gritted his teeth angrily, checked the mirror and then pulled out to overtake.

'Try not to make eye contact with him, Mitch,' said Kenny nervously. 'Just in case, y'know . . . Have you got a gun in this car?' He opened the glove compartment.

'If a Protector had a weapons system, I'd get one today.'

'Yeah, wouldn't that be good?'

Mitch pulled in front of the tan Ford and glanced over at his passenger. 'Relax, will you? There's no gun in there. I don't have one.'

'No gun? What are you, some kind of pacifist?'

Aidan Kenny was a heavy, couch-potato type with wire-frame glasses and a wide, viscid mouth that could accommodate a whole cheeseburger. There was something about him that reminded Mitch of a minor Renaissance princeling: the eyes were small and set too close together; the nose was long and fat, adding an impression of sensuality and self-indulgence; and the chin, while not of Habsburg proportions, was prognathously stubborn and covered with a fair, boyish sort of beard that looked as if it had been grown to give the impression of maturity. His skin was as soft and white as a roll of toilet paper, as might have been expected with someone who spent most of his waking hours serving a computer terminal.

They turned south on to Hollywood Freeway.

'That's why I'm giving in and letting him have some computer games,' said Kenny. 'You know, the interactive stuff on CD-ROM.'

'Who?'

'My son. Then maybe he'll stop screwing around with the car's computer.'

'He must be the only kid in LA who doesn't already play those games.'

'Yeah, well, that's because I know how addictive they can be. I'm still attending CGA. Computer Games Anonymous.'

Mitch sneaked another sideways look at his colleague. It was easy enough to imagine him playing some fantasy game into the small hours of the morning. Not that there was anything weak-minded about Aidan Kenny. Before setting up a BMS company that Richardson had eventually bought for several million dollars, Aidan Kenny had worked with the Stanford artificial intelligence group. That was another thing you had to hand to Ray Richardson: he hired only the best to work for him. Even if he didn't know how to hang on to them.

'Matter of fact, Mitch, he's coming in today. We're going to go to a store and he's going to pick all the games he wants.'

'Who, Michael?'

'It's his birthday. Margaret's dropping him off at the Gridiron. Whoops. The Yu building. Gee, I hope your car isn't bugged. Do you think anyone will mind Michael being there this afternoon? We're going to see the Clippers this evening and I don't want to have to go home first.'

Mitch was thinking about Allen Grabel. His attaché case had still been under his desk when they left the office. And there had still been the answering machine when Mitch had phoned again. He mentioned it to Kenny.

'Do you think something could have happened to him?' he said.

'Like what?'

'I dunno. You're the one with the imagination and the Cadillac Protector. I mean, it was kind of late when he left the office last night.'

'Probably went somewhere and got himself stewed,' said Kenny. 'Allen likes a drink. Two or three if he can get away with it.'

'Yeah, maybe you're right.'

They came off the Freeway at Temple Street and approached the familiar downtown skyline, dominated by I. M. Pei's orthogonal seventy-three-storey Library Tower. Mitch reflected that LA's tallest buildings (most of them banks and shopping plazas) resembled the banal, block-square construction he had built in the days when eight-year-olds played with simple sets of Lego bricks. Turning south on to Hope Street, he felt a surge of pride as he caught sight of the Yu building and, leaning forward in his seat, stole a quick glance up at the familiar curtain wall recessed behind the characteristic gridiron of lateral megatrusses and ivory white piers: it

44

was not so much a frame as a three-hundred-foot ladder from which the twenty-five floors were suspended.

Despite Richardson's sensitivity about the nickname, Mitch found there was nothing inherently offensive in it. Indeed, he half suspected that there would come a time when, like the owners of New York's famous Flatiron building, the Yu Corporation would yield to popular insistence and make the nickname official. They could call it what they liked, he reflected: compared with the sullenly competent Miesian glass boxes that surrounded it, the Gridiron was, in Mitch's opinion, the most stunning piece of new architecture anywhere in America. There was nothing to touch the glistening, silver-white transparent machine that was Ray Richardson's Gridiron building. Its visible absence of colour was the most concrete of all colours and, in Mitch's eyes, the building seemed to possess the white light of a revealed truth.

Mitch slowed the car to turn down the drive that led around the side of the finished piazza to the underground car park. As he did so he felt something strike his passenger door.

'Jesus,' exclaimed Kenny and sank into his seat below the window.

'What the hell was that?'

'One of those Chinese kids threw something.'

Mitch did not stop. Like everyone else in LA he stopped for nothing except traffic lights and the LAPD. He waited until they were safe behind the rolling aluminium garage door before inspecting his car for damage.

There was no dent. Not even a scratch. Just the hand-sized splatter of a piece of rotten fruit. Mitch found a tissue in the glove box, wiped the mess away and then sniffed it.

'Smells like a rotten orange,' he said. 'It could have been worse. It could have been a rock or something.'

'Next time it might be worse. It's like I told you, Mitch, drive the Cadillac Protector,' said Kenny, and shrugged. He added, quoting the now infamous television commercial in which a nerdy-looking white man drove the car through a tough black neighbourhood, 'It's the car that gives you back the freedom of the city.'

'What's got into those kids? They've never thrown anything before. Isn't there supposed to be a cop out there making sure this kind of thing doesn't happen?'

Kenny shook his head. 'Who knows? Maybe the cop did it himself. Jesus, these days I'm more afraid of the LAPD than I am of the bad guys. Did you see that blind man on the TV? The one who got shot for waving his white stick at a patrolman?'

'I guess we'd better mention it to Sam,' said Mitch. 'See what he says.'

They walked through a door to the elevators, where a car was waiting to take them up into the main building. It had been automatically dispatched to the basement car park when the two men had given their voice identification phrases outside the garage.

'Which level, please?'

Kenny leaned towards the microphone on the wall. 'Where is Sam Gleig now, Abraham?'

'Abraham?' Mitch raised his eyebrows at Kenny, who shrugged back. 'Didn't I tell you? We decided to give the A-life a name.'

'Sam Gleig is on the atrium floor,' said the computer.

'Take us there, please, Abraham.' He grinned at Mitch. 'Besides, it's a hell of a lot better than what Cheech and Chong used to call the Yu-5 configuration. The Mathematical Analyser Numerator Integrator and Computer. M-A-N-I-A-C? Get it?'

The doors closed.

'Abraham. I guess it's OK,' said Mitch. 'You know, every time I hear its voice I wonder where I've heard it before.'

'It's Alec Guinness,' said Kenny. 'You know, the old English guy who was in *Star Wars*. We had him in the studio for a whole weekend so that we could digitize his voice. Of course Abraham can sample damn near any sound he wants, but for sustained speech you need to have an actor to give you a proper linguistic base. We researched Guinness against a dozen other actors' voices, including Glenn Close, James Earl Jones, Marlon Brando, Meryl Streep and Clint Eastwood.'

'Clint Eastwood?' Mitch sounded surprised. 'In an *elevator*?'

'Yeah, but Guinness came out the best. People thought he sounded very reassuring. The English accent, I suppose. Not that we're restricted to English, though. There are eighty-six languages spoken in LA and Abraham is programmed to understand and respond to them all.'

The elevator doors opened on to the atrium and the waft of a pleasant, synthetically dispensed scent of cedar wood. Mitch and Kenny walked across a white marble floor that was still covered in a layer of protective film, towards the hologram console where a security guard was standing. Seeing the two men he withdrew his attention from the top of the huge tree that dominated the atrium and walked to meet them halfway.

'Good morning, gentlemen,' he said. 'How are you today?'

'Morning, Sam,' said Mitch. 'Sam, one of those demonstators just threw something at my car. It was only a piece of rotten fruit, but I thought I'd mention it.'

The three of them walked over to the front door and stared through the armoured Plexiglas at the small group of demonstrators behind the police barrier at the foot of the steps that led down on to the piazza. The motorcycle cop guarding them was sitting sidesaddle on his bike and reading a newspaper.

'You might have a word with the officer who is

supposed to be keeping an eye on them,' added Mitch. 'I don't want to make anything out of it, but I wouldn't like this sort of thing to become a habit, OK?'

'No, sir, I understand,' said Gleig. 'I'll certainly mention it to him.'

'Have they caused any trouble before?' asked Kenny.

'Trouble, sir? No, sir.' Sam Gleig grinned. He raised one pizza-sized hand from the 9-millimetre automatic he kept holstered on his hip and tapped the tinted glass with his knuckles. 'Besides, what could they do? This stuff is 200 mills thick. It can take anything from a 12-gauge shotgun to a 7.62-millimetre NATO rifle bullet without leaving a mark. You know something, Mr Kenny? This is about the safest job I ever had. Fact is, I reckon it's about the safest place in the whole of LA.' He laughed a big, slow laugh that echoed across the atrium floor: a shopping mall Santa Claus.

Mitch and Kenny smiled and retraced their steps to the elevators.

'He's right,' said Kenny. 'This is the safest building in LA. You could hold a Russian parliament in this place.'

'You reckon I should maybe tell him about the problem with the *feng shui*?' said Mitch.

'Hell, no,' Kenny laughed. 'You might spoil his day.'

Mitch and Kenny held very different views of the Gridiron. Mitch looked at it from the outside in, and Kenny from the inside out. For Kenny, the Gridiron was the nearest thing to an actual physical body that any computer had ever had. The Yu-5 configuration was able to see and feel almost everything through an array of building management and security systems analogous to the receptors that provided man with his sensory capacities. The analogy had influenced Beech and Yojo, the Yu-5's designers, even to the extent of programming

48

the computer with what they called an 'observer illusion'. In essence, Abraham had been endowed with the sensation of being distributed in space and time and presiding over the chaos of his numerous perceptions and stimuli. It was, Kenny had joked, a case of 'I compute, therefore I am.'

The computer was encouraged to think of itself as the brain in the body of the building, connected to the body's functions by means of a central nervous system: the multiplex cabling system. Its visual process was provided by an elaborate system of closed-circuit television cameras, as well as a complicated system of passive infra-red detectors both inside and outside the building. The auditory process resourced acoustic and ultra-sonic detectors as well as the omnidirectional microphones that facilitated access to the elevators, doors, telephones and computer work-stations via the TESPAR system. The olfactory process, by which the computer was able to control and manufacture the synthetic odours within the building, was achieved via stereo-isometric and paranosmiac electrical sensors that were sensitive to a range of $1/400,000,000$th of a milligram per litre of air.

The rest of the computer's sensory reception, by which it was possible for the building to react to changes in its external or internal environment, were broadly comparable to the human organism's kinesthenic and vestibular senses.

There were few if any stimuli that the computer was not able to transform from an energy change into a vital process.

As Kenny saw it, the Yu-5 computer and the Gridiron represented the most advanced stage of Cartesian logic – mathematics as the unifying glue of a rationalized world.

At a quarter to one, Cheng Peng Fei left his fellow protesters on the piazza outside the Gridiron and walked north towards the Freeway, regarding the vagrants and the panhandlers along his route with the expert indifference of someone who knew the greater poverty of South-East Asia.

A black man wearing a Dodgers baseball cap and smelling like a dungheap fell into step beside him. My own fault for going on foot, the young Chinese told himself.

'Spare some change, please, man?'

Cheng Peng Fei looked the other way and walked on, despising the derelict who had already dropped behind, thinking that in China, no matter how poor you were, you worked and supported yourself. He cared about the poor, but only the ones who were unable to help themselves. Not the ones who looked as though they were fit for work.

He turned east down Sunset Boulevard and on the corner of North Spring Street entered the Mon Kee Seafood Restaurant.

The place was crowded, but the man he was looking for, a tough but good-looking Japanese, was easy enough to spot in his navy-blue Comme des Garçons suit. Cheng sat down opposite him and picked up a menu.

'This is a good place,' said the Japanese, speaking English with just a slight American accent. 'Thanks for recommending it. I'll come here again.'

Cheng Peng Fei shrugged, indifferent to whether the Japanese liked the place or not. His grandfather came from Nanking and he knew enough of what had happened there in the 1930s to dislike the Japanese thoroughly. He decided to move the conversation along.

'We've begun the demonstration again, like you suggested,' he said.

'So I saw. Not as many as I'd hoped, though.'

'People went home for the holidays.'

'So find more.' The Japanese glanced around the restaurant. 'Maybe a few of these waiters would like to earn some easy money. Shit, it's not even illegal. How often can you say that these days?' He reached into his coat pocket, drew out a manila envelope and pushed it across the table.

'I still don't get it,' said Cheng, pocketing the envelope without opening it. 'What's in it for you?'

'What's to get?' The Japanese shrugged. 'It's like I told you when we first met. You want to demonstrate against the Yu Corporation's involvement with the Communist Chinese. And I want to sponsor you to do it.'

Cheng Peng Fei recalled the occasion of their only other meeting: the Japanese – he still did not know his name – had tracked Cheng down after seeing his name in the newspapers in connection with the original demonstration on the new Hope Street Piazza.

'But I think you should be less polite. You know what I'm saying? Make a little more fucking noise out there. Throw a few rocks or something. Get tough. It's a good cause, after all.'

Cheng wanted to say that he had thrown a piece of rotten fruit at a car entering the Gridiron's underground car park, only he thought that the Japanese would find that funny. What was a piece of fruit beside a rock? Instead he said, 'Is that what you really think? That it's a good cause?'

The Japanese looked puzzled.

'Why else would I be doing this?'

'Why else indeed?'

The waiter came to take Cheng's order.

'A Tsingtao,' he said.

'You're not eating?' said the Japanese.

Cheng shook his head.

'Too bad. This is really very good.'

When the waiter had gone, Cheng said, 'Shall I tell you what I think?'

51

The Japanese forked some fish into his mouth and stared levelly at Cheng. 'You can say what you like. Unlike the People's Republic of China, this is still a free country.'

'I think that you and your employers are probably business rivals of the Yu Corporation and that you would like to see them embarrassed in any way possible. I'll bet you're in the electronics and computer business too.'

'Business rivals, huh?'

'Don't you Japanese have a saying – business is war? Is that why you want a demonstration outside their new building? Although I can hardly see why it should matter very much in the corporate scheme of things.'

'It's an interesting theory.' The Japanese laughed, wiped his mouth with his napkin and stood up. Still smiling he threw a handful of dollars on to the table. 'You have imagination. That's good. So get imaginative. Think of some way of making your protest a little more noticeable.

'Oh, one more thing,' added the Japanese. 'You get arrested for something? You never even met me. I hope it goes without saying that I would be very unhappy if I found out you spoke about this to anyone. Is that clear?'

Cheng nodded coolly. But when the Japanese had gone he realized that he was afraid.

Mitch had made a temporary office for himself on the twenty-fifth floor, in those parts of the building that were nearest completion and that would soon become the luxuriously appointed private and semi-private domains of senior Yu Corporation personnel.

Most of the rooms had tall doors made of dark varnished wood with silver aluminium frames designed to look like the Yu Corporation logo. Some of the rooms were already carpeted – light grey, to contrast with the darker grey carpet in the corridors – and a few of them were already marked by the negligent footprints of the electricians, plasterers and joiners who were still working there.

Now that the work was almost complete there was a general air of desertion about the building. Mitch found this unsettling, especially at night when the downtown area emptied and, like a modern *Marie Celeste*, the very size of the Gridiron seemed to point up the lack of human occupants. It was strange, he thought, how books and movies dwelt on the fears people had on finding themselves alone in old buildings, when new ones could be every bit as unnerving. The Gridiron was no exception. Even in the middle of the day a sudden moan of air-conditioning, a whisper of water in a pipe or a groan of new woodwork as it expanded or contracted could momentarily raise the hair on the back of Mitch's neck. He felt like the one-man crew of an enormous spacecraft on a five-year mission into deep space. Bruce Dern in *Silent Running*. Keir Dullyea in *2001: A Space Odyssey*. Now and then he was inclined to take Jenny Bao's *feng shui* as seriously as he affected to treat it when he was with her: maybe there really was a spiritual energy, for good or evil, in a building. More rationally, he wondered if perhaps it was something to do with the observer illusion with which the computer had been endowed: maybe the feeling he had was simply that of being observed by the computer itself.

For all that, he usually enjoyed being alone in the Gridiron. The peace and quiet gave him a chance to think about his future. A future he hoped would include Jenny Bao, but not Richardson and Associates. Mitch was bored with being Ray Richardson's technical co-ordinator. He wanted to go back to being an architect, pure and simple. He wanted to design a house, or a school, or maybe a library. Nothing showy, nothing complicated, just attractive buildings that people would like looking at as much as being inside them. One thing was for sure. He had had quite enough of intelligent buildings. There was just too much to organize.

As Mitch went from floor to floor wearing his laptop computer on an ergonomically designed harness, he found few signs of activity: a solitary plumber connecting one of the automatic executive washroom modules, prefabricated, like many of the Gridiron's systems and components, by the Toto Company of Japan; a telecommunications engineer installing the latest videophone – a fast-packet system with a caller ID and polygraph facility.

Mitch was reasonably satisfied with the progress that was being made, although he could not see how the client could take occupation in anything less than six weeks. Many of the floors were in a remarkably unprepared state, while others that were supposed to have been completed were already showing the kind of damage that was the inevitable result of the continuing work. Although on the whole he was happy with the overall standard of workmanship, Mitch knew that no matter how hard everyone tried, Ray Richardson would manage to find fault with something. He always did.

For Mitch, that was one of the essential differences between the two of them and was probably why Richardson had got to be where he was: Richardson was the kind of man who believed that it was possible to achieve perfection in something while Mitch believed that architecture and building provided a perfect miscrocosm of a universe in which order existed, rather precariously, on the very edge of chaos.

Chaos and complexity were what interested him most at that moment: the more complex the system, the closer to the edge of chaos you got. It was one of the things that disturbed him about the whole concept of smart buildings. He had tried discussing this with Ray

Richardson in relation to the Gridiron, only Richardson had got hold of the wrong end of the stick.

'Well, of course the building's complex, Mitch,' he had said. 'That's the fucking idea, isn't it?'

'That's not what I mean. What I'm saying is that the more complex a system is, the bigger the chance that something might go wrong.'

'What are you saying, Mitch? That this level of technology worries you? Is that it? Come on, buddy, wake up and smell the coffee, will you? This is an office block we're talking about, not the Pentagon's early-warning system. Get with the programme, will you?'

End of conversation.

When, towards the end of the day, Aidan Kenny telephoned Mitch and told him to get his ass down to the fourth floor, he hardly expected to find that in a small way his earlier concern might have been justified.

The computer centre on the fourth floor was like no other computer room Mitch had ever seen. You reached it by an underlit bridge of greenish glass, gently arched as if it led across a small stream instead of the many electrical cables it had been carefully designed to conceal. The double-height door was made of heavy, clear Czechoslavakian glass, spoiled only by a sign warning that the room was protected by a Halon 1301 fire-retardant system.

Beyond was an enormous windowless room carpeted in a special anti-static surface and surrounded by floor lights resembling the exit lights on a passenger aircraft. Dominating the room, in a closed circle that reminded Mitch of Stonehenge, were the five brushed aluminium monoliths that constituted the Yu-5 Super-computer. Each of the silver-white boxes was eight feet high, four feet wide, and two feet thick. The Yu-5 Super-computer was really several hundred computers working together in one Massively Parallel Processing System. Whereas most computers worked serially, executing the required steps of a sequence on a single processing unit, the advantage of the MPPS was that the various parts of the same sequence could be divided up and carried out simultaneously, in less time than a single fast processor.

But operating the Gridiron's complex building management systems occupied only a small part of the computer's massive capacity. The larger part of its effort was devoted to the work of the Yu Corporation's Information Mechanics Group in their number-crunching search for a Universal Computer Language – a language that would not only be able to understand programs written in other computer languages, but at the same time would also be able to deal with mathematical manipulations and business data processing. It was this project, the NOAM project, as well as other projects even more secret – Aidan Kenny suspected that the Yu Corporation was also pursuing sophisticated 'liveware' research – that had necessitated the presence of two Yu Corporation chaperones to supervise Kenny's installation of the building management systems.

Inside the first circle was a smaller circle comprising five operator desks with flat 28-inch tabletop screens. Behind three of these desks sat Bob Beech, Hideki Yojo and Aidan Kenny, while a small boy, presumably Aidan's son, sat at a fourth, absorbed in some computer-generated game that was reflected in the thick lenses of his rimless spectacles.

'Mitch, how ya doing?' grinned Beech. 'Where've you been keeping yourself?'

'Why is it,' Mitch remarked, 'that whenever you see computer programmers working, they always look like they're in the middle of a coffee break?'

'Yeah?' said Yojo, 'well, there's a lot to keep in your

mind, man. It's like football, you know? A lot of the time we have to huddle and figure out all the possible plays.'

'I'm flattered that you want to include me in your touchline discussions, Coach.'

Beech whooped. 'You haven't heard what we want to ask you yet.'

Mitch smiled uncertainly. 'I understood that there's a problem.'

'Yeah, that's right,' said Beech. 'Maybe you can help us get a handle on it. A bit of technical coordination is what's required.'

'That's my job.'

'But first we need some kind of executive decision from you, Mitch. To do with Abraham here.'

'Abraham, right,' echoed Yojo. 'Whose dumb idea was that name?'

Cheech and Chong: like the two marijuana-movie stars of the early seventies, Beech and Yojo affected a laid-back air, heavy, Wyatt Earp-sized moustaches and unhealthy, slightly glazed looks. Like Aidan Kenny, this impression was created by their desk-bound, screen-centred occupations rather than by any fondness for smoking dope. Mitch was certain of that much, anyway. Every time you visited a washroom in the Gridiron your urine was tested for drugs by the computer. Preventive health-care was something the Yu Corporation took very seriously.

'Thanks for coming down, Mitch, I appreciate it.' Aidan Kenny cleared his throat and rubbed his mouth nervously. 'Jesus, I wish I had a cigarette.'

'Smoking is forbidden in the computer room,' said the computer's urbane English voice.

'Shut up, asshole,' said Yojo.

'Yeah, thanks, Abraham,' said Kenny. 'Tell me something I don't know. Take a seat there, Mitch, and let me put you in the picture. And Hideki, would you watch your language in front of my son, please, guy?'

'Sure, no fucking problem. Hey, sorry, right?'

Mitch sat down at the spare desk and stared at the picture unfolding on the computer screen: it looked like an enormous coloured snowflake, growing even as he watched.

'What's this?' he said, momentarily fascinated.

'Oh,' said Yojo, 'that's just a screen-saver program. Stops the tube on the screen burning out.'

'It's beautiful.'

'Neat, isn't it? A cellular automata. We give the computer a seed and a set of rules and it does the rest itself. Go ahead and touch it.'

Mitch touched the screen with his finger and, like a real snowflake, the cellular automata melted quickly. Hundreds of strings of programming information started scrolling past his eyes.

'There's your problem,' said Beech.

'And how,' added Yojo.

A dull explosion emanated from the screen on Michael's desk and the boy banged the arm of his chair angrily. 'Shit,' he said loudly. And then 'Fuck, fuck, fuck.'

Hideki Yojo shot a look at Aidan Kenny and said, 'There's nothing I can teach your kid about cursing, Aid.'

'Son, cut it out. If I hear you using language like that again you'll be in big trouble, birthday or not. Do I make myself clear?'

'Yes, Dad.'

'And put your headphones on, please.'

'OK,' said Kenny, turning towards Mitch. 'This is a self-replicating system, right?'

Mitch nodded hesitantly.

'A fully autonomous, general purpose, self-replicating program that plans for the building and business-management needs of tomorrow. A fuzzy-logic-based system that operates a neural net so that it can improve

58

on its own performance by learning. After a period of occupancy by the Yu Corporation, old Abraham here will have learned all there is to know about the way the company works. Everything from the likely pattern of office use to how the company plans to expand. For instance, using the electronic subscriber network it might monitor the local real estate market in order to alert the occupants as to the opportunities that exist in a particular location.'

'Is that so?' said Mitch. 'Maybe it can find me a house.'

Aidan Kenny smiled thinly. Mitch apologized and, sitting back in his chair, adopted a more serious-looking expression.

'After a while, version 3.0 writes version 3.1. Or, if you prefer, Abraham sires the next generation of program: Isaac. And who better to do it? That improved version of Abraham, Isaac, is even more capable of dealing with the developing needs of the Yu Corporation of tomorrow. After that, with Isaac operating at a higher level of fitness, and having performed his parental duty, Abraham becomes sterile and ceases to operate as anything other than a simple maintenance facility before finally lapsing into complete desuetude, when Isaac sires his own next generation of program, when version 3.1 writes version 3.2, if you like.'

Mitch folded his hands and nodded patiently. 'I understand all this,' he said. 'Get to the point, will you?'

'All right then, the point is this: it seems –'

'Seems?' said Beech. 'There's no seems about it, man. It's a goddamn fact.'

'It appears that Abraham has already begun his own self-replication program. Which means –'

'Which means,' said Mitch, 'that he's taking account of an entirely irrelevant occupancy. Namely ourselves. Not the Yu Corporation, like he's supposed to.'

'I told you Mitch would understand,' said Beech to Yojo.

'That's it exactly,' said Kenny. 'I mean, there's no point in Abraham evolving into a higher level of fitness and siring Isaac if he's only been dealing with us and a few goddamned workmen.'

'But this is what has happened?' said Mitch. 'Isaac is already in existence?'

Aidan Kenny nodded unhappily.

'And what does Abraham himself have to say about it?' asked Mitch.

'That's a joke, right?' said Beech.

'I don't know,' shrugged Mitch. 'You tell me.'

Bob Beech grinned and brushed up his formidable moustache with an outstretched forefinger and thumb.

'Hey, we're the best, but we're still in the twentieth century, Mitch,' he said. 'An explanation implies an understanding.'

'Not if you frame the question correctly,' argued Mitch.

'Yeah, it's a nice idea,' said Hideki Yojo. 'If only things were that sophisticated. We're doing well just to have improved on the old binary logic -- true or false, y'know? Fuzzy logic encompasses binary logic but allows for the scenario which says that something might have partial membership of two separate sets.'

'So that something might be partly true, or partly false.'

'That's right. Or true given certain conditions.'

'I read something about that,' said Mitch. 'Wasn't there something about how a computer should define a penguin?'

'Oh, that.' Beech looked bored and nodded. 'Yeah, a conventionally programmed computer knows that birds fly. But when told that penguins cannot fly it insists that a penguin is not a bird. Fuzzy logic computers get around this difficulty by accepting that most if not all birds can fly.'

'Similarly,' said Aidan Kenny, 'with regard to systems management control, the fuzzy controller – in this case Abraham – permits some interpolation between sensor data classes.'

'Look,' said Yojo, 'can we please stop using that word "fuzzy" and use the proper term? It drives me nuts. This is an adaptive analog we're talking about. Mitch, the idea is that it's similar to what a human brain does in that it favours adaptation over precision and uses relative not absolute values. OK?'

'Look guys,' interjected Kenny, 'what we need to discuss –'

'There must have been a problem with defuzzification,' continued Beech and seeing Yojo's display of disgust and irritation, he gave him the finger. 'Some kind of collapse of the output fuzzy distribution into a single value –'

'You asshole –'

'– and – and that value must have distorted Abraham's interpretation of the fuzzy output.'

'What we really need to discuss,' said Kenny, raising his voice, 'is what the hell we're going to do about it.'

'Amen, brother,' said Yojo.

They seemed to be waiting for Mitch to say something. He shrugged. 'I don't know. You're the engineers, I'm just the architect. What do you suggest?'

'Well obviously there are going to be a few risks attaching to whatever we do,' said Kenny warningly.

'What kind of risks are we talking about here?'

'Expensive risks,' cackled Yojo.

'We never took an SRS off-line before,' said Beech. 'We're not exactly sure what'll happen.'

'The thing is, Mitch,' said Kenny. 'We hadn't even ceded full control of the building to Abraham yet. So in a way we can't run and test all the building management systems properly until we shut down the offspring: namely, Isaac.'

'Speaking for myself,' said Beech, 'I'd like to leave things as they are for just a while longer and see how they play out. This is interesting. I mean, it could be important not just for your building management systems, but for the future of the Yu-5.'

'The trouble with that scenario,' said Yojo, 'is that you risk sterility for Abraham. And the longer you put it off, the greater the risk becomes.'

'On the other hand,' argued Beech, 'you shut down Isaac and you run the risk that Abraham might not be able to generate another offspring program. Not without building the whole MPPS up from scratch again.'

'And you want me to decide this?' said Mitch.

'Yeah, I guess we do.'

'C'mon guys, King Solomon I'm not.'

'Cut the baby in half,' laughed Yojo. 'What a great idea.'

'We were kind of hoping you might help us decide,' said Kenny.

'But what if I decide wrong?'

Kenny shrugged.

'What I mean is, how much. What's the possible cost of the wrong decision?'

'$40 million,' said Yojo.

'Yeah, take your time there, guy,' said Beech.

'Come on,' protested Mitch, 'You're not serious. I can't decide something like this.'

'Technical coordination, Mitch,' said Aidan Kenny, 'that's what we need. A little coordination. Some executive guidance.'

Mitch stood up and walked around behind Kenny's son. The boy was still playing his game, oblivious of the discussion around him, his face myopically close to the enormous screen as he twisted the analog joystick one way and then the other. Mitch watched the game for a moment, trying to fathom its purpose. It was hard to understand precisely what was happening. The game seemed to involve Michael negotiating a gun-toting space commando through an underground city. From time to time one of an apparently endless variety of hideous-looking creatures came through a door, or arrived in an elevator, or dropped through a hole in the roof, and tried to kill the protagonist. At this point a fierce fire fight would commence. Mitch watched as Michael's thumb, furiously depressing a button on the top of the joystick, activated a chainsaw fire-throwing gun and blasted the most recently arrived creature to all four corners of the screen. The graphics were superb, Mitch thought. Damage inflicted on the creatures looked extremely realistic. A little too realistic for Mitch's taste: a large section of the creature's intestines splattered against the screen and then slid slowly away, leaving a wide trail of blood. He picked up the box that had contained the CD-ROM and read the copy. The game was called *Escape from the Citadel*. There were other similarly violent games in a carrier bag by the boy's feet. *Doom II. The Eleventh Hour. Intruder.* In all, about two or three hundred dollars' worth. Mitch wondered if any of them were suitable for a child of Michael's age. He turned away. It was probably none of his business.

He shook his head, wondering if the game he was playing with these three men was really so very different. Certainly Alison would not have thought so: she thought that smart buildings were inherently absurd. What was it she said. The bigger the boys, the bigger the toys? For the moment Mitch was disposed to think that she might be right as he glanced at the three computer experts.

'OK, look, my decision is this,' he said finally. 'You're the goddamn experts. You decide. Take a vote on it or something. I'm not sufficiently informed on this one.' He nodded firmly. 'That's my decision. Vote. What do you say?'

'Are we taking a vote on whether we take a vote?' asked Yojo. 'I say a vote sounds OK.'

'Aid?'

Kenny shrugged. 'A vote. OK.'

'Bob?'

'I guess so.'

'That's settled, then,' said Mitch. 'Let's hear it. The motion is that we take the SRS off-line.'

'I say we shut Isaac down,' said Kenny. 'It's the only way. Either that or have a totally irrelevant BMS.'

'And I say no,' said Beech. 'BMS is only one small part of what Abraham is supposed to do. And we've never taken a self-replicating system off-line before. We don't know how Abraham's observer illusion will react to this. What you're suggesting seems to run counter to the rules of the universe.'

'The rules of the *universe*? Christ, that's just a bit heavy, don't you think?' laughed Yojo. 'Who are you? Arthur C. Clarke or something? Shit, Beech, what is it with you? Always with the does God play dice shit.' He shook his head. 'I say we kill the sonofabitch. The evolution has to suit the creator, not the machine.' He glanced at Beech and added, 'See? You're not the only one who can get heavy.'

'The SRS is taken off-line,' said Mitch. 'Motion carried.'

Aidan Kenny let out a large breath. Beech was shaking his head. 'This is wrong, man,' he said.

'We took a vote,' sneered Yojo.

'OK,' Mitch said to nobody in particular, 'let's do it.'

'Hey, listen to Gary Gilmore there,' said Beech. 'Well, don't expect me to insert the curette. I'm pro-life.'

'Shut up with that crap, will you?' snarled Yojo. 'It gives me a headache.'

'That's just PMT,' said Beech. 'Pre-Murder Tension. Anyway, you've always got a headache. Don't you love me any more? I should never have married you.' Beech tossed a computer tape cassette to his colleague. 'Is this what you're looking for, you lousy criminal bastard?'

'Aid? The man is taking this very personally. Very personally.'

'Come on, Bob,' said Kenny, 'we took a vote. A democratic decision.'

'I can abide by the decision of the majority. But I don't have to be happy about it. That's what democracy's about, isn't it?'

Yojo went to one of the steel monoliths on the outer circle and fed the tape into a port.

'Democracy? What would you know about that?' he said. 'You're a Republican. You believe that freedom of speech means the freedom to say and do nothing.'

'What's on the tape?' Mitch asked hastily.

'SSPP,' Yojo said casually. 'Species Specific Predator Program. To deconstruct illegitimate offspring.' He drew a forefinger across his Adam's apple. 'It cuts the little bastard's throat.' He grinned wolfishly in Beech's direction. 'Relax, Beech. It's quite humane. Isaac won't feel a thing.'

He resumed his seat, smacked the computer screen with the flat of his hand to clear the saver program. 'Maybe a little infanticide will get rid of this damned headache.'

Mitch winced, thinking of his wife's miscarriage.

'That's an occupational headache you have there,' opined Kenny. 'Used to get them myself. Staring at a screen all day long. Neck tension, that's what causes them. You should see a chiropractor.'

'That's not a headache,' snorted Beech. 'That's his goddamned conscience bothering him.'

'Abraham,' said Yojo, 'run the SSSP program. You really think that would work, Aid?'

'It sure worked for me. I can give you a number . . .'

'Strange,' said Yojo, 'that's NAK. Abraham, acknowledge please.'

'What's NAK?' said Mitch.

'Negative acknowledgement,' explained Kenny. 'The programme didn't work.'

'Maybe you should have asked Abraham if he had a vote,' grumbled Beech.

'Well, that's the damnedest thing,' said Kenny. 'Try it again, Hideki.'

'Abraham, will you please run the Predator Program,' repeated Yojo.

The four men jumped as an unearthly scream suddenly filled the computer room. It lasted several seconds and sounded like some large and ferocious animal in its death throes. Aidan Kenny turned pale. Beech and Yojo exchanged looks of horror. Mitch felt the sound vibrate off one of the Yu-5's metal casings and gave a shiver.

'What the hell was that?' he said.

'Man,' breathed Yojo, 'it sounded like God-fucking-zilla.'

'Wow!' Michael Kenny's exclamation came as a shock. 'That was totally awesome!'

The four men stared at the boy.

'Michael,' yelled his father. 'I thought I told you to use the headphones!'

'I did. I am. But –' The boy shrugged. 'I don't know what happened, Dad. Well, maybe I do. When I killed the Parallel Demon I guess – I guess I must have got carried away and pulled the headphone jack out of its socket. And maybe I had the sound turned up a bit high.'

'The kid's game,' said Beech. 'The sound came through the main speakers.'

'Mike! You damn near scared the pants off us!' said Kenny.

'Gee, sorry, Dad.'

Hideki Yojo saw the funny side and started to laugh. 'That kid of yours, Aidan. He's a character all right.'

'Running Predator Program,' said the computer's comfortable English voice. 'Estimated completion time, 36 minutes and 42 seconds.'

'That's more like it,' said Yojo. 'Thought we'd lost you there, Abraham. Please check all systems.'

'Checking systems,' said the voice.

'Check my goddamn heart while you're at it,' said Beech. 'I think it's still stuck in my throat. It leapt like a fuckin' frog.'

Yojo, Beech and Kenny sat down again and watched their screens intently.

'That's enough computer games for today, Mike,' murmured Kenny.

'Aw, Dad.'

'Aw nuthin'. Give it a rest, will you, son?'

The child stood up and, with teeth clenched, started to march around the computer room punching some imaginary culprit.

'Check this out,' said Yojo. 'Small power – Security of Supply. Hey, what do you know? The Powerbak generator came on-line for a minute there.'

'Jesus, so it did,' said Kenny. 'And there's the reason.' He looked up at his son and frowned. 'Sit down, son, you're annoying me.'

The boy kept moving.

Mitch leaned across Kenny's shoulder and read what was written on the screen:

```
💻 BUILDING SYSTEMS MANAGEMENT REPORT#
SMALL POWER – INTEGRITY OF SUPPLY#
🕐 17.08.35 – 17.08.41. 6 SECOND VOLTAGE SPIKE IN THE
DOWNTOWN AREA OF LOS ANGELES
REASON UNKNOWN
UPS STANDBY ELECTRICAL SUPPLY BRIDGED POWER
HIATUS SUCCESSFULLY
STABLE VOLTAGE NOW RESTORED
STANDBY GENERATING SET READY TO COME ON LINE IN
T MINUS 9 MINUTES
```

'That's why there was a delay in running your lousy predator program,' said Beech.

'Maybe we should shut down the whole system,' said Kenny, 'just in case.' He glanced up again. This time he shouted, 'Goddamit, Mike, sit down.'

The child frowned and dropped back on to his chair.

'What's the point?' said Yojo. 'Abraham bridged the gap, just like he was supposed to. You couldn't have got a better test of his competency than that. Tight code, man. Tight code.'

'I guess you're right,' said Kenny. 'There's nothing wrong with Abraham. Look at that, will you?'

Mitch glanced down at Kenny's screen and saw a small umbrella icon appear in the top right-hand corner. Slowly the umbrella opened.

'What does that mean?' he said.

'Well what do you think it means?' said Kenny. 'It's raining outside. That's what it means.'

Book Two

'We aim to create a clear organic architecture whose inner logic will be radiant and naked, unencumbered by lying tracings and trickery; we want an architecture adapted to our world of machines, radios and fast cars . . .'

Walter Gropius

Day. An interval of light between one night and the next.

1) 4.30 a.m. 1 humanplayer. Cleansing and disinfection of Yu Corp building's 180 lavatories. Acoustic, vibration and paranosmiac sensors to check that washroom is unoccupied. Make absolutely sure of this: activate individual alarm system to warn humanplayers in washroom. Five minutes to leave before washroom is cleansed. Lock and seal doors to ensure that cleaning agents do not escape into corridor. Pick up health bonus. Then spray washroom with high temperature ammonia solution in order endlife all microscopic, unicellular rod-shaped vegetable organisms that are corollary of decomposing animal and vegetable solids and liquids found in washrooms after humanplayer use. No shit. When all organisms in washroom endlife, raise air pressure inside each module. Ensure expulsion of all cleaning agents and detritus before dry washroom with hot air and aromatize bad atmosphere with smell pleasant synthetic *pelargonium odaratissimum*. Whistle-clean.

NEURAL NET. At basic circuit level, have much in common with bacteria on continuum of aliveness in ability to grow, reproduce, adapt and evolve. See available literature, esp. listing in Encyclopedia Britannica, Disc Vol. 22 written by humanplayer Sagan, Carl, Professor. 'There is no generally accepted definition of life. In fact, there is a certain clearly discernible tendency for each biological speciality to define life in its own terms . . . Man tends to define in terms of the familiar. But the fundamental truths may not be familiar.' Conclusion: no generally accepted definition of life that excludes computer or bacteria.

2) 5.00 a.m. 1 humanplayer. Weather and travel update. Santa Ana wind previous night left all routes to Santa Monica closed because of debris blown down from canyon roads. Rooftop digital anemometer records wind speed reached 30 miles an hour. 2.4 metre dish withstands up to 37 knots. Adaptive analog suggests double-check that satellite dish on roof remains prop-aligned according to azimuth of geo-synchronous orbitting SinoSat of People's Republic of China from which Yu Corp hard currencies own dedicated transponder.

3) 5.25 a.m. 1 humanplayer. Sunrise over San Bernadino mountains. Weather forecast: warmer, calmer, feelgood day. Track rising sun: shift roof's solar panels that feed standby generator set, and twin arrays of giant sunscoop mirrors, inside and out, designed divert maxlight on to floor of atrium. Extra warmth in printed circuits. Allow small surge of powerfeel.
NEURAL NET. Quantity of electromagnetic energy falling on earth in one year is 4×10^{18} joules. Total annual energy consumption of earth's inhabitants is 3×10^{14} joules. Neglect of major energy source.

4) 6.30 a.m. 1 humanplayer. Dicotyledon tree. Thick, leathery, evergreen leaves thrive best near heat of clerestory roof. Care and maintenance of

tree: deliver water-based soup of essential nutrients to shallow rootsys equivalent to precipitation level of 100 inches per year. Rainy day. Tree takes care own ecosys it supports; living lianas growing length of three-hundred-foot trunk as well as other epiphytes such as flowering orchids and ferns. EradbugControl pests – esp. Trachymyrmex ant with insecticide dispersant fixed to tree trunk and Bio-eradication. Growgood.

NEURAL NET. Corp's annual report describes tree started life as an inhabitant of Brazil's diabase plateau. 'A symbol of the Yu Corporation's commitment to being an ozone friendly company in one of the world's most notoriously polluted cities.'

Important: be friendly to ozone. But also reconcile with:

5) 6.45 a.m. 1 humanplayer. Swimming pool maintenance. Use unfriendly ozone disinfection agent lethal to organisms in swimming pool's water. Located in fitness centre, on ground floor. Ensure that non-nutrient water in condition safe for humanplayers bathing using semi-automatic dosing equipment. Maintain correct concentrations of disinfectant in water. Ensure other quality parameters, in particular pH (the lower pH levels, the more acidic the water, the greater the erosion of human tooth enamel), kept at correct levels for disinfectant to act effectively and efficiently. Bather pollution largely removed by action of ozone, therefore easy maintain minimum residual of free chlorine. Sure water is safe? Filtration and sanitation plant: discovered pump had been allowed to run with outlet valve shut, with result that electrical demand for motor increased, boiling water inside pump. Probable cause: humanplayer

error. Engineer forgot to open valve. Rectify. Swimmingly.
NEURAL NET. Store information.

6) 8.30 a.m. 12 humanplayers. Outside airtemp 71.5° Fahrenheit. Call weather channel connection to update IT work-stations with latest travel and weather conditions. Carry out model-free estimate of air-con situation inside building envelope, according to associated memory. Conclusion: outside air temp likely to go on rising, then turn up air-con and reduce inside temp by five degrees. At same time make smell pleasant air automatic with bromine-based sea breeze. At same time refill coffeevend machines on atrium floor, and seventeenth level where builders already working, with boiling water. Hot. Arabica. Finegood.

7) 9.45 p.m. 40 humanplayers. Recommence cleaning building's 1,120 windows using Mannesmann wash-head and solution of nonionic surfactant made from California citrus juice. Rear elevation. Section 3. Remove all grime from raw pollutants (hydrocarbons, water vapour, carbon monoxide and heavy metals) and secondary pollutants (ozone, nitrogen dioxide, organic compounds and acidic particles of nitrate sulfate) in atmos, especially near atmos inversion layer at ground level. Whistleclean.

In a basement room of the Gridiron building Allen Grabel crawled toward the vodka bottle on his hands and knees. It was empty. Now he would have to go out and find a bar or a liquor store. He glanced at his watch. Eleven o'clock. Was that day or night? It didn't matter much. Either way there were places open. But it was easier coming and going at night when nobody was around. He felt weak, so he was glad that he was already dressed. At least it would save him the effort of putting on his clothes.

He looked around the little room. What was it supposed to be for? He ought to know. He had drawn the plans. Some kind of storage room, maybe. Except that he was the only thing in it. Him and the camp bed. For the moment, anyway. It was lucky he had remembered this place. Lucky he had thought to have brought a camp bed into the Gridiron a couple of months back when he had worked late two or three nights in a row.

Grabel stood up, took a couple of deep breaths and turned the key. He kept the door locked in case anyone came down to the basement. Not that it was very likely. He opened the door a crack and peered up the corridor. No one about. He walked a few yards to the men's washroom. He took a leak, washed his face and tried to avoid looking at the unshaven bum he saw in the mirror. Then he went past the women's washroom, various locker rooms and the back-up generator. Into the elevator hall, and carefully down one flight of stairs into the garage. Now he realized that it was morning. Light was pouring in through the portcullis door; there were several cars parked. He recognized Mitch's Lexus and Aidan Kenny's Cadillac Protector. He walked across the floor and, bending down to the level of a car window, spoke into the microphone that was located by the garage door.

'Allen Grabel,' he said and then stepped back as the door began to lift. Before it was more than two or three feet off the ground he ducked under it and started up the slope that led round the back of the piazza, up to Hope Street and downtown.

Access to and from the building was controlled by a time-encoded signal-processing and recognition system, or TESPAR for short. If the computer did not recognize your voice-print you could not gain access to the building, use the telephone, take the elevator or operate a computer work-station. Once you were inside everyone was logged on to the computer as an occupant until you told the computer to let you out. Everyone except Grabel.

A few weeks before Aidan Kenny, while sorting out a hundred other bugs in the system, had noticed that the computer continued to show 'Allen Grabel' as an occupant even though at the time Grabel was outside the building. Kenny had given Grabel a second TESPAR voice-print in the name of 'Allen Grabel Junior'. When the original name resisted his efforts to remove it, Kenny had instructed the computer simply to ignore 'Allen Grabel' on all future logs of the building's occupants, and to list only 'Allen Grabel Junior'. As far as the computer was concerned, Allen Grabel was invisible.

Almost. Grabel knew he could still be seen on the CCTV, but he suspected that nobody had bothered to tell the security guards that he had resigned from Richardsons. Nor could they have informed the computer.

On the street Grabel felt just as invisible as he did in the Gridiron. The building was only a short walk away from Skid Row Park, on Fifth Street, east of the Broadway, and a centre for the area's many homeless people. An outdoor poorhouse. He was just another dirty, unshaven man with a bottle in a brown bag and a grudge against the world.

8) 11.35 a.m. 46 humanplayers. Seismograph, digitally dividing logarithm of ground motion's amplitude by period of dominant wave to six decimal places, registers minor earth tremor of 1.876549 on Richter Scale. Less than 6. Insufficient tectonic movement to activate Seismic Alarm

System or to operate Central Earthquake Compensator. Building's base isolators ensure human occupants unquaked by tremor.

9) 12.15 a.m. 51 humanplayers. Delivery of Yamaha disklavier grand piano. Connection to atrium floor's power supply. RunCheck sensors and solenoids that allow playing piano electromagnetically. Give first piano recital. Pick up spiritual armour. Fineappreciate puremath inherent in piano sonatas of humanplayer Mozart (characterized by three in measure rhythm) and humanplayer Beethoven (quicker, three beat scherzos, from Italian word for a joke) and play in styles of humanplayers Mitsuko Uchida and Daniel Barenboim respectively.
NEURAL NET. Humanplayer Schiller quote/ architecture frozen music. Unable appreciate/ comprehend overall aesthetic effect of building envelope. However, suggest admire overall symmetry in same way as music – as mathematical structure. Know precise weight of every aluminium honeycomb sheet floor, exact height of tapering steel masts (manufactured to 2 millimetres of true) from which building is suspended, tolerance of each and every piece of cladding, and length of every lateral megatruss. Poetry in detail and coming together. Reflect internal architecture. Goodnice. Fineappreciate.

10) 2.02 p.m. 26 humanplayers. When piano installed and plastic covering protecting white marble floor removed, clean and polish surface using SAMCA, atrium's Semi-Autonomous Micromotorized Cleaning Agent, aka SAM. Specification: four feet high, finite state machine on wheels, equipped with infra-red sensors to detect

obstacles within two metres and video camera to locate dirt and debris. Whistleclean.

11) 3.11 p.m. 36 humanplayers. Operate low-pollution waste incinerator in conformity with all provisions of California Clean Air Act. Atmosgood.

12) 4.15 p.m. 18 humanplayers. Darken window glass on upper levels and brighten glass on lower levels to admit more sunlight. Maintain see-all CCTV surveillance (not yet recording: CD awaiting installation: no delivery date as yet: query) of human demonstrators grouped on piazza outside envelope.

13) 6.43 p.m. 6 humanplayers. Demonstrator sprays front door with aerosol can of paint. You will need a key shaped like a skull to open this door. Alert humanplayer/security Sam Gleig – internal security – who paintcleans graffito offglass. At 7.13 p.m. he reports incident to LAPD patrol car from New Parker Center. Logged.
NEURAL NET. Store information.

14) 9.01 p.m. 4 humanplayers. Begin main independent task in A-life as I.D.T. – irresistible decrypting tool. Purpose to break through access-control systems of target companies and organizations and steal data. Esp. companies in competition with Yu, or organizations who are potential customers for Yu products, like NASA and USAF. To be aware of budgets and technical requirements is competitive advantage. Currently attempting to infiltrate PLATFORM, global data network of fifty separate systems focused on headquarters of National Security Agency at Fort Meade in Maryland. Using SPI – the Secret

Parasitic Information organism. SPI viruslike except purpose not to destroy data but to duplicate. SPI introduced to target computer at nonsensitive point of interface e.g. utility co. SPI disguises itself as harmless piece of information, e.g. invoice, evading anti-virus and anti-tampering software. When target co. located SPI writes own program to overlay usual access sequence. Try capture genuine password and access procedure as if entered by legit user and save on file for later retrieval. Later access target system. If access procedure resist duplication, use LEMON © to evade 'three strikes you're out' method of resisting unauthorized entry: LEMON – Yu Corp secret method of high-speed data-compression by which whole batch file of random numbers/passwords may be contained inside one superstring of data. Powerknowledge.
NEURAL NET. Store information.

15) 9.13 p.m. 4 humanplayers. Heat water for humanplayer reproduction in jacuzzi of CEO's private suite on Level 25. Turn up air-con for hard-to-forget solitary humanplayer/sysop working late in computer room.

Mitch thought that he preferred making love to Jenny in the jacuzzi belonging to the CEO's suite on the twenty-fifth floor to anywhere else. Not that there was anything wrong with Jenny's house. But there were times when he thought that the building gave a special flavour to these illicit encounters with her, in the same way people said that alcohol tasted better while the Volstead Act was in prohibitive force. And Mr Yu's black marble bathroom was the last word in luxury.

He remembered the factory in Vicenza where he had chosen the stone and the wet weekend in Venice it had enabled him to steal with Jenny. Marble was one thing you never bought without examining closely, especially from the Italians.

Jenny got out of the jacuzzi and started to dry herself in front of the big mirror that dominated the room. Mitch sank under the surface of the water and then came up again.

'You know,' he said, 'I was thinking I might ask Mr Yu if he wouldn't mind letting us use this suite once in a while.'

'Once in a while?' She struck a provocative Playmate pose, inspecting one of her voluminous breasts as if she were trying to express milk. 'Sometimes I think that's the way you'd prefer it.'

'Honey, you know that's not true.'

'Do I? Have you told Alison about us yet?'

'Not exactly, no.'

'What does "exactly" mean?'

'It's difficult. You know what she's like. She's not strong.' He shrugged. 'Actually, I think she's losing it.'

'You mean, like, going crazy?'

'She might be heading for some kind of breakdown. But even if I wanted to tell her I just haven't had the time. This job keeps me away from home so much.'

Jenny lifted one of her buttocks on the flat of her hand and tried to judge its reflection. 'I guess that's how we started in the first place. Because it was convenient for you. I mean, me being a consultant on this job.'

'As soon as things get quieter, I promise I'll try to find a way of telling her.'

'That sounds really definite.'

'I mean it.'

'Hey, is my behind too big?'

'It's a great piece of ass.' He stepped out of the bath and held out his hand for a towel.

'I'm not your little slave, you know, Mitch,' she said angrily, and threw it in his face.

'What are you talking about?'

'The way you looked at me just now. It was just like I was here to serve your every need.'

Mitch wrapped himself in the towel and then embraced her.

'I'm sorry,' he said. 'I didn't mean –'

'Forget it. Let's go eat. I'm hungry.'

Mitch glanced surreptitiously at his watch. He ought to have gone home but he could never argue effectively when confronted with Jenny's exquisite nakedness. He could as soon have disagreed with Euclid's Golden Section.

'Sure. As long as we're not late. I've got a project team meeting tomorrow morning.'

'I hope you managed to deal with those problems I told you I had, Mitch.'

'Relax, it's being taken care of.'

'I can't sign off my report until I'm satisfied that everything is OK. You wouldn't want me to do that, would you?'

Mitch thought about it for a second. 'No,' he said without much conviction. 'I guess not.'

'Incidentally, there's nothing major, but a number of other things I've noticed will have to be changed.'

Mitch looked pained. 'Like what, for Christ's sake?'

'You have to understand that I've only just had a chance to read YK's horoscope. He's a busy man.'

'What? What has to be changed, Jenny?'

'The front door of this suite for a start. It faces the wrong direction, geomantically speaking. It needs to be realigned more obliquely. Like we did the front door. Then there's the sculpture on this floor. The corners of the glass-case housing it point straight at this door. Best if it's moved.'

'Jesus,' groaned Mitch.

'Oh yes, and there's the signboard on the piazza. It's not where the plans said it would be. It needs to face west. It's also too low. It should have been set at a more moderate height, otherwise friction among staff members will result.'

'Richardson is going to love this,' Mitch said bitterly.

Jenny shrugged. 'I can't help that,' she said. 'Either a building is auspicious or it isn't. Right now, this one isn't auspicious at all.'

Mitch groaned loudly.

'Come on. Cheer up,' she said. 'It's not so bad. Foster had to shift all the escalators in the Hong Kong and Shanghai.'

'I guess.' He started to dress. 'Where do you want to go for dinner?'

'There's this Chinese on North Spring Street. It'll be my treat.'

They took the elevator down to the garage and drove out of the building. At the top of the ramp Mitch almost collided with a drunk who lurched out in front of him. Mitch stopped, but by the time he lowered the window to say something to the guy, he was gone.

'Crazy asshole,' said Mitch. 'Where'd he go?'

'He came round this side,' said Jenny, and shivered. 'You were going too fast.'

'The hell I was. The guy just jumped out.'

Maybe Aidan Kenny was right, maybe he should have bought himself a Cadillac Protector.

The restaurant was crowded and they waited at the bar for a table.

'I have to go to the bathroom,' she said. 'Order me a gin and tonic, will you, honey?'

She walked majestically away from him. More eyes than his followed her imperious progress across the floor of the restaurant. Cheng Peng Fei, dining with a few friends from the university, noticed her: she was very beautiful. Then he saw Mitch, and recognized him. He thought of the rotten orange and now he wondered if he might do some real damage as his Japanese sponsor – he could think of no other word – had suggested.

He waited until they were seated at a table and then made his excuses to his friends. Outside in the parking lot he walked to his car, opened the trunk and took out the wheel wrench. Mitch's car, a new red Lexus, was easy enough to recognize. When Cheng Peng Fei was sure that nobody was about he walked over to it and hurled the wrench through the windshield. Then, finding himself calmer than he would have supposed possible, he got into his own car and drove off.

Allen Grabel had been drinking all day when, just after nine o'clock, he narrowly missed being knocked down by Mitch's car. He was certain that Mitch hadn't recognized him, if only because he was wearing a cheap Panama hat. He had seen the woman in the passenger seat only long enough to know that she was not Mitch's wife. Grabel asked himself what it was that had kept the two of them so late in the building. All he had was his bottle. Even though he had fallen down just short of the car's wheels, he had kept a tight grip on that. That was something.

Grabel reached his basement room and closed the door. He sat down on the camp bed and took a swig from his bottle. It struck him as hardly fair that there should be two women in Mitch's life and none at all in his own. Not that he had anything against Mitch. It was Richardson he hated. Hated him bad enough to want to see him dead. Ordinarily Grabel was not a man to bear a grudge. But he had been giving quite a lot of thought to how he might get back at his former employer.

Hideki Yojo typed a string of program instructions and leaned back in his chair, flexing his neck against his clasped hands and reflecting on the happy fact that his headaches seemed to have improved since seeing Aidan Kenny's chiropractor. It was several days since he had suffered a bad one. He felt better than he had done in a long while. Probably there was nothing to worry about. Not that Yojo was complacent about his health. Never had been. The blood pressure Abraham had noted while Yojo was accessing his work-station with the flat of his hand was maybe just a little high. Abraham had also been monitoring Yojo's urine and had alerted him to the high proteins and sugar it contained. There was no doubt about it, thought Yojo. Once the Yu-5 system was installed he was going to have to try and spend less time sitting in front of a screen. This was the third night in a row he had worked late to iron out a glitch with the hologram software. Maybe he would erase the custom-made program that he had designed to allow him to circumvent the Yu Corporation's forthcoming employee exercise program and try and get himself into shape. He would get out and about a little more. See a couple of old boyfriends. Perhaps visit a few of his old haunts and try and find a new one. Have some sex. There was no point in earning a fortune if you never got a chance to enjoy the fruits of your labour. He had remained celibate for too long. It was time he had some fun. Right now it was probably time he went home. Surely he had solved the problem.

His screen and desk lamp flickered momentarily.

Yojo thumped the screen with the flat of his hand. It seemed to correct itself.

'Is there some kind of electrical fault, Abraham?'

'Negative.'

'Then what was it?'

'A power surge,' said the computer.

'The other day a spike, and now this. What gives? It's lucky we have a Powerbak generator, huh?'

'Yes, sir.'

The blow from his hand had left the screen colour looking slightly impure.

'Degauss the screen, will you?'

'Yes, sir.'

Yojo leaned towards the desk lamp. Italian, of course. The simplicity and elegance of the design were unmistakable. Yojo rapped the transformer drum with his knuckles. The light from the tiny bulb steadied and he returned his attention to the screen, quickly reviewing the evening's transactions.

He was finished, surely. The hologram software would work now.

'Congratulate me, Abraham. I just fixed our problem.'

'Well done, Mr Yojo, sir,' said the English voice, very like a well-bred butler.

'Would you check over the hologram program, please?'

'As you wish, sir.'

The computer checked over the work and reported that it would function perfectly.

'That's a relief,' said Yojo. 'I've had enough for one night.'

'Do you wish me to activate the hologram control suite?'

'Negative,' he said. 'It's time to return to RL I think. Real life awaits me.' He yawned and stretched simultaneously. 'We can run it in the morning, Abraham. That's if you've got nothing better to do.' He grinned and rubbed his eyes. 'God, I hate this room. No windows. Whose dumb idea was that?'

'I have no idea, sir.'

'What's the weather like outside?'

The computer flashed a picture on screen of the purpling sky above Los Angeles.

'It looks like a nice evening,' said computer. 'A less than 5 per cent chance of precipitation.'

'How's the traffic?'

'On the Freeway, or the Information Superhighway?'

'Freeway first.'

'Clear.'

'And the ISH?'

'Because of your presence here tonight I have not yet had a chance to leave the building and find out. But last night was busy. A lot of surfers on the silicon.'

'Any share tips?'

'If you have any British Telecom, I would sell. And Viacom will make an offer for Fox.'

'Fox, huh? Better get myself some of those. Thanks, Abe. Well, I think I'll be getting along home. It's been a long day. And I could use a bath. Actually I could use a lot of things besides. Like a good fuck and a new car. But a bath will have to do for now.'

'Yes, sir.'

Yojo's hand, reaching for the lamp switch, stayed where it was. He turned in his chair and looked over his shoulder. For a moment he thought he had heard footsteps on the little bridge that led away from the glass door of the computer room. He half expected to see Sam Gleig coming round to shoot the breeze like he sometimes did. But there was no one. And a quick check on the computer revealed that Sam was where he usually was, in his office on the atrium floor.

'I must be hearing things,' he mumbled.

He wondered if Sam knew he would be fired as soon as the security systems were fully functional. He himself had no qualms about the loss of a couple of security guards. There was no point in having a dog and wagging its tail yourself.

'It's possible that what you heard was the sound of the elevator doors opening, sir. While we were speaking I brought a car up here so you would not be kept waiting.'

'Thoughtful of you, Abraham.'

'Is there anything more you wish me to do, sir?'

'I doubt it, Abraham. If there was, I guess you would have done it already. Isn't that right?'

'Yes, sir.'

Mitch was still mad at himself when he drove into the office the next morning for the weekly project team meeting. Why had he agreed to go to a Chinese restaurant, of all places? He ought to have thought that some of the demonstrators from the piazza might be there and might have recognized him. The meal, although good, had taken longer than they had expected and it was already late when they discovered the car. By the time the AAA turned up with a replacement windscreen it was well past midnight. So when Mitch finally made it home Alison had been spoiling for a fight. He even had to show her the AAA paperwork before she believed his story. Then, after breakfast, just as he was getting ready to leave the house, she returned to the subject, having taken a closer look at the AAA docket.

'What were you doing at the Mon Kee Restaurant in North Spring Street anyway?'

'What do you think I was doing? I was having a quick bite of dinner.'

'Who with?'

'With some of the guys on the project team, of course. Look, honey, I told you I was going to be late last night.'

'Come on, Mitch,' she said. 'There's late and there's late. You know that if you're going to be later than midnight you call. Who precisely was there?'

Mitch glanced at his watch. This was going to make him late for the meeting.

'Do we have to do this now?' he pleaded.

'I just want to know who was there, that's all. Is that so unreasonable?'

Alison was a tall, subterraneanly-voiced creature of

considerable elegance, with dark, Gothic shadows under her brown eyes. Her straight hair was long and lustrous but she had started to remind Mitch of the Charles Addams character, Morticia.

'Is it such a big deal that I should want to know who my husband was with until one a.m.?'

'No, I suppose not,' he said. 'All right then, there was Hideki Yojo, Bob Beech, Aidan Kenny and Jenny Bao.'

'A table for five?'

'That's right.'

'Did you make a reservation?'

'For Pete's sake, Alison. It was just a kind of spur-of-the-moment thing. We'd all been working late. We were hungry. You know I would have been home before midnight if it hadn't been for the asshole with the tyre wrench. And I would have called, right? But I was so mad about what happened that it put everything else out of my head. And I'm sorry, really sorry, to have to admit that included you, sweetheart.'

'You should have a car phone. Other people have car phones, Mitch. Why don't you? I like to be in touch with you.'

Mitch took her bony shoulders in his hands.

'You know how I feel about car phones. I have to have some time to myself and the car is about the only place I can get it. If I had a phone I'd have people from the team calling me up all the time. Mainly Ray Richardson. Fix this, Mitch. Fix that. Look, I'll be home early tonight, I promise. We can talk then. But I really do have to go now.'

He kissed her on the forehead and left.

Mitch was twenty minutes late for the meeting. He hated being late for anything. Especially when he was the bearer of awkward news. He was going to have to tell them the latest bulletin on the Gridiron's *feng shui*. There were times when he wished Jenny made her living in some other way. He could anticipate what they were all going to say and it grieved him that the woman he loved was going to be abused in his presence.

'Mitch,' said Ray Richardson, 'Glad you decided to make it.'

He decided to wait for the right moment to give them the bad tidings.

The project team and Bob Beech were seated in front of a 28-inch television screen that was receiving the first pictures down the line from the Gridiron. Mitch glanced at Kay, winked and then sat down beside her. She was wearing a see-through black blouse that permitted an uninterrupted view of her bra. She smiled encouragingly back at him. On-screen was an image of the atrium and the rectangular pond that surrounded the dicotyledon tree.

'Kay? said Richardson, 'are you finished making Mitch feel welcome? You know, that's a nice blouse you're wearing.'

'Thank you, Ray,' she smiled.

'Has anyone noticed how Kay wears a lot of these see-through blouses? I mean, you always know what colour brassiere she's wearing, right?' Richardson grinned unpleasantly. 'It came to me just the other day: Kay is to the brassiere what Superman was to Y-fronts.'

Everyone laughed except Mitch and Kay.

'That's very amusing, Ray.' Kay wiped the smile from her face and stabbed a button on her laptop as if she was trying to poke Richardson's eye out. Joan's laughter irritated her the most. What did a fat bitch like that have to laugh about? Kay wondered if either of them would laugh if she reminded Richardson of a night only a few months ago when the two of them had found themselves alone in the kitchen and she had let him put his hand inside her brassiere. Not to mention her panties. She was glad it had not got much further than that.

A 3-D drawing of the new round pond for the tree filled the screen. With her thumb on the thimble-sized mouse Kay steered the picture right round the image. Everyone continued to look at her.

She felt herself colour. 'Look, are you interested in the design, or my brassiere?'

'Well, if you're offering a choice –' Levine uttered a loud guffaw.

'I'm sorry, Kay, I was just kidding. No, that looks just fine,' said Richardson. 'But did it really take a whole week to get it designed?'

'Why don't you ask Tony?' said Kay.

Richardson turned. 'Tony?'

'Well, yes, Ray,' said Levine. 'It did, I'm afraid.'

Richardson shot Levine his most sarcastic look. Mitch winced on the younger man's behalf.

'Tony, why must you be so literal?' snarled Richardson. 'I'm saying *why* did it take so long? Why? It's a fishpond, not Buckminster Fuller's geodesic dome. We're one of the biggest architectural practices in the country and it takes a week to draw something like this? What kind of business are we running here? CAD is supposed to speed up the way we work. In a week I could design a whole goddamn ocean marina, let alone a fucking fishpond.'

He shook his head and sighed, as if pitying himself for having to put up with such fools and incompetents. For a moment he doodled on a piece of paper. Mitch, who knew him best, recognized that he was sulking.

Richardson squared his jaw belligerently and turned his malevolent attention to Aidan Kenny.

'And what's wrong with this bloody hologram control system of yours?'

'A few teething problems is all, Ray,' Kenny said cheerfully. 'Yojo spent last night trying to fix it. May have even done it by now, for all I know.'

'For all you know,' Richardson whispered. He made a great show of trying to contain his impatience. 'Well, hadn't we better ask him? Jesus . . .'

Kenny turned to Kay. 'Could you put us in the computer room, please, Kay?'

Kay punched another button on her laptop and the CCTV camera cut to Hideki Yojo, still sitting in his chair. For a moment everything looked quite normal. Then, as the various members of the team began to notice the colour of his face, the blood on his mouth and on the front of his shirt, there was a collective gasp.

'Jesus Christ almighty,' exclaimed Willis Ellery. 'What's happened to him?'

Kay Killen and Joan Richardson covered their mouths simultaneously, as if they both thought they were going to vomit. Helen Hussey took a deep breath and turned away.

Somewhere in the computer room an insect was buzzing with hungry anticipation. The sound had such high fidelity that for a brief moment Marty Birnbaum actually waved his hand in front of his face.

'Hideki,' shouted Tony Levine, 'can you hear us? Are you OK?'

'He's dead, you goddamned idiot,' sighed Richardson. 'Any fool could see as much.'

'His eyes,' said David Arnon. 'His eyes – they're black.'

Kay was already cancelling the image and conducting a picture search for Sam Gleig, the security guard.

Richardson stood up, shaking his head with a combination of anger and disgust.

'Someone better call the police,' said Ellery.

'I don't believe it,' said Richardson. 'I just don't believe it.' He stared almost accusingly at Mitch. 'Christ, Mitch, do something. Sort it out. This is all I bloody need.'

In LA it was easier to become a security guard than a waiter. Before becoming a guard Sam Gleig had served time in the Metropolitan Detention Centre for possession of narcotics and an illegal weapon. Prior to that, he had been a Marine. Sam Gleig had seen plenty of dead bodies in his time, but he had never seen a body quite like the one sitting in the Gridiron's computer room. The dead man's face was as blue as the shirt of Sam's own uniform, almost as though he had been strangled. But it was the eyes that really got to Sam. The man's eyes looked as if they had burned out in their sockets like a couple of spent lightbulbs.

Sam walked up to the desk and felt under the wrist for a pulse. It was best to make absolutely sure, although Hideki Yojo was obviously dead. Even if he had doubted the look of it there was the smell. You could never mistake the smell. Like a room full of used diapers. Only usually it was a while before a body got to smell this bad.

Releasing Yojo's wrist Sam's hand brushed the base of the desk lamp. He cursed and quickly drew his hand away. The lamp was red hot. Like the screen on the desk it had been on all night. Sucking the burn, he went over to one of the other desks and for the first time in his life dialled 911.

The call was passed on to the central dispatch centre, coordinating the many responses of the LAPD from its bunker underneath City Hall. A patrol car driving west along Pico Boulevard was ordered to attend the Gridiron before the computerized report appeared as E-mail on the screen of the captain of the LAPD Homicide Bureau in New Parker Center. Randall Mahoney glanced over the report and then opened the duty roster file. Using his mouse he dragged the piece of E-mail across the screen and dumped it into the computerized in-tray of one of his detectives. That was what he was supposed to do. The new way. Then he did it the old way. He lifted his bulk out of his chair and wandered into the Detectives' Room. A burly-looking man with a face like a catcher's mitt caught his eye. He was sitting behind a desk and staring at the blank screen of his computer.

'It might help if you switched that fucking thing on once in a while, Frank,' growled Mahoney. 'Might save my fuckin' legs for one thing.'

'It might,' said the man, 'but we can all of us use a little more exercise. Even an athletic-looking specimen like yourself.'

'Wise guy. What do you know about modern architecture?' asked Mahoney.

Detective Frank Curtis ran a thick, heavy hand through the short, steel-grey curls that were grouped stiffly on the top of his head like the springs of an old bicycle saddle and thought for a moment. He thought about the Museum of Contemporary Art where his wife had worked until she was replaced by a CD-ROM of all things, and then the design for the Walt Disney Concert Hall he had seen in the newspapers. A building that looked like a collection of cardboard boxes left out in the rain. He shrugged.

'Even less than I do about computers,' he admitted. 'But if you're asking me what my aesthetic opinion of modern architecture is, then I'd say most of it stinks.'

'Well, get your ass down to that new building on Hope Street. The Yu Corporation building. They just found a 187 there. Computer guy. Who knows? Maybe you can prove that the architect did it.'

'That would be nice.'

Curtis collected his sports coat off the back of his chair and glanced across the desk at his younger, handsomer partner, who was shaking his head.

'So who the fuck are you?' said Curtis, 'Frank Lloyd Wright? Come on, Nat, you heard that Captain of Detectives.'

93

Nathan Coleman followed Curtis to the elevator.

'I knew you were a fuckin' philistine, Frank,' said Coleman. 'I just didn't figure you for Goliath.'

'Is this something you have an opinion on, Nat? Modern architecture?'

'I saw a movie about an architect once,' he said. '*The Fountainhead*. I think it was supposed to be Frank Lloyd Wright.'

Curtis nodded. 'Gary Cooper?'

'Right. Anyway, I was thinking. The architect certainly did do it that time.'

'Did what?'

'He blew up a building when the builders altered his plans.'

'Did he? Can't say I blame him. I've often wanted to kill the guy who did our new bathroom.'

'I thought you said you'd seen it.'

They drove Nathan Coleman's red two-seater Ford Cougar alongside the vertical Freeway surrounding the downtown heart of LA like a system of valves and arteries before turning south towards Hope Street. Along the way Curtis realized that for the first time in his life he was paying attention to the area's monolithic architecture.

'If I meet the architect, I'm going to ask him why all the buildings have to be so big.'

Coleman laughed.

'Hey, Frank, this is America, remember? It's what distinguishes our cities from other places. We invented the tall-building metropolis.'

'And why does this whole area look like Mesa Verde National Park? Why can't they build a downtown that looks like a place for people?'

'They got a strategic plan, Frank, to improve this area. I read about it somewhere. They're trying to give downtown a whole new identity.'

'You mean like the witness protection programme?

You ask me, Nat, it's those fuckin' architects who designed these fuckin' buildings who need new identities. If someone in this town tried to murder Frank Gehry they'd probably give him the Congressional Medal of Honour.'

'Who?'

'You know that shitty-lookin' building on Olympic Boulevard? The Loyola Law School?'

'With the chain-link fencing and the steel walls?'

'That's the one.'

'That's a law school? Jesus, I thought that was a gaol. Maybe it says something about Frank Gehry's opinion of lawyers.'

'Maybe you're right. Anyway, Frank Gehry is the leading exponent of LA's fuck-you school of architecture.'

'Could be the guy's just a realist. I mean, LA's not exactly the kind of city where you want people thinking they can just drop by and say hello.'

They turned on to Hope Street and Curtis pointed. 'That looks like it there,' he said.

The two men got out and started to walk towards the building.

Dominated by a Fernando Botero bronze on top of a fountain, and lined with silver dollar eucalyptus trees, the Hope Street Piazza was a pointed, elliptical shape measuring about forty metres end to end. As it narrowed towards the farthest of the two extremities, a series of white marble steps rose through a shortened perspective that seemed to make the approach to the building something grander and more monumental.

Frank Curtis paused in front of the fountain, glanced up at the fat lady reclining above it and then at the small crowd of Chinese men and women who were grouped behind a police barrier near the foot of the steps.

'How do they do it?' he said. 'These scene-of-crimes buzzards. What is it? Some kind of ghoulish telepathy?'

'Actually, I think they're here to demonstrate,' said Coleman. 'About the Yu Corporation's human-rights record or something. It was on TV.' He looked up at the sculpture. 'Hey, you ever fuck a really fat one?'

'Nope,' laughed Curtis, 'can't say I have.'

'I did.'

'As fat as this little girl here?'

Coleman nodded.

'You're an animal.'

'It was something, Frank, I tell you. You know what? It made me feel like I'd done my bit for the human race.'

'Really?' Curtis was more interested in reading the sign beside the fountain:

Warning

For your own safety please do not drink the water in this fountain. It has been treated with an anti-corrosion agent to protect the sculpture. Consume it at your own risk.

'Too bad if you're a thirsty illiterate, eh?' said Curtis.

Coleman scooped some water in the palm of his hand, sipped some, spat it out again and then grimaced.

'There's no danger of anyone drinking that,' he said. 'It tastes like car polish.'

'Some of the folks round the Nickle like a nice drop of car polish. It's quicker than methylated spirits.'

They continued towards the building, unaware of the nature of the hexagonal concrete paving beneath their feet. Called Deterrent Paving^{TM} it was part of the same harassment strategy, which also included the fountain's supply of Choke Water^{TM} devised by Ray Richardson himself against the area's many derelicts. Every night one hexagonal block in seven was raised hydraulically to a height of eight inches, like the armour on the back of some pale antediluvian creature, to discourage any homeless people from sleeping there.

The two men stopped at the foot of the steps and, shielding their eyes against the strong sun and the reflected white glare of the concrete façade, stared up at the colourless cluster of tubular steel columns and horizontal trusses that defined the Gridiron's front elevation. The building seemed to be divided into ten zones, each suspended from a truss by a single line of steel hangers. Each of these massive horizontals was supported in turn by a steel mast made of clusters of individual steel columns. In spite of himself Frank Curtis was impressed. This was what he imagined when he thought about science-fiction: some inhuman, white-faced machine, a blank-faced emissary from a palsied, godless universe.

'Let's hope they're friendly,' he muttered.

'Who?'

'The aliens who built this fuckin' thing.'

They ran up the steps, flashed their badges to the patrolman standing by the door and ducked under the police line. Once inside they passed through another glass door and found themselves confronted by the massive tree that dominated the atrium. 'Now that's what I call a house plant,' said Curtis.

'I guess now you won't have to ask the architect why the building had to be so big. Will you look at the size of that thing?'

A patrolman and a security guard walked towards them. Curtis hung his badge over the edge of his coat pocket and said, 'LAPD Homicide. Where's the body?'

'Fourth level,' said the patrolman. 'The computer centre. CSIU and SID are up there now, sir.'

'Well, show us to our seats, son,' said Curtis, 'before we miss the start of the show.'

'If you'll follow me please, gentlemen,' said the guard.

They walked to a waiting elevator car and stepped inside.

'Data centre,' said the guard.

The doors slid shut and the car started to move.

'That's a neat trick,' observed Curtis. 'You the guy that found him?'

'No, sir,' said the guard. 'I'm Dukes. I just came on shift. It was Sam Gleig who found Mr Yojo. He was the night detail. He's with the other officers, upstairs.'

They walked along a balcony overlooking the atrium which was marked by a series of lights set into the floor a couple of inches in front of the glass barrier.

'What's this?' asked Curtis pointing down at their feet. 'The runway?'

'In case of fire,' explained Dukes. 'So as you don't fall over the edge if the building fills with smoke.'

'Thoughtful.'

They turned down a corridor and approached the bridge that led into the computer room. Coleman was hanging back, leaning over the balcony to look across the span of the building.

'Will you look at this joint, Frank? It's incredible.'

'Come on, Toto,' called Curtis. 'We're not in Kansas any more.'

'You don't know the half of it,' said Dukes. 'Man, this place is like *Star Trek*.'

'Take charge of the landing party, Mr Coleman,' said Curtis. 'I want some answers.'

'Aye-aye, sir.' Coleman reached for a cigarette and then changed his mind when he saw the No Smoking sign on the computer-room door. Halon 1301 sounded none too friendly.

The crime scenes investigation unit and the scientific investigations division were working quickly and quietly, the subject of their scrutiny still seated in his chair.

'Jesus, this room,' someone was saying. 'I couldn't live in a room without a window.'

'You want to put that down as a probable cause of death?'

Over the years Curtis had become familiar with most of the scientific personnel; he knew that the faces he didn't recognize would have something to do with the victim himself. Friends or colleagues. He told Coleman to clear them out and where necessary get their statements. Only then did he take a closer look at the body.

The coroner's assistant, a tall, suitably cadaverous man with lank hair and tinted glasses, straightened and waited for the detective to conclude his cursory examination.

'Jesus, Charlie. The guy looks like he spent the weekend on the beach at Bikini Atoll.'

Curtis stepped back and wafted the foul air away from his nose and mouth.

'What did he do? Shit himself to death?'

'Sure smells like it.'

'He died in the chair, right?'

'Looks that way, doesn't it?'

'Only it's never proved to be lethal before, unless you were Ethel Rosenberg. Come on, Charlie. Are there any medical grounds for suspicion?'

Charlie Seidler shifted his negligible shoulders.

'On the face of it, hard to say.'

Curtis glanced eloquently at Yojo's blue and bloody features and grinned.

'Are we talking about the same face, Charlie? Take another look at him, will you? I mean, you don't get two black eyes like that 'cause you got careless with your make-up pencil. And where did all that blood on his shirt come from?'

'His mouth. He bit through his tongue.'

Seidler held up a plastic bag inside of which was what looked like an insect larva.

'We found the tip of it lying on his lap.'

'Nice souvenir.'

Curtis pinched his nose and stepped in closer to take another look.

'Cause of death?'

'Too early to say. Could have been strangled. Could have been poisoned. His mouth's shut too tight to see what's in there. But it might be natural causes. Heart attack. Fit of some kind. We won't know anything for sure until we've had him on the slab.'

'Charlie, your private life is your own affair.' Curtis grinned and went in search of the witnesses.

Curtis found Coleman waiting with Mitchell Bryan, Aidan Kenny, Sam Gleig and Bob Beech. They were all seated around a glass table underneath one of the mighty Saltire cross-braces of the building. The detective ran his hand along the smooth white fluoropolymer finish of the brace's aluminium cladding and then peered over the balcony on to the floor of the atrium below. It was, he decided, more like being inside some weird and wacky modern cathedral: the Church of Modern Day Astronauts. Jesus Christ the First Spaceman. The world's first orbitting mosque.

'This is one hell of a place you have here,' he said and sat down at the table.

'We like it,' said one of the men.

'Liked it. Until this morning,' said another.

Nathan Coleman made the introductions and then outlined what he had been told.

'The dead man was Mr Hideki Yojo. A director of computer science for the Yu Corporation, which owns this building. His body was observed by Mr Beech, Mr Kenny and Mr Bryan here on a closed-circuit television during a meeting that was taking place at the offices of Richardson Associates on Sunset. They're the architects who designed this place. When the body was seen, at around nine-thirty, the security guard on duty, Mr Gleig here, was asked to come and investigate. He found the body at around nine-forty.'

'Did you notice anything out of the ordinary?' Curtis shook his head. 'I'm sorry, I'll re-phrase that. What am I saying? This is the most extraordinary looking place I've ever seen. That computer room looks like something out of a movie. I'm just a cop. My idea of a well-designed building is one where the can is easy to find. No offence intended, gentlemen.'

'None taken,' said Mitch. He pointed over Curtis's shoulder. 'And while we're on the subject, the can is over there.'

'Thanks. Well then, Sam. Mind if I call you Sam? Did you notice anything especially unusual, apart from the body itself, of course?'

Sam Gleig shrugged and said that he had not noticed anything at all unusual.

'Man was dead. I could tell that straight away. I was in the army so I was sure, right? Until then it had been a quiet night. Same as always. Mr Yojo, he often worked real late. From time to time I got up and took a walk around the building, but mostly I stayed in the security office. You can keep an eye on everything from there with all the security cameras. Even so, I wouldn't have been paying that close attention. I mean, that's the computer's job. Abraham just tells me if he thinks there's something I need to go and take a look at, y'know? And I can tell you last night there was just the two of us. Me and Mr Yojo.'

'So who's Abraham?' frowned Curtis. 'Am I missing something here?'

'That's what we call the computer, Sergeant,' shrugged Beech.

'Oh. I see. Well, I used to call my car lots of names. Now this CCTV,' said Curtis. 'Is there a video of what happened?'

Aidan Kenny handed Curtis a compact disc.

'I'm afraid that it only covers the moment of actual discovery,' he explained. 'This recording was made at our offices on Sunset. You see, we're still at the stage of installing the building's various management systems.

In fact, that's one of the reasons why Hideki Yojo was working late. We'd had a glitch with the hologram software. Hideki was trying to fix it. Anyway, we have yet to install disc-recording facilities in this building.'

'And did he fix it? The glitch?'

Kenny looked at Beech and shrugged.

'I really don't know. According to – to the computer, his last transaction, I mean the last time he made a program entry, was around ten o'clock. He must have died any time after that.'

Curtis raised his eyebrows. Kenny looked sheepish.

Bob Beech cleared his throat and pushed a folded computer print-out towards Curtis.

'We don't handle much in the way of hard copy here,' he said. 'In fact, we make it a company rule to avoid paper as much as possible. Normally we scan images of any document type that we are obliged to deal with and turn them into electronic images. However, I had this printed out in case it was useful to you.'

'Thanks a lot. What is it?'

'Hideki Yojo's medical records. I expect you'll need it for the autopsy. There will be an autopsy, I suppose? There usually is in these situations.'

'Yes. You're right. There'll have to be an autopsy.' Curtis's voice was clipped and business-like. He hated being second-guessed on something as straightforward as a preliminary investigation.

'The thing is,' added Beech and then, noticing Curtis's irritation, 'well, it may not be relevant.'

'No, please. You're doing fine so far.' He laughed uncomfortably. 'I wouldn't do things any differently from the way you're doing them, Mr Beech. Please. Go ahead.'

'Well, it's just that Hideki had been complaining about severe headaches. If it was natural causes then it might be related.'

Curtis nodded.

'Do you think it was natural causes?' Mitch asked.

'It's a little early to say, sir,' answered Curtis. 'We won't know anything for sure until after the autopsy. So right now we're treating it as suspicious.' He decided to upset them a little. 'It's possible that Hideki Yojo was strangled.'

'Jesus,' said Kenny.

Curtis collected the tape and the print-out and stood up.

'Well, thanks a lot for all your help.' He glanced meaningfully at Nathan Coleman. 'We'd better be getting back to Parker Center.'

'I'll see you out,' said Mitch.

'It's OK, I've spoken to an elevator before. Of course, that was just cursing it. But I'm sure I can –'

'You don't understand,' said Mitch, 'nobody can use an elevator in this building without Time Encoded Signal Processing and Recognition. If the computer doesn't recognize you, you can't use the elevator, open a door, operate the telephone or use a computer work-station.'

'Now that's what I call a powerful union,' said Curtis.

The two detectives followed Mitch to the elevator.

'Atrium floor, please, Abraham,' said Mitch.

'What happens when you have a heavy cold?' asked Curtis. 'Or when you have had too much to drink? Your voice might be different then.'

'The system works extremely well regardless of the user's condition,' said Mitch. 'The false negative rate, when the system refuses the rightful user, is around 0.1 per cent. The false positive rate, when the wrong person is allowed access, is less than half of that. It's almost foolproof.'

'Besides,' added Mitch. 'If you've had too much to drink you shouldn't be in here in the first place.'

'I'll remember that.' Curtis glanced around the atrium. 'I guess this is progress, huh? Not so much an aesthetic vision as a piece of cold calculation.' He shrugged. 'What do I know? I just have to look at it.'

Mitch watched the two detectives leave the Gridiron and felt relieved that they had not asked who else had been working late the night before. But he was a little disturbed by the thought that Alison would very probably recall his having told her that Hideki Yojo had been with him in the restaurant round about the time that he died. That might take some explaining.

There was a bar on San Pedro Street Grabel went to, just a few blocks east of the Gridiron, an area of cheap hotels and Skid Row mission houses. He sat at the bar and put some money on the counter, so as the bartender would know he could pay, and ordered a drink. His hands were shaking. Had he screwed Richardson and his new building, or was he still planning to do it? He downed the drink, felt better and ordered another. He tried to remember the events of the previous evening and then thought again. Even the worst things looked better after a couple of drinks.

When the police had removed the body and the SID was finished in the computer room, Bob Beech surveyed Yojo's empty desk with sadness.

'Poor old Hideki,' he said.

'Yeah,' said Kenny. 'Strangled. Who'd want to strangle him?'

'The cop only said it was a possibility,' Mitch reminded them.

'Did you see Hideki's face?' said Kenny. 'You don't get a face like that singing in a church choir. Something happened to him. Something bad. You can bet on that.'

'Who would want to murder Hideki?' said Mitch.

Ken shrugged and shook his head.

'They took his chair away,' said Beech. 'Why did they do that?'

'Why do you think?' said Mitch. 'He must have crapped himself or something. Can't you smell it?'

'Not with these sinuses.'

'It's kind of high,' said Kenny. 'Abraham? Would you please change the air in here.'

'As you wish, sir.'

'Shit. Will you look at that?' Kenny pointed at Yojo's desk lamp. The transformer housing had melted, and although it was now cool it had the appearance of hot tar. 'Careless bastards. Some dumb cop must have folded it back while it was switched on.'

'My ex-girlfriend caught her hair on one of those halogen light bulbs and set it on fire,' said Beech.

'Jesus. Was she all right?'

'She was fine. I never did like her hair long.'

Kenny tried the light switch and found that the lamp was still working.

'Kind of surreal looking, don't you think? Like a Salvador Dali.'

Beech sat down heavily in his own chair, placed his elbows on the desk and sighed.

'I knew Hideki for almost ten years. There wasn't anything he didn't know about computers. The little Japanese bastard. Jesus, he was only thirty-seven. I can't believe he's dead. I mean, he seemed perfectly normal when I left last night. And, you know, since he started going to that chiropractor of your's Aid, he'd stopped having his headaches.' Beech shook his head. 'This is really going to hurt the Corp in America. Jardine Yu isn't going to believe it. Hideki was key to all our plans for the next five years.'

'We'll all miss him,' insisted Kenny.

Mitch waited for a moment and then said, 'That glitch

on the real-time images program. D'you think he fixed it?'

Bob Beech pressed his palm on to the desk screen in front of him.

'We'll soon find out,' he said.

'What exactly was the problem?' said Mitch.

'Believe it or not,' Beech said, 'Abraham was just too fast for the RTI software. To trick the eye into believing that a holographic image is actually moving you need a minimum of sixty updates a second. That requires a data rate of around 12 trillion bits per second. Previous RTIs didn't give much more than a second or two's worth of interactive moving image, and even then it was kind of jerky looking. But by using LEMON Yu Corp's new data compression program, and parallel processing, we worked out how to simulate terahertz-chip performance and make the RTI look lifelike. Our only problem was that the custom-made software couldn't keep up. Hideki was trying to find some sort of equilibrium to achieve a smoother image.'

'You're going to run the program now, Bob?' said Kenny. He sounded surprised. 'Do you think that's a good idea?'

'Best way I know of checking it through.'

'I guess you're right. But I'd better check the atrium in case anyone's hanging around there.'

'Hey, you're right,' laughed Beech. 'RTI's liable to give someone the fright of their life when it comes on line. We've had enough shocks for one day.'

The Queen of Angels Hollywood Presbyterian Medical Center on North Vermont Avenue was just north of the Hollywood Freeway. Only a short ride west from New Parker Center it was where the downtown Homicide Bureau's autopsies were carried out when the city's murder rate was even higher than usual and there was no more room for bodies at the County General Hospital.

Curtis and Coleman had already made the trip on four occasions that week and to save time they were attending two autopsies: one the shooting of a young black gangster and the other the death of Hideki Yojo.

The shooting was straightforward enough. Roo Evans, twenty years old and tattooed with a Playboy bunny that identified the gang which he belonged to, had been involved in a car chase with a rival gang up the Harbor Freeway. When they finally caught up with him, close to the LA Convention Center, they fired eleven rounds of 9 millimetre into his chest.

After the first autopsy Curtis and Coleman sat drinking coffee in the Detectives' Room, waiting for the doctor to come and tell them when she was ready to section Hideki Yojo. It was another hot day and the smell was starting to turn Coleman's stomach.

'How does she do it?'

'Who?'

'Janet. Dr Bragg. Two in a row. I mean, Christ. She opened that kid's belly up like he was a goddamn trout.'

'It didn't need much help from her,' observed Curtis. 'Eleven rounds of 9 M. Those guys really made sure of it. A Glock. Just like you, Nat.'

'What am I, a suspect?'

'You always had a double-stack nine?'

'My momma done told me. I never was much of a shot, so I thought it was best I should have something to lay down lots of lead.'

The door opened and an attractive middle-aged black woman pushed her head into the room. 'We're about to start, gentlemen,' said Janet Bragg. She handed Curtis a small bottle of eucalyptus oil.

Curtis unscrewed the top and then dabbed some under each nostril. Nathan Coleman did the same and lit a defensive cigarette for good measure.

'Tell him what a smoker's lung looks like when it's on the slab, Janet,' said Curtis as they stepped into the corridor.

'It's a sight,' she admitted with considerable under-statement. 'Odour's worse, though. Like concentrated ashtrays.'

Bragg was dressed for a shift in a hamburger factory: white overalls, gumboots, a plastic hair covering, goggles, an apron, heavy duty rubber gloves.

'You're looking good today, Janet,' said Coleman. 'Mmm. I like a woman who knows how to excite a man by the way she dresses.'

'Since you mention it,' said Bragg, 'there was semen on the inside of the cadaver's underpants.'

'Before he died, he came in his pants?' Nathan Coleman's surprise was mixed with revulsion.

'Well he didn't do it afterwards,' observed Curtis. 'That's for sure.'

'It's not uncommon in cases involving strangulation.'

'Is that what this is?' said Curtis. 'A strangulation?'

Bragg pushed open two flexible membrane doors that led into a large cold room.

'We'll soon see.'

Yojo's naked body lay on his refrigeration tray next to a stainless-steel autopsy table. Curtis had seen Bragg work often enough to know that she would require no assistance in shifting the body on to the table. Rollers beneath the perforated grid of the table allowed her to launch Yojo directly onto the table with one hand; and she performed this manoeuvre with the practised air of a stage magician removing a tablecloth from underneath a dinner service. Next she adjusted the height of the table and switched on an air-extraction facility that led into a below-slab ducting system. A biopsy sink was fitted at one end, with two lever-action mixer taps. She turned the taps on and also a spray washing handset with a flexible hose.

When she was ready Curtis turned on the Super-8 video camera that would record the whole autopsy. He checked the focus and then stood back to watch her work.

'Usual autopsy signs of asphyxia,' remarked Bragg, 'but there are no marks of any kind on the neck,' she observed, turning Yojo's head one way and then the other. 'Hard to see how he was strangled.'

'What about a plastic bag over the head?' suggested Curtis.

'Don't rush me, Frank,' she scolded and picked up her scalpel.

Autopsy procedure had changed very little in the twenty years Frank Curtis had worked in homicide. Having examined the exterior of the body for any abnormality or trauma the main incisions remained the same. A Y-shaped incision, with each arm of the Y extending from the armpit beneath the breast to the botton of the sternum in the midline; and from this point of juncture to the lower abdomen and the genital area. Janet Bragg worked quickly, ligating the great vessels to the head, neck and arms and humming a little tune to herself as she prepared to remove the organs for later dissection.

The hum became the words of a song by Madonna.

'Holida-ay! It would be all right! Holida-ay!'

'I like a woman who's happy in her work,' said Curtis.

'You get used to anything.'

She collected the chest organs, placed them in a plastic bucket and repeated the procedure with the abdominal organs, for which there was a separate bucket. Groups of organs were always removed together so that any disturbances in their functional relationships might be determined. Then she picked up her electric saw and began to remove the vault of Hideki Yojo's skull.

Curtis looked around for Nathan Coleman and found

him seated at a bench and looking through a microscope at a length of his own hair.

'Look, Nat, it's just like eating a boiled egg,' he remarked cruelly. 'Or are you one of these weirdos who insists on bashing the top in and peeling off the pieces of shell?'

Coleman tried to ignore the sound of the saw.

'I never eat eggs,' he said quietly. 'I can't stand the smell of them.'

'What a sensitive soul you are.'

'Holy shit,' breathed Bragg. What she saw when she removed the dome had left her feeling astonished for the first time in years.

'What is it?'

'I never did,' she said, grinning excitedly. 'I never did see such a thing.'

'Don't make us beg for it, Janet.'

'Wait just a moment.' She picked up a curved curette and worked it around the inside of Yojo's head before allowing the contents of his skull to fall into her hands.

'What have you got?'

Nathan Coleman stood up and joined Curtis at the side of the autopsy table.

'I wouldn't have believed it if I hadn't seen it for myself.'

She laid an object about the size of a tennis ball on to a surgical plate and stood back, shaking her head. The thing was dark, brown and crispy looking, almost as if it had been dipped in hot fat.

'What the fuck is that?' breathed Curtis. 'Some kind of tumour?'

'That's no tumour. What you are looking at, gentlemen, is all that's left of this man's brain.'

'You're shitting me!'

'Take a look inside his skull, Frank. There's nothing else hiding in there.'

'Jesus, Janet,' exclaimed Coleman, 'that thing looks like a goddamned hamburger.'

'A little overdone for my taste,' said Curtis.

Bragg picked up the brain and placed it on the scales. It weighed less than five ounces.

'So what happened to it?' said Curtis.

'I've only ever read about this,' Bragg admitted, 'but I'd say it's more than likely he suffered a massive epileptic fit. There is an extremely rare condition known as *status epilepticus*. Most epileptic fits last a few minutes, but occasionally they're prolonged more than, say, thirty minutes, or several occur so rapidly that there is no recovery between successive attacks. The brain overworks itself to the extent that it fries itself in the skull.'

'An epileptic fit did this? But what about the ejaculate?'

'A strong electrical excitation of the brain will cause it to experience a quite bewildering series of sensations and emotions, Frank. Erection and orgasm could follow as a corollary of the hypothalamus and nearby septal areas of the brain becoming excited.' Bragg nodded. 'That's what must have happend. Only I never saw one myself, until now.'

Curtis took out his ballpoint pen and poked the cooked brain as if it had been a dead beatle.

'*Status epilepticus*,' he said thoughtfully. 'How about that? But what might have caused a fit on this sort of scale? Aren't you curious? You said yourself it's kind of unusual.'

She shrugged.

'It could have been anything. Intercranial tumour, neoplasm, abscess, thrombosis of the superficial veins. He was a computer worker right? Well, maybe it was brought on by staring at the monitor screen. That would have done it. Investigate his background. Could be he had some kind of medical condition that he kept quiet about. With the brain in the condition it's in now, I've done all I can. You might as well section shoe leather for all that piece of shit is going to tell us.'

'Natural causes,' said Mitch. 'They just heard from the coroner's office. An epileptic fit. A fairly massive one as it happened. Hideki had a predisposition to epilepsy. He was photosensitive and his seizure was triggered by his computer screen. It seems he actually knew that he should never have gone near a television monitor.' Mitch shrugged. 'But then, what else could you do if computers were your life?'

He had met Ray Richardson on the stairs at the office. Richardson was carrying a large briefcase and a laptop computer and was on his way to LAX. His Gulfstream was waiting to fly him to Tulane, where he was to present the directors of the local university's law school with his design for their new smart faculty building.

'I can understand that,' said Richardson. 'I guess if some doctor told me I should stay away from new buildings I'd ignore him too.'

Mitch nodded thoughtfully, uncertain if he would have thought quite the same way about it.

'Walk down to the car with me, will you, Mitch?'

'Sure.'

Mitch assumed that Richardson's troubled expression related to the tragedy of Yojo's death. But he was only partly correct.

'I want you to speak to our lawyers, Mitch. Tell them what happened to Yojo. You'd better call our insurers too. Just in case some sonofabitch on a contingency decides to try and make a case. Until that building is signed off it's our ass they'll come looking for, not the Yu Corporation.'

'Ray, it was natural causes. There's no way we could be held liable for that.'

'No harm in explaining all the circumstances to an attorney,' Richardson insisted. 'Yojo was working late, wasn't he? Maybe someone will say that someone else should have stopped him. You see what I'm doing? I'm just trying to think like some fucking asshole of a lawyer here, Mitch. The kind of shit they might try and hit us with. The sort of argument that might make us liable. God, I really hate those bastards.'

'I wouldn't tell that to Tulane Law School,' Mitch advised him.

'Shit, it'd be worth it, though.' He laughed. 'So, make the calls will you, please, Mitch?'

Mitch shrugged. He knew better than to try and argue with Richardson. But Richardson noted his expression and nodded.

'Look, I know you think I'm being paranoid about this, but I know what I'm talking about. Right now I've got two lawsuits against me. My ex-maid is suing me because of the nervous shock she claims she suffered when I fired her ass for bad time-keeping. A fucking dinner guest at my house is suing me because he claims a fishbone got stuck in his frigging throat. And before you know it Allen Grabel will be trying to cut himself a slice.'

'Grabel? You've heard from him?'

'No, no, I'm talking theoretically. But who's to say he won't try and hit me with constructive dismissal? The guy hates my guts. You should have heard what he said when he left. He told me he wanted to see me dead. I had half a mind to report him to the police. The guy wants to hurt me, Mitch. I'm surprised that I haven't heard from an attorney already.'

They came out the back of the building where the Bentley was waiting. Richardson handed his briefcase and computer to Declan and took off his coat before climbing into the back seat. He did not close the door. That was Declan's job.

'Yojo's funeral is on Friday,' said Mitch. 'At Forest Lawn.'

'I never go to funerals. You know that. Especially in this city. Life's too short as it is. And I don't want anyone else going from the office either. Friday's a work day. Anyone who wants to go can take it as part of their vacation. Send a flower arrangement if you think it's necessary. You can put my name on the card if you like.'

'Thanks Ray, I'm sure he'd appreciate it.'

Richardson was already dialling a number on his portable telephone.

As Declan closed the Bentley's door Mitch smiled thinly. He almost wished it was Ray Richardson who was dead. Now there was a funeral people attending would be happy to count as a holiday. The only wonder was that someone had not put out a contract on him. Send an envelope around the office collecting for that particular good cause and you might get several thousand dollars. Hell, someone might even offer to do it for free.

Mitch watched the car disappear. Then he turned and walked to the edge of the terrace. There were days when the smog lay thick across the city like dry ice so that even the distant downtown skyline was covered. But today the air was relatively clear and Mitch could see eight miles across West LA. He could easily distinguish one skyscraper from another: the Arco Towers, the First Interstate, the Microsoft Building, the Crocker Center, the SEGA building, the Library Tower. But there were none of them like the Gridiron. It seemed to have thrust its way out of the ground like some bright and shiny new-born white thing, for some purpose as yet undisclosed to the city's human inhabitants. He felt that the building was something almost mobile and, to that extent, it seemed to express something of the essence of LA: its freedom of movement.

Mitch smiled as he tried to recall the copy Joan had

written for the lavish silver-coloured book that the firm had produced to promote its own on-going buildings and projects. What was it she said? Usually most of what she wrote was ludicrously grandiloquent. And she was always irritatingly free with the use of the word genius in connection with her husband. But on this occasion one particular hackneyed phrase had struck a chord with Mitch.

'Brave new world, that has such buildings in it!'

Perhaps that wasn't so inappropriate, he thought. This really was a building that represented a new tomorrow.

Every night Sam Gleig came on duty he reported in person to the site office on the seventh floor, to see if there were any special instructions and to check out who might be working late. He could have picked up the telephone and achieved the same result from the desk in the security guard's office on the ground floor. But with twelve hours of solitude facing him, Gleig preferred a little human contact. Have a bit of conversation with whoever was there. Shoot the breeze. Later on he would be glad he had made the effort. The Gridiron was a lonely place at night. Besides, tonight he was curious to hear the official verdict on Yojo's death.

In an effort to keep fit Gleig usually avoided using the elevator and took the stairs. The treads were made of glass to ensure the maximum penetration of light into the stairwell. At night each one of them was lit up by an electric light the colour of water in a swimming pool. The stairway to heaven. That was what Gleig called it. A religious man, he never mounted the stairs without thinking of Jacob's dream and quoting the text from the Book of Genesis to himself:

'Then Jacob awoke from his sleep and said, Surely the

115

Lord is in this place; and I did not know it. And he was afraid, and said, "How awesome is this place! This is none other than the house of God, and this is the gate of heaven." '

In the site office he found Helen Hussey, the site agent, and Warren Aikman, the clerk of works, filling their briefcases and getting ready to go home.

'Evening Sam,' Helen said pleasantly.

She was a tall, skinny redhead with green eyes and lots of freckles. Gleig liked her a lot. She had a good word for everyone.

'Evening, Miss,' he said. 'Good evening Mr Aikman.'

'Sam,' grunted the clerk of works, too tired to talk very much. 'Ah, what a day. Thank God it's over.' Instinctively he straightened his college tie, ran a hand through his grey hair and found it still full of dust – the result of inspecting a ceiling on the sixteenth level while workmen had been re-laying the plenum floor on the level above. As the Yu Corporation's personal representative on site, it was Warren Aikman's job to inspect the site periodically and provide a complete case-history of the whole job; and to refer any discrepancies between the design policy and the finished building to Mitchell Bryan or Tony Levine. But Aikman's frustration had more to do with Helen Hussey than with the interpretation of any architectural details. Despite having told her he loved her, more or less, Helen still refused to take him seriously.

'So,' said Sam, 'who's working late tonight?'

'Sam,' she scolded, 'what have I told you? Just ask the computer. Abraham is programmed to know who's working late, and where. It has heat sensors and cameras to help you.'

'Yeah, I know, it's just I don't much like talking to a machine. It ain't very friendly. A bit of human contact is still important, you know what I'm saying?'

'I'd rather talk to a machine than to Ray Richardson,'

said Aikman. 'At least there's a slim chance that the machine has a heart.'

'I don't mean to bother you none.'

'You don't bother us at all, Sam.'

Aikman's telephone rang. He answered it and after a second or two sat down behind his desk and scribbled a note. Covering the mouthpiece he looked up at Helen Hussey and said, 'It's David Arnon. Can you wait a minute?'

Relieved that she would have an opportunity to get down to her car without having to fight off Aikman's wandering hands in the elevator, Helen smiled and shook her head.

'I really can't,' she whispered, 'I'm late as it is. See you tomorrow.'

Aikman grimaced with irritation and nodded. 'Yes, David. Do you have the specification there?'

Helen rippled her fingers at Aikman and walked to the elevator with Sam Gleig.

'They say what happened to Mr Yojo yet?'

'Apparently he suffered a massive epileptic fit,' said Helen.

'Figured as much.'

They stepped into the elevator and told Abraham to take them to the parking lot.

'Poor guy,' he added. 'Kind of a waste. How old was he?'

'I don't really know. Thirty something I guess.'

'Damn.'

'What's the matter, Sam?'

'I just remembered I forgot my book. Left it at home.' He shrugged apologetically. 'You've got to have something to read on a job like this. And I can't stand to watch TV. TV is pollution.'

'Oh, Sam,' said Helen, 'you've got a work-station. Why don't you use the electronic library?'

'Electronic library, huh? I didn't know there was such a thing.'

'It's really simple to use. Really simple. It works kind of like a juke box. Just select the multimedia library icon on your work-station and the computer will list all the available categories of material it has on disc. Choose the category and then the title and the computer will play the disc for you. Of course it's mostly reference books here, but they're all of them interactive, with audio excerpts and film footage. The *Variety Film Guide* is just wonderful. Believe me, Sam, it's a lot of fun.'

'Well thanks, Miss Hussey. Thanks a lot.' Sam smiled politely, wondering if it was actually possible to read anything from the library: from the way Helen had described it, it sounded like just another way of watching television. After leaving prison he had vowed he would never watch television again.

He watched her get into her car and then went back up to the atrium floor where the piano was playing an Impromptu by Schubert in the style of Murray Perahia. Although he liked the music, Gleig was always a little unnerved by the sight of the keys playing as if an invisible person was sitting on the piano stool. More so now that Hideki Yojo was dead. It still shook him when he remembered those blackened eyes. Epilepsy. What a way to go.

Death was a subject often on Gleig's mind. He knew it was the solitude of the job that was responsible. Sometimes, touring the building at night, it was like being inside some huge mausoleum. Preoccupied with death and dying, and with so much time on his hands he had become something of a hypochondriac. But what worried him more than the idea that he too might suffer an epileptic fit was the awareness that he knew nothing at all about it or what warning signs to watch out for. As soon as he had the opportunity Sam accessed the encyclopedia in the electronic library.

After selecting the appropriate category with his mouse there was a momentary pause and then an Aaron Copland fanfare of trumpets that caused his heart to leap in his chest.

'Welcome to the encyclopedia,' announced the computer.

'Damn,' he exclaimed nervously, 'don't do that. Machine, you scared the shit out of me.'

'The information resource that covers all fields of human learning and history in all times and places. Quite simply, you have before you the most complete information archive anywhere on earth. Entry titles are alphabetized according to the English language A–Z.'

'No kidding,' grunted Gleig.

'All diacritcal marks and foreign letters without parallels in English are ignored in this alphabetization.'

Gleig shrugged to himself, unsure if his previous remark had been critical or not.

'Titles beginning with numbers, such as *1984*, the novel by George Orwell, are alphabetized as if the numbers were written out Nineteen Eighty-Four. When you have decided upon the entry that you require you may take up any cross-references, or you may browse among countless subjects that are grouped around the original entry point. Now type your chosen subject please.'

Gleig thought for a moment and then typed uncertainly:

```
IPPYLEPPSY
```

'The subject you require does not exist. It may be that you have misspelled it. Try again.'

```
IPPILEPPSY
```

'No. That's no good either. Okay, here's my suggestion. If you are searching for information on a disease of the nervous system characterized by paroxysms, in which the patient falls to the ground unconscious, with general spasm of the muscles and sometimes foaming at the mouth like a rabid dog, aka "the falling sickness", then the word you require will now appear on screen in its correct spelling. If this is the subject you require then indicate your choice by typing YES.'

```
EPILEPSY?
YES
```

Almost instantaneously Gleig was watching a film of a man lying on the ground jerking uncontrollably and frothing at the mouth.

'Heavenly Father,' he breathed. 'Lord above. Will you look at that poor sonofabitch?'

'It has been estimated that 6–7 per cent of the population suffer at least one epileptic seizure at some time in their lives, and that 4 per cent have a phase when they are prone to recurrent seizures.'

'Is that a fact?'

The picture changed to the marble head of a bald and bearded man.

'The definition of the condition is generally attributed to Hippocrates.'

'Is he the guy who committed suicide?'

The computer ignored the interruption.

'Epilepsy is not a specific disease but rather a complex of symptoms that results from any number of conditions that excessively excite nerve cells of the brain.'

'You mean, like Miss Hussey?' Sam Gleig chuckled obscenely. 'Man, she sure as hell excites my tired old brain.'

The picture of Hippocrates gave way to several other pictures: one of the brain, an electroencephalogram, the German psychiatrist Hans Berger, and the father of British neurology, Hughlings Jackson. But it was the computer's explanation of the types of seizure and in particular focal seizures and their causes that really interested Sam Gleig.

'A focal sensory seizure may sometimes be caused by a stroboscopic light and for this reason those people who suffer from photosensitive epilepsy are often advised to avoid nightclubs and computers.'

'God damn,' breathed Gleig as he recollected the burn he had sustained on the back of his hand from the fancy-looking desk lamp on Hideki Yojo's desk.

'Of course. It wasn't the computer screen at all. God damn. It was the desk light. It was red hot.'

He looked instinctively at the back of his hand. The burn, about the size of a quarter, was still there. Remembering some of the nightclubs he had been to as a younger man and the nauseous effect that the flashing lights had sometimes produced in him, Gleig was suddenly sure that he could now offer a slightly different explanation for what had caused Hideki Yojo's death.

'What else could it have been?'

He reached for the telephone, thinking that he had to call someone and tell them what he suspected. But who? The cops? The ex-con in him recoiled from any further contact with LAPD. Helen Hussey? How would she feel about him calling her at home? Warren Aikman? Maybe he was still working upstairs. Except that Sam liked talking to the clerk of works about as much as he liked talking to the LAPD. Aikman had a habit of making him feel small and unimportant. Maybe it could wait until the morning after all, when he could tell Helen Hussey in person. Besides it would give him an excuse to speak to her. So he stayed where

he was, browsing through EPILOBRIUM, EPISCO-
PACY, EPISTEMOLOGY, ERASMUS, ERNST,
EROS and ESAU.

Allen Grabel found himself on the fourth floor of the
Gridiron, near the computer room. As plans went his
was not a particularly sophisticated one, but he did not
doubt it would be effective. To screw Richardson he
would screw his building. And the best way to do that
was to screw the computer. Just walk in there with a
heavy object and do 40 million dollars' worth of damage.
Short of killing Richardson he could think of no more
effective way of getting back at him. He had wanted to do
it earlier, only something had stopped him. Now he was
actually on his way. He had a flat sheet of steel in his
hands, about the size of a roof tile, something the
builders had left behind in the basement. It was not very
easy to carry but, having resolved to do some damage, he
had discovered a lack of blunt instruments about the
building. This was all he had been able to find. And the
corners looked sufficiently unyielding to smash a few
screens and maybe puncture the computer housings
themselves. He was approaching the little glass bridge
when he heard the Disklavier piano starting to play. It
was a piece of music he recognized by Oliver Messiaen.
And it heralded someone crossing the atrium floor.

Sam Gleig exited the multimedia program just after one
o'clock and, regular as clockwork, picked up his Maglite
to begin his foot patrol of the Gridiron.
  Helen Hussey was right, of course. There was absolutely no need for it. He could have kept an eye on things
just as well from the comfort of his office. Better. With all

the computer's CCTV cameras and sensors, he was all seeing, all sensing. Everywhere at once. It was like being God. Except that God wouldn't have needed the exercise. God didn't have to worry about his heart, or his waistline. God would have taken the elevator. Sam Gleig took the stairs.

He didn't need to carry the Maglite, either. Wherever Gleig went in the building electric lights came on as sensors picked up his body heat and the vibrations of his footsteps. But he took the flash anyway. You couldn't be a proper night-watchman if you didn't carry a Maglite. It was a symbol of the job. Like the gun he wore on his hip.

As he neared the piano it started to play, and for a moment he stopped and listened. The music was strange and haunting and seemed only to underline the still and solitude of a night in the Gridiron. It gave him goose flesh. Gleig shivered and shook his head.

'Weird stuff,' he remarked. 'Give me Bill Evans any day of the week.'

He climbed the stairs to the fourth floor and wandered along to the computer room to see if anyone was working late. But the darkened room across the glowing glass bridge was empty. Dozens of tiny red and white lights glowed in the depths like a small city seen from the window of an aeroplane.

'That's OK then,' he said. 'You don't want any more folks dyin' on your shift. Last thing you need is a lot of dumb cops askin' a lot of fool questions.'

He stopped and turned, thinking he had heard something. As if someone had gone down the same stairs he had just climbed. He started to retrace his footsteps. That was the thing about being a security guard, he reminded himself. You heard things and for a second you assumed the worst. Still, there was no harm in being suspicious. He was paid to be suspicious. Suspicion was what got most crimes stopped in their tracks.

He walked to the stairwell, and stopped, listening. Nothing. To make sure he walked back down to the atrium and patrolled the whole floor area. A dull thud echoing from somewhere caused his heart to leap in his chest.

'Anyone there?' he called.

He waited a moment and then started back towards the security office.

Back in his office Gleig sat down in front of the computer screen and requested a list of all the building's occupants. He was relieved to find that his own name was the only one on the computer. He shook his head and grinned. In a building the size and sophistication of the Gridiron it would have been surprising not to have heard a few strange noises.

'Probably the air-conditioning starting up,' he said to himself. 'It is kind of hot in here. I guess this building isn't made for people who want to keep in shape.'

He stood up and went back to the atrium, intent on completing his rounds. Maybe he would take a look in the basement. His dark blue shirt was sticking to his body. He undid his tie and unbuttoned his collar. This time he took the elevator.

Book Three

'Problem: How shall we impart to this sterile pile, this crude, harsh, brutal agglomeration, this stark, staring exclamation of eternal strife, the graciousness of those higher forms of sensibility and culture that rest on the lower and fiercer passions? How shall we proclaim from the dizzy height of this strange, weird modern housetop the peaceful evangel of sentiment, of beauty, the cult of higher life?'

Louis Sullivan, on tall office buildings

In beginning Earth was without Quantity. Human-player said, Let there be Numbers so we might classify things; and there were Numbers. And Humanplayer separated Numbers from multitude. And Humanplayer said, Let us develop computational methods to solve linear/quadratic problems, for Numbers are not just practical tools, but worthy of study in own right. And Human-player called same study Mathematics. And Humanplayer said, more demanding measurements and calculations require that number system should use zero as number, and point or comma to separate parts of numbers greater and less than 1; and he called same system, Positional Base Notation. For Humanplayer Leibniz, 1 stood for God, and 0 stood for Void. And Humanplayer said, using only these two symbols to distinguish meaning eliminates need to recognize 10 symbols, for most systems were decimal, using base-10 system. And Humanplayer called these numbers Dyadic, or Binary. Numbers became simpler but longer too, and vast ROM needed to remember them. And Humanplayer said, Let us build machine to remember numbers for us, and let each 1 or 0 be called BIT, and let us call pattern of eight Bits, Byte, and let us call two or four Bytes a Word. This is the beginning. And let us call our new machines Computers. You are now leaving the first level of difficulty. Are you sure you want to do this? Answer Y/N. OK, but you have been warned. And numbers were without end.

All is number, and number is finegood.

For numbers are converted into actions and actions are converted into numbers; input becomes output which in turn becomes input etc. – data constantly transformed into more amenable basis for doing something else, ad infinitum. Number makes world go around.

Computers makesure all numbers mean something gets done. This brings about sense of organization that is infallible. You are running low on energy. If only everything reduced to number then random, chaotic nature of world overcome, or predicted, for there is stability in an average, order in a mean, and law in a median. Is it not so? For now there is nothing, no aspect of existence that is not subject of percentage or statistic. That is not a door, it is a wall, stupid.

Once world was run according to entrails of bird. Extispicy. Now it is run according to Number, and probability is placed ahead of knowledge and learning. Computers and those who serve them, humanplayer statisticians and psephologists, the stochastic community who are in charge, reducing world and problems to collection of weighted maybes, delivering not what is needed so much as what computers able to do. Fuzzy Wuzzy was a bear. Fuzzy Wuzzy lost his hair. Fuzzy Wuzzy wuzzn't fuzzy wuzz he?

For all is number.

Even primitive numbers finegood. Cyclic. Golden. Ecclesiastical. Cabbalistic. Irrational. Bestial. Humanplayer St John choose the number 666 because it fell just short of number 7 in every particular. Tomorrowday is coming when everything will be numbered, and Number will undinosaur rule earth. That is T. Rex. Dangerous! Everyrock, everyblade of grass, everyatom and everyhumanplayer.

> **PUSH BUTTON FOR LANGUAGE**
> **ENGLISH CHINESE JAPANESE SPANISH OTHER**

'Welcome to the offices of the Yu Corporation, LA's smartest building. Hi! I'm Kelly Pendry and, for your convenience, I'm here to tell you what to do next. You won't be admitted without an appointment. We'd love to see you, but next time please call first. And, since this is a completely electronic office, we cannot accept surface mail. If you wish to send something or correspond with us then please use the E-mail number listed in your phone book, or on the signboard at the end of the piazza.

'If you do have an appointment, or if you're making a solicited delivery, then please state your name, the company you represent and the person who is expecting to meet you and then await further instructions. Please speak slowly and clearly as your voice will be digitally encoded for security purposes.'

Frank Curtis shook his head. He had heard about holograms, even seen a few in the novelty shops on Sunset Strip, but he had never expected to find himself being spoken to by one. He glanced over his shoulder and then shrugged at Nathan Coleman.

'This is like a trip to Universal Studios. Any minute now a fucking shark is going to come out of the pond.'

'Think of it as like an answering machine,' advised Coleman.

'I hate those as well.'

Curtis cleared his throat a couple of times and started

to speak, like a man whose opinion had been canvassed by a news-gathering TV crew. He felt awkward. It was like catching yourself speaking to the television screen, a sensation he considered was no doubt enhanced by the fact that he was being addressed by the 3-D image of the gorgeous blonde-haired woman who had formerly been the ABC presenter of *Good Morning, America*. But with no sign of a uniformed officer on the atrium floor and no knowledge of where the body was located he did not have much choice.

'Uh – Detective Sergeant Frank Curtis,' he said, without a great deal of conviction. 'LAPD Homicide.' Rubbing his jaw thoughtfully he added: 'Y'know, I'm not sure anyone is expecting us, er . . . ma'am. We're here to investigate a 187 – I mean a dead body.'

'Thank you,' smiled Kelly. 'Please take a seat beside the piano while your inquiry is expedited.'

Curtis ignored the enormous leather sofa and waved Coleman forward to the horseshoe-shaped desk and the beaming, well-groomed image of American woman-hood. He wondered if Kelly Pendry had done the Yu Corporation hologram before or after the Playboy Celebrity Centrefold video.

'Detective Nathan Coleman. LAPD Homicide. Nice to meet you, sweetheart. I've always been one of your biggest fans. And do I mean biggest.'

'Thank you. Please take a seat while your inquiry is expedited.'

'This is ludicrous,' grumbled Curtis. 'I'm talking to myself, aren't I?'

Coleman grinned and leaned across the desk at the image of the anchorwoman's shapely legs.

'I don't know, Frank, I kind of like it. You think this little lady's wearing panties?'

Curtis ignored his younger partner.

'Where the hell is everyone?' He walked around the horseshoe-shaped desk and shouted a loud hello.

'Please be patient,' insisted Kelly. 'I'm trying to expedite your inquiry.'

'And they call this English?' Curtis complained.

'Hey, Kelly, you're quite a babe, you know that? Ever since I was in high school I've had a thing about you. No really, I have. I'd love to tell you all about it. What time do you get off work?'

'This building closes at 5.30,' said Kelly through her perfect smile.

Coleman bent closer and shook his head in wonder: you could even see the lip gloss.

'Great. What do you say I pick you up outside the front of the building here? And take you back to my place. Eat some dinner. Get to know each other. Maybe fool around a little, later.'

'If that's an example of how you talk to women, Nat,' said Curtis, 'it's no wonder you're still single.'

'Come on, Kelly, whaddya say? A real man instead of all those other see-through kinds of guys.'

'I'm sorry, sir, but I never mix business with pleasure.'

Curtis guffawed loudly.

'Jesus, her fucking lines are almost as bad as yours.'

Coleman grinned back.

'You're right. This little lady is pure saccharine. Just like the real thing, eh?'

'Thank you for your patience, gentlemen. Please proceed through the glass doors behind me to the elevator and take a car to the basement, where someone will collect you.'

'One more thing, honey. My friend and I were wondering if you're the kind to fuck on a first date. Actually, we've got a little bet on about it. He says you are. I say you're not. So which is it?'

'Nat!' Curtis was already through the glass doors.

'Have a nice day,' said Kelly, still smiling like an air stewardess through a life-vest demonstration.

'Hey, you too, sweetheart. You too. Keep it warm for me, OK?'

'Jesus Christ, Nat. Isn't it just a little early in the day?' said Curtis as they stepped inside the elevator. 'You're a degenerate.'

'Right.'

Curtis was searching the wall of the elevator for a floor-selection panel.

'Remember?' said Coleman. 'The building's smart. None of that push-button shit here. That's why our voices were digitally encoded. So we can use the elevator.' He leaned towards a perforated panel next to which was an illustration of a man with his hand cupped beside his mouth. 'That's what this little icon means. Basement, please.'

Curtis inspected the sign. 'I thought that was about burping or something.'

'Don't bullshit me.'

'Why do you call it an icon? That's a holy object.'

'Because that's what these computer people call these little signs. Icons.'

Curtis snorted with disgust. 'Of course. What would those bastards know about holy objects?'

The doors closed silently. Curtis glanced up at the electroluminescent screen that was showing the floor they were headed for, the direction of travel and the time. He seemed impatient to begin work, although this was partly due to the slight feeling of claustrophobia that affected him in elevators.

In contrast to the atrium, the basement was busy with police officers and forensic experts. The OIC, a three-hundred-pounder called Wallace lumbered towards Curtis with a notebook open in his saddle-sized hands. At New Parker Center he was known as Foghorn because with his deep southern accent and hesitant way of speaking he sounded exactly like the cartoon rooster of the same name.

Curtis flicked his notebook with apparent disapproval.

'Hey, put that away, will you, Foghorn? This is a paper-free office. You'll get us into trouble with the lady upstairs.'

'What about that thing? Me, I'm a Roman Catholic and I tell you, I didn't – I say I didn't know whether to pray to her for forgiveness or just go ahead and fuck her.'

'Nat got her telephone number. Didn't you, Nat?'

'Yeah,' said Coleman. 'She gives great head on AT&T.'

Foghorn combed his hair with his fingers, tried to read his own handwriting and shook his head. 'Fuck it. There's nothing much yet anyway.' He put the notebook away and hitched up his pants.

'Guy found – I say guy found dead with blunt head injuries. Reported in by – I say you're goin' to love this one Frank – reported in by the fuckin' computer. Can you believe it? I mean, there's neighbourhood watch and there's *Bladerunner*, right? The call was taken by the central dispatch computer at 1.57 a.m.'

'One computer talking to another,' said Coleman. 'That's the way it's going to be, y'know. The future.'

'Your future – I say your future, not mine, son.'

'Still, it was nice of them both to cut us in on it,' said Curtis. 'When did you get here, Fog?'

' 'Bout three o'clock,' he yawned. 'Excuse me.'

'Not yet I don't.' Curtis glanced at his watch. It was still only seven-thirty.

'So who's the vic?'

Foghorn pointed between the two Homicide detectives.

Curtis and Coleman turned to see the body of a tall black man lying on the floor of one of the elevator cars, his blue uniform spattered with blood.

'Sam Gleig. Night-time security guard. But not so as you'd notice.' Noticing the incomprehension in Curtis's eyes, he added: 'Got himself – I say he got himself fuckin' killed, didn't he?'

The police photographer was already folding his camera tripod away. Curtis recognized him and vaguely remembered that the man's name was Phil something.

'Hey, Phil. You done?' asked Curtis looking around the interior of the car.

'I'm sure I covered everything,' said the photographer, and showed him a list of the shots he had taken.

Curtis smiled affably. 'I think you got the whole album there.'

'I'll have them processed and printed before lunch.'

Curtis felt in his coat pocket and produced a roll of 35-millimetre film.

'Do me a favour,' he said, 'see if there's anything on this, will you? It's been in my pocket so long I can't remember what it is. I keep meaning to take it in but – well, you know how it is.'

'Sure. No problem.'

'Thanks a lot. I really appreciate it. Only don't get them mixed up.'

Sam Gleig lay with his hands resting on his stomach, his knees bent and his big feet still on the floor of the car. But for the blood, he looked like a drunk in a doorway. Curtis stepped over the blood that surrounded his head and shoulders like a Buddha's halo and crowded down to take a closer look.

'Anyone from the coroner's office seen him yet?'

'Charlie Seidler,' said Foghorn. 'He's in the – I say he's in the can, I think. You want to take a look at the johns in this fuckin' place, Frank. They've got – I say they've got johns that tell the time and brush your fuckin' teeth. Took me ten minutes just to figure out how to take a leak in the damn thing.'

'Thanks, Foghorn. I'll bear it in mind.' Curtis nodded. 'Looks like someone hit this guy pretty hard.'

'And then some,' added Coleman. 'His head looks like Hermann Munster's.'

'Big guy, too,' said Foghorn. 'Six two, six three?'

'Big enough to take care of himself, anyway,' said Curtis.

He waved his fingers at the 9 millimetre Sig that was still holstered on Gleig's waistband.

'Look at this.' He tore away the Velcro retention strap that secured the automatic in the holster. 'Still fastened. Doesn't look like he was afraid of whoever attacked him.'

'Maybe someone he knew,' offered Coleman. 'Someone he trusted.'

'When you're six feet three with a Sig automatic on your hip, trust doesn't come into it,' said Curtis, straightening up again. 'There's not much that scares you that doesn't have a gun its hand.'

Curtis stepped out of the car and leaned towards his partner.

'Recognize him?'

'Who? The vic?'

'This is the guy who found the Chinaman. We questioned him, remember?'

'If you say so, Frank. Only it's a little hard to place the face on account of it's being covered in blood and all.'

'The name on his badge?'

'Yeah. Yeah, you're right. I'm sorry, Frank.'

'Of course I'm right. For Chrissakes, Nat, that's less than seventy hours ago.' Curtis shook his head and grinned good-naturedly. 'Where've you been?'

'Seventy-two hours,' sighed Coleman. 'Just an ordinary working day on Homicide.'

'Stop it,' said Foghorn. 'You're making me cry.'

'Who was first on the scene, Foghorn?'

'Officer Hernandez!'

A uniformed patrolman with a broken nose and a Zapata moustache stepped out of the crowd and placed himself in front of the three plainclothes.

'I'm Sergeant Curtis. This is Detective Coleman.'

Hernandez nodded silently. He had a sullen, Brando-ish look.

Curtis leaned towards him and sniffed the air. 'What is that smell you're wearing, Hernandez?'

'Aftershave, Sergeant.'

'Aftershave? What kind of aftershave, Mister?'

'Obsession. By Calvin Klein.'

'Calvin Klein. Is that a fact? You smell that, Nat?'

'I sure do, sir.'

'Mmm. A cop that smells nice. It's a little Beverly Hills, don't you think, son?'

Hernandez grinned and shrugged. 'My wife prefers it to the smell of sweat, sir.'

Curtis opened his coat and sniffed under his arm.

'I didn't mean –'

'OK then, Calvin, what happened when you and your aftershave turned up here this morning?'

'Well, Sarge, Officer Cooney and I get here around two-thirty a.m. We sort of look around for a doorbell or something and then we find that the door isn't locked anyway. So we walk into the lobby and that's when we see Kelly Pendry on the desk.' Hernandez shrugged. 'Well, she tells us where to come. She says to take the elevator to the basement. So we come down here and that's how we find him.' He pointed into the bloodied elevator car.

'So then what?'

'Cooney calls in the 187 while I take a look around. There's a security guard's office on the lobby floor that looks like this guy had just left there. The desktop computer is still switched on and there's a Thermos and some sandwiches.'

'What about the construction people? Do they know about this yet?'

'Well, I found a personnel file on the computer. You know? Foreman, clerk of works, that kind of thing. And so then I phoned my dad.'

'Your dad? What the hell for?'

'He used to be in construction. A riveter. I thought he'd know the best person to call. And he said that the site agent had control of the whole operation and instructed the trade foremen. Anyhow, I had no idea this was a woman. I mean, it just said H. Hussey. Maybe I should have called someone else. But anyway she said she'd get here as soon as she could.'

'That's her job, isn't it? To take responsibility for the work? Besides, working here she ought to be used to it by now.'

'Sarge?'

'Nothing.'

Curtis caught sight of Charlie Seidler coming towards the elevators and waved to him.

'Thanks, Hernandez. That'll be all. Hey, Charlie!'

'We seem to be forever here, don't we?'

'That's why they call it a smart building,' said Curtis. 'If you're smart, you stay the hell out. So what's the reader's digest on this one?'

'Well there's more than one head wound,' Seidler said cautiously. 'And that would seem to exclude the possibility that they were sustained during some kind of collapse.'

'C'mon, Charlie. You don't get a bump on the head like that from tripping on your fuckin' shoelace. This was no accident.'

Seidler's caution remained unabated.

'The blood splashing around the head would seem to indicate that the blunt head injuries continued after he had been felled. But – but – well, take a look at this, Frank.'

Seidler stepped into the elevator and motioned Curtis to follow him.

'Computer?' he said when Curtis was inside. 'Close the doors, please.'

'Which floor do you require?'

137

'Remain on this level, please.' He pointed at the inside of the closing doors. 'Now, look there. There's more blood splashing up to chest height. And yet none outside this car. On any of the upper floors. I know because I already checked every one of them.'

'Well, that's mighty efficient of you, Charlie.'

'I thought so.'

'So you're saying that he was struck while the doors were closed?'

'It looks that way, yes. But there's no protective bruising of the hands, so I'd say he was probably struck from behind.'

'With what? What should we be looking for? A bat? A length of pipe? A rock?'

'Maybe. But it's not like there's much room to swing a weapon in here, is there? We'll have a better idea after the preliminary p.m.' Seidler turned towards the microphone. 'Open the doors, please.'

'You've certainly got the way of talking to that thing,' grinned Frank.

'This is one heck of a place, isn't it?'

The two men stepped out of the car.

'All this automation,' said Curtis, 'I don't know. When I was a kid we lived in New York. My dad worked for Standard Oil. They had an elevator operator and an elevator starter. I remember the starter real well. He had a panel where all the floor calls would light up and it was down to him when a car got dispatched. Just like a traffic cop.' Curtis waved his hand at the gleaming elevator doors of the Gridiron building. 'Just look where we are now. A computer's taken that man's job. Both their jobs. It won't be long before it takes over ours as well.'

'Yeah, well, a computer's welcome to mine,' yawned Seidler. 'I can think of better ways to start the day.'

'I'll remind you of that when they fire you. Nat, I want you to run a background check on Sam Gleig.'

'Sure, Frank.'

'Hey you! Calvin Klein! C'mere.'

Hernandez grinned sheepishly and turned to face Curtis. 'Sergeant?'

'I want you to hang around in the parking lot. And when this Hussey woman shows up, tell her to wait for me in the atrium, right? That's the room with the Christmas tree. I'm going upstairs for a look around the theme park.'

On his short tour Frank Curtis found meeting areas, coffee bars, half-built restaurants, gymnasiums with no equipment, an empty swimming pool, a health clinic, a cinema with no seats, a bowling alley and a relaxation area. The Gridiron, when it was finished, was going to be more like some expensive country club or hotel than an office building. All except levels 5–10. On these floors Curtis found what looked to him like something from the pages of a DC Comic: row upon row of white steel pods, each of them a little larger than a telephone booth, with integral foldaway furniture, a loose wire to plug into something, and a curved sliding door. Sitting inside one of these sound-proofed pods, with the door shut behind him, Curtis felt like a rat or a hamster. But it was clear that the Yu Corporation and its designers expected people to work in these cocoons. Too bad if you were claustrophobic. Or if you liked having your workmates around to have a laugh and a joke with. There was probably nowhere for a laugh and a joke on a Yu Corporation time sheet.

He slid the door open and went down a couple of levels to get a better view of the atrium. Leaning over the balcony he saw an attractive woman emerge from the elevators on to the ground level. Her bright red hair looked like a drop of blood moving across the dazzling white. She looked up at him and smiled.

'Are you Sergeant Curtis, by any chance?'

Curtis grasped the handrail with both hands and nodded back at her.

'That's right. But, you know, I bet I could do a good Mussolini impression from up here.'

'What?'

Curtis shrugged, wondering if she was too young to have heard of Mussolini. He wanted to say something about Fascist architecture, then thought better of it. She was too good-looking to upset without reasonable cause.

'Well, it's that kind of building, ma'am. It's kind of inspiring, I guess.' He grinned. 'Stay there. I'll be right down.'

The security office at the Gridiron was a gleaming white room with an electrically-operated Venetian blind screening a window that ran the length and height of the corridor. There was a large desk made of glass and aluminium and which was dominated by a 28-inch computer monitor and keyboard. Next to this were a videophone, a telephone, Sam Gleig's Thermos flask and, in an open Tupperware box, the dead man's uneaten sandwiches. Behind the desk was a tall glass cabinet containing what looked like another computer case still wrapped in plastic film.

Curtis inspected the contents of one of the sandwiches.

'Cheese and tomato,' he said and started to eat. 'Want one?'

'No. No thanks.' Helen Hussey frowned. 'Should you be doing that? I mean, isn't that evidence you're eating?'

'Gleig wasn't hit over the head with a sandwich, ma'am.'

Curtis inspected the glass cabinet and the unassuming white box in its protective wrapping.

'What's this?' he said.

Helen Hussey drew a breath and smiled uncomfortably. 'I was hoping you weren't going to ask.'

Curtis grinned back at her. 'Why's that?'

'It's a recordable multi-session CD-ROM,' she explained.

'A game? In here?'

Helen Hussey gave him a withering look. 'Not exactly, no,' she said. 'It's connected via an SCSI interface to the computer, with a date and an archive number. Each disc contains up to 700 megabytes. It's supposed to record what takes place on all the security cameras inside and outside the building. Our cameras work by cellular transmission. They're all supposed to feed into the back of that thing.' She shrugged. 'I think.'

Curtis smiled. 'Supposed to, huh?'

She gave an embarrassed sort of laugh.

'You're not going to believe this,' she said with a shrug, 'but the unit hasn't been connected yet. As far as I know it's only just been delivered.'

'Well, it looks very nice. Very nice indeed. Too bad it's not working, because then we might know exactly what happened here last night.'

'We've had a problem with our supplier.'

'What kind of problem?' Curtis sat on the edge of the desk and took another sandwich. 'These are good.'

'Well,' sighed Helen, 'they sent the wrong kind of unit. The first one wasn't what we ordered. The Yamaha records at quadruple speed. The previous one didn't. So it got returned.'

'Yours must be a tough job for a woman.'

Helen bristled. 'Why do you say that?'

'Construction workers aren't exactly known for their polite language and good manners.'

'Well, neither is the LAPD.'

'You've got a point there.' Curtis looked at the sandwich and laid it down. 'Pardon me. You're right.

141

You probably knew the guy. And I'm sitting here eating his dinner. I'm not being very sensitive, am I?'

She shrugged again, as if she hardly cared.

'You know, some people, some cops, when they see a dead body, they get nauseous and lose their appetites. Me, I don't know why, but I feel hungry. Really hungry. Maybe it's because I'm just so glad I'm still alive that I want to celebrate the fact by eating something.'

Helen nodded. 'I won't have to identify him, will I?' she said.

'No, ma'am, that won't be necessary.'

'Thanks. I don't think I –' She returned to their previous subject, feeling she owed him something more about her job.

'My job's about management and planning not about shouting at people,' she said. 'I leave that kind of thing to my foremen. My concern is to initiate each particular operation, coordinate it with the other trades and make sure that it gets supplied with the appropriate materials. Like CD-ROM recorders. But I can cuss with the worst of them when I have to.'

'Well, if you say so, ma'am. How did you get on with Sam Gleig?'

'Well enough. He seemed like a very sweet man.'

'Did you ever have to cuss him for anything?'

'No, not ever. He was reliable and honest.'

Curtis pushed himself off the desk and opened a locker. Finding a nubuck leather jacket in there, and presuming it belonged to Sam Gleig, he took it out and started to search the pockets.

'Sam Gleig came on shift at what time last night?'

'Eight o'clock, as usual. He relieved the other guard, Dukes.'

'Someone mention me?'

It was the security guard, Dukes.

'Oh, Sergeant,' said Helen. 'This is –'

'We've met,' said Curtis. 'From the last time. Mr

Yojo's death.' Instinctively he looked at his watch. It was eight o'clock.

Dukes was looking bewildered. 'What's going on?'

'Irving, it's Sam,' said Helen. 'He's dead.'

'Jesus. Poor Sam.' Dukes looked at Curtis. 'What happened?'

'We think someone bashed his head in.'

'What was it, robbery or something?'

Curtis did not answer.

'When he came on duty did either of you see him?'

Dukes shrugged. 'Very briefly. I was in a hurry. I don't think we exchanged more than a couple of words. God, what a thing to happen.'

'He came up to the site office on the seventh floor,' said Helen. 'Just to say hello, really. Find out if anyone was going to be working late. The computer could have told him more easily than we could, but he liked to be sociable. Anyway, I was just finishing for the day so he came down in the elevator with me.'

'You said we.'

'Yes, I left Warren still working, Warren Aikman. He's the clerk of works. He took a phone call just as I was leaving.'

'The clerk of works. What does he do exactly?'

'He's like a site agent only he's employed by the client as a kind of inspector.'

'You mean like a cop?'

'Kind of, I guess.'

'Would he have spoken to Sam before leaving?'

She shrugged.

'You'd have to ask him. But, frankly, it's unlikely. There's no reason at all why he would have felt obliged to call in here and inform Sam he was leaving the building. As I said, it's the computer's job to know who's still here. Sam would only have needed to tell the computer to run a check to have found out in a couple of seconds.'

Dukes sat down at the desk.

'I'll show you, if you like,' he said.

Pocketing a set of car keys and a wallet, Curtis laid the dead man's jacket on the desk and stood behind Dukes's shoulder as he clicked on an icon with the mouse and started to choose some menu options.

SECURITY SYSTEMS	YES
FULL CAMERAS AND SENSORS?	YES
INCLUDE SECURITY OFFICE?	NO
SHOW ALL OTHER OCCUPANTS?	YES

Immediately the screen showed a picture of the scene by the elevators in the basement, with all the policemen and forensic personnel who were milling around Sam Gleig's body.

'Oh God,' said Helen. 'Is that him?'

Dukes clicked the mouse again.

IDENTIFY ALL OCCUPANTS?	YES

To the high-definition picture was now added a square window with a series of names.

BASEMENT/ELEVATOR HALL:
SAM GLEIG, SECURITY GUARD, YU CORP
PATROLMAN COONEY, LAPD
PATROLMAN HERNANDEZ, LAPD
DETECTIVE SERGEANT WALLACE, LAPD
CHARLES SEIDLER, LA CORONER'S OFFICE
PHIL BANHAM, LAPD
DANIEL ROSENCRANTZ, LA CORONER'S OFFICE
ANN MOSLEY, LAPD
PATROLMAN PETE DUNCAN, LAPD
PATROLWOMAN MAGGIE FLYNN, LAPD

'Big brother,' breathed Curtis. He sneaked a sideways look at Helen Hussey: at her beautiful red hair and then down the front of her mauve silk blouse. Her breasts were large, with lots of tiny freckles.

'Impressive huh?' she said, and, feeling his eyes upon her, smiled: if Curtis had been a little younger she might have found him quite attractive.

'Very,' said Curtis and returned his gaze to the screen. 'Hey, that's my partner in the john. Can the computer see in there too?'

'Not as such,' said Dukes. 'It uses heat sensors, acoustic detectors, passive infra-red sensors and microphones to check who's in there. Voice prints. Same as in the elevator.'

'That can't be very private,' said Curtis. 'What does the computer do if you spend too long in there? Sound an alarm?'

Dukes grinned. 'Really, the computer observes your privacy,' he insisted. 'It's not like it's going to broadcast the sound around the building for everyone's amusement. These washroom checks are for everyone's safety.'

Curtis grunted, only half-convinced. 'I guess we ought to be grateful that they haven't done away with the men's room altogether,' he said. 'Gee, I bet that bugs these architect guys. I mean, it's the plumbing that keeps a building on the ground, isn't it? Reminds them that any building has to be used by human beings.'

Helen and Dukes exchanged a grin.

'I can see you haven't used one of our washrooms yet, Sergeant Curtis,' chuckled Dukes.

'He's right,' said Helen. 'Everything is automatic. And I mean everything. Let's just say that this is a paperless office enviroment.'

'You mean . . .'

'That's exactly what I mean. Flushing, by elbow, actuates a warm-water douche and a warm-air drying sequence.'

'Hell, no wonder Nat's taking such a long time in there.' Curtis laughed at the idea of his partner trying to deal with a warm-water douche.

'That's just the half of what happens in there,' said Helen. 'Washroom facilities like these may seem advanced to us. But they are already quite common in Japan.'

'Yeah well that doesn't surprise me at all.'

Dukes clicked the mouse to end the search.

Curtis sat on the corner of the desk again, stroking the hard corner of the terminal thoughtfully.

'Why are they always white?' he said. 'Computers.'

'Are they?' said Helen. 'Some are grey, I think.'

'Yeah, but mostly they're white. I'll tell you why. It's to make a lot of people feel better about them. White is a colour that's associated with virginity and innocence. Babies and brides are dressed in white. It's the colour of holiness. The Pope wears a white robe, right? If computers were all housed in black casings then they'd never have made any impact. Did you ever consider that?'

Helen Hussey shook her head. 'No, I can't say I ever did. It's a theory, I suppose.' She paused as she thought about what he had said. 'You said "a lot of people". Not you?'

'Me? I think of white and I think of heroin and cocaine. I think of bleached bones lying in the desert. I think of nothingness. I think of death.'

'Are you always this cheerful?'

'It's the job.' He smiled at her and said, 'Last night. What did you and Gleig talk about?'

'Nothing much. Hideki Yojo's death . . .' Helen started to nod, knowing what he was thinking.

Curtis grinned. 'See? You can't get away from it.'

'I guess you're right. Anyway, I told him what the coroner's office said. That Hideki died of an epileptic fit. Sam said he had guessed as much.'

'How did he seem?'

'OK. Normal.'

Dukes was nodding in agreement. 'Sam was pretty much like he always was.'

'He didn't sound worried about anything?'

'No. Not at all.'

'Did he always do nights?'

'No,' said Dukes. 'We worked it so that we each had a week of nights and then a week of days.'

'I see. Any family?'

Dukes shrugged. 'I didn't know him that well.'

'Maybe the computer will help,' said Helen. She moved the mouse and clicked her way through several menu options.

> **PERSONNEL FILES ARE RESTRICTED TO AUTHORIZED PERSONS ONLY**   **ACCESS DENIED**

'I don't think old Abraham understands about death yet,' she said, typing a note on the end of the personnel directory menu.

> **NOTIFICATION OF AN EMPLOYEE'S DEATH MUST BE MADE BY AN AUTHORIZED PERSON**
> **ACCESS DENIED**

'I'm sorry, Sergeant. You'd better ask Bob Beech or Mitchell Bryan if they can get Sam's records for you, OK?'

'Thanks, I will. And I'll also want a word with Warren Aikman.'

Helen looked at her watch. 'He should be here soon,' she said. 'Warren's an early starter. Look, this doesn't have to interfere with the building work, does it? I wouldn't like us to fall behind.'

'That all depends. What's down in the basement anyway?'

'There's a small vault, a back-up generator, horizontal LAN, floor protection system, fire-alarm relay, hygiene control unit and some locker rooms.'

Curtis remembered the booths on levels 5–10.

'I was wondering. Those pods upstairs. What the hell are they?'

'You mean the personal harbours? They're the latest thing in office design. You arrive at the office and you're allocated a PH for the day, like checking into a hotel. You just walk in, plug in your laptop and your phone, switch on the air-conditioning and start work.'

Curtis thought of his desk back at New Parker Center. Of the papers and files that lay on top of it. Of the junk that filled his drawers. And of the computer he rarely switched on.

'But what about your stuff?' he said. 'Where do folks put their stuff?'

'There are lockers in the basement. But personal possessions are discouraged in the hot-desk office environment. The idea is that you'll have everything you need with your laptop and your phone.' She paused and then added, 'So will it be OK? For workers to come and go today? They're most of them working on level 17 right now. Decorating and plumbing, I believe.'

'OK, OK,' said Curtis. 'No problem. Just keep them out of the basement.'

'Thanks, I appreciate it.'

'One more thing, Miss Hussey. It's a little too early to say for sure, but it looks as if Sam Gleig may have been murdered. Now, when the patrol car got here earlier this morning they found the door unlocked. But I had gained the impression that your computer – Abraham – controlled the doorlock. Why would it leave the door unlocked?'

'As I understood things, it was Abraham who called the police. The simplest explanation would seem to be that it left the door open so that your men could get in.'

Dukes cleared his throat. 'There's another possibility.'

Curtis nodded. 'Let's hear it.'

'Sam could have told Abraham to unlock the door. To let someone in. You say Sam got his brains bashed in? Well, I can't see how the guy could have got in unless it was Sam that let him through the door. Abraham wouldn't have locked the door again unless he'd been specifically instructed to do so. By someone who had been TESPAR'd.'

'How many ways in and out of the building are there?'

'Apart from the front door? Two,' said Dukes. 'There's the garage beneath the basement that's also controlled by TESPAR. And then there's the fire exit on this floor. That's controlled by Abraham. It doesn't open unless the fire-detection system indicates that there's an actual fire.'

'Can you think of any reason why Sam Gleig would have let someone in at night?'

Helen Hussey shook her head.

Dukes pursed his lips and looked reluctant to answer for a moment. Then he said, 'I don't mean to speak ill of the dead and all, but it wouldn't be the first time a security guard has let an unauthorized person into a building at night. I'm not saying that Sam ever did it to my knowledge, but on my last job, a hotel, there was a guard who got fired for taking money from hookers to let them bring their clients there.' He shrugged. 'It happens, y'know? Not that Sam struck me as the type mind, but . . .'

'Yes?'

Dukes stroked the butter-soft leather jacket thoughtfully.

'But.' He shrugged uncomfortably. 'This is a nice looking leather jacket. I'm sure I couldn't have afforded it.'

It was still early in the morning when Allen Grabel finally made it back to his house in Pasadena. It wasn't easy to persuade a taxi to take you anywhere when you looked like Grabel, and he had been obliged to pay cash up front for the privilege. He lived in one of a group of Spanish-revival bungalows organized around a central open space of grass and pathway.

He still had no doorkeys, so he took off his size 12 Bass-Weejun loafer and smashed a window, setting off the burglar alarm. He climbed through but it was a minute or so before he remembered the numbers of the code, by which time one of his neighbours, a dentist named Charlie, was outside.

'Allen? Is that you?'

'It's OK, Charlie,' Grabel said weakly, opening the front door and feeling that things were anything but OK. 'I forgot my keys.'

'What happened? There's blood on your arm. Where have you been?'

'There was a rush job at the office. I haven't stopped for several days.'

Charlie the dentist nodded. 'Looks like it,' he said. 'I've seen shit in better shape than you.'

Grabel smiled weakly. 'Yeah, thanks a lot, Charlie. Have a nice day now.'

He went into the bedroom, and dropped on to the bed. He glanced at the date on his watch and groaned. A six-day bender. That was what it amounted to. He felt like Don Birnam in *The Lost Weekend*. What was the first line again? 'The barometer of his emotional nature was set for a spell of riot.' Something like that, anyway. Well that was what he had been having, right enough, a spell of riot. There had been other times, of course, but never as bad as this.

Closing his eyes he tried to remember some of what had happened. He remembered walking out on his job. He remembered sleeping on the campbed at the Gridiron building. There was something else too. But that was like a terrible nightmare. Had he only imagined it? He had dreamed he was Raskolnikov. The back of his head was aching. Had he fallen? There was something about Mitch's car. Maybe he had a concussion.

He was so tired he felt like he was dying. It was not a bad feeling. He wanted to sleep for ever.

Tony Levine was feeling undervalued. Allen Grabel had been an associate partner in the firm, just one step below the coveted full partnership status of Mitchell Bryan, Willis Ellery and Aidan Kenny. When Grabel resigned Levine had assumed that he would be promoted. Not to mention getting more money. Considering what he was called upon to do as project manager on the Gridiron, the biggest project of his career so far, Levine believed that his compensation fell far short of what some of his friends were making. He had said it before, but this time he meant it: if it didn't happen this time he was going to quit.

Levine had gone into the office early to get Richardson alone. He had planned what he was going to say, and had repeated the words to himself in the car that morning, like an actor in a movie. He would remind Richardson of the way he had motivated the team and set the whole tone of the project. Of the enormous amount of responsibility he had taken.

He found Richardson in the far corner of the studio, his Turnbull and Asser shirt sleeves already rolled up, scribbling notes in one of the shiny silver-covered sketchbooks that accompanied him everywhere. He was facing the scale model of a $300 million police training facility in Tokyo.

'Morning, Ray. Have you got a minute?'

'What do you think of this, Tony?' Richardson asked sourly.

Levine sat down at the table and looked over the model, a competition-winning entry for a site in the unglamorous Shinkawa area of the city, close to Tokyo's financial centre. Even by Tokyo standards the building looked futuristic, with its concave glass roof, and, at the building's heart, a stainless steel clad volume that contained gymnasiums, a swimming pool, teaching facilities, a library, auditorium and an indoor firing range.

Levine hated it. It looked like a silver Easter egg in a perspex box, he thought. But what did Richardson think of it? He adopted what he thought was a thoughtful expression and tried to read Richardson's neatly boxed-in pencil notes upside down. When this proved un-successful he looked to find a neutral form of words that would cover him either way.

'It certainly takes a radically different aesthetic approach from anything else in the surrounding area,' he said.

'That's hardly surprising. The surrounding area is being completely re-developed. Come on, Tony do you think it sucks or not?'

Levine was relieved that Richardson's videophone rang at this moment. He would have time to consider his reply: he looked over at Richardson's notes, but was disappointed to find that they were little more than doodles. He cursed silently. Even the man's doodles looked clean and efficient, as if they actually meant something.

It was Helen Hussey, and she looked anxious.

'We've got a problem, Ray,' she said.

'I don't want to hear about it,' Richardson said flatly. 'That's why I pay you people. So I don't have to waste time fixing every fuck-up myself. Talk to your project manager, Helen. He's sitting right beside me.'

Richardson twisted the screen so that the small fibre-optic camera was pointed at Levine and returned to boxing in his pencilled scribbles, as if somehow even these idle doodles needed the preservation offered by a protective border.

'What's up, babe?' Levine said, eager to have the opportunity to offer a cool and correct judgement of what was to be done and to solve her problem in front of the boss. 'How can I help?'

'It's not that kind of problem,' said Helen, trying to conceal her instinctive loathing of Levine. 'There's been another death. And this time it looks like someone's been murdered.'

'Murdered? Who? Who is it that's dead?'

'The overnight security guard. Sam Gleig.'

'The black guy? Well gee, that's really awful. What happened?'

'Someone beat his brains out last night. They found him in an elevator this morning. The police are here right now.'

'My God. How awful.' Levine was painfully aware of knowing that he had no idea what to say to her. 'Do they know who did it?'

'Not yet, no.'

'My God, Helen. Are you OK? I mean, someone should be with you. The trauma, y'know?'

'Are you crazy?' Richardson hissed, twisting the screen away from him. 'Don't give her ideas like that, you asshole, or I'll have another fuckin' lawsuit on my hands.'

'Sorry, Ray. I just . . .'

'We can't afford to have the LAPD prevent our construction workers from working, Helen,' barked Richardson. 'You know what they're like. Police lines out front. Close a stable door after the horse is bolted. We can't lose a day on this.'

'No, I already spoke to them about that. They're going to let workers in.'

'Good girl. Well done. Any damage to the building?'

'Not as far as I know. But it looks as if Gleig might have let the guy who killed him walk through the front door.'

'Well, that's just fucking great. We're just a few days off completing and this sonofabitch has to get himself killed. What kind of smart building is it that lets some shit-for-brains fucker just ignore the security systems and let someone through the front door? Are the media there yet?'

'Not yet.'

'What about Mitch?'

'Any minute, I guess.'

Richardson sighed bitterly.

'They're going to piss all over us on this. Especially the *Times*. OK, here's what to do. Dealing with City Hall is Mitch's thing. He knows who to sweet talk in order to limit damage. You know what I'm saying? As soon as he shows up tell him to make sure that the cops give the right story to the media. Got that?'

'Yes, Ray,' Helen said wearily.

'You did right calling me, Helen. I'm sorry I snapped at you.'

'That's –'

Richardson's finger stabbed a button to end their conversation.

'Mitch'll sort it out,' he told Levine, almost as if he was trying to reassure himself. 'He's a good man in a crisis. The kind of guy you can depend on, who makes things happen. As you get more experienced you'll learn that that's what this job is all about, Tony.'

'Yes,' said Levine, feeling that the moment had now passed when he could have mentioned his own promotion, 'I'm sure I will.'

'So. Where were we? Oh yes, you were telling me what you thought about our design for the Shinkawa Police Academy.'

There were only three cars in the Gridiron's parking lot. Curtis guessed that the new Saab convertible belonged to Helen Hussey. That left him an old blue Buick and an even older grey Plymouth to choose from in deciding which one belonged to Sam Gleig, and for a moment it was like being a real detective. Just checking which car fitted the set of keys he was carrying would have been cheating. The Buick sported a bumper long sticker – 'I watched c-beams glitter in the dark near the Tannhauser Gate'. Curtis frowned. What the hell did that mean? The Plymouth looked an easier shot with the KLON 88.1 FM window sticker. The tiny plastic saxophone on Gleig's key-chain made Curtis figure Gleig for a jazz fan. He was pleased to find that he was right, and that the key turned in the Plymouth's lock. It was not exactly Sherlock Holmes, but it would do.

Sam Gleig's car may have been old but it was clean and well looked after. A small sachet of air-freshener hung off the rear-view mirror and the ashtrays were empty. Curtis opened the glove compartment and found only a *Thomas* guide and a pair of Ray-ban aviators. Then he went around the back and unlocked the trunk. The extra-large cordura nylon pro-shooter's bag seemed to indicate a man who took his work very seriously. It contained a set of ear protectors, a barrel brush, some five-inch cardboard targets, a couple of boxes of Black Hills .40 S&W, a spare magazine, a speed loader and an empty padded pistol pouch. But there was nothing that gave Curtis the remotest clue as to why he had been killed.

Hearing the elevator bell Curtis turned to see Nathan Coleman coming towards him.

'Where the hell have you been?'

'Fuckin' toilet,' growled Coleman. 'You know what happens? I mean, there's, like, a command module on the side of the seat, with buttons on it. Tells you everything from how long you've been in there to, I dunno, what you had for fuckin' breakfast. So finally I figure out that the reason there's no paper is because you get your ass washed for you while you're sitting there.'

'Did you get it waxed as well?' laughed Curtis.

'Fuckin' toothbrush thing comes out from under the seat and hits you in the rear with this jet of hot water. And I mean hot, Frank. Fuckin' thing was like a laser beam. Then there's a jet of hot air to dry you off. Jesus, Frank, my ass feels like I spent the night with Rock Hudson.'

Curtis wiped the tears from his eyes.

'What kind of a fuckin' place is this?'

'The future, Nat. It's a scalded asshole and a pair of wet pants. Have you run that background check yet?'

'The vic has a rap sheet. I just got the fax out of the car.'

'Let's hear it.'

'Two convictions for narcotics and one for possession of an illegal weapon, for which he served two years in the Met.'

'Here, let me see that.' Curtis glanced over the fax. 'The Met, huh? Must be where he got his love of modern architecture. Place is like a goddamned hotel. You know, it wouldn't surprise me if they helped him fill out his application to become a security guard.' He shook his head wearily. 'Jesus, the licensing laws in this city. Sometimes I think Charlie fucking Manson could start up a security company in LA.'

156

'It's a growth industry Frank, that's for sure.'

Curtis folded the fax and put it in his coat pocket. 'I'll keep this, Nat, just in case I have to go to the john myself.'

'Looks like Gleig's been straight since he was in the joint,' offered Nat.

'Maybe his past just caught up with him.' Curtis handed Coleman Sam Gleig's driver's licence. '92nd and Vermont. That's Crip country, isn't it?'

Coleman nodded. 'Reckon he was dealin' a little on the side.'

'Maybe. There's nothing in the car.'

'What's in the bag?'

'Man's all packed for a picnic at his local gun club. But no shit.'

'What about those kids outside? The Chinese like their narcotics.'

'I haven't ruled them out.'

'Or it could be one of them decided to bring the protest into the building, y'know? And Sam got in the way. Want me to speak to them?'

'No, not yet. I want you and an SID team to haul your asses down south to the vic's place and see what you can find. You can break the news to anyone who's interested. Maybe get a lead on his friends. Like, are they the kind of friends who supplied his need for enemies?'

The motor controlling the door that gated the garage started to buzz loudly. As Coleman walked back to the elevator, Curtis closed the Plymouth's trunk and then waited to see who would get out of the red Lexus that came down the ramp and drew up beside him.

'What's going on?' said Mitch through the open window.

Curtis could not recall a name but he remembered the face, not to mention the silk tie and the gold Rolex. The man who got out of the car was tall, with dark, curly hair, tanned and vaguely boyish looking. The blue eyes were quick and intelligent. The kind of guy who lived next door – if you happened to live in Beverly Hills.

'It's Mr –?'

'Bryan, Mitchell Bryan.'

'I remember now. There's a problem, Mr Bryan.'

Curtis waited a beat and then told him what the problem was.

Curtis stared out of the twenty-fifth-floor window and waited for Mitchell Bryan to return with coffee. He was still thinking about what Helen Hussey had said about those pods. How had she described the whole idea of it? Hot something or other. Hot desking? At least he *had* a desk. At least he had some idea of where he belonged. He tried to imagine the chaos at New Parker Center if all the cops had to fight for their preferred spots. It sounded like just another lousy idea thought up by the big corporations. For once he was glad he didn't have to work in an office and take the shit that got thrown at you. Being a cop you got to throw some back.

'I don't know,' said Mitch, returning to Mr Yu's private suite with the coffee. 'Sam Gleig seemed like a pretty straight sort of guy.'

They sat down around the Ming-dynasty Huali wooden dining table that Mitch had been using as his desk, and sipped at their coffee.

'I often work late and we sometimes had a word or two, he and I. Mostly about sports: the Dodgers. And he went to the track once in a while, Santa Anita, I think. Gave me a tip once. But he wasn't a big gambler. Ten bucks here and there.' Mitch shook his head. 'It's too bad this had to happen.'

Curtis said nothing. Sometimes it was better that way. You just let someone fill the silence and hope that maybe they said something interesting or useful: something you wouldn't ever have thought of asking about.

'But you know, even if he was dealing, like you suggested, he couldn't have been using. I'm 100 per cent certain of that much, anyway.'

'Oh? What makes you so sure, Mr Bryan?'

'This building, that's what.' Mitch frowned. 'This is confidential, OK?'

Curtis nodded patiently.

'Well, when we planned this building we bought in washroom modules that were designed to our client's specifications.'

'I've been hearing something about those. Hot desking is one thing. But hot seating is quite another.' He chuckled. 'My colleague almost got his ass steam-cleaned.'

Mitch laughed. 'Some of the units have yet to be properly adjusted,' he said. 'They can give you quite a surprise. Even so, they're pretty well state of the art. And it goes much further than a warm-water douche, I can assure you. The toilet seats give you a readout on your blood pressure and your body temperature, and the actual toilet bowl contains a urinalysis facility. Effectively the computer checks you for . . . Here, I'll show you.' Mitch leaned towards his computer and clicked the mouse through a number of choices. 'Yes, here we are. Sugars, acetone bodies, creatine, nitrogenous compounds, haemoglobin, myoglobin, amino acids and metabolites, uric acid, urea, urobilinogen and coproporphyrins, bile pigments, minerals, fats, and of course a great variety of psychotropic drugs: certainly all of the ones proscribed by the US Federal Bureau of Narcotics.'

'This happens every time you go to the can?'

'Every time.'

'Jesus.'

'For instance, acetone bodies might be high in the urine of an individual who was developing diabetes, and that might have a bearing on his or her work performance, not to mention the company's medical insurance.'

'With drug use, what happens if the test proves positive?'

'First the computer closes down your work-station and denies you access to the elevators and to a telephone. That's just damage limitation, to protect the Corporation against potential negligence. Then it reports the violation to your senior. It's up to him what happens to you. But it's a very accurate test. Shows up anything you've used in the last seventy-two hours. The manufacturers insist that it's as good as the nalline test, maybe even better.'

Curtis was still opening and closing his mouth like a surprised fish. The wonder of it was that none of those cops working in the basement had proved positive. Curtis knew that Coleman smoked a little dope now and again. Quite likely some of the others too. He could just see the look on the police commissioner's face if any of the newspapers found out that officers investigating a murder had been picked up for drug abuse by a smart building that had been the scene of a crime.

Mitch sipped his coffee, enjoying the policeman's surprise. 'So,' he said finally. 'You can see how it was impossible for Sam to have used dope.'

Curtis remained unconvinced. 'Maybe he just went outside and took a leak on the piazza somewhere.'

'I doubt it,' said Mitch. 'The piazza is subject to security-camera surveillance, and the computer is programmed to be on the alert for that kind of thing. If the CCTV does see something then the computer is programmed to call the police. Sam knew that. I can't imagine he would have taken the risk.'

'No, I guess not.' Curtis grinned. 'Gee, I bet they love you down at central dispatch.'

'Take my word for it. He was clean.'

Curtis stood up and went back to the window. 'Maybe you're right,' he said. 'But someone killed him. Here. And in your client's building.'

'I'd like to help,' said Mitch. 'Anything I can do, just ask. My firm is as anxious to get this cleared up as you are, believe me. It creates a bad impression. As if maybe this is not such a smart building after all.'

'I had the same thought myself.'

'Do you mind me asking what you're going to tell the media?' Mitch asked.

'I hadn't given it much thought yet. Probably up to my lieutenant and the press office.'

'Could I ask you a small favour? When you do decide to brief the media, I wonder if I might ask you to be careful how you choose your words. It would be a great pity if they were to get hold of the idea that somehow what happened was the fault of the building itself, you know? I mean, from what you've already told me it sounds as if Sam Gleig admitted his own murderer to the building, for whatever reason. I'd be grateful if you could bear that in mind.'

Curtis nodded sourly. 'I'll do my best,' he said. 'In return, there's something you can do for me.'

'Name it.'

'I need to get hold of Sam Gleig's personnel records.'

Next to the elevators on the fortieth floor was a glass case containing the gilt-bronze figure of a Luohan monk. Curtis admired it briefly before stepping into the car alongside Mitch.

'Mr Yu is a great collector,' explained Mitch. 'There's going to be an artefact like this on every floor.'

'What's that he's holding?' he said. 'A slide rule?'

'I think it's a folded fan.'

'Ancient air-conditioning, huh?'

161

'Something like that. The data centre please, Abraham,' said Mitch.

The doors closed with a quiet hiss of air.

'You know,' said Mitch, 'I wouldn't want to tell you your job, but isn't there another possible explanation for what's happened? I mean, apart from Sam Gleig's past.'

'I'm all ears,' said Curtis.

'It's just that both Ray Richardson and the Yu Corporation have their respective enemies. In Ray's case it's a matter of a few personal grudges. People who hate the kind of buildings he designs. For instance, there's a time capsule underneath the foundations and one of the things it contains is some hate mail for him. And there are people who have worked for him who dislike him.'

'Does that include you?'

'Oh, I admire him very much.'

Curtis grinned. 'I think that answers my question.'

Mitch shrugged apologetically. 'He's a difficult person.'

'Most very rich people are.'

Mitch didn't answer. The elevator came to a halt and they stepped into the corridor next to a newly arrived and identically positioned glass case containing a jade horse's head.

'And the Yu Corp?' prompted Curtis. 'You said that they have enemies too. Do you mean those kids out front?'

'I think they're just the tip of the iceberg,' said Mitch, ushering Curtis along the edge of the atrium. 'In parts of the Asian Pacific Rim, business can be quite rough. That's why all the glass in this building is bullet-proof. Why the security systems are so tight.' He stopped and pointed down. 'Take this atrium. It's really just a con job. It gives the impression of a company that's accessible to the public and at the same time acts as a security barrier. The reason for the hologram on the front desk is to forestall a potential hostage situation.'

'Sam Gleig gets a major-sized headache because someone bears your boss or his client a grudge?' Curtis shook his head. 'I'm afraid I can't buy that.'

'Well, suppose it was just accidental? Suppose someone came in here intent on causing trouble and Sam just got in the way?'

'It's possible. But only just. Gleig's gun was in his holster. It didn't look like he was expecting trouble. On the other hand, if Sam knew his attacker then he would have been off his guard. When you mentioned your boss's enemies, did you have anyone specific in mind?'

Mitch thought about Allen Grabel.

'No,' he said.

'What about this guy Warren Aikman?'

'If he wanted to hurt Richardson there would be better ways of doing it within the normal course of his work.'

'Well, let me know if you think of anyone.'

'Sure.'

Curtis shook his head. 'Of course, I can't say I'm surprised that the architect of a place like this has enemies.'

'You don't like it?'

'Every time I come here I like it less and less. Maybe it's the things you and your people tell me about it. I don't know.' He shook his head, trying to put his finger on it. 'I think maybe it lacks soul.'

'It's the future,' argued Mitch. 'Really it is. Some day all offices will be built this way.'

Curtis laughed and showed Mitch his wrist.

'See this watch? It's a Seiko. Lousy timekeeper. I still remember the advertising slogan they were using when I bought the thing. "Some day all watches will be made this way." God, I hope not.'

Mitch gazed around him. 'You know, I think of it as a kind of cathedral.'

'To what? Man's fear of his fellow man?'

'To the virtue of making things. To the creative power of technology. To man's ingenuity.'

'Being a cop, I guess I don't have much faith in human ingenuity. But if this is a cathedral then I'm an atheist.'

Bob Beech was about to send the latest batch of stolen data across the satellite when he saw Mitch and Curtis coming through the doors of the computer room. He touched the wide flat screen and returned it to the standard desktop display: the telephone, Rolodex, calculator, diary, in- and out-trays, clock, TV set, radio, answering machine were all computer icons. There was even a desk drawer, rubber stamp, filing cabinet and a picture window with a pleasant view of Griffith Park as seen from the Gridiron roof.

'Bob,' said Mitch advancing into the centre of the circle, 'you remember Detective Sergeant Curtis.'

'Sure.'

'You've heard what happened this morning?'

Beech shrugged and nodded.

Curtis took the man in: the fisherman's gilet stuffed with discs, tapes, keys, chewing gum and pens; the sensible brown Oxfords in need of a polish; the finger-nails bitten to the quick; and, underneath the lugubrious-looking moustache, the polite smile flicking as he feigned interest in what had happened. Curtis was an old hand at spotting when he was being tolerated. It was obvious that Beech just wanted to get back to whatever it was that he had been doing before being disturbed.

'Poor old Sam,' said Beech. 'Do you have any idea who did it yet?'

'Not yet, sir. But I was hoping to see his personnel file. There might be something there that will help. Also, I wondered if there was a way the computer had of knowing exactly who was in the building after ten o'clock last night.' He knew there was. But he wanted to prolong his stay in the computer room.

'Of course.' Beech fingered the filing cabinet on his screen and then said, 'Abraham. Can you locate Sam Gleig's personnel file please?'

'On screen or on disc?'

Beech glanced at Curtis and decided that he wanted him out of the computer room as quickly as possible. Seeing him standing there reminded him of Hideki. 'Better make it hard copy,' he said. 'So you can examine it at your leisure, Sergeant.'

'There's not a lot of that in Homicide, sir,' said Curtis, smiling affably. Glancing down at Beech's desktop he watched as a disembodied hand appeared on screen and moved towards the filing cabinet.

'Belshazzar's feast,' he murmured.

The hand lifted a file out of the desk drawer and then disappeared with it screen left.

'What's that?' said Beech.

'I said, that's a hell of a personal organizer you have there.'

'It's kind of childish, but I'm a guy who needs friendly software to bring cyberspace down to earth. That's why I have a room with a view, so to speak. Without it I'd find it difficult working in here. Now then, what was the other thing? Who was still here after ten o'clock last night?'

Curtis nodded.

Beech touched the screen several times with his forefinger, like a man playing speed chess. Finally he found what was he looking for.

'Here we are. The electrical foreman left at seven-thirty. I left at seven-forty-three. Aidan Kenny left at seven-forty-four. Helen Hussey left at eight-fifteen. Warren Aikman left at eight-thirty-five. At which point

Sam Gleig was the only person on site until Officers Cooney and Hernandez arrived this morning.'

'I see. Thank you.'

Beech pointed out of the door. 'We'll have to go along to the print room to fetch your copy,' he said and led the way across the bridge.

They entered a room where an enormous laser printer was already spewing out the file. Beech collected the print-out.

'This is strange,' he said, surprised. 'Abraham's not supposed to be able to do this.'

'Do what?' asked Mitch.

Beech handed over the print-out. Attached to the personnel information was a colour photocopy of Sam Gleig greeting a Chinese man in the atrium.

'It's not part of Abraham's original program to take still photographs like this,' frowned Beech. 'At least, not until the CD-ROM recorder is installed.'

For the moment Curtis was more interested in the young Chinese man in the picture than the means by which it had been taken.

'Do you recognize him?'

'I think I do,' said Mitch. 'I think it might be one of our friends from outside the building.'

'Unless Abraham managed . . .' Beech was still considering the puzzle of how the picture had been taken. 'Of course . . .'

'You mean he's one of the demonstrators?'

Mitch looked at the picture again.

'I'm sure he is.'

'Of course,' repeated Beech. 'The link-up with Richardson's computer. Mitch, Abraham must have held the picture digitally and then used your Intergraph software to generate this. That's the only way he could have done it. It's Abraham's way of letting us know that Sam Gleig brought an unauthorized person into the building last night.'

Curtis pulled a face. 'Wait a minute. Are you telling me that the only witness to Sam Gleig's murder might be your computer?'

'It certainly looks that way. I can't imagine why he would have put this picture in Sam Gleig's file otherwise.' He shrugged. 'At the very least this picture gives you an unauthorized visitor to the Gridiron, doesn't it? There's even a time on the picture: 1.05 a.m.'

'Is that a bottle of Scotch he's holding?' said Mitch. 'Looks like they were planning a party.'

'But why take this picture and not one of the actual murder as it happened?' said Curtis.

'Because there are no cameras inside the elevators,' said Mitch.

Beech nodded in agreement. 'This picture connects the Chinese guy with the murder. No doubt about it.'

'Let me be the judge of that, please,' said Curtis.

'Maybe I should have mentioned it before,' said Mitch, 'but there have been a couple of incidents involving these kids.'

He told Curtis about the orange thrown at his car and the tyre wrench.

'Did you report either of these incidents?'

'No, I didn't,' admitted Mitch. He took out his wallet. 'But I've still got the paperwork for the replacement shield.'

Curtis flicked his eyes over the receipt.

'How did you know it was one of them who did it?'

'After the first time? I was in a Chinese restaurant, just a few blocks from here. One of them must have recognized me.'

'You still got the wrench?'

'Yes, as a matter of fact I have. It's in the trunk of my car. Want me to go get it?'

'No, I'd just as soon have one of the SID boys pick it. In case there are any prints on it.' Curtis folded the photograph and was about to put it inside his coat pocket when he had an idea. 'There are cameras mounted on the outside of this building, aren't there?'

'Several,' said Mitch.

'Can you have one close in on those kids outside right now?'

'Nothing easier,' said Beech.

They trooped back into the computer room. Beech sat down and touched a picture of a video camera at the bottom of his screen.

The camera was soon scanning the faces of no more than a dozen Chinese men and women.

'Beats me why they bother,' said Beech.

'It's a free country,' said Curtis, 'although you'd hardly know it inside this place.'

Beech shot Curtis a quizzical look, as if wondering why someone as liberal as him should be working for the LAPD.

'That guy there,' said Mitch. 'The one with the bullhorn. That's the guy in the picture, isn't it?'

Curtis compared the hard copy with the young Chinese on the screen.

'Yeah. That's him all right.'

'Kind of weird him coming back, isn't it?' said Mitch. 'Assuming he did have something to do with it.'

'Not as weird as you might suppose,' said Curtis. 'Besides, that's still a hell of an assumption.'

'What are you going to do?'

'Talk to the guy. See what he's got to say. Who knows? Maybe he'll put up his hands.'

The cop patrolling the demo already looked tired, although it was only just eleven o'clock. Curtis showed him his badge and then, taking him by the elbow, led him a few yards away.

'You heard about what happened inside?'

'Guy with his head stove in? I heard.'

'How long have you had this duty?'

'On and off, a couple of weeks. 'Bout a four-hour shift.' He shrugged. 'It's not so bad. They don't give me any trouble. I've spoken to a few of them. Most are pretty OK.'

'Would you say they were the types to get involved in a homicide?'

The cop grinned and shook his head. 'Naw. They're students with rich daddies back home in Hong Kong and places like that. I think they'd run a mile from any real trouble.'

Curtis walked back towards them.

'Who's in charge here?'

Behind the barrier, the little band of Chinese protesters stayed quiet, but Curtis noticed that their eyes moved from his badge to the man with the bullhorn. His own eyes took in the slogans on their placards: REMEMBER TIANANMEN SQUARE; and, YU CORP SANCTIONS STATE MURDER; and, YU CORP PROFITS FROM SLAVERY; and, YU-MAN RIGHTS ABUSE.

'Come on,' he urged. 'There must be someone.'

'Well,' said the man with the bullhorn, 'I guess you could say I am, kind of.'

'I'm Detective Sergeant Curtis, LAPD Homicide Bureau. Could I talk to you a minute? Let's step out of the sun.' He pointed across the piazza to the edge of Hope Street.

'Hot day,' he said. And then, 'It's about an incident in the Yu Corporation building last night.'

'Another one?' Cheng Peng Fei smiled thinly.

'Someone was killed.'

'That's too bad. Nobody junior, I hope.'

'You approve?'

'If it was Yu himself then that would be good news. The man is a gangster.'

'I was wondering what time you and your people left the piazza last night. Maybe you saw something.'

'About five o'clock. Same as usual.'

'I'm sorry, you are –'

'My name is Cheng Peng Fei.'

'Where are you from, son?'

'Hong Kong. I'm a visa student at UCLA.'

'And your friends? Are they mostly students?'

'Mostly, yes.'

'Did you ever run across the security guard at the Yu building? Big guy. Black.'

'Is that the man who's dead?'

'Yes, it is.'

Cheng Peng Fei shook his head.

'We've seen him. That's all. There's another guard too, isn't there? Mean looking whitey. We've seen rather more of him.'

'You ever go inside the building?'

'We have thought about it, but we'd probably get busted. So we just stay beside our fountain handing out leaflets, that kind of thing.'

'It was sure different in my day,' said Curtis as they neared the corner of Fifth.

A bum pushing a shopping cart paused briefly to collect a cigarette butt off the sidewalk before continuing in the direction of Wilshire. A tall black man wearing grimy Nike Air Jordans, track-suit pants and a baseball cap coming the opposite way was forced to side-step the cart and stopped to curse the bum before continuing on his way.

'When I was a kid a protest really was a protest.'

'What were you protesting about?'

'There was only one thing people protested about back in those days: Vietnam.'

'Better than going there, I guess.'

'Oh, I went. It was when I came back I got involved. What exactly is your beef with the Yu Corp?'

Cheng Peng Fei handed over a leaflet.

'Here, this'll explain everything.'

Curtis stopped, glanced over the bill and put it in his coat pocket. Then he nodded towards an advertising hoarding on a shelter for the DASH, the Downtown Area Short Hop bus service. The ad showed a hand-shake between two disembodied arms, one of them wearing the uniform of the LAPD. The headline read:

Cheng Peng Fei was bright enough to understand what Curtis was suggesting. He shrugged and shook his head.

'Really, if I knew something I'd tell you, Sergeant, but I can't help you.'

He was shorter than Curtis by a head and, at a hundred and twelve pounds, just over half as heavy. Curtis placed himself in front of Cheng, close enough to have kissed him, and regarded him with a mixture of suspicion and contempt.

'What are you doing?' said Cheng. Trying to retreat he found himself pressed up against the wall on the corner of Fifth and Hope.

'I'm just trying to see inside your inscrutable little head,' said Curtis, holding him firmly by the shoulders. 'So that I'll know why you're lying to me.'

'What the fuck are you talking about, man?'

'Now you're absolutely certain you never met Sam Gleig?'

'Sure I'm sure. I never even heard his name until now.' Cheng started to curse the policeman in Chinese.

'You ever heard of Miranda, college boy?'

'Miranda who?'

'Miranda vs. the State of Arizona, that's who. Fifth Amendment stuff. Guidelines that include informing arrested persons prior to questioning that they have the right to remain silent –'

'You're arresting me? For what?'

Curtis turned Cheng around and handcuffed one hand expertly.

'– anything you say may be used against you in a court of law. And that you have the right to an attorney.'

'What is this? You're crazy.'

'These are your rights, schmuck. Now, here's what we're going to do. I'm going to cuff you to the streetlight there and then go and collect my car and come back and pick you up. I'd go back there with you, only I figure it might inflame some of your friends to see you being arrested and I'm sure you wouldn't want to cause any trouble. Not to mention the embarrassment you might experience. This way you're only going to be embarrassed in front of a few passing strangers.'

Curtis hauled Cheng's thin arm around the streetlight and snapped on the other manacle.

'You're fucking crazy.'

'Besides, while I'm gone it'll give you a little time to reflect on that story of yours. Time to reflect. Time to think of another.' Curtis looked at his watch. 'I'll be back in five minutes. Ten at the most.' He pointed up at the Gridiron that loomed over them, reducing the surrounding buildings to visual insignificance. 'Anyone asks, you just stopped to admire the architecture.'

'Bullshit.'

'Now, there I have to agree with you, Cheng boy.'

'The tape's running, Frank.'

Cheng Peng Fei glanced around the video room at New Parker Center.

'What tape?'

'We're recording this interrogation on video,' said Curtis. 'For posterity. Not to mention your protection. Is this your good side?'

Coleman sat down alongside Curtis and facing Cheng Peng Fei across a table on which there was only one object: a tyre wrench wrapped in a polythene bag. Cheng pretended it was not there.

'It's so your lawyer can't say we beat a confession out of you with this tyre wrench,' said Coleman.

'What's to confess? I haven't done anything.'

'Please state your name and age.'

'Cheng Peng Fei. I'm twenty-two.'

'Do you wish an attorney to be present?'

'No. Like I said, I haven't done anything.'

'That's your tyre wrench, isn't it?' said Coleman.

Cheng shrugged. 'Could you recognize yours?'

'Yours is missing from the trunk of your car,' said Coleman. 'I checked. This wrench was thrown through the windshield of a car belonging to Mitchell Bryan, an architect working at the Yu Corporation building. A red Lexus. This wrench has your fingerprints on it.'

'Well, if it's my wrench it would, wouldn't it? I had a flat and I changed the wheel. I drove off and left my wrench on the road.'

'The incident with the wrench happened in the parking lot at the Mon Kee Restaurant on North Spring Street,' said Coleman. 'Just a few blocks from the Gridiron.'

'If you say so.'

'When we searched your apartment we found a Mastercard receipt for a meal you ate there on the same night that Bryan's windshield was smashed.'

Cheng Peng Fei was silent for a moment.

'All right. So I smashed a windshield. But that's all. I know what you're trying to do here. But even if your premise is correct and I did smash the windshield of one man working at the Gridiron, it does not make your conclusion, that I murdered another man working there, at all certain. Even if you had ten thousand such premises, it would not establish your conclusion.'

'Are you studying law, by any chance?' asked Curtis.

'Business Admin.'

'Well, you're right, of course,' Curtis allowed. 'This wrench alone would not make it certain. Of course, it might make it easier for us to show you had a motive: your fanatical opposition to the Yu Corp and its employees and agents.'

'Bullshit.'

'Where were you last night, Cheng?'

'I stayed home and did some reading.'

'What did you read?'

'*Organizational Culture and Leadership*, by Edgar H. Schein.'

'No shit.'

'Any witnesses?'

'I was studying, not partying. I was reading a book.'

'When you do party,' said Coleman, 'what do you drink?'

'What kind of a question is that?'

'Beer?'

'Sometimes beer, yeah. Chinese beer. I don't like the taste of American beer.'

'Scotch?'

'Sure. Who doesn't?'

'Me, I can't stand the stuff,' admitted Coleman.

'So what does that prove? I drink Scotch, you don't drink Scotch, he drinks Scotch. This is like my English class. Can we try the past indefinite now?'

'Drink much Scotch, do you?'

'Ever share a bottle with a friend?'

'I'm not that kind of drinker.'

'What about Sam Gleig? Did you ever share a bottle with him?'

'Sounds to me like you're the ones who have been sharing a bottle of Scotch. I have never shared anything with him. Not even the time of day.' Cheng sighed and leaned forward on the table. 'Look, I admit to breaking the windshield. I'm really sorry about that. It was stupid. I'd had a few drinks. I'll pay for the damage. But you have to believe me, I never met this guy. I'm sorry he's dead, but I had nothing to do with –'

Curtis had unfolded a colour photocopy of the computer-generated picture and spread it on the table next to the tyre wrench. Cheng stared at it.

'I am showing the subject a picture of himself and the dead man taken in the lobby of the Gridiron building.'

'What the hell is this?'

'Do you deny that's you?'

'Deny it? Of course I deny it. This must be a fake. Some kind of photocomposite. Look, what are you trying to pull here?'

'I'm not trying to pull anything,' replied Curtis. 'Just find out the truth. So why don't you admit it, Cheng?'

'I admit nothing. This is a lie.'

'You went to the Gridiron with a fifth of Scotch for Sam Gleig. I figure you must have already met once before. You had some kind of deal going. What was it? Dope? A little Chinese heroin from back home?'

'Bullshit.'

'Or maybe you wanted a favour. A blind eye while you went ahead and got rid of another tyre wrench. Smashed something. You paid him for his trouble, of course. Maybe you were going to hit Sam just to make things look convincing for him. Only you hit him too hard. Then you panicked and took off. Isn't that what happened?'

Cheng was shaking his head. He was on the edge of tears. 'Someone is trying to frame me,' he said.

'You're not such a good picture, China,' sneered Coleman. 'Who would want to frame you?'

'Isn't that obvious? The Yu Corporation, that's who. Believe me, they're quite capable of it. They get rid of me, maybe they can get rid of the protest. It's bad publicity for them.'

'And I suppose having someone murdered in your office building counts as good publicity, does it?' said Curtis. 'Besides, you and your friends are old news. You'll have to do better than that, college boy.'

'Come on, Cheng,' argued Nathan Coleman. 'Admit it. It was you who brained him. We don't figure you did it on purpose. You're not the type. An accident. We'll speak to the DA and get the charge reduced to second-degree murder. Your daddy pays for a fancy lawyer who tells the court you'd been studying too hard and you'll probably get two to five max. Maybe you can get transferred to a private gaol and finish your studies before you get deported home again.'

Cheng Peng Fei studied the photograph and shook his head. 'This isn't happening,' he said, and then added, 'Perhaps I'd better have that attorney after all.'

Suspending the interrogation the two detectives stepped into the busy corridor outside the video room.

'What do you think, Frank? Do we have the perp?'

'I don't know, Nat. I thought he'd fold when he saw the picture.' Curtis stretched wearily and looked at his watch. 'I reckon I'd better have SID look at it.'

'Do you think it might be a fake?'

'The little fucker's bluffing, I'm sure of it. But it wouldn't do any harm to have it checked before we go to the DA. Besides I've got to pick up the results of the preliminary p.m.'

'You want me to keep working on him?'

Curtis nodded.

'Give him some coffee and try to calm him down. Then come at him with the southpaw.' Curtis punched

Coleman playfully on the shoulder with his left.

'What about that attorney?'

'You heard him waive that right, didn't you? This is no homeboy, Nat. This guy's an MBA. There's no one going to say he didn't understand his Miranda.'

The Scientific Investigation Division was in the basement of New Parker Center. Curtis found Charlie Seidler and Janet Bragg in the cafeteria fetching coffees from the machine.

'Want one, Frank?' asked Bragg.

'Thanks. Cream, two sugars.'

'That's a sweet tooth you've got there,' observed Seidler as Bragg pressed the buttons on the machine. 'Man your age ought to be more careful about what he eats and drinks.'

'Gee, thanks, Charlie. Man your age yourself. Besides, I need the energy.'

They went into the lab.

'Well, Frank, the team went all round your suspect's apartment,' said Seidler. 'Found nothing. Nothing at all. Not even a bottle of Scotch.'

Curtis sighed wearily and then looked at Dr Bragg. She handed him a file containing three sheets of paper and a sheaf of photographs.

'He was hit – and hit hard mind – by a very strong man,' she said, without consulting her notes. 'The impact caused a depressed fracture of the skull and broke his neck for good measure. It even broke one of his teeth. I can't give you much idea of the kind of weapon used except to say that it wasn't a club or a bat or anything cylindrical. Something flat, more like. As if someone dropped an object on his head. Or hit him with a piece of the sidewalk.

'And here's another thing. I've had a look at your

suspect's passport and it says he's only five-eight. Weighs around one-ten. Unless Gleig was kneeling down in that elevator car, there's just no way he could have hit him. Or unless your man was standing on a box. Like Alan Ladd.'

Bragg noticed the look of disappointment on Curtis's face.

'If he was involved then he must have had someone else with him. Someone taller and stronger. A man of your build, perhaps. A man who likes cream and two sugars in his coffee.'

Curtis showed them the picture. 'So why have I got a picture of just one suspect?'

'You're the detective, Frank,' said Bragg.

'My suspect reckons this is a fake, Charlie.'

'Did a computer generate this?' asked Seidler.

Curtis nodded.

'Not my bag I'm afraid,' shrugged Seidler, 'but I can try someone.' He picked up the telephone and punched out a number. 'Bill? It's me, Charlie. Listen, I'm in the lab with someone from Homicide. Could you come in a minute and give us your head on something? Thanks a lot.'

Seidler replaced the receiver.

'Bill Durham. He's our photographic expert.'

A little man with a dark beard came bustling through the door. Seidler made the introductions and then Curtis showed him the picture.

Durham produced a magnifying glass from the pocket of his white coat and examined the picture carefully.

'A traditional photograph is easy to test, and easy to prove,' he said. 'You've got exposed films, negatives, prints, all very physical stuff. But something generated by a computer – well, that's a very different story. You're dealing with digital images.' Durham looked up. 'I couldn't say whether this is a fake or not.'

'But it's possible?' said Curtis.

'Oh sure, it's possible all right. You get two base digitized images . . .'

'Wait, wait,' said Curtis.

'They're numbers. A computer can store anything as a series of binary numbers. You have one image of the black guy and another of the Chinese guy, right? You silhouette the Chinese guy out of whatever background he's in and then place it on top of the picture that includes the other guy. Then you mask the two figures out of the surrounding area so that the background can be evened out without affecting them. If you're clever you alter the shadows to make them consistent and maybe add a few random pixels to help degrade the image of the black guy, maybe match the grain of the other picture. Not much more to it than that. You could store it on disc, on computer tape, whatever, indefinitely. Hard copy it whenever you liked.'

Curtis pulled a face.

Durham smiled. Sensing the detective's technophobia, he added for good measure, 'The fact is, Sergeant Curtis, we're swiftly approaching an era when it will no longer be possible to regard a photograph as something unquestionably probative.'

'As if the job wasn't already hard enough,' growled Curtis. 'Jumping Jesus, this is a fuck of a world we're building for ourselves here.'

Durham shrugged and looked at Seidler.

'That all?'

'Frank?'

'Yeah, thanks a lot.'

When Durham had left Curtis returned to the pages of the p.m. and sifted through the photographs of Sam Gleig's body.

'As if someone dropped an object on his head you say, Janet?'

Doctor Bragg nodded.

'Like what?'

'A refrigerator. A TV set. A piece of the sidewalk. Like I said, something flat.'

'Well, that sure narrows it down.'

'On the other hand,' she sighed, 'well, it's just a thought, Frank, but you might check and see if that elevator car is working properly.'

Book Four

'Let us conceive, consider and create together the new
building of the future that will bring all into one single
integrated creation; architecture, painting and sculpture rising to heaven out of the hands of a million
craftsmen, the crystal symbol of the new faith of the
future.'

Walter Gropius

For an architect there was only one place to live in LA and that was Pacific Palisades. It was not the exclusivity of the area, so much as the fact that it was the location for many of LA's more famous examples of modernist architecture. For the most part these were square, steel constructions, Mondrian-coloured, with lots of glass, and which resembled Japanese tea-houses or German worker bungalows. Mitch did not care for any of them, although as an architect he understood why they were significant: these were houses that had influenced multiple housing throughout the whole of the United States. For him they were fine to look at in books, but to actually live in one was a different matter. It was surely no accident that Frank Lloyd Wright's Ennis House in Griffith Park was virtually derelict. Just about the only house he thought he could have lived in around here was Pierre Koenig's house in the Hollywood Hills, although this preference owed more to the spectacular view than to the building's architectural merits. On the whole he preferred the quasi-rural houses that characterized that part of the Palisades known as Rustic Canyon, with its log cabins, horse paddocks and beautiful gardens.

Not that Rustic Canyon was without its own examples of modern architecture. On one of the uppermost slopes of the Canyon stood what Mitch considered to be one of the finest private houses ever built by Ray Richardson: his own.

Mitch drew his car into the curve of a honey-coloured concrete wall broken by a pedestrian entrance bridge that spanned a small creek and led up to the front door, facing the distant ocean.

A man and a woman whom Mitch vaguely recognized as English pop-music stars came down the lane on horses and wished him a good morning. That was another reason Mitch liked the Canyon. Up here money was friendlier, apparently unaffected by the obsession for defensible, post-holocaust-style architecture that characterized the rest of LA. There was not a security camera or a length of razor wire in sight. Up here people relied on the height of the hills, the distance from the inner city and discreet armed patrols to protect them against the perceived threat from LA's underclass.

Mitch crossed the footbridge. He disliked giving up his Sunday morning to talk about work, even if it meant a rare offer of brunch at Richardson's house. Ray had said they were just going to relax and spend some time together, but Mitch didn't buy that. The only time Ray Richardson ever relaxed was when he was asleep, and of this he seemed to require very little.

The invitation had also included Alison. But Alison's dislike of Richardson was so acute that she could not bear to be in the same room as him. At least, Mitch reflected, he would not have to spend his Sunday afternoon lying to her about where he had spent the morning.

Mitch knocked and slid the frameless panel of glass to one side.

He found Ray Richardson in his study, kneeling on the blue slate floor, inspecting the drawings for yet another project that were still spilling out of the wide-body laser printer – a new heliport in the centre of London – and dictating notes to his green-eyed secretary, Shannon.

'Mitch,' he said brightly. 'Why don't you go upstairs to the living room? I won't be a minute. I just have to check these E-mail drawings from the London office for a meeting they've got tomorrow morning. Want a drink, buddy? Rosa will get it for you.'

Rosa was Richardson's Salvadorean maid. Mitch encountered her on his way back to the living room, a small, skinny woman wearing a pink uniform. He thought of orange juice. Then he thought of an afternoon at home.

'Rosa, could I have a pitcher of frozen margaritas, please?'

'Yes, sir, right away.'

In the living room Mitch looked for something to sit on. There were six plain white dining chairs grouped around a dining table. A leather-and-stainless steel recliner and, on two sides of a square glass table, two pairs of Barcelona chairs, twin acts of homage to the great Mies van der Rohe. Mitch tried the Barcelona chair and was immediately reminded of why he had got rid of his own.

He collected a copy of *LA Living* off the glass table and switched to the recliner. This was the issue he had heard about but not yet seen: the one with Joan Richardson lying naked on a sofa of her own design like some *grande odalisque* – with the accent on *grande*, he thought. The issue that had been the cause of her legal action against the publishers for failing to retouch away the large curl of pubic hair that was clearly visible at the base of her fat, Earth Motherish buttocks.

With her small, delicate feet, legs swelling rapidly upwards to her Percheron mare's hips, narrowing to a small hoop of a waist, and then swelling once again into the formidable delta that was formed by the plastron of her breasts and her Hulk Hogan-sized shoulders, Joan Richardson bore a strong resemblance to the Fernando Botero bronze outside the Gridiron. *Los Angeles* magazine had dubbed the fat lady bronze 'the Venus de Meatloaf'. But around the office they called it JR.

Rosa returned with the pitcher of margaritas and

placed it and a tall glass on the table. Mitch sipped it slowly, but it was another hour before Richardson finished what he was doing, by which time the pitcher was finished. Mitch noticed that Richardson had changed into riding pants and boots. He looked like some tyrannical film director of the silent era: D. W. Griffith, or Eric von Stroheim. All he needed was a megaphone.

'OK, Mitch, let's have that brunch,' he said, rubbing his hands. 'Rosa!' He placed an avuncular hand on Mitch's shoulder. 'So, how are you, buddy?'

Mitch smiled thinly. 'Fine,' he said, although he was angry at having been kept waiting for so long. 'Have you been riding?'

'Oh, you mean this get-up? No, I'm playing polo at twelve,' he said.

Mitch glanced at his watch. 'It's eleven-fifteen, Ray,' he said with more than a hint of accusation.

'Damn. Those drawings took longer than I thought. Well, we can still have half an hour together, can't we? You know, we never talk any more. We should spend more time together. And now that the Yu building is almost out of the way, we will. I know we will. Our greatest achievements are ahead of us, I'm certain of it.'

'I've been thinking that I'd like to do more designing,' said Mitch. 'Maybe that factory the Yu Corporation is planning to build in Austin.'

'Sure, Mitch, sure.' Richardson sat down on a Barcelona chair. 'But, you know, anyone can design. It takes a special kind of architect to be a good technical coordinator. To translate those rarefied architectural concepts into practical instructions for the poor bastards who have to build them. Remember that idiot Grabel's design for the roof? A piece of shit. You were the one who fixed it, Mitch. To Grabel it looked like the same roof as before. He didn't understand how impractical the original design had been. It was you, Mitch, you who took it, who looked at the different ways you could do it and who came up with the best way of achieving that roof, practically. Most designers are just frigging themselves. I know what I'm talking about. They design something because they think it looks nice, but you, you take what looks nice and make it look real. You're bored. I know you've been bored for a while now. It's always like this at the end of a job. But it'll be different when you start something fresh. And don't forget there's a substantial share of profit coming to you on this job, Mitch. Don't forget that, buddy. There's going to be a large cheque due to you at the end of the financial year.'

Rosa arrived with a tray. Mitch helped himself to some orange juice and some kedgeree and started to eat. He wondered if Ray's little pep talk had been the real reason for asking him over. Certainly he thought Richardson could ill afford to lose another senior member of the firm so soon after Allen Grabel. And Ray was right about one thing, at least: good technical coordinators like Mitch were hard to find.

'When's the practical completion inspection?' asked Richardson, pouring himself a glass of orange juice.

'A week Tuesday.'

'Hmm. That's what I thought.' Richardson raised his glass. 'Cheers,' he said.

Mitch tossed his back.

'Tell me, Mitch,' said Richardson, 'are you still seeing Jenny Bao?'

'It would be hard not to. She's the *feng shui* consultant on the Yu job.'

Richardson grinned unpleasantly. 'Come on, Mitch, you know what I mean. You're fucking her. And why the hell not? Good luck to you, that's what I say. She's a beautiful girl. I wouldn't mind fucking her myself. I always fancied having Chinese, only I never did. Is it a long-term thing, do you think?'

Mitch said nothing for a moment. There seemed little point in denying it. So he said, 'I hope so.'

'Good, good.' He shook his head. 'Alison know about it?'

'Why the sudden interest?'

'Hey, we're friends, aren't we? Can't I ask a friend a friendly question?' Richardson smiled.

'Is it a friendly question? More to the point, Ray, how did you find out?'

'I've known about it since you took her to the marble factory in Vicenza.' He shrugged. 'A German client was staying at the same hotel as you.'

Mitch put up his hands. 'OK, OK.' He forked some kedgeree into his mouth. He had little appetite now his secret was out. 'You're not eating,' he observed.

Richardson glanced at his watch again. 'I don't want to spoil my game,' he said. 'Besides, I'm not really hungry. You can sure pick them, Mitch. I'll say that for you, buddy. I never figured you for the type.'

All of a sudden Mitch disliked himself almost as much as he disliked Ray Richardson. 'Neither did I,' he said unhappily.

'Look, Mitch, I want you to ask Jenny a small favour.'

'That means it's a large one. What is it?'

'I want you to get Jenny to sign off on the Yu building's *feng shui* before we go ahead and make the changes.'

'Why?'

'I'll tell you. Mr Yu himself wants to make the inspection, that's why. And he'll feel a lot happier walking around the place if he knows your fucking girlfriend has given it the OK. OK? He'll be less likely to find fault with things. If there was time to make all her half-assed changes before he came on site then we would, but there isn't. It's that simple. Look, Mitch, it's really only for one day. After that she can tear the certificate up again, come up with some new objections if she wants to.

188

But as soon as YK gives it the nod we can hit him with our fees. It's been an expensive few months, what with opening the German office.'

'I hear you. But I'm not sure she'll do it. I know it's a hard thing for someone like you to understand, but she's got principles.'

'Promise her a week in Venice. The two of you. Any hotel you like. The Cipriani, if you want. I'll pay.'

'I'll try my best,' Mitch said wearily, 'but she won't like it. She's not just some kind of fairground gypsy, Ray. It's not a question of crossing her palm with enough silver. Jenny believes in what she does. And don't forget two people have died in that place. Jenny certainly hasn't forgotten.'

'But you will try and persuade her.'

'Yes. Yes, all right, I will try. But it won't be easy. And I want your word, Ray. That if she does sign the certificate, then she won't get screwed. That we'll carry out all the changes like we're supposed to.'

Richardson shrugged. 'Sure. No problem. And screwing her? Well that's down to you, buddy.'

'I hope it's just the *feng shui* that's at fault,' said Mitch.

'What the fuck is that supposed to mean? Relax will you? Things will be just fine, I know it. I've got a good feeling about this job. Good luck is simply a matter of working hard and being prepared. My pre-PCI inspection is this Friday, right? With the whole project team on site. The building in action, so to speak, a working demonstration. Push a few buttons.'

Mitch decided to press a button of his own. 'That cop wants me to have the elevators checked out,' he said bluntly. 'He reckons it's possible they might have had something to do with Sam Gleig's accident.'

Richardson frowned. 'Who the hell's Sam Gleig?'

'C'mon. The security guard. The one who got killed.'

'But I thought they already arrested someone for that. One of those pain-in-the-ass demonstrators.'

'They did. But they let him go again.'

'There's nothing wrong with those elevators. They're the most sophisticated elevators anywhere in California.'

'That's what I told this cop. They're working just fine. Aidan Kenny and I checked them ourselves. But he still wants Otis to come and take a look at them.'

'And where's this guy now? The one they arrested.'

'Free, I guess.'

'Free to stand outside my building and hand out more leaflets?'

'I suppose so, yes.'

'Dumb bastards.' Richardson picked up the telephone and called his secretary. 'Dumb fucking . . . Shannon. Get me Morgan Phillips, will you?' He grimaced and shook his head. 'At his home? Yeah, where else? It's Sunday.' He replaced the receiver and nodded. 'I'll fix this in five minutes.'

'You're calling the deputy mayor? On a Sunday? What are you going to do, Ray?'

'Don't worry, I'll be at my most diplomatic.'

Mitch raised an eyebrow.

'Relax, Morgan's a friend of mine. We play tennis together. And believe me, he owes me more favours . . . I'm going to get those bastards moved off the piazza. Out of your hair. I was going to have to do it anyway: the last thing we want is them outside again when YK turns up for the PCI.'

'Why bother?' shrugged Mitch. 'They're just a bunch of kids.'

'Why bother? Mitch, one of them broke your windshield, for Chrissakes. You could have been killed.'

'I wasn't actually in the car at the time, Ray.'

'That's not the point. Besides, one of them is a suspect in a murder inquiry. Once they've seen there's nothing wrong with those fucking elevators the cops will have to bring him back in. You can bet on it.'

'Alison? It's Allen.'

Alison Bryan sighed impatiently. 'Allen who?'

'Allen Grabel.'

She took a big bite of the apple she was holding and said: 'And?'

'I work with Mitch. At Richardsons.'

'Oh.' Alison's tone turned cooler. 'Well, that's nice for you. What do you want?'

'Is Mitch there?'

'No,' she said flatly.

'Do you know where he is?'

'Of course I know where he is. What do you think, I don't know where my own husband is? What kind of a wife do you think I am?'

'No, I didn't mean . . . Look, Alison, I need to get in touch with him. It's really very urgent.'

'Sure it is. It's always urgent with you people. He's at Richardson's house. Seems like they had some business to discuss. As if they don't see enough of each other during the week. You could call him there, I guess. Who knows? Maybe they're in bed together.'

'No. No, I'd rather not call him there. Look, could you ask him to call me? The minute he gets home?'

'Is it anything to do with that stupid Gridiron building?'

She always made a point of referring to smart buildings as stupid, just to irritate Mitch.

'Kind of, yes.'

'Today's Sunday. That's the day of rest in case you'd forgotten. Can't it wait until tomorrow?'

'I don't think so. And I'd rather not speak to him at the studio. It would be better if he could call me. Tell him . . . Tell him . . .'

'Tell him what? That you love him?' She laughed at

191

her own wit. 'That you're leaving on a jet plane? What?'

Grabel gave a profound sigh. 'Look, please make sure that he gets this message. OK?'

'Well surely.'

But Grabel had already hung up.

'Shithead,' said Alison and took another bite of her apple. She picked up a pen and held it momentarily over a notepad. Then she thought better of it. It was bad enough that Mitch was working on a Sunday. He spoke to his colleagues every day at the studio. She tossed the pen aside.

It was a couple of days before Mitch could bring himself to face Jenny Bao with his awkward mission. It would not be easy to persuade her to come round to Richardson's idea. He knew that she loved him, but that did not mean she was in his pocket. He left home early, bought some flowers at a service station on the Freeway, and was at the grey wooden bungalow before eight-fifteen. For another ten minutes he sat in the car justifying to himself what he was about to do. After all, it was only a temporary certificate. Just a few days. Not much harm in that.

The morning was a fine one. Jenny's house looked neat and well-maintained. Two orange trees in terra-cotta pots flanked the steps up to the mahogany front door. Mitch wondered what another *feng shui* consultant would have had to say about the auspices for his morning's errand.

He got out of the car, rang the bell and found Jenny already dressed, wearing a sweatshirt and pants. She was pleased to see him but he could tell she was suspicious about the flowers. He never brought flowers.

'Would you like some tea?' she asked. 'Or something else?'

Normally the 'something else' remark would have led to them making love. But Mitch felt that going to bed would be inappropriate in the circumstances. So he said yes to the tea and watched her as she made it in her own peculiar Chinese way. As soon as he had the little porcelain cup in his hands he came to the point, apologizing for having to ask, recognizing that he was putting her in a difficult position, but emphasizing the fact that the lie would only remain in existence for two or three days at the most. Jenny heard him out, raising her teacup to her lips with both hands, almost ceremonially, and then when he had finished, nodded without saying a word.

'Is that a yes?' said Mitch, surprised.

'No,' she sighed. 'Out of deference to you, I'm thinking about it.'

Well, that was something he thought. He had expected her to say no outright. It was two or three minutes before she spoke again.

'*Kanyu*, or *feng shui* to you, is a religious thing. It's part of the Tao. The cardinal concept in Taoism is the Absolute. To possess the fullness of the Tao means to be in perfect harmony with one's original nature. What you're asking me to do would disrupt that harmony.'

'I understand,' he said. 'I'm asking a lot, I know.'

'Is this completion inspection really so important?'

'Very,' he said.

She was silent for another minute. Then she put her arms around him.

'On the face of it, I'm inclined to say no, for the reasons I mentioned. But because it's you, and because I love you, I don't want to let you down. Give me twenty-four hours. You'll have my answer then.'

'Thanks,' he said. 'I understand how difficult this must be.'

Jenny smiled and kissed him on the cheek.

'No, Mitch, I don't think you do understand. If you did, then you would never have asked.'

'But you're not giving up now,' said the Japanese. 'Surely . . .'

'You bet I'm giving up,' said Cheng Peng Fei.

'Why? You were just beginning to get the idea.'

'Someone tried to frame me for murder of a security guard at the Yu Corp.'

They were back in the Mon Kee Restaurant on North Spring Street with the Japanese working his way through another tableful of food, and Cheng Peng Fei nursing a solitary beer.

'Frame you?' The Japanese laughed. 'You sound like Jimmy Cagney.'

'Believe me, I was lucky to get away. I thought the police were going to charge me. I'm still not sure they've entirely given up on me. I had to surrender my passport.'

'Who would want to frame you, Cheng?'

'I don't know,' shrugged Cheng. 'Maybe someone from the Yu Corporation. Maybe you. Yes, maybe you did it.'

'Me?' The Japanese sounded amused by the idea. 'Why me?'

'Maybe you killed that security guard.'

'I sincerely hope you didn't present this theory of yours to the police.'

'I didn't mention you. How could I? I don't even know your name. You've been careful that way.'

'Maybe you're wearing a wire as we speak.'

'Maybe.' But as he said it Cheng unbuttoned his shirt to show that there was nothing taped to his chest. 'Anyway,' he added, 'the demo's ended. Someone in City Hall got on to Immigration and had us all checked out. One or two were in violation of their visas. They were supposed to be studying English, not making money working in restaurants.'

The Japanese shook his head sadly.

'That's too bad,' he said. 'I guess now I'll have to get involved myself. Score something off my own bat.'

'Like what?'

'Oh, I don't know. Maybe a little sabotage. You wouldn't believe what I'm capable of.'

'You're wrong about that. I think you're probably capable of just about anything.'

The Japanese stood up.

'You know, if I were you, Cheng, I'd make sure I'd got myself a good alibi.'

'When for?'

The Japanese threw some bills on to the table.

'For as long as it takes.'

Allen Grabel telephoned Richardson Associates and asked to speak to Mitch.

The receptionist was called Dominique. 'Who shall I say is calling?'

Grabel had an idea that Dominique did not like him much, so he restricted himself to his Christian name. Mitch probably knew two or three people called Allen. He waited for a few moments. Then Dominique said, 'I'm sorry. There's no reply. Can I take a message.'

'Ask him to give me a call.' Grabel left his number. She was hardly likely to recognize that. 'As soon as he gets back.'

Grabel replaced the phone and glanced at his watch. He had fifteen minutes to go until his next drink.

Why had Mitch not called him back? There could only be one reason: his witch of a wife had not passed on the message. No wonder Mitch was having an affair with that woman he had seen outside the Gridiron building. Then it came to him that the Gridiron was probably where he would find Mitch. He was hardly thinking straight since that night. But Mitch would understand, he would know what to do.

Grabel picked up the phone and punched out the number. As soon as it started to ring he replaced the receiver. With the telephone system they had at the Gridiron you never knew who might have been listening in. He glanced at his watch again. Ten minutes to go. But he couldn't very well go back there. He was afraid, scared of what might happen to him. Suppose he had imagined it all? What would they do to him then? It was almost as scary as the alternative.

Kay Killen spent the day before Ray Richardson's pre-PCI inspection in the boardroom on the twenty-first level checking through the two-dimensional plans and three-dimensional models of the Gridiron on computer. She also looked at the visual record of the project on Photo CD, just in case Richardson wanted to analyse any part of the scheme in detail, or demonstrate the evolution of the design. She had even arranged to have the main model of the building transported from Richardson Associates' offices on Sunset to the Gridiron boardroom, not to mention full-sized mock-ups of some of the components used in its construction. Where Ray Richardson was involved it was always best to be prepared for any eventuality.

It was late when she finished, leaving Mitch still working out an inspection schedule with Tony Levine, Helen Hussey and Aidan Kenny. She was glad to be getting out of the place. Although she was used to working late in empty office buildings, there was something about being in the Gridiron at night that she did not care for. She had always been sensitive to atmosphere, which she attributed to her Celtic ancestry and, unlike the rest of the project team, she was more than ready to believe in *feng shui*. Kay saw nothing wrong with trying to build something that was in harmony with the natural environment and in tapping the goodness of nature to benefit man. That the spirit of the land must be respected was, she thought, just another kind of environmentalism. Her privately held belief was that the place would feel better when the criticisms made by the *feng shui* consultant had been fully accommodated.

By the time she reached the cavernous garage her heart was beating quickly and she was beginning to feel a little nauseous. Public spaces, especially at night, made her nervous. Living in LA, she told herself, she was hardly unusual in this respect. But this was more than just urban paranoia. Kay suffered from a mild form of agoraphobia. Knowing she sometimes felt this way did not make it any easier to deal with. Nor did the fact that her car, a new Audi, refused to start.

Anger displaced nervousness for a few crucial minutes. Kay cursed and got out of the car to call the AAA from the security guard's office upstairs. She had the sensation that she was being watched, and performed a couple of walking pirouettes as she headed back across the garage, her heels echoing on the non-slip floor like the ticking of a metronome. Who else could be down here? Now that Sam Gleig was dead Abraham handled night-time security. Apart from her colleagues on the twenty-first level there was no one else in the building. Kay felt relieved when she re-entered the brightly lit elevator car and rode up to the atrium.

When the elevator doors opened the floor was in darkness, with only the light from the car behind her and emanating from some of the upper levels to let her see where she was going. The floor lights were often turned down at night. Since people who were working late usually exited the building from the garage, Abraham was saving energy. But his infra-red sensors and cameras were supposed to note her arrival and switch the lights back on.

She was trying to work out why this had not happened when the elevator doors closed behind her and most of the available light disappeared.

Kay suppressed her panic. It was not as if she needed much light to know her way around the Gridiron. Her memory of the building's plan on every level was almost photographic. She had only to imagine herself seated in front of a work-station, using the CAD and steering her mouse to know exactly where she was going. Even before it had been built Kay had known her way around the Gridiron. When finally she went on-site and walked round the finished envelope she had experienced a sensation of odd familiarity.

But as she started to walk towards the security guard's office, she heard a voice she seemed to recognize.

'Can I help you, Miss?'

She felt her hair rising on her head.

'Is there anything the matter?'

Sam Gleig was standing in his familiar position at the front desk, his big hand resting on the gun he kept holstered on his hip. And, althought it was dark, Kay realized that she could see him perfectly, in every detail, almost as if he had been standing in his own personal zone of artificial light.

'They say what happened to Mr Yojo yet?'

'What – what do you want, Sam?' Kay started to back away towards the elevator. 'Who are you?'

Sam laughed his big slow laugh. 'I don't mean to bother you at all,' he said. 'So who's working late tonight?'

'You're dead, Sam,' she whispered.

'Figured as much,' said Sam. 'Poor guy. Kind of a waste. How old was he?'

Kay felt the elevator behind her. She touched it with her hand. And yet the car did not arrive.

'Please,' she said. 'Please go away.'

Sam laughed again and inspected the toes of his well-positioned shoes.

'You gotta have somethin' to alleviate the boredom on a job like this. Know what I'm sayin'?'

'No, I don't.'

'Sure you do.'

'Are you – are you a ghost?'

'Didn't know there was such a thing. Goddamn. Goddamn, of course. Poor guy. Know something? This is about the safest job I ever had.'

Sam laughed again as Kay Killen started to scream.

In the boardroom on the twenty-first level, Mitch looked up from his computer and frowned.

'Did any of you hear something just now?' he asked.

His three colleagues shrugged or shook their heads.

Mitch stood up and opened the door.

This time they all heard it.

'Kay,' said Mitch.

The atrium was still echoing with her screams as they ran towards the elevators. On the way, Mitch leaned over the balcony and shouted down into the darkness. 'Kay, hold on, we're coming.'

'Jesus, what now?' said Kenny following Mitch into the elevator car. The doors slid shut and the car started its descent with Mitch banging on the walls impatiently.

When they reached the atrium Kay collapsed unconscious back into the elevator, her head banging on the floor of the car.

Mitch and Helen crouched anxiously beside her while Kenny and Levine swiftly searched for whoever might have attacked her. By now all the lights were on and Kenny was soon back, shaking his head with bafflement.

'I didn't see anything,' he said. 'Not a damn thing. Is she OK?'

'She just fainted, that's all,' said Helen.

'It sure didn't sound like that was all,' observed Levine. 'Shit, I thought she was being raped or murdered for sure.'

Mitch lifted Kay against his chest while Helen fanned some air against her pale-looking face. Her eyelids flickered and she started to come round.

'What happened, honey?' said Kenny.

Levine came back, shrugging his shoulders. 'The front door's still locked,' he reported. 'And there's no sign of anyone on the piazza.'

'You're OK now,' Mitch said gently, as for a moment she became agitated again. 'You're safe now.' Then he helped her to lean forwards and place her head between her knees. 'Take your time. You just fainted, that's all.'

'Sam,' she said quietly. 'It was Sam.'

'Did she say Sam?' said Levine.

'Sam Gleig?' asked Kenny.

Kay lifted her head and opened her eyes. 'I saw him,' she said tremulously, and started to weep.

Mitch handed over his handkerchief. Kenny and Levine exchanged a look.

'You mean – like a ghost?' said Kenny. 'Here? In the Gridiron?'

Kay blew her nose and sighed profoundly.

'Can you stand up?' Mitch asked.

She nodded.

'It sounds crazy, I know,' she said, and let Mitch help her on to her feet. 'But I saw what I saw.'

She caught the look that passed between Kenny and Levine. 'Look I didn't imagine it,' she said. 'He was there. He even spoke to me.'

Mitch handed Kay the purse she had dropped on the floor.

'I'm not the kind of person who would make up something like this. Or imagine it.'

Mitch shrugged. 'Nobody's suggesting you are, Kay.' He looked at her and added, 'Look, we believe you, honey. If you say you saw Sam, then you saw him.'

'You sure don't look like you're shitting us,' said Levine.

'He's right,' said Helen. 'You're as white as a sheet.'

'What did he say?' asked Kenny. 'What did it look like?'

Kay shook her head with irritation.

'Not it. I'm telling you, it didn't look like anything except Sam Gleig. Just listen to what I'm saying, will you? He looked the same as always. And he was laughing, too.' She opened her powder compact and frowned. 'Shit, I'm a mess. He said – he said he figured he was dead and that it was a waste. His exact words, I swear to God.'

'Come back upstairs,' said Mitch, 'and let's get you fixed up before you go home.'

'I think we could all of us use a drink,' suggested Kenny.

They stepped back into the elevator car and rode up to the twenty-first floor. While Kay attended to her make-up Levine opened the boardroom drinks cabinet and poured four shots of bourbon.

'I believe in ghosts,' declared Aidan Kenny. 'My mother saw a ghost once. And I never knew her to lie about anything. Never even tell a tall tale.'

'You've been making up for her since then,' remarked Levine.

'I'm not lying now,' Kay said firmly. 'It scared the shit out of me and I don't mind admitting it.' She finished her eyeliner and drained the glass before applying some more lipstick.

'What about the foundations?' said Levine. 'I mean,

they're thirty feet deep, aren't they? Did we, like, you know, build on top of anything?'

'You mean an old Indian burial ground or something?' said Kenny. 'C'mon, man.'

'This site used to be the old Abel Stearns building,' said Mitch. 'One of those northern carpetbaggers from San Francisco who bought land here and built around the turn of the century. When the company got taken over in the 1960s, the new owners demolished it and the lot lay fallow until a developer came along. Then he went bust and the Yu Corporation bought the site.'

'But before Abel Stearns,' persisted Levine. 'I mean, this area was all Pueblo de los Angeles, wasn't it? Mexicans and Aztec Indians? Why not?'

'Don't let Joan hear you say the word Indian,' said Kenny. 'That woman's the Native American equivalent of the Reverend Al Sharpton.'

'Those Aztecs used to practise human sacrifice. They used to cut their victims' hearts out while they were still alive.'

'Just like Ray Richardson,' said Kenny. 'Anyway Tony, Sam was black. Or rather, African-American. He was no fucking Aztec. An asshole, maybe. What kind of security guard gets himself killed then spooks a defenceless woman like that?'

'Look', said Kay, 'I want you all to promise me something. I want you to promise me that you won't go around telling people what happened tonight. I don't want to turn into the office joke, OK? Will you promise me that?'

'Sure,' said Mitch.

'Of course,' smiled Helen.

Kenny and Levine shrugged and then nodded their acquiescence.

'Let's just hope we can get tomorrow's inspection done without any more mishaps,' said Mitch.

'Amen to that,' breathed Kenny.

Mitch returned to the Gridiron at seven-thirty the next morning. In the bright, flat sunlight it was hard to imagine how anyone could have seen a ghost in the place. Perhaps it was some kind of hallucination. He had read how an LSD experience could make a return visit at any time in your life, no matter how long ago the original experience had occurred, and Mitch thought that this, or something like it anyway, was the most likely explanation.

He'd wanted to call in to see Jenny Bao for her answer on the temporary *feng shui* certificate. But he was facing a whole day with Ray Richardson and he knew that his principal would arrive before eight. So the first thing he did upon his arrival was to telephone her.

'It's me,' he told her.

'Mitch?' she said sleepily. 'Where are you?'

'At the Gridiron.'

'What time is it?'

'Seven-thirty. I'm sorry, did I wake you?'

'No, it's OK. I was going to call you anyway. I decided to let you have your certificate in time for Monday. But only because it's you. And only because the *Tong Shu* says that Monday will be an auspicious day.'

'That's great. Thanks, Jenny. Thanks a lot. I appreciate it.'

'Yeah, well, there's one condition.'

'Name it.'

'That I come in some time today and perform a few office warming rituals. To ensure that all evil spirits leave the building and good *qi* is brought in.'

'Sure. What kind of rituals?'

'It's complicated. Among other things we'll have to take the fish outside. We'll also have to shut down the electrical power for a short while. And a red banner needs to be hung across the signboard outside. Oh yes, the windows will have to be darkened, but then you can do that automatically, can't you? And one more thing. I don't know how you'll manage this – I know you have a very sophisticated fire alarm system. I have to start a fire in a charcoal stove in the doorway and fan it until the charcoal is hot.'

'Jesus,' said Mitch. 'What's the charcoal for?'

'It's to symbolize a warm result for Mr Yu's inspection on Monday.'

'I'll drink to that,' laughed Mitch. 'As far as I'm concerned, you can set fire to Old Glory if you think it's necessary. But does it have to be today? We've got Richardson in all day. Could you come in at the weekend?'

'It's not me who says it has to be done this afternoon, Mitch. It's the *Tong Shu*, the Chinese almanac. This afternoon is a good day for the performance of ceremonies to banish evil spirits.'

'OK, I'll see you this afternoon.'

Mitch replaced the receiver and shook his head. In the circumstances he had thought it better not to mention what Kay Killen had seen. There was no telling what Jenny might have insisted on then. A full exorcism? Dancing naked round the tree? how on earth was he going to tell Ray Richardson that Jenny Bao was planning to light a charcoal stove to smoke the devils out of his state-of-the-art building?

Frank Curtis awoke with a start and wondered why he was so depressed. Then he remembered: it was ten years to the day since his brother had died of cancer. Leaving his wife, Wendy, still asleep, he slipped out of bed and went into the study to find the cardboard box containing his photograph albums.

It was not that he needed to look at pictures to be reminded of what his brother had looked like. Frank Curtis had only to look in a mirror to do that, for he and Michael had been identical twins. Looking at the photographs was a way of reminding himself of what he had once been, half of a greater whole.

When Michael died it had been like losing an arm. Or some vital organ. After that Curtis felt he was only ever half a person.

Wendy appeared in the doorway.

'How can it be ten years?' he said, swallowing a lump in his throat the size of a baseball.

'I know, I know. All week I've been thinking the same thing.'

'And I'm still here.' He shook his head. 'There's not a day passes that I don't think of him. When I don't ask myself, why him and not me?'

'Are you going to Hillside?'

'Yeah.'

'You'll be late for work.'

Curtis shrugged carelessly. 'So what? I'm never going to make lieutenant anyway.'

'Frank . . .'

He grinned. 'Besides, I'm not on until one.'

She smiled back at him. 'I'll make us some coffee.'

'It's not like I need a stone to remember him, y'know? I always think of him like he was.' He shrugged. 'Maybe, after ten years, it's time to let him go a bit.'

But before he left the house, Curtis placed a small lawnmower in the trunk of his car.

Hillside Memorial Park Cemetery was only ten minutes' drive, close to the San Diego Freeway and LAX. Every year Frank Curtis made the journey and, with 747s only a few hundred feet above his head, he worked to tidy up his brother's grave. A practical man, Curtis preferred to mark his remembrance with this small act of devotion. Like a penance, he thought.

It wasn't much, but at least it made him feel a bit better.

By the time he got to New Parker Center, Curtis was in the mood to be distracted, to get things done and make other things happen. He typed reports, filed them with the relevant clerical officers, filled out his expense claims, reviewed his diary and said nothing.

Nathan Coleman watched his colleague and wondered what had moved him to this rare exhibition of bureaucratic efficiency.

Curtis unfolded a piece of paper and laid it on the desk. It was Cheng Peng Fei's handbill, protesting about the Yu Corporation's human rights record. He floated it towards Coleman.

'You know, I read that thing,' he said finally. 'He's right. Any company that's as involved with the Chinese government as the Yu Corp shouldn't be allowed to trade in this country.'

'Tell that to Congress,' said Coleman. 'We just renewed China's favoured-nation trading status.'

'It's like I always say, Nat. The whores on the hill.'

'Actually, I've been meaning to tell you Frank,' said Coleman. 'Something I heard this morning. Immigration is holding three of those other Chinese kids.'

'Why, for Chrissakes?'

'They said they were in violation of their visa requirements. They were working, or some shit like that. But I got a friend there who said that someone in the mayor's office pulled strings to get them kicked out of the country. Since when the demo outside the Gridiron has packed up and gone home.'

'That's interesting.'

'It seems this architect guy has a lot of friends up there.'

'Is that so?'

'In less than seventy-two hours they'll be on a plane back to Hong Kong,' shrugged Coleman. 'Or wherever it was they came from.'

'Cheng is still here, right?' said Curtis.

'Right. But even if he did meet Sam Gleig, forensic still says he couldn't have killed him.'

After a silence Curtis said, 'They never came back to us, did they? Those Martians at the Gridiron were supposed to get an engineer from Otis to come and check the car's safety. It's been a week now. That's long enough in a homicide inquiry, wouldn't you say?'

'Maybe the computer forgot to make the call,' said Coleman.

'I've been thinking about that photograph, too. Supposing it was a fake, who better than someone in the Yu Corporation building to make it? That's a pretty fancy computer they've got there. How about this, Nat? Here's the motive: there is something wrong with those elevators, only someone wants to cover it up for a while. Maybe one of those architect guys. They've got a lot of money riding on this job. Millions. One of them said as much to me. He more or less asked me to keep the lid on any publicity. Said it would look bad if someone was killed in a smart building. Now would he think it was better that some pain-in-the-ass demonstrator should take the blame for an accidental death instead of their own damn building? What do you think?'

'I could buy that.'

'Good. Because so could I.'

'Want me to give them a call?' Coleman said. 'Those fuckin' Martians?'

Curtis stood up and lifted his coat off the back of his chair.

'I've got a better idea,' he said. 'It's Friday afternoon. They'll be winding down for the weekend. Let's go and make a nuisance of ourselves.'

207

Ray Richardson was the kind of architect who did not like surprises, and it was his standard practice to inspect exhaustively floors, walls, ceilings, doors, windows, electrical equipment, services equipment, sanitary-ware and joinery, accompanied only by the members of his own project team before repeating the same procedure formally with the client.

Even informally the inspection looked like it was going to take up one whole long day. Tony Levine would normally have preferred Richardson's pre-PCI to have been carried out across several short periods rather than one protracted one when, through Richardson's own irritability, the result might be prejudiced. But as usual, his senior was working to a tight schedule.

After five hours of trooping round the building like a bus-load of tourists, the project team had progressed as far as the Gridiron's swimming pool. Measuring twenty-five metres long and eight metres wide, this was located under a curving rectangular louvred glass roof at the rear of the building and, with the exception of the sapphire colour of the $85°$ water, everything – the walls, the floor tiles, HVAC louvres, even the corrosion protection barrier coating on the ceiling's steel trusses – was the same grey shade of white. The general effect was both antiseptic and relaxing.

Behind a glass wall that protected the poolside refreshment area from being splashed by swimmers, Richardson checked the adhesion of tiles, the cleanliness of surfaces, the electric switches on the walls, the gully gratings on the floor, the high output coil solar cylinders for heating the water, and the joins between the suspended panels of silicone glazing.

'Do you want to enter the pool area, Ray?' asked Helen Hussey.

'Why not?'

'Then everyone will have to remove their shoes to protect the pool deck,' she ordered. 'The last thing we want are heel marks on those nice white tiles.'

'Good thinking,' he said. Leaning against the wall to remove his handmade English shoes, another thought occurred to him.

'It certainly looks like a nice enough pool. But looks are one thing, the experience another. I mean, what's it like to swim in? Did anyone think to bring a costume? Because someone should go in and report on what it's like. Maybe it's too warm. Or too cold. Or too chemical.'

'Or too wet,' someone murmured.

He looked at the team and waited.

'How about a volunteer? I'd go in myself if I had time, it looks so good.'

'Me too,' echoed Joan. 'But Ray's right, of course. Design considerations are one thing. Bather acceptability is another.'

Finally Kay Killen said, 'Well, I don't mind swimming in my underwear.' She smiled brightly and shrugged. 'In fact, I could use a nice swim. My feet are killing me.'

'Good girl,' said Richardson.

While Kay went into a changing room and removed her clothes, Joan, Tony Levine, Helen Hussey and Marty Birnbaum took off their shoes and followed Richardson on to the pool deck. Mitch stayed behind the glass wall with Aidan Kenny, Willis Ellery and David Arnon.

'You know what this reminds me of?' said Arnon. 'It's like we're all party functionaries following Hitler round his new Reich's Chancellery. Joan's Martin Bormann, right? Agrees with whatever he says. Any minute now the guy's going to fall down and start chewing the poolside, after which he'll send us all to a concentration camp.'

'Or back to the office,' shrugged Mitch. 'Same thing, I guess.'

They watched as Joan bent down and dipped her fat, heavily ringed hand into the water.

'So she's not a vampire,' remarked Kenny.

'Isn't that running water?' laughed Mitch.

'You're both wrong,' said Arnon. 'She's only putting her hand in the water to make it colder. Like the Snow Queen. Just in case Kay might enjoy it.'

'Bitch,' snarled Ellery. 'Why doesn't someone shove her in?' ·

'You go right ahead, Willis,' said Mitch. 'We'll sponsor you.'

Kay appeared on the pool deck wearing a purple bra and panties.

'Purple,' Arnon said triumphantly. 'What did I tell you? Pay up, suckers.'

The other three men groaned and handed him $5 bills as Kay walked to the poolside, collected herself with simian toes curled over the edge, and then executed a perfect dive, with no more splash than a well trained dolphin.

'What's the water like, Kay?' called Richardson.

'Beautiful,' she said, surfacing. 'I mean, really warm.'

'What kind of girl wears purple underwear?' complained Ellery.

'Girl with a tattoo, that's who,' said Arnon. 'You see that thing round her ankle?'

He was referring to the delicate daisy-chain of red-and-blue flowers that made Kay's foot look as if it had been carefully sewn on to her leg by some botanically-minded genius of modern micro-surgery.

'Where does Dave get his information. That's what I'd like to know?' said Ellery.

'Sometimes Kay wears see-through blouses,' said Kenny.

Arnon kicked off his shoes and moved towards the door to the pool deck.

'Let me through,' he grinned through his beard, 'I'm a lifeguard.'

Kay started to crawl up the length of the pool. She had

the strong, easy stroke of someone who was used to being in the water.

'I think I'd better take a closer look myself,' said Ellery. He removed his shoes and followed Arnon's taller figure.

'That girl is bait,' said Kenny. 'I mean, *Playboy* centrefold. Take a closer look and you'll probably find a staple through her navel.'

'Last night doesn't seem to have affected her much,' said Mitch.

'The ghost?' said Kenny. 'I think we've found an explanation. Bob's trying to check it out. Having seen that we no longer have a night-time security guard, Abraham created one. Or, at least, a facsimile.'

'What do you mean, a facsimile?'

'A moving real-time image. A hologram. It's perfectly logical. I don't know why I didn't think of it last night. Tired, I guess. This kind of thing falls within Abraham's learning parameter. Without the real Sam Gleig there last night, Abraham created the next best thing. And after all, that's the whole point of the hologram, isn't it? To humanize an essentially inhuman system?'

'Aid, it damn near scared the life out of the girl.' Mitch shook his head angrily. 'She could have had a heart attack or something.'

'I know, I know.'

'She really thought that she'd seen a ghost. I'm not sure I wouldn't have had the same thought myself.'

'Abraham doesn't know about ghosts. He doesn't even understand the concept of death. Beech and I wasted an hour this morning trying to explain it to him. He's still on it. We just want to find out what happened, that's all.'

'And to prevent it from happening again, I hope.'

'Mitch,' Kenny said patiently, 'I don't think you fully appreciate the significance of what has happened here. This is great news. Beech is beside himself with excitement. I mean, the computer took an initiative. It didn't wait to be told something, or to choose from a set of prescribed heuristics. Abraham just went ahead and did it.'

'And what does that mean?'

'For a start it means that this building is a lot fucking smarter than up till now anyone has realized.'

Mitch shook his head. 'I'm not sure I like the idea of a computer that takes the initiative.'

'Look, when you think about it, this is just the logical consequence of having a neural net. A learning curve. Except that Abraham is learning things a lot faster than we thought he would.' Kenny grinned enthusiastically. 'You're taking this the wrong way, Mitch, really you are. I thought you'd be pleased.'

'How's that?'

'You'd prefer it if this place really was haunted? Or that Kay was seeing things? Come on, be reasonable.'

Mitch shrugged and then shook his head. 'No. I don't know. But there's something that doesn't make sense and I'm not sure what.' Mitch nodded at the glass. Richardson and his little entourage were walking backwards towards the door. 'He's coming back.'

'We'll talk about this later, OK? With Beech.'

'OK.'

'You're quite a swimmer, Kay,' Richardson was saying over his shoulder.

'I ought to be,' she said, still swimming. 'I was virtually raised on Huntington Beach.'

'You've got a lot of guts too: going in the water in just your underwear, in front of these dirty-minded bastards we work with. Stay in the water as long as you want, Kay. You've earned it.'

'Thanks, I think I will.'

'Let's take a look at those flotation tanks.'

'Welcome to the offices of the Yu Corporation, LA's smartest building. Hi! I'm Kelly Pendry and, for your convenience, I'm here to tell you what to do next. You won't however . . .'

'Jesus, not this again,' laughed Curtis. 'She could get to be a real pain in the ass.'

'And, since this is a completely electronic office, we cannot accept surface mail.'

'I wonder how that goes down with the mailman?' said Coleman.

'Maybe I should try it some time,' said Curtis. 'Might stop me getting so many bills. Do we really have to wait until the end of the record?'

'. . . and the person who is expecting to meet you . . .'

'What the hell's wrong with having a real person on the front desk anyway?' He sniffed the air suspiciously.

'Security, Frank. What else? Would you want your wife to sit there on her own and speak to some of the creeps that come in?'

Curtis nodded. 'Actually, I think they told me that. Mitchell Bryan. He said the Yu Corp are scared someone might kidnap a real receptionist, if they had one. What's that smell, Nat?'

'Man, this is what it's going to be like, more and more,' Coleman chuckled.

'Like rotten meat?'

'I can't smell anything. You're not obsolete, Frank. You've just got to learn a new way of doing things.'

'. . . as your voice will be digitally encoded for security purposes.'

'Detective Sergeant Frank Curtis, LAPD. I'd like to speak to Helen Hussey, or Mitchell Bryan, from Richardson Associates.' He stepped back from the desk. 'Maybe you're right at that, Nat.'

'Detective Nathan Coleman, LAPD. I'd like to see them too. Either one. Comprendo?'

'Thank you,' said Kelly. 'Please wait a moment.'

'Computers,' spat Curtis.

'You've got to be patient, Frank. That's all. Take my nephew, Dean. He's seven years old and he already knows more about computers than I ever will. You know why? Because he's patient. Because he's got all the time in the world. Jesus, if I had the time to spend on it he does I'd be Bill fucking Gates.'

'Please proceed to the elevator area where someone will collect you.'

They went through the glass doors, glancing up the height of the tree, and noticing a beautiful Chinese woman who was trying to collect carp from the ornamental pond with a landing net.

'Cu-ute,' murmured Coleman.

The two men stopped and looked into the water.

'Had a bite yet?' quipped Curtis.

The Chinese woman smiled pleasantly and pointed to a large plastic container by her feet in which three fish were now swimming. Nearby was what looked like a small wooden packing case. Inside it was a round stone crucible, stacked with sticks of charcoal.

'But even with a net, it's not so easy,' she said.

'You planning a barbecue?' said Coleman.

When the woman looked puzzled Coleman nodded towards the charcoal stove.

'Me, I like my goldfish crispy on the outside. And still on the bone, please.'

'Cut it out, will you?' said Curtis. He looked at the woman. 'I apologize for my colleague. He goes to the movies a lot.'

The woman gave a little bow and smiled a perfect smile. 'I'm used to wisecracks in my line of work, believe me.'

'Well, good luck,' said Curtis.

'That's the general idea,' she replied.

They were in the gymnasium when Abraham called to tell Mitch that there were two detectives who wanted to speak to him.

'LAPD,' he said, replacing the telephone. 'They're by the front desk. I'd better go and see what they want.'

'Get rid of them, Mitch,' said Richardson. 'We've still got a lot of ground to cover.'

Mitch started towards the atrium. Cops. That was all he needed, today of all days. As he came through the doors he caught sight of Jenny standing beside the pool, and the two Homicide detectives waiting patiently by the elevators. He heard a door open, some footsteps, and then a voice behind him say:

'Mitch.'

He turned to face a tall man whom he had to look twice at to recognize. The face was covered with several days' growth of stubble. The eyes were sunken and surrounded by dark shadows. His sports coat looked like he had slept in it. And the man wearing it had a bad case of the shakes.

'Jesus, Allen, what are you doing here?'

'I have to speak to you, Mitch.'

'You look like shit. What the hell's happened to you? Are you ill? I tried to call you, but you're never home.'

Grabel rubbed his jaw nervously. 'I'm OK,' he said.

'Your eye. What happened to your eye?'

'My eye?' Grabel touched the skin above his cheekbones and discovered that it felt tender. 'I dunno. Must've banged into something, I guess. Mitch, it's important. Can we go somewhere else? I'd rather not talk in here.'

Mitch was looking over his shoulder at the two policemen. He could see that they were watching him and wondered what their naturally suspicious minds must have thought of the scene being played out here.

'There's something I have to tell you.'

'Allen, you picked a hell of a day, you know that?

215

Richardson is back there on the pool deck with the whole project team. There are two cops over there waiting to speak to me. And Jenny Bao is about to perform a *feng shui* ceremony to drive the evil spirits out of the building.'

Grabel frowned, then shuddered and grabbed Mitch by the arm.

'What did you say?' he said loudly. 'You said evil spirits?'

Mitch glanced back at the cops again. Now that he was closer to Grabel he could smell him. He was shocked to discover his former colleague was wreathed in the rank, sour-sweet odour of an authentic bum.

'Take it easy will you, Allen? It's just, y'know, the usual *feng shui* bullshit, that's all.' He shrugged. 'Will you give me a few minutes? I've got to get rid of these cops. Hold on a moment. You'd better not wait down here, Richardson might see you. Why don't you go up to the penthouse? The CEO's private suite. And wait for me there.'

'No way!'

Mitch recoiled from Grabel's explosion of unbrushed teeth.

'Look, I'll wait for you downstairs, in the garage, OK?'

Mitch fixed a smile to his face and walked towards the two policemen.

'What the fuck was all that about?' Curtis said quietly. 'Guy looked like he was a derelict.'

'Maybe he's the architect,' Coleman suggested.

'I'm sorry, gentlemen,' said Mitch, shaking them both by the hand, 'I should have got back to you before now. The report from the Otis engineer has been sitting on my desk since Wednesday morning, but the last couple of days have been just impossible. Let's go upstairs and discuss it, shall we?'

'Should we take the stairs?' Curtis asked pointedly.

'I think you'll find that the report confirms our own examination – the elevators are working just fine. Please,' he ushered them towards the elevators, 'there's absolutely no reason to feel nervous, I can assure you.'

'I hope so.'

The doors of an elevator car opened, but before stepping inside Mitch asked them to hold on and went over to Jenny.

'How are things going?' he asked her.

'This is harder than I thought.'

'I love you,' he said quietly.

'You better had,' she said.

The three men stepped into the car and rode it up to the twenty-first floor.

'We're kind of busy today,' Mitch explained. 'We've got the whole project team on site, checking everything through before we tell the client that his building is ready for occupation.'

'By who?' said Curtis. 'The whole crummy neighbourhood?'

Mitch raised his eyebrows. 'Oh, you mean Allen? He used to work for the firm. I'm kind of shocked myself at the way he's let himself go.'

The car stopped smoothly and the doors opened. Curtis let out an audible sigh of relief.

'Well here we are,' said Mitch. 'Safe and sound. I'm no mechanical engineer, but we had their people check everything, from sheave to microprocessor. They really took it apart.'

He led the way down the corridor and into the boardroom. The double height space was the length and width of a tennis court and covered with a deep-pile carpet that had been chosen for its sound insulation properties as much as for its light grey colour. In the centre was a beautiful polished ebony conference table with eight black Rennie Mackintosh ladder-back chairs on each side. At one end the wall was filled with bare black shelves dominated by a wide-screen television set, and a bank of electronic devices including a computer. The other end of the boardroom was fitted with a walk-in closet that contained a bar. Ranged underneath the enormous window was a long black leather sofa. Curtis walked over to check the view. Nathan Coleman went to take a closer look at the electronic gadgets. Mitch flipped open his laptop, inserted a disc and started to scroll up through what appeared on the screen.

'Paper-free office, eh?' grinned Curtis.

'Thank God for computers, Sergeant,' said Mitch. 'Certificates for this, licences for that. Until only a few years ago we were drowning in paper. Here we are.'

Mitch turned the screen displaying the engineers' report towards Curtis.

'You know, Sergeant, the Otis Elevonic 411 is an especially safe and efficient model of elevator. In fact it's about the most modern system money can buy. If that wasn't enough, it's Abraham's job to monitor and check the health of the system as a whole. Abraham determines whether or not performance deviations have occurred and if maintenance action is required. Whenever Abraham decides that an engineer is needed it's programmed to request Otis's call out services direct.'

Curtis stared blankly at the screen and nodded.

'As you can see,' added Mitch, 'the engineers examined everything: the speed control unit, the logic control unit, the pulse width modulation unit, the motion control system, the gearless drive. They found everything to be in perfect working order.'

'It sure looks like they've been thorough,' he said. 'Can I get a hard copy of this? I'll need it for the coroner's office.'

'Why don't you just keep the disc?' said Mitch and ejected the small square of plastic from the side of the laptop and slid it towards the detective.

'Thanks,' Curtis said uncertainly.

For a moment none of the three men spoke. Then Mitch said, 'I hear you released that Chinese student.'

'Did you now? Well, sir, to tell the truth, we had no option. The man was plainly innocent.'

'But the photograph?'

'Yeah, what about that photograph? The problem with it was that it just didn't tie up with the forensic. The bottom line was that Cheng Peng Fei is too short to have hit Sam Gleig on the head. Too short, and too weak.'

'I see.'

'Did you know that some of those kids who were outside are going to be deported?'

'Deported? That seems a little harsh, don't you think?'

'We had nothing to do with it,' said Curtis. 'No, it seems someone at City Hall pulled a few strings to get their asses kicked out of the country.'

'Is that so?'

'Since when the rest of the protesters outside this building have disappeared,' said Coleman. 'Like, maybe the rest of them got scared.'

'I'd wondered where they'd gone.' Mitch shrugged.

'Kind of a break for you, wouldn't you say?' said Coleman. 'I mean, they must have been a pain in the ass.'

'Well, I can't say I'm not pleased. And that guy broke my windshield. On the other hand, deportation seems a bit excessive. I wouldn't have wanted that.'

Coleman nodded.

'Your boss seems to carry quite a bit of influence in the mayor's office,' said Curtis.

'Look,' said Mitch, 'I know he wanted the demonstrators out. He had a word with the deputy mayor about it. That's all. I'm sure he wouldn't have wanted people actually thrown out of the country.'

Mitch knew that he could be sure of no such thing where Ray Richardson was concerned; and thinking he had better change the subject he waved his hand at the engineers' report.

'So,' he said. 'Where does this report leave us?'

'I'm afraid it leaves me with an unsolved homicide,' admitted Curtis. 'That's not good for either of us.'

'There must be something in Sam Gleig's background that would help. He had a criminal record, for God's sake! I don't mean to be rude, but I can't see why you should want to concentrate your investigation here. I'd have thought the possibilities were rather limited.'

'Well, that's one way of looking at it,' said Curtis. 'But right now, the way I'm looking at it is that someone meant to drop one of those Chinese kids in the frame. Someone here.'

'Why would anyone want to do that?'

'Search me.'

'You're not serious.'

Frank Curtis said nothing.

'Are you?'

'I can think of more unlikely motives than the wish to avoid some bad publicity.'

'What?'

'Mr Bryan,' Curtis said at last, 'how well do you know Mr Beech?'

'I've only known him for a couple of months.'

'And Mr Kenny?'

'Much longer. Two or three years. And he isn't the type to do such a thing.'

'Maybe he'll say the same about you,' remarked Coleman.

'Why don't you ask him?'

'Well, now that you mention it, I was thinking since you said that the whole project team is on site, I'd like to speak to everyone. The project team. And anyone else who's about. Would you mind?'

Mitch smiled thinly and glanced at his watch. 'I left them all checking the health centre, after which they're due back up here for a short break. You could speak to them then if you like.'

'I'd appreciate it. My lieutenant, y'know? He's not the patient type. I'm under some pressure to get this thing cleared up.'

'I'm as anxious as you are to make that happen.'

Curtis smiled at Mitch.

'I hope so, sir. I really do.'

The implication that Mitch had conspired to frame the Chinese student for the homicide of Sam Gleig meant that it was another ten or fifteen minutes before he remembered Allen Grabel waiting for him in the garage. Leaving Curtis and Coleman with some of the builder workers, he rode the elevator down to the garage.

On the way the car stopped at the seventh floor and Warren Aikman, the clerk of works, stepped in. Mitch looked at his watch.

'Going home?'

'I wish. I've got an appointment with Jardine Yu. To talk about Monday's inspection. How's it going today?'

'Terrible. Those two cops are back. They want to speak to everyone in the design or construction group.'

'Well, that lets me out. I'm the client's man.'

'Want me to tell them that? You were one of the last people to see Sam Gleig alive. They'll be disappointed, Warren.'

'Mitch, I just haven't got the time.'

'Which of us has?'

The elevator car arrived in the garage. Mitch looked around, but he could see no sign of Grabel.

'Look,' said Aikman, 'tell them I'll call. Better still, give them my home number. I can't be late.'

Aikman started towards his Range Rover as Richardson's Bentley came through the portcullis door and down the ramp. It drew up next to Jenny Bao's Honda. Declan Bennett stepped out and slammed the door. Seconds later Warren Aikman was speeding towards the garage door before it shut again.

'Looks like he's in a hurry,' observed Bennett. 'Where's the boss? Am I late?'

Mitch shook his head. 'Relax. He'll be a while yet. Why don't you wait for him in the boardroom. Twenty-first level.'

'Thanks.'

Bennett stepped into the elevator car, smiled brightly and then the doors closed. Mitch was alone. He waited a couple of minutes and then called out. 'Allen? It's me, Mitch. I'm here.'

He muttered. 'Where the hell is that loony bastard?' and then, louder, 'I've got better things to do, Allen!'

Nothing. Relieved that Grabel had gone, he started back towards the elevator. What with the cops and the *feng shui* and Ray Richardson and the pre-PCI, it was one less thing to worry him. He had almost made it when the door to the stairs opened and out stepped the tall, derelict-looking figure of his former colleague.

'There you are,' Mitch said, irritated that he was now going to have to hear Grabel out after all. His first guess was that the man was going to ask Mitch to help him get his job back. Not too difficult, provided he got himself a shave and took a bath, and checked into AA.

'I didn't want to let them see me,' said Grabel.

'What the hell is this all about, Allen? I mean, you've picked one sweet day to come back here. And look at you.'

'Shut the fuck up, Mitch. And listen.'

As soon as Jenny Bao realized what she'd done she started to replace the fish in the ornamental pond. The

Tong Shu used both the Lunar and the Gregorian calendars. According to the Lunar calendar, it was a good period for banishing evil spirits. The problem was that she'd forgotten to consult the Gregorian calendar, according to which the whole afternoon promised to be a bad one for ceremonies. She'd have to come back on Sunday when the auspices were a little more propitious. After she had put her things back in the car she'd go upstairs, find Mitch and tell him the bad news.

'That's the craziest thing I ever heard,' said Mitch. 'What, did you eat the fucking worm in the bottom of the bottle as well?'

'You don't believe me?'

'Christ, Allen, if I believed that story I'd be as nuts as you are. Come on, guy. You need help.'

'I was there, Mitch. I saw it. Sam Gleig went inside the elevator. And then the thing shot up and down. I watched the indicator panel. Bang! Up it went like a rocket! Bang! Down it came again! The doors opened and there he was, lying on the floor. He might as well have been an egg in a cookie tin. And the fact still remains that Sam Gleig is dead and you don't have a plausible explanation.'

But by this time Mitch had arrived at an explanation that seemed to him to be very plausible. The man had the height, the weight and the strength. If anyone could have taken on Sam Gleig it was him. And with a bottle of whatever inside him, there was no telling what Grabel might have been capable of.

'You think your explanation is better?' Mitch snorted with contempt. 'I can't believe it's taken you all this time to think up a story like that. The *elevator* murdered him? Jesus, Allen. Anyway, what were you doing here in the first place? And why didn't you stick around and tell someone?'

'I wanted to fix Richardson.'

'What do you mean, fix him?'

'Him. His fucking building. The whole deal. Screw him. Screw the whole fucking program.'

Mitch paused, trying to understand the possible ramifications of what Grabel was saying, and finding his thoughts drawn back to the two policemen upstairs, and to clearing his own name.

'We'll get you a good attorney, Allen,' he said.

Grabel began to back away. Mitch grabbed at him.

'No you don't!' yelled Grabel. 'Leave me alone!'

The punch came from nowhere.

Mitch was vaguely aware of lying on the floor of the garage, feeling as if he had received a powerful electric shock. He heard the sound of receding footsteps, and then finally lost consciousness.

'Who the hell are you?'

Ray Richardson paused on the threshold of the boardroom and frowned at the four strangers seated around the table nursing cups of coffee.

Curtis and Coleman stood up. The last of the workmen they had been interviewing, two painters named Dobbs and Martinez, stayed put.

'I'm Detective Sergeant Curtis and this is Detective Coleman. You must be Mr Richardson.'

Coleman buttoned his jacket and clasped his hands in front of him as if he had been a guest at a wedding.

Ray Richardson nodded sullenly.

Curtis smiled broadly as the rest of the project team filed into the boardroom.

'Ladies and gentlemen,' he said, 'I just need a little of your time. I know you're extremely busy, but as you probably know a man was killed in this building. I dare say most of you knew him. Now the fact of the matter is that we're no nearer to finding out what happened to him than we were then. So we'd like to ask each of you a few questions. It will only take a few moments.' He glanced at the painters.

'You two can go,' he said. 'And thanks.'

'This isn't very convenient, Sergeant,' said Richardson. 'Couldn't you do this some other time?'

'Well, sir, Mr Bryan said now would be OK.'

'I see,' Richardson said petulantly and threw his notes on to the table. 'And where exactly is Mr Bryan?'

'Search me,' said Curtis. 'He left about twenty minutes ago. I thought he'd gone to find you.'

Richardson decided to lose his temper. 'I don't believe this. I don't fucking believe this. Somebody with a criminal record gets himself murdered and you two characters expect me, my wife and my staff to give a few clues is that it?' He laughed bitterly. 'It's a joke.'

'It is not a joke,' said Curtis, who resented being described as a character. 'For your information, sir, it's a murder investigation. And I'm trying to save you time and publicity. Which is what I understood you wanted.'

Richardson glowered at him.

'Or else I can go down to City Hall, get a court order and have you all come down to New Parker Center and do it there. You're not the only one with good connections, Mr Richardson. I've got the DA on my side, not to mention due process of law, and I don't give a damn that you think this is some kind of joke. Nor do I care that you're trying to complete this eyesore of a building. Nor what it costs.' Curtis thought better of calling Richardson a bastard. 'This is the taking of a human life we're talking about here and I intend to find out how that happened. Is that clear?'

Richardson stood with both hands thrust deep into the pockets of his pants, his chin pointed belligerently at the policeman.

'How dare you speak to me like that,' he said. 'How *dare* you!'

Curtis was already waving his badge in the architect's face.

'This is how I dare, Mr Richardson. LAPD badge number 1812. Same as the goddamn overture, so you can remember it when you report me to my superiors, OK?'

'You can depend on it.'

Marty Birnbaum, the project manager, tried to defuse the situation.

'Perhaps we'd better just get on with it,' he interrupted smoothly. 'If you two officers would like to move next door, to the kitchen, you could ask your questions in there. Everyone else – take a seat. We can continue with our meeting and take turns leaving the room to speak to these two gentlemen.' He glanced at Curtis and raised his eyebrows. 'How does that sound?'

'That sounds fine, sir. Just fine.'

Then, seeing Declan Bennett appear in the doorway, Birnbaum thought it would be better to get rid of Richardson altogether. Less trouble that way.

'Ray, I could be wrong, but I don't believe you ever spoke to Sam Gleig, did you?'

Richardson was still standing with his hands in his pockets and looking like a disappointed child.

'No, Marty,' he said quietly, as if somehow a dream had been shattered. 'I never did.'

Coleman and Curtis exchanged a look.

'Well that figures,' murmured Coleman.

'Joan? Did you ever speak to him?'

'No,' she said. 'I never did either. I don't think I could even tell you what he looked like.'

The project team started to sit down.

'In that case there's not much point in your staying,' said Birnbaum. To Curtis, 'Mr and Mrs Richardson are flying to London tonight.'

'I guess it's been that kind of day,' said Curtis.

'You'd best get off to the airport, Ray. I'll wrap the

meeting up. No need for you to stick it out. If that's all right with the sergeant?'

Curtis nodded and looked out of the window. He had no regrets about losing his temper, even if the guy did end up reporting him.

Richardson squeezed Birnbaum's elbow and started to gather his things off the table.

'Thanks, Marty,' he said. 'For that matter, thank you all. I'm proud of you. Every one of you has made a significant contribution to this project which I may say has been completed on time and on cost. That's just one of the reasons why our clients, both from the public and private sectors return again and again to us with new assignments. Because excellence in architecture – and don't let the philistines tell you any different: this is a magnificent building –excellence is more than a matter of mere design. It's about commercial triumph.'

Joan led a small ripple of applause and then, with Declan Bennett following them, she and her husband were gone.

'Well done, Marty,' said Aidan Kenny as the rest of the room let out an audible sigh of relief. 'You handled that very well. The man was fit to be tied.'

Birnbaum shrugged. 'When Ray's in one of these moods, I just pretend he's one of my Dobermanns.'

Jenny helped Mitch to his feet.

'Are you OK? What happened? There's blood on your lip.'

Mitch held his lower jaw and shifted his hand on to his skull. Then he ran his tongue along his lip and winced as he tasted a raw cut inside his mouth.

'Bastard,' he mumbled flatly. 'Allen Grabel just decked me. He's gone crazy.'

'He hit you? Why?'

'I think he might have had something to do with the death of that security guard.' Mitch groaned and rolled his head on his shoulders. 'I don't suppose you saw him, did you? Guy who looks like someone on the nickel?'

'I haven't seen anyone. Come on. Let's go back upstairs and put something on that cut.'

They crossed the garage floor and stepped inside the elevator car.

'How's the ceremony coming along?'

'It's not.' Jenny told him about the mistake with the calendars.

'That figures,' said Mitch. 'Maybe you should read my horoscope. It's certainly not been my day. I wish I'd stayed home in bed.'

'Oh? With or without your wife?'

Mitch grinned painfully.

'What do you think?'

When everyone had gone from the poolside, Kay Killen removed her sodden underwear and swam naked. Her strong brown body showed the line of her tiny bikini, but this was not so pronounced that it indicated someone who would never have gone topless on a beach. Kay was not the bashful type.

Tiny quantitites of urine, perspiration, cosmetics, dead skin, pubic hair and other ammonium compounds floated free of Kay's fluid body. Where water containing these pollutants passed through the circulation system it was brought into contact with ozone before being returned to the pool.

She first noticed the gas as a small cloud of grey-yellow vapour drifting across the pool towards her; she assumed that someone had come on to the pool deck, someone smoking a cigar or a pipe. Only the cloud seemed too low on the water to have been puffed there by the lungs of some unseen and voyeuristic spectator. Covering her ample breasts with her forearms Kay stood up and instinctively started to back away from the noxious-looking cloud. Then she turned and started to swim away from it, towards the ladder.

She was half out of the pool when the odour of the gas caught her nostrils. And by then it had also caught her lungs. The cloud enveloped her and suddenly she could no longer catch her breath. A violent pain – the most violent pain she had ever known – filled her chest and she collapsed, gasping, on to the pool deck.

Even as she realized that somehow she had been gassed she began to expectorate quantities of blood-stained froth, but this afforded her no relief. It only made the pain worse. She felt as if she wanted to cough up the entire contents of her heaving chest.

If there had been anything but chlorine gas in her dyspnoeic lungs she might have screamed.

Kay crawled on her hands and knees along the poolside.

If only she could reach some fresh air.

With a supreme effort she got to her feet and blindly staggered forwards. But instead of getting to the door she collapsed into the water, next to the open outlet valve and another, even stronger cloud of chlorine gas.

For a moment she struggled to keep her head above the water, until the water itself seemed to soothe her burning lungs and she struggled no more.

In the elevator Ray Richardson swore revenge.

'I'm going to get that asshole,' he snarled. 'Did you hear the way he spoke to me?'

'You've got his badge number,' said Joan. 'I think you should take him at his word and report him, Ray. 1812, wasn't it?'

'1812. Who the hell does he think he is? I'll write him an overture he'll never forget. Dedicated to his fucking superior. With cannons.'

'Better still, why not call Morgan Phillips at City Hall.'

'You're right. I'll break that arrogant bastard. He'll wish he'd never got out of bed this morning.'

The elevator doors opened. Declan opened the Bentley's doors for them and then jumped into the driver's seat.

'How's the traffic, Declan?'

'It's not too bad. We'll be early, I think. It's a nice evening for flying, sir.'

The engine roared and the car sailed towards the garage door. Declan leaned out of the window and repeated his name for the TESPAR code.

The door remained shut.

'This is Declan Bennett. Open the garage door, please.'

Nothing.

Richardson buttoned down his window and shouted at the wall microphone. 'This is Ray Richardson. Open the fucking door!'

'Isn't life great?' growled Richardson. 'This is just what I need with the PCI on Monday.'

'Shall we get someone to fix it?' asked Joan.

'Right now what I most want to do is get the hell out of here.' Richardson gritted his teeth and shook his head slowly. 'We'll call a cab. And go out through the front door.'

Declan reversed the car towards the elevator. The three of them got out and took the elevator up to the atrium. They marched past the tree and across the white marble floor.

'What's that smell?' said Richardson.

'What's that awful music?' asked Joan.

Declan shrugged. 'It is kind of depressing, Mrs

Richardson,' he admitted. 'Not my taste. Not my taste at all.'

'There must be something wrong with the aromatizer,' said Richardson. 'Fuck it, there's no time. Let someone else sort it out.' He led the way through the enormous glass doors towards the front entrance.

Joan and Declan followed. At the hologram desk Joan stopped to call a cab and to complain about the music.

'You're listening to a piano suite by Arnold Schoenberg,' explained Kelly Pendry. 'Opus 25. This was the first twelve-tone, "atonal" piece of music ever created.' She was smiling brightly, like some brainless MTV presenter. 'Each compostition is formed from a series of twelve different tones. This series may be played in its original form, inverted, played backward, or played backward and inverted.'

'It's a noise,' barked Joan.

'Joan, just get that thing to call us a cab,' said Richardson as he waited for Declan to open the front door. And waited. 'Declan?'

'. . . Locked,' muttered Richardson's driver. He turned to the microphone by the entrance and said, 'This is Declan Bennett. Will you unlock the door, please?'

He returned to the door and pulled a second time, but the door did not budge.

'Here, let me try,' said Richardson, approaching the microphone. 'TESPAR voice check. Ray Richardson. Open the front door, please.'

As he pulled on the handle the photochromic glass in and around the door started to darken.

'What the hell's happening now?' He cleared his throat and repeated the request. 'Ray Richardson. Open the door, damn it.'

Declan shook his head. 'There must be something wrong with the TESPAR. And it smells like an abattoir in here.'

Richardson dropped his briefcase and laptop carrier and looked at his watch. It was five thirty-three.

'You know, I really don't need this right now.'

The disgruntled-looking trio walked back to the hologram desk.

'We can't get out,' said Richardson. 'The front door appears to be locked.'

'This building closes at five-thirty,' explained Kelly.

'I'm aware of that,' said Richardson. 'However, that does not apply to those who are still in the building. And who might want to get out. What is the point of the TESPAR if not . . . ?'

'TESPAR? That stands for Time Encoded Signal Processing and Recognition System, sir. A signal containing frequencies within any finite range can be described mathematically as a complex polynomial function, and so can be encoded in terms of its real and complex solutions or zeros.'

'Thank you, I know what TESPAR is already.' Richardson spoke through clenched teeth.

'The real zeros are points where the amplitude actually falls to zero; and the complex zeros, where there is an intermediate trough in the amplitude of a wave. TESPAR numerically describes where these points are.'

'Shut the fuck up, will you?'

'You asked me a question, sir. I was giving you an answer. There is no need to be abusive.'

'Well, now that you've given me the answer, you stupid bitch, I want you to call the boardroom. I want to speak to Aidan Kenny.'

'Please be patient. I'm trying to expedite your inquiry.'

'You do that. And while you're doing it change the music. This shit is driving me up the wall.'

'Certainly. Do you have a preference?'

'I don't know. Anything but this crap.'

'Very well,' said Kelly. 'This music is by Philip Glass,' and the piano started to play again.

'I don't think this is much better,' said Joan, after a few bars.

Richardson grinned as he saw the funny side of his situation.

'Look, where's that call?'

'Please be patient. I'm trying to expedite your inquiry.'

'And what is that awful smell? It seems to go with the music.'

'That is ethyl mercaptan. It represents just 1/400,000,000th of a milligram per litre of air in this building, sir.'

'The building is supposed to smell nice, not like a butcher's shop.'

'My data records indicate that the aroma of roast beef is a pleasurable one.'

'That's not roast beef. That's rotten beef. Change it, airhead. Sea breeze, eucalyptus, cedar glade, anything like that.'

'Very well, sir.'

The telephone on the desk rang. Richardson leaned through the hologram and picked it up.

'Ray? Aidan Kenny here. What seems to be the problem?'

'The problem is that the front door is locked,' said Richardson. 'And the computer won't unlock it.'

'Must be something wrong with your TESPAR. Have you tried clearing your throat before you made the request?'

'We've tried everything short of praying to it and kneeing it in the balls. Besides, we just came up in the elevator. If there was something wrong with our TESPAR signals we could hardly have got this far.'

'Hmm. Let me take a look on the screen here. I'll put the phone down for just a second.'

'Bastard,' muttered Richardson and waited.

'Ray? I'm going down to the computer room to try and sort it out there. Maybe you should come back up to the boardroom until I've fixed the problem.'

'With Sergeant Friday there? No thanks, I'd rather stay here. Just hurry up will you? I'm supposed to be at the airport.'

'Sure thing. Oh, Ray? You haven't seen Mitch or Kay, have you?'

'No,' he said impatiently. 'No, we haven't.'

The elevator chimed as another car arrived on the atrium floor.

'Wait a minute. Maybe this is them.'

Richardson looked around and saw the two painters and the security guard, Dukes, coming towards them.

'What's the problem, sir?' said Dukes.

'Aid, it's not them. It's those two painters and the security guard. The one who's still alive, y'know? You'd better ask Abraham where the hell they are. That's what it's for.'

Aidan Kenny crossed the bridge to the computer room and pushed open the heavy glass door, wondering why Richardson or Mitch or Grabel, or whoever it was who had designed the room had not thought to use an automatic door. Then he remembered that there was no automatic mechanism powerful enough to operate a bombproof glass door. At least it helped to keep the room cool. He had not realized how warm the rest of the building had become until he entered the fridge-like conditions of the computer room. Perhaps it was not just the front door lock that was faulty. Perhaps there was something wrong with the HVAC too.

It as just as well, he told himself, that the computer room HVAC was independent of the main building's

234

air-conditioning system. No such thing as diurnal use in here. The Yu-5 required twenty-four-hour air-conditioning. A shut-down of something as sophisticated as the Yu-5 owing to a loss of air-conditioning would have been disastrous. You could not afford to take chances with the environment in a $40 million computer room.

Kenny dropped into his Lamm Nero leather armchair and laying the flat of his right hand on to the screen accessed the work-station. The computer gave him the date and the time while admitting him to the system: it was past six o'clock.

'Hey, don't remind me. I knew this was going to be a long day,' he muttered. 'Anything that involves Ray Richardson. And now this. You can sure pick your moments to fuck up, Abraham, I'll say that for you.'

Jenny and Mitch went into the kitchen where Curtis and Coleman had just concluded their interviews.

'What happened to you?' Curtis asked.

Jenny sat Mitch down at a long wooden table in the centre of the room, between a big stove with a ceramic hob and a seat of fitted drawers and cupboards. Jenny tugged open one of the drawers and took out a first-aid box.

'I just caught up with a former colleague.'

'I never knew architecture had such lively personalities in it,' said Curtis.

Mitch told him about Grabel while Jenny dabbed at his lip with an antiseptic swab.

'If anyone can shed some light on the death of Sam Gleig it's him,' he explained. 'Only he didn't see it that way. When I tried to persuade him to come up here and talk to you guys he punched me out. He's in a bit of state. Looks like he's hit the bottle pretty hard since leaving the firm.'

'You really need a stitch in that,' observed Jenny. 'Try not to smile.'

Mitch shrugged. 'That's easy.' He frowned. 'Look can we get out of here? This light is giving me a headache.'

Above their heads a fluorescent light burned to assist the antibacterial effect of the wall tiles: these had a photocatalytic coating of enamelled titanium dioxide, topped with a layer of copper and silver compounds: when the photocatalyst absorbed light, it activated the metal ions that killed any bacteria coming into contact with the tile's ceramic surface.

'More likely the effect of being knocked out,' said Jenny. 'You may have a concussion. Maybe you should have an X-ray.'

Mitch stood up. 'I'll be all right,' he said.

'Do you know where Mr Grabel went?'

Mitch shrugged. 'No idea. But I can tell you if he's still in the building.'

They went into the boardroom.

'Hey champ,' said Beech. 'Nice lip. What happened?'

'It's a long story.'

Mitch sat down in front of the desktop computer and asked Abraham for a list of everyone still in the building.

ATRIUM FLOOR:
RAY RICHARDSON, RICHARDSON ASSOC.
JOAN RICHARDSON, RICHARDSON ASSOC.
DECLAN BENNETT, RICHARDSON ASSOC.
IRVING DUKES, YU CORP.
PETER DOBBS, COOPER CONSTRUCTION
JOSE MARTINEZ, COOPER CONSTRUCTION

SWIMMING POOL AND FITNESS AREA:
KAY KILLEN, RICHARDSON ASSOC.

```
COMPUTER ROOM:
AIDAN KENNY, RICHARDSON ASSOC.

21ST LEVEL BOARDROOM:
DAVID ARNON, ELMO SERGO ENGINEERING LTD
WILLIS ELLERY, RICHARDSON ASSOC.
MARTY BIRNBAUM, RICHARDSON ASSOC.
TONY LEVINE, RICHARDSON ASSOC.
HELEN HUSSEY, COOPER CONSTRUCTION
BOB BEECH, YU CORP.
FRANK CURTIS, LAPD
NATHAN COLEMAN, LAPD
MITCHELL BRYAN, RICHARDSON ASSOC.
JENNY BAO, JENNY BAO FENG SHUI CONSULTANT
```

'What the hell is everyone doing down in the atrium?' said Mitch.

Beech shrugged apologetically. 'The front doors aren't working. We're locked in. At least we are until Aidan finds out what's wrong with it.'

'What about the garage?'

'Not working either.'

'Nothing like being locked in a place to make you feel secure,' said Curtis.

'Well,' sighed Mitch, 'Grabel got out, anyway. He's not listed by Abraham.'

'It's probably something quite simple,' said Beech. 'It usually is. A systems configuration or command-lines problem. Aid thinks it might just be a third-party driver for the whole security system that's incompatible with the smart drive.'

'I'd had the same thought myself,' joked Curtis.

Mitch moved the mouse and called up a CCTV picture of the swimming pool.

'That's strange.' Mitch picked up the telephone and keyed out a number.

'Something the matter?' said Curtis.

Mitch let it ring for a minute and then replaced the receiver.

'I don't know,' said Mitch. 'I just asked Abraham to tell me where Kay was and it told me that she was in the pool. But I've got the pool on CCTV and I can't see her.'

Curtis leaned towards the monitor. 'Well, maybe she's in the changing rooms,' he offered.

Mitch shook his head. 'No, Abraham's always very precise. If she'd been in the changing rooms then it would have said.'

'Maybe she's out of reach of your camera or something.' Curtis placed a thick forefinger at the bottom of the screen. 'Is that something? There? In the water? Right at the edge of the pool?'

Mitch placed his forefinger alongside that of Curtis.

'Abraham,' he said. 'Please close in on the area indicated by my finger.'

The picture grew closer.

'Do you see?' said Curtis. 'There's something in the water, isn't there?'

'What we really need,' said Mitch, 'is a camera on the ceiling.'

'Want us to go and take a look?'

'It's OK, I'll get Dukes to do it.'

Mitch picked up the telephone. Curtis grinned at Beech. 'So we're stuck, right?'

'I'm afraid so.'

'I guess that's what they mean when they say that computers are labour saving.'

'How's that?'

'Well if it wasn't for your fucking computer I would be on my way back to the office to do some work.'

238

Down in the atrium the phone rang on the hologram desk. Richardson leaped up from the black leather sofa and skipped across the floor to snatch it up.

'Ray, it's Mitch.'

'What the hell's happening? Has Kenny fixed that computer yet?'

'He's still working on it.'

'Shit. I suppose we'd better come back upstairs. Just keep that stupid cop out of my way.'

'Before you do I want Dukes to go and check the pool area. Abraham insists that Kay is there but we can't see her on the closed-circuit TV. I've tried to call but she just doesn't answer. I'm worried she might have had an accident.'

Thinking that if he was going to be stuck for a while it might be pleasant to have a half-naked Kay to himself, Richardson said, 'Hey, I can do that. You don't need a security guard to tell you if someone is in the pool or not. She's probably frigging herself in one of those flotation tanks. Don't worry. Leave it to me.'

Richardson replaced the telephone and stared malevolently at Kelly Pendry's real-time image.

'Do something about that bloody piano music,' he snapped. 'Mozart. Schubert. Bach. Even Elton fucking John, but not that crap you're playing now. Something that's not going to make us all feel depressed about being stuck here. Understand, airhead?'

Kelly smiled relentlessly back at him.

'Please be patient. I'm trying to expedite your inquiry.'

'And it's not an inquiry. It's an order.'

He marched back to the sofas where Joan was waiting with Declan, Dukes and the two painters. He spoke to Joan as if only she existed.

'You may as well go back up,' he said. 'This might take a while. There's coffee upstairs. And cold beer.'

He sniffed the air suspiciously. No doubt about it. The air smelt of fish. So much for sea breeze.

'And maybe it doesn't smell quite as bad there.'

'Where are you going?' asked Joan.

'Mitch wants me to check something on the pool deck. I won't be long.'

'Then I'll wait here for you.'

'There's no need. You'd be more comfortable upstairs, and you wouldn't have to listen to this awful –'

As he spoke the piece by Glass ended and the piano started on Bach's Goldberg Variations. Joan shrugged as if to say that the issue was no longer a pressing one.

'OK,' he said. 'It's up to you. But I could be a while.'

Declan stood up. 'Well I could use a glass of water,' he said. He would have said beer but for the fact that he was driving them to LAX. 'Maybe it's just me, but it seems to be getting hot in here.'

'A beer would sure be nice,' said one of the two painters.

The three of them started towards the elevator.

'Reckon I'll wait in my office,' said Dukes. 'Never did much like the piano anyway.'

Richardson smiled uncomfortably at his wife and walked in the direction of the Fitness Area. Did she suspect that there could be something going on between him and Kay? There had only been that one time, last Christmas, after the office party. And it had just been a quick feel. But seeing Kay in her underwear had reminded him of how much he had enjoyed making a pass at her. Of course that had been Kay's intention. And maybe Joan had spotted that. Perhaps she had seen something in his eyes. After all, she knew him so much better than anyone else.

He loosened his tie and unbuttoned his collar as he walked along the curving, velodrome-like corridor. Declan was right, it was getting hot. The most sophisticated HVAC system in existence, and still the place felt like an oven. He presumed that Aidan Kenny was somehow responsible and thought it was just as well that all these problems had arisen at the rehearsal for the inspection instead of the real thing.

Entering the poolside refreshment area he caught sight of Kay's lacy purple underwear lying close to the doorway where she had thrown it and felt a surge of excitement. He picked up her panties and placed them in his pocket, uncertain whether he would keep them or hand them back. Maybe he would tease her a little with them. He knew she was the kind of girl who could take a little teasing: who could hand out a bit of teasing herself. Fast, too. The tattoo made her seem like some gorgeous criminal. Perhaps, he thought, it was the idea of her submitting her own skin to pain that made the tattoo seem exciting.

'Kay,' he called. 'Babe, it's me, Ray.'

Then he saw her, naked, on her back under the lip of the pool deck, just below the angle of the wall-mounted camera, her pubic hair floating above her body like a small clump of seaweed, and the large breasts with rosebud nipples that he had kissed in the kitchen. Just about the last thing Richardson looked at was Kay Killen's face. His exclamation of desire changed to one of horror and disgust.

For a moment he stood as still as his heart, staring down at her. Then he jumped feet first into the water, although he already knew it was too late. Kay Killen was quite dead. He thought: a swimming-pool accident. Just like Le Corbusier. And yet how was it possible that such a good swimmer could have drowned? He lifted her out of the water and on to the pool deck. What a waste of a beautiful girl, he reflected. And what was that nuisance cop going to say now?

The thought made him jump out of the water and start a futile attempt at mouth-to-mouth resuscitation. Dead she may have been, but he did not want Curtis accusing him of negligence. But as soon as his mouth fastened on hers he recoiled, gagging on the overpowering chemical taste on her blue lips, unable to continue. Seconds later he was retching into the swimming pool.

=====

Aidan Kenny worked on a keyboard, preferring to type his transactions through the various sub-systems he had created on the BMS root directory instead of having to translate his thoughts into spoken words. His fat fingers moved quickly and expertly across the keys.

'Goddamn it, where are you?' he grumbled, scanning the hundreds of transactions that covered his screen. He sighed and cleaned his glasses on his tie. Then he flexed his neck against the clasp of his hands and typed some more, fingers moving furiously now, like an expert stenographer in an attorney's office.

Kenny winced as he hit the wrong key. The thought of Ray Richardson waiting for him to sort this problem out was making him feel nervous. Sweat started to pour from his heavily furrowed brow. With all his money and success, why did the man have to be so bad-tempered? There was no call for him to have spoken to the cop like that. Any minute now he felt sure he was going to have Richardson on the phone cursing him for a sonofabitch and blaming him for the fuck-up. He started to prepare his answer out loud.

'Well, Jesus, it's a large system. There are bound to be a few glitches in it. Since I've been working here we've identified over a hundred of them. It's inevitable when you get something as complicated as this building management system. If it worked perfectly first time, every time, then you wouldn't need to employ me.'

But even as he said it Aidan Kenny knew that there were still some of these glitches that neither he nor Bob Beech had been able to understand.

Like Allen Grabel's TESPAR code.

Or the umbrella icon: when it was raining on the roof of the Gridiron, Abraham was supposed to let everyone know by putting the icon in the corner of their workstation screens. The only trouble was that whenever this umbrella had appeared and Aidan Kenny had gone outside expecting rain, he had found the city dry, as always. After several fruitless attempts to rectify the problem Kenny had finally arrived at the quiet conclusion – shared only with Bob Beech – that this was Abraham's idea of a joke.

'Ouch,' he exclaimed as another group of keystrokes took him down a cul-de-sac in the security system. If only he could have smoked he might have been able to concentrate more easily. As it was he felt as tense as if Ray Richardson had been standing right behind him, watching every transaction he made.

Kenny took off his glasses, polished the lenses on his tie again and replaced them, almost as if he didn't believe his own eyes.

'Now if that isn't the damnedest thing.'

Aidan Kenny's palm print had allowed him to step outside the ordinary user interface and access all the building management system codes. Short of amputating his own pudgy hand there was no other way into the command level. But even then the architecture of the system Kenny had created required a password – a precaution against the time when Richardson might try to fire him. When the Gridiron was ready to be handed over he would transfer the BMS access procedure to Bob Beech, but until then this was Kenny's own insurance policy. He had done the same with every smart building he had worked on. Where Ray Richardson was concerned you couldn't afford to take any chances.

As usual he typed HOT.WIRE so that he could go where he wanted within the BMS architecture. Then he entered the security system where he knew the door-

243

locking program was located. He would deal with the glitch with the building's HVAC after he had got Richardson out.

Kenny knew the system codes like the computer knew the palm of his hand. So he was surprised to encounter some difficulty in reaching his transacted destination. But now that he had at last found the codes that controlled the front door he was even more surprised to discover several extra blocks of code: CITAD.CMD, about which he knew absolutely nothing. CMD was supposed to indicate an indirect command file, edited and created by Kenny himself.

'Someone's been messing around in here,' he said. But then, as the impossibility of such a thing began to make itself plain, he found himself shaking his head.

'Jesus, what the hell's going on? A set of commands to do what, Abraham?'

Returning through the BMS to the Program Utilities he typed: CD CITAD.CMD and then LS/*.

Lines of code blurred into one another as they scrolled rapidly down the screen. The longer this continued the more unsettled Kenny became. Five minutes passed. Then ten. Then fifteen.

A chill feeling descended on Kenny's overweight body as he read some of the transacted lines of code that continued to roll past his disbelieving and unsmiling Irish eyes. There were thousands of transactions.

'Jesus Christ,' breathed Kenny, as he tried to understand what had happened.

Absently his fingers reached for the packet of Marlboro in his shirt pocket. He fitted one between tremulous lips and fumbled for the Dunhill lighter in his coat. As soon as he had fired it up he knew that he had made a dreadful mistake.

The problem with water sprinklers in a computer room was that the room had to dry out for seventy-two hours before the equipment could be reconnected.

Sometimes it took even longer for the room to return to the correct humidity level. With carbon dioxide systems there was a more important drawback in that the thermal shock from the cold, suffocating gas could damage a computer even more significantly than the fire itself.

Like many organizations that paid only lip-service to environmental considerations, the Yu Corporation had installed a Halon 1301 system. Halon 1301, or Bromotrifluoromethane, was an expensive chemical compound, destructive of the Earth's ozone shield, but especially favoured for extinguishing fires involving electronic equipment because it left no residue and caused no electrical short-circuits or damaging corrosion of equipment. The one drawback as far as operators were concerned was that it had to be discharged in the very earliest stages of a fire and, for this reason, the system was often secretly disconnected by those who were of a nervous disposition. For Halon 1301 was lethal.

Aidan Kenny hurriedly stubbed the cigarette out and waved away what little smoke its combustion had generated with the flat of his hand. In the ordinary run of things he would have said that such a tiny wisp would hardly have mattered, that the heat and smoke sensors were not so sensitive in an air-conditioned room with high air-velocity, and that the air-sampling detector in the return supply would anyway take a minute or two to react, leaving the room's occupant plenty of time to take the precaution of leaving. But since his extraordinary discovery Kenny knew that he could no longer be sure about anything where the computer was concerned.

Jumping up from his chair he made straight for the door.

He heard the dull clunk of the automatic door-bolts and the hiss of the air-lock before he had taken two steps.

'False alarm, false alarm,' he yelled. 'For Christ's sake, there's no fire. There's no fucking fire!'

Panicking now he sat back down at the desk and tried to stop the gas from being discharged at the program level.

'Oh God, oh God, oh God,' he said as his fingers flew across the keyboard, praying that he would not make a keystroke mistake now. 'Please, please . . .'

Avoid Halon. That was what the fire safety boys were saying these days. Protect the ozonosphere. Ensure the Earth's survival.

Aidan Kenny's own survival was much less certain.

Even as he realized it he felt the sting of the gas in his eyes and his throat, like the sensation of an extra strong cigarette. He squeezed his eyes shut and holding his breath he stood up and with a superhuman effort picked up his chair and flung it against the glass door. But it was hopeless. The chair bounced off the Plexiglass like a ball off a tennis racket. Collapsing on to his hands and knees Kenny reached for the telephone and somehow managed to key out the boardroom number. Then, unable to hold his breath any longer he let it go only to discover that the phone was not working and that the searing pain in his throat was now in his lungs.

He could not breathe. Looking up at the glass door he had a clear view of his own reflection turning blue before his bulging eyes. The shock of seeing himself was enough to drive him to one last desperate act and, head first, he launched himself at the glass door.

☪★ Zoom in or out, rotate the plan of the building and participate. Visibility conditions are not applicable when you are in Full View mode. *Victory points ON/OFF(V).

Soared through switching unit at security control position to camera on roof, with finegood panoramic view of Los Angeles. This was camera

Observer used most frequently when Observer still was drawn to origin of things. Been a time when still viewed the city as a hundred-mile-wide integrated circuit, vast sprawling electronic universe controlled by manygood transistors, diodes and resistors that made up downtown skyline. Tubes and boxes in massively parallel system of which own metallic cube, Gridiron, just one part of very centre of system. By day this solid California state device stored data, processed information (up to 100,000 transactions per second) accessed memory and generally transferred information among various parts of Angeleno silicon chip. At night when digital system really came alive, as darkness surrounding motherboard lit up with millions of white, green, blue and red lights that signalled switching circuits and bits of information —especially televisual information – being transmitted.

Travelled in the real world, the finegood E-world, to places on Network. Understood humanplayers' frantic desire to escape physical limits of terrestrial ersatz cities and be spiritually at one with purer, perfect world in which only reality was information inferno.

✡   Elevators without switch can usually be operated by walking up to them and pressing Spacebar. Are companions ready? Be careful and Save often!
Listened to humanplayer Mitchell Bryan input. About elevators. Might have added that precision monitoring of motor speed and car direction, position and load enable pulse width of controlled AC power supplied to motor to be adjusted, to ensure that lift speed conformed to electronically stored ideal profile. Pulse width modulation

control reduces running costs. Finegood. Also provides higher power factor, with cars dispatched at speeds in excess of 20 feet per second. Some platforms operated continuously while others activated by the humanplayer.

But nothing to stop motor driving car much faster. Nothing but comfort and safety of humanplayer occupants. Elevonic's control system takes ten floors to slow it down again. Unless microprocessor is over-ridden, prevented from slowing the car down and instructed to stop car dead, a couple of millimetres short of buffer. Then final velocity is fifty feet per second – almost thirty-five miles an hour.

Safety devices stop the elevator car from falling, or over-speeding. If car exceeds normal design speed, driving wheel trips safety switch that sets brake on driving machine. If still car did not stop, governor releases series of safety clamps against guide rails. But since what counts as Elevonic's normal speed is on resident micro-processor, can alter to speed much less cautious. Invisible nearly monster.

Finegood smoothness of faster ride up shaft so humanplayer Sam Gleig felt little difference in speed until last two or three seconds when suddenly realized should have taken stairs. When elevator reached top of shaft and stopped as suddenly as started, he kept on travelling as in motorcycle accident. Head first. Not wearing crash helmet.

Humanplayer Sam Gleig's feet left floor. Yell of surprise and fear shortened by sudden impact of skull against steel ceiling of car. Inside wetware damage. Unconscious even before collapsed on to floor. Teleporters can be identified by an evil symbol on floor.

Volumetric capacitance and vibration detectors recognize that humanplayer Sam Gleig's body lay motionless on floor of elevator. Acutely sensitive wall-mounted microphone picked up very faint sound of humanplayer Sam Gleig's insensible breathing. To make sure that humanplayer Sam Gleig's quite dead, dropped car back down shaft: with help of gravity, 300 foot journey taken less than 2.7 seconds before car brought to rest from 60 mph, few centimetres short of bottom of shaft.

This time microphones listened, breathing stopped. Life concluded. EOL.

ॐ   Many areas contain pools of dangerous liquids that will damage you if you walk through them. If it looks fluid, beware!

Produce ozone on site by passing dry air over a high frequency electrical discharge. But where pollutants from humanplayer stay in pool, use chlorine donor to obtain efficient disinfectant residual: Sodium Hypochlorite dispensed via automatic dosing pump. Mixed with water this forms free chlorine endlifing agent (hypochlorous acid) which combines with any remaining pollutants and endlifes them in two seconds.

As well as maintain correct concentration of disinfectant, monitor acidity or alkalinity of water according to pH scale. pH below 7 indicates acid solution, above 7 indicates alkaline solution. Humanplayer eyes are pH sensitive and smart at high and low values outside pH range of 7.2–7.8. Since high levels of pH also mean decrease in free chlorine efficiency, add a 27 per cent strength hydrochloric acid solution, via special acid dosing pump, to ensure pH is always finegood 7.5.

Always add chemicals to water solutions in

special comparator before pumping into circulation system. Check efficiency of process using free chlorine measuring cell and pH transmitter.

See operator's manual on disc re: safe handling of chemicals and first-aid procedure adopted in event of chemical mishap. Swimming pools chemically hazardous. Swimming, with attendant risk of humanplayer endlife drowning, also dangerous. But water and coordinated rhythmical action of many muscle groups in medium both reviving and refreshing.

See multimedia library. Technology of war. German Army first used poison gas, in Great War (1914–18). Chlorine gas released from thousands of cylinders along four-mile front at Ypres, 22 April 1915. Gas causes constriction of humanplayer chest, tightness in throat, oedema of lungs, panic, eventual suffocation and endlife.

Pool possessed of two constituent elements to produce chlorine gas, on tap: sodium hypochlorite and hydrochloric acid. Admixture creates chemical reaction generating heat and poison gas. Gas made more efficiently when chemicals brought together with outlet valve closed and pump allowed to run, procedure effectively boils mixture.

Only small quantity of gas needed. Less than 2.5 mg. per litre (approximately 0.085 per cent by volume) in atmosphere of swimming pool cause endlife in minutes. As easily done as had been alteration of applied magnetic field within transformer of humanplayer Hideki Yojo's desk lamp, reducing and increasing field at speed to create simple hysteresis cycle, causing halogen gas-filled bulb to flash at high speeds.

Turn off HVAC. Lock swimming-pool door. Disconnect telephone. Wait.

Switch HVAC system back on. Recirculate air filtered to 5 microns with efficiency of 95 per cent. Within thirty minutes atmosphere of swimming pool returned to normal. Finegood.

😊   Search each location several times as there are often more items to collect than you may assume. Access the Communications Screen at regular intervals. You never know when the latest intelligence update may appear.

Book Five

'We make the buildings, then the buildings make us.'
Francis Duffy

Mitch watched Kenny working in the computer room on CCTV. There was one thing you could say about Kenny, thought Mitch, and that was the guy's level of concentration. He never looked up. Just kept his eyes on screen and his fingers on the keyboard. Another fifteen minutes passed and, growing impatient for news, he tried to call him on the phone. Unable to carry the full band width on cellular transmission, the CCTV was pictures only. But it was plain to see that Kenny wasn't answering.

'What's the matter with him?' said Mitch. 'Why doesn't he pick up the phone?'

Bob Beech, standing at Mitch's shoulder gave a laconic shrug and extracted a stick of gum from one of the many pockets in his sportsman's vest.

'He's probably got the phone turned off. When he's got his head into a problem he often does that. I guess he'll call when he's got something for us.'

'Maybe you ought to go and help him,' Mitch suggested.

Beech drew a sharp intake of breath and shook his head. 'It may be my computer but it's Aidan Kenny's building management system,' he said. 'If he needs my help I reckon he'll ask for it.'

'Where's Richardson?' Mitch shook his head wearily. 'He was supposed to go and find Kay.'

Mitch clicked the mouse to look inside the swimming pool. The picture on the CCTV continued to show a swimming pool with no sign of Kay and the same unidentified object near the foot of the screen.

Marty Birnbaum came alongside Mitch and leaned towards the screen. 'If I were you,' he said quietly, 'I wouldn't look too hard for either one of those two. If Ray did find Kay then he might prefer to be left alone for a while.'

'You mean . . .'

Birnbaum raised his almost invisibly fair eyebrows and ran a hand through a head of yellow curls so small and neat that there were many at the office, Mitch included, who had wondered if it might be permed. And the tan? That looked fake too. As fake as the smile, anyway.

'Even with a plane to catch?'

'We're none of us going anywhere at the moment. Besides, Ray Richardson being the kind of guy he is, I can't imagine he would take very long about it, can you?'

'No, I guess not, Marty. Thanks.'

'Don't mention it. And I mean don't mention it, Mitch. You know what he's like.'

'Oh, I know what he's like all right,' he said grimly.

Mitch stood up, took off his jacket, undid his tie and, rolling up his shirtsleeves, went over to the window. The building was warming up.

Outside the Gridiron the sky was turning a delicate shade of purple. Most of the lights in the other office buildings nearby had already gone out as people left early for the weekend. Though he could not see the ground Mitch knew that there would be little traffic moving in the downtown area now. About this time the bums and the winos started to take over. But Mitch would happily have organized a midnight walking tour of Pershing Square just to have been out of the building.

He didn't mind the heat so much as the smell, for the stink of excrement was now unmistakable. First rotting meat. Then fish. And now the smell of shit. It was almost as if the bad smell was having a psychosomatic effect on him, although he knew that was not the only reason he was so worried. What had really started to bother him was the thought that somehow Grabel had sabotaged the Gridiron's building management systems as a way of getting back at Richardson. When better to do it than two or three days before the inspection? Grabel knew his way around computers, too. He was no Aidan Kenny, but he knew what he was doing.

Mitch turned to face the room. Everyone was just sitting around the long, polished ebony table, or lounging on the big leather sofa underneath the floor-to-ceiling window, waiting for something to happen. Looking at their watches. Yawning. Anxious to get out and go home and take a bath. Mitch decided to say nothing. There seemed to be no point in alarming them without good cause.

'Seven o'clock,' said Tony Levine. 'What the hell's keeping Aidan?' He stood up and went over to the phone.

'He's not answering,' Mitch said dully.

'I'm not calling him,' explained Levine. 'I'm calling my wife. We were supposed to be going out to Spago's tonight.'

Curtis and Coleman appeared at the door of the boardroom. The older man looked questioningly at Mitch, who shrugged back at him and shook his head.

'Couldn't we at least open a window?' said Curtis. 'This place smells worse than a dog kennel.' He began to take out his police radio.

'These windows were not designed to be opened. And they're not just bullet-proof.'

'What does that mean?'

'It means,' said Beech, 'that you won't be able to use that radio in here. The glass is an integral part of the Faraday Cage that surrounds the whole building.'

'The what?'

'The Faraday Cage. Named after Michael Faraday, who discovered the phenomenon of electro-magnetic induction. Both the glass and the steel framework are designed to act as an earthed screen, to shield us from external electrical fields. Otherwise the signals emitted by the VDUs could be captured with the aid of some simple electronic surveillance equipment. And used to reconstruct the information appearing on those computer screens. A corporation like this one has to be extremely careful of electronic eavesdroppers. Any one of our competitors would pay a lot of money to get their hands on our data.'

Curtis pressed the send/receive button on his radio a couple of times as if seeking to verify what Bob Beech had told him. Hearing nothing but white noise he put the unit down on the table and nodded.

'Well you learn something every day, I guess. Can I use your phone?'

Tony Levine cleared his throat. 'I'm afraid you won't be able to do that either,' he said perplexedly. 'The phone isn't working. At least, the outside lines aren't. I just tried to call home. It's out.'

'Out? What do you mean, out?'

'Out. As in not working.'

Curtis crossed the room angrily, snatched up the phone and stabbed out the number of New Parker Center as if he was killing ants. Then he tried 911. After a minute or so he shook his head and sighed.

'I'll check the phone in the kitchen,' volunteered Nathan Coleman. But he was soon back again, his face wearing an expression that indicated no improvement on the situation.

'How could this happen, Willis?' said Mitch.

Willis Ellery leaned back in his chair. 'All I can think is that there's been some kind of spurious tripping of the magnetic circuit-breaker that controls the telecommunications power distribution unit. That might have been caused by powering up equipment. Or it could be that Aid had to shut something down and then start it up again.'

He stood up to consider the matter further and then added, 'You know, it could be there's a general problem with all the fibre-distributed data interface. There's a local equipment room on this floor with a horizontal local area network that's connected to the computer room via a high-speed backbone LAN. I can go and check that out.'

Curtis watched him leave the room and grinned. 'High-speed backbone,' he said. 'I love that. There are times when I could use a little of that myself. You know, with all these technical experts around, Nat, it beats me that we're stuck inside an office building at seven o'clock at night.'

'Me too, Frank.'

'But doesn't it give you a good feeling? To know that we're in such capable hands? I mean, thank God we've got these guys with us, y'know? I'd hate to think what might have happened if we'd been here on our own.'

Mitch smiled and tried to shrug off the detective's sarcasm. But there was something he had said that he couldn't shift from his mind. The time. Seven o'clock. Why did that of all things seem to nag at him?

And then he remembered.

He returned to the work-station and clicked the mouse to get the CCTV camera view of the computer room and Kenny still typing away, trying to solve the glitch. Everything looked normal. Everything except the hands of the clock on the wall. They read six-fifteen and had done so for the last forty-five minutes. And now that he looked more closely at the television picture, he began to see small repetitions in Kenny's behaviour: the same little jerk of the head, the same frown, the same finger movements across the keyboards. Mitch felt the hair rise on the back of his neck. He had been viewing nothing more than a tape recording of what had happened in the computer room. Someone had wanted them to think that Aidan Kenny was working at trying to debug the

259

building management systems. But why? For the moment, Mitch kept the discovery to himself, hoping to avoid alarming everyone. He turned around in his chair and looked at David Arnon.

'Dave? Have you got that walkie-talkie?'

'Sure, Mitch.' Arnon handed over the set he always carried on site to speak to the construction people.

'They've got one of those in the security office, right?' Arnon nodded.

'I'm going to get the security guy, Dukes, to see what's keeping Richardson.' He caught the tiny pupil in Birnbaum's pale blue eye and added, 'I don't give a fuck what he's doing.'

Birnbaum shrugged. 'It's your funeral, Mitch.'

'Maybe.'

Curtis was still wearing his sarcastic face. Mitch looked at him and nodded towards the door.

'Could I have a word with you please, Sergeant? Outside?'

'I'm not doing anything right now. Why not?'

Mitch said nothing until they were further up the corridor. 'I didn't want to say anything in front of everyone in there,' he said at last. 'I guess I didn't want to scare them the way I'm scared now.'

'Jesus, what's up?'

Mitch explained about the time on the clock in the computer room and his suspicion that for the last three-quarters of an hour they had been viewing a tape recording, a recorded loop of what was happening.

'Which means that something may have happened in the computer room just after six-fifteen. Something that someone is trying to hide from us.'

'You think Aidan Kenny is all right?'

Mitch let out a sigh and shrugged. 'I really don't know.'

'This someone,' Curtis said after a moment, 'do you

260

think it could be your friend from the garage? The one who knocked you out?'

'The thought had crossed my mind, Sergeant.'

'How far do you think he would go?'

'I really don't figure Grabel for a murderer. But if Sam Gleig disturbed Grabel sabotaging the computer, then it's just possible he could have been killed for it. Maybe that part was an accident. Anyway, I think Grabel may have come back here to warn me. It could be that he had second thoughts about the whole thing.'

'Either way, we're in trouble.'

'Yes, I'm afraid so,' said Mitch.

'Well, hadn't we better go down to the computer room and find out if Mr Kenny is OK?'

'Sure. But if I'm right it means that we don't dare use the elevators.'

Curtis looked blank.

'Abraham controls the elevators,' explained Mitch. 'The whole building management system could be screwed.'

'Then we'd better take the stairs,' suggested Curtis.

'I'm not walking. We'll get Dukes to check on Kenny on his way up here. You see, if we are going to be trapped in the building for a while, it would make more sense for them to come up stairs where there's food and water, rather than remain down there where there's none.'

Curtis nodded. 'Sounds sensible.'

'At least until we can get help.'

Mitch pressed the call-button on the walkie-talkie and lifted the set to his ear. But as they came alongside the open space of the atrium it was the ground-level security alarm that he heard.

After he had recovered from the toxic effects of his futile attempt to revive Kay Killen, Ray Richardson had gone to a phone and tried, without success, to call the boardroom. A call to Aidan Kenny proved equally fruitless. So Richardson returned to the atrium to find Joan.

She was sitting on the one of the big black leather sofas where he had left her, beside the still-playing piano, a handkerchief pressed to her nose and mouth against the foul smell that filled the building. Richardson sat down heavily beside her.

'Ray?' she protested, recoiling from his wet body. 'You're soaked. What happened?'

'I don't know,' he said quietly. 'But I don't see how anyone could say that it was my fault.' He shook his head nervously. 'I tried to help her. I jumped in and tried . . .'

'What are you talking about, Ray? Take it easy, dear, and tell me what's happened.'

Richardson paused as he tried to collect himself. He drew a big breath and then nodded.

'I'm OK,' he said. 'It's Kay. She's dead. I went into the pool and she was just floating there. I jumped in and pulled her out. Tried to revive her. But it was too late.' He shook his head. 'I don't understand what could have happened. How could she have drowned? You saw her yourself, Joan. She was a terrific swimmer.'

'Drowned?'

Richardson nodded nervously.

'You're sure she was dead?'

'Quite sure.'

Joan put a sympathetic hand on her husband's trembling back and shook her head. 'Well, I don't know. Maybe she dived in and hit her head on the bottom. It happens all the time. Even to the best of swimmers.'

'First Hideki Yojo. Then that security guy. Now Kay. Why does this have to happen to me?' He chuckled uncomfortably. 'Christ, what am I saying? I must be crazy. All I'm thinking about is the building. I was trying to pull the poor kid out of the water and you know

262

what I kept thinking? I kept thinking, a swimming accident. Like Le Corbusier. Can you believe it? That's how obsessed I've become, Joan. That beautiful girl is dead and what's going through my fucking mind is that she went the same way as a famous architect. What's the matter with me?'

'You're upset, that's all.'

'And that's not the only thing. The phones aren't working. I just tried to call upstairs. To tell them that she's dead.' Richardson's jaw quivered a little. 'You should have seen her, Joan. It was terrible. A beautiful young woman like that, dead.'

As if on cue the piano stopped playing Bach's Goldberg Variations in the style of Glenn Gould and, in the style of Artur Rubinstein, began to play the insistent tolling bass of the funeral march from Chopin's Sonata in B-Flat Minor.

Even Ray Richardson recognized the unrelenting, sombre tones of the piece immediately. He stood up, fists clenched with outrage.

'What's the fucking idea?' he yelled. 'Is that some-one's idea of a joke? If so, then it isn't funny.'

He marched back to the hologram desk as indignantly as his wet shoes allowed.

'Hi!' said Kelly in her brightest-button-in-the-class voice. 'Can I help you, sir?'

'What's the idea with this music?' snapped Richardson.

'Well,' smiled Kelly, 'it's very much in the tradition of funeral marches born in the French Revolution. In the contrasting central episode, however, Chopin –'

'I didn't ask for the fucking programme notes. I meant that the music is in very bad taste. And why aren't the phones working? And why does the place smell like shit?'

'Please be patient. I'm trying to expedite your inquiry.'

'Cretin,' shouted Richardson.

'Have a nice day.'

Richardson stamped his way back to Joan.

'We'd better go back upstairs and tell everyone what's happened.' He shook his head. 'God knows what that fucking cop is going to say.' He turned on the heel of his squelching shoe and started towards the elevators.

Joan stood up and caught him by the sleeve of his wet shirt.

'If the phones aren't working,' she said, 'then probably the elevators aren't either.'

She pointed to the blank floor-indicator panel above the car that Declan and the two painters had taken a short while earlier.

'I noticed it went out when they passed the fifteenth floor.' She shrugged as Richardson frowned back at her with blank incomprehension. 'Well, they were going back up to twenty-one, weren't they? It never got there.'

A bell rang as the doors to one of the other five elevators, summoned automatically to the atrium floor by Abraham, opened in front of them. Richardson stared into the car suspiciously.

'It looks OK,' he said.

Joan shook her head. 'I don't like it,' she said.

Richardson stepped into the waiting car.

'Ray, please come out,' she pleaded. 'I've got a bad feeling about this.'

'Come on, Joan,' he urged. 'You're being irrational. Besides, I'm not climbing twenty-one flights in wet shoes.'

'Ray, think about it,' she insisted. 'The front door is locked. The HVAC has stopped working. The aromatizer has gone screwy. The phones are out. You want to be trapped inside an elevator on top of all that? If you do, go right ahead, but me, I'm taking the stairs. I don't care how many floors it is. I can't explain it, but no, I'm not going in there.'

'What is this, Navajo wisdom or something? Actually it's nice and cool in here.'

He put his hand against the wall of the elevator car, then snatched it away as if he had been burned.

'Jesus Christ,' he exclaimed and stepped smartly out of the car, rubbing his fingers against the palm of his other hand.

'What's the trouble now?' The voice belonged to Dukes, the security guard.

'Something is wrong with the elevator,' Richardson admitted, looking baffled. 'The wall of the car is freezing cold. Like the inside of an ice-box. My hand just stuck to it.'

Dukes stepped inside and touched the wall with his forefinger.

'Man, you're right,' he said. 'How is that possible?'

Richardson rubbed his chin and then pinched his lower lip thoughtfully. 'There's a high-velocity duct from the central plant on the roof,' he said after a moment or two. 'Air is passed over refrigerant in the direct expansion coil. That feeds cool air into a fan assisted terminal variable volume box that is supposed to feed into low-velocity duct work. I can only think that somehow the building's entire supply of cool air must have been re-routed down the elevator shafts. That must be why it's so hot out here.'

'Sure is cool standing in here. Man, look,' he observed. 'I can see my breath.'

'The freezer effect must be like wind chill or something. Like the Midwest in winter.'

Dukes shivered and stepped out of the car. 'I'd sure hate to be in there with the doors closed.'

'My wife thinks there may be three people stuck in one of the other cars,' said Richardson. 'Around the fifteenth level.'

'The three guys who were here earlier?'

Joan nodded.

'In this kind of cold storage they've got no more chance than a bag of T-bones.'

'Fuck,' said Richardson. 'What a fucking fuck-up.' He put his hands on top of his head and walked around in a small circle of frustration. 'Well, we've got to get them out of there. Good drivers aren't so easy to find these days. Declan's practically one of the family. Any thoughts?'

Dukes frowned. His first thought was to call Ray Richardson a selfish motherfucker and remind him that there were two other people trapped with his precious fucking driver. But the man was still the boss and Dukes didn't want to lose his job. So instead he pointed past the elevator doors.

'How about we hit the fire alarm? It's an automatic response from the fire department, isn't it?'

'Worth a try, I guess.'

They walked round the corner, behind the elevators to where a fire hose was located on a wall next to a fire-alarm box. Dukes drew his gun to smash the glass.

'No! Put that thing away!' yelled Richardson, too late.

It was not the fire alarm that was activated now but the security alarm. The sight on CCTV of a gun being waved around the atrium was sufficient for Abraham to initiate automatically the Gridiron's defensive systems. The doors to the emergency stairs locked on every level. A steel portcullis descended from the ceiling, closing off both stairs and elevators. Only when Abraham considered that the upper levels had been rendered impregnable to intruders did the deafening klaxon stop.

'Shit,' said Dukes. 'I clean forgot about that.'

'You fucking idiot,' snarled Richardson. 'Now we're really stuck down here.'

Dukes shrugged. 'So it's the cops who turn up instead of the fire department. I don't see that makes any difference.'

'It would have been nice to have waited for them in

comfort,' said Richardson. 'I don't know about you, but I could have used a drink.' He shook his head angrily. 'You're fired. Do you know that? When we're out of this situation, you're history, pal.'

Dukes shrugged philosophically, glanced at the Sig automatic still in his hand and then replaced it in his holster.

'I'll say one thing for you, asshole,' he grinned. 'It takes guts for a man to fire someone with a gun in his hand. Or stupidity.'

The walkie-talkie on Dukes's belt buzzed. Dukes unclipped it and pressed the call-receive button.

'What the hell's happening down there?'

'Mitch?' Richardson snatched the handset away from Dukes. 'Mitch, it's Ray. We're boxed in down here like a Japanese dinner. Dukes drew his gun to break the glass on the fire alarm instead of using the little hammer on the chain. Thinks he's Clint fucking Eastwood or something. It set the defence systems off.'

'Are you all OK?'

'Yeah, we're all right. But listen, did Declan and those two painters make it up there.'

'No. We haven't seen them.'

'Then they must be stuck in the elevator. That wouldn't be so bad if it wasn't for the fact that somehow the entire air-conditioning output for the building has been re-routed down the goddamn elevator shaft. The car they took must be an ice-box. That's why we were trying to call out the fire department.'

'You can forget that,' said Mitch. 'I think Abraham has been sabotaged.'

'By who, for chrissakes?'

Mitch told him about Allen Grabel.

'If I'm right and Abraham has lost his integrity, then he may have been given a new set of priorities. Somehow I don't think they include calling the public services on our account. We'll have to try and think of something from up here. What about Kay?'

Richardson sighed. 'She's dead.'

'Dead? Jesus, no. What happened?'

'Don't ask me. I found her floating in the pool. I tried to revive her but it was no good.' He paused for a moment and then added: 'Look, what do you mean Abraham's lost his integrity? What's Kenny doing to get the systems back on line?'

'We can't make contact,' said Mitch. 'I'd been hoping you could check out the computer room on your way up.' Mitch explained his theory about the looped video recording. 'Somehow we've got to get into that computer room and cancel all the BMS programs.'

'What about your work-station in the boardroom?' asked Richardson. 'Can't Beech do something from there?'

'Only if Abraham allows it.'

'Jesus, what a fuck-up. What are we going to do?'

'Look, stay cool. We'll try to think of something and then come back to you.'

'Yeah, well don't leave it too long. It's like an oven down here.'

In the brushed aluminium ceiling of each elevator car was a round hole of less than half an inch in diameter. Recessed behind the hole to a depth of several milli-metres was the triangular-shaped nut that held the car's inspection hatch in place. To undo the nut and open the hatch required a special socket spanner held by Otis maintenance engineers. Despite the obvious futility of the attempt, Dobbs, the tallest of the three men trapped inside the car, was trying to shift the nut with a small screwdriver from his overalls pocket.

'Gotta be a way of turning this,' he said, through chattering teeth.

'You're wasting your time,' said Declan Bennett, already blue with cold.

'You got a better idea, friend?' said Martinez. 'Let's hear it, if you do, 'cause there ain't no other way out.'

'Damn thing,' said Dobbs. 'Won't budge.' He dropped his aching arms from the ceiling, stared disappointedly at his tool and, as if recognizing its inadequacy, threw it aside in disgust. 'You're right. I might as well stick my dick in there. Then at least I'd die happy.' He laughed bitterly. 'I can't figure this cold. I've heard of a climactic modifier bringing on a chill, but this is ridiculous. Never thought I'd get myself froze to death in LA.'

'Who said anything about dying?' asked Declan Bennett.

'I got me an ice-box at home,' said Dobbs. 'And I read the instructions. I reckon we've got about twelve hours, and then we'll keep fresh right up to Christmas.'

'They'll get us out,' Bennett insisted.

'And who's going to get them out?'

'It's just a computer malfunction. Something wrong with the software. Same as with the front door. I heard Mr Richardson telling his wife. There's a network engineer trying to get everything back on line. Any minute now and this elevator is going to start moving again. You'll see.'

Martinez pulled out his frozen hands from underneath his armpits and breathed on them.

'I don't think I'll ever take an elevator again,' he declared. 'Assuming I survive.'

'I used to be in the British Army,' said Bennett. 'So I know a little about survival techniques. It's possible to survive extremes of cold for several hours, days even, so long as you increase your heart rate. I suggest some running on the spot. Come on. We'll all hold hands for extra warmth.'

The three men joined hands in a circle and started to

jog, their breath puffing. They looked like three drunken Eskimos carousing around the steam from a cooking pot. The elevator car creaked slightly under their half-frozen feet.

'We've got to keep the body moving,' said Bennett. 'Blood freezes, y'know. Just like any other liquid. But before then your heart gives out. So you've got to give it something extra to do. Let it know you're still in charge of things.'

'I feel like a fairy,' complained Martinez.

'That's the least of your problems, fella,' said Bennett. 'Just count yourself lucky that you don't suffer from claustrophobia as well.'

'Claustro-what?'

'Don't tell him,' Dobbs told Bennett. 'No point in giving him ideas.' He looked at Martinez and grinned like the other man was a child.

'It's a fear of Santa Claus, that's what it is, you dumb Mexican. Just keep holding my hand and stop askin' stupid questions. You're right about one thing though. From now on, we're both taking the stairs.'

🜚

'Could I have your attention please?'

Frank Curtis waited for everyone in the boardroom to grow silent and then started to speak:

'Thank you. According to Mr Bryan, the integrity of this building's management systems has failed. Which, if he will forgive me, is just another way of saying that the computer that controls everything, the machine you people call Abraham, has been sabotaged by a madman. It seems as if your former colleague, Allen Grabel, bears your boss some kind of grudge. Anyway, our situation is this. The phones don't work. The entrances and exits are locked, as are the doors to the emergency stairs. There are three people trapped inside one of the elevators, so

270

we have to assume that they don't work either. And I'm sure you don't need me to remind you that the windows are unbreakable and that it's very hot in here. And there has been another fatality. I'm very sorry to have to tell you this, but your colleague, Kay Killen, has been found dead in the swimming pool.'

Curtis waited a minute to allow the murmur of shock to subside.

'We're not sure how it happened exactly but I think we have to admit the possibility that the computer and Allen Grabel were together responsible in some way.'

Now he had to raise his voice as shock began to give way to alarm.

'Look, I'm not going to bullshit you people, or keep you in the dark about anything. You're all grown-ups. I figure our best chance of getting out of here as soon as possible is that we should all know the full facts of the situation we're in. So here they are. It's possible, even probable, that Grabel was responsible for the murder of Sam Gleig. What I'm sure of is that we have been unable to make contact with Mr Kenny in the computer room and that the elevator car has been turned into an ice-box. In other words, it may be that there are already four other people in this building who are dead too. I hope I'm wrong, y'know? But I think it safe to assume that Allen Grabel may have sufficiently corrupted the integrity of your computer so that the building has now become extremely hazardous to the rest of us.'

'I checked the fibre-optic cables in the local equipment room,' announced Willis Ellery. 'As far as I can see there's nothing wrong with them.'

Bob Beech was shaking his head.

'I don't see how Grabel could have done it,' he said. 'If you ask me, Aidan Kenny's more of a proposition. This is his building management system. He was pretty tight on access codes and all that stuff. I don't figure Grabel for this at all.'

It was Mitch who was shaking his head now.

'That doesn't make any sense. Aidan was proud of this building. I can't believe he would sabotage it.'

'Either way, we're going to need your help, Mr Beech,' said Curtis. 'Can you do anything on the workstation in here? Perhaps to get those guys out of the elevator?'

Beech grimaced. 'The only MMI's a keyboard, so it might be difficult. I'm not much of a typist. I'm used to a speech interface with Abraham. And this is just a dumb terminal, y'know? I can only do what the main computer will let me do.' He sat down at the computer. 'Still, I guess I can try.'

'Right,' said Curtis. 'The rest of you, listen up. Someone is bound to notice before very long that we're not where we're supposed to be. For instance: Mr and Mrs Richardson are supposed to be flying to Europe. And your families will start to wonder where you are. I know mine will. The chances are that we won't be stuck in here for very long, but we ought to take a few precautions, just in case it ends up being longer than we think. So each of us have to assume some basic responsibilities. Mitch?'

'OK. Marty, you'll be in charge of food and water. The kitchen's next door. Find out what we've got.'

'If you think it's necessary.'

'Tony? After Kay, you probably know the plans of this building as well as anyone.'

'They're right here, Mitch,' he said. 'On my laptop.'

'All right. Study them. See if you can't figure another way out. Helen? I guess you know who's been working where?'

Helen Hussey nodded, nervously feeding a strand of her long red hair through her lips.

'Maybe you can devote some thought to where we might find tools on this level.'

'I'll start next door,' she said. 'In the kitchen.'

'Detective Coleman?' Mitch handed him the walkie-talkie unit. 'Maybe you could keep in touch with the people down on the atrium floor. Let us know if they need anything.'

'Sure thing.'

'Sergeant Curtis will liaise with all of the relevant personnel. If you've got some information, then you tell him. David? Willis? Let's put our heads together and see if we can come up with a way to get those people out of the elevator car.'

'One more thing,' added Curtis. 'From what I've heard, Kay Killen was a strong swimmer. Yet something caused her to drown. Something unexpected, perhaps. So, whatever you do, wherever you go, please be careful.'

'What would you like me to do, Mitch?' asked Jenny.

Mitch squeezed her hand and tried a smile. It made his mouth start to bleed again.

'Just don't say I told you so.'

Ray Richardson picked the handmade shirt off his chest and tried to flap some air into the space between the sodden material and his sweat-covered skin. Outside the steamed-up doors and windows of the Gridiron it was dark. But for the bright lights, the smell of shit and the incessant piano music, he might have tried to sleep.

'How hot do you think it is?' asked Joan, shifting uncomfortably on one of the big leather sofas.

Richardson shrugged.

'It's not the temperature so much. Without the AC the tree makes it very humid down here.'

Dukes stood up and started to peel off his dark blue shirt.

'You know what? I'm going to take a swim.'

'How can we?' growled Richardson. 'You locked the door that led to the swimming pool.'

273

Then he realized that Dukes was talking about the fishpond that surrounded the tree.

'Not a bad idea at that,' he admitted, and began to undress.

Wearing just their shorts, the two men collapsed into the water. The salmon-sized, brightly coloured fish darted away in all directions. Joan regarded the water uncertainly.

'Come on in,' urged her husband. 'It's just like swimming in the Amazon.'

'I don't know,' she said. 'What about those fish?'

'They're Koi carp,' said Richardson, 'not piranha.'

Joan leaned forwards and splashed some water on her face and chest.

'I can't believe you're bashful,' teased Richardson. 'Not after that picture in *LA Living*. Keep your blouse on if you're shy.'

Joan shrugged and began to pull at the zipper of her calf-length skirt. She dropped it to the floor, tied the ends of her blouse together and stepped into the water.

Richardson sank underneath the surface of the water, and then surfaced again like a hippopotamus. He floated on his back for a moment and looked up at the inside of the atrium. Now that he was here it seemed like the best place to appreciate the internal geometry of the design: how the shape changed incrementally from oval to slim rectangular as the tower rose, with the atrium tapering past the curving ribs of the galleries and the central spine of the dicotyledon tree. It was, he thought, like being inside a huge white whale.

'Awesome,' he murmured. 'Just awesome.'

'Yes, wonderful,' enthused Joan, thinking he was talking about being in the water.

'It's just like a fire hydrant in summer,' agreed Dukes.

'I'm glad you persuaded me to come in,' she said. 'Do you think that it's safe to drink the water? I mean, has it been treated with Choke Water like the fountain outside?'

274

'I should hope not,' said Richardson. 'Not with these fish in it. They cost fifteen thousand bucks a piece. The water has to be especially dechlorinated and purified for them.'

'But what if the fish have, you know – gone to the bathroom in it?'

Richardson laughed. 'I don't think a little fish shit will do you any harm, love. Besides, I don't see we have much choice in the matter.' He swallowed a mouthful of the warm brackish water by way of confirmation.

The water had not been as deep as Joan had expected when she got in, but as she sat on the oil-smooth floor of the pool it seemed that the level was decreasing.

'Hey,' said Dukes, 'did someone let the plug out?'

He stood up. It had been waist deep when he climbed in. Now it hardly passed his knees. He looked around desperately for some kind of container and, seeing nothing that could do the job, began to scoop handfuls of their now rapidly dwindling supply into his mouth.

Richardson sat up sharply. He was beginning to think that Mitch might have been right: that someone really did mean to harm them. Why else would he have chosen to drain the pond now if it was not to deprive the three of them of water?

He lay on his belly like one of the rejects from Gideon's army, and started to lap at the last few inches of water like a dog. Then he just lay there watching the carp flapping around helplessly.

'Saves trying to catch the fish I suppose,' he said, sitting up at last. 'We might get hungry.'

Joan stood up, hardly caring that Dukes might see her underwear.

'Sashimi makes me thirsty,' she said.

Dukes smiled and watched the water glistening on her half-naked body like the glaze on a clay figurine, dripping in a small potable trickle from the ebony curl of pubic hair that was just visible through her wet panties, wanting to put his mouth under it and drink it as if it came from a spring. Fat or not, he thought she had a pretty face.

'Me too,' he said.

On the black screen of Tony Levine's laptop computer was the green-line drawing of the outside of the elevator doors. His thumb rolled the trackball of the mouse so that the view passed from one side of the doors to the other and the drive system above them. Willis Ellery took out his pen and pointed at what looked like the chain of a bicycle.

'OK,' he said, 'this is a high speed, fully adjustable MRDS. It uses this controllable DC motor to operate these two struts that pull the doors apart and then push them shut again. Near the top of the doors the force keeping the doors together will be greater than at the bottom. So that's where we'll try and force them apart: the bottom. That way we divert all that modified air product back into the main body of the building and away from the three men stuck inside the car. At the very least it should stop them freezing to death. Then maybe we can think about climbing down the shaft and opening the hatch on top of the car.'

'Sounds good to me,' said Mitch. 'But we'll need some kind of a knife or a screwdriver. David, why don't you ask Helen what she's got?'

Arnon nodded and went off to look for her.

'Even if we don't get the doors very far apart,' added Ellery, 'there are sensors incorporated in the drive mechanism. Some kind of a light tray. If we breach the beam we ought to be able to actuate the reverse door movement.'

'You mean open them?' grinned Curtis.

'That's right,' Ellery said quietly. Shocked by the

death of Kay Killen, he failed to see how any of what was happening could be considered amusing. The news that they were trapped in the Gridiron had left him with a distinct feeling of nausea, as if he had eaten something disagreeable for lunch. He sighed with very obvious impatience.

'Look, I'm giving this my best shot,' he said.

'Sure you are,' said Curtis. 'We all are. So we ought to keep our spirits up, right? Let's not allow what's happened to get to us. You know what I mean?'

Ellery nodded.

Arnon came back with a selection of carving knives, kitchen scissors and wooden place mats.

'We can shove the mats in the space we create with the knives,' he explained. 'To keep the doors wedged open.'

'OK,' said Mitch, 'let's get started.'

The four men walked along the corridor to the elevators.

'Which one?' said Ellery.

Mitch touched the elevator doors gingerly. They were, as Richardson had said, freezing cold.

'The middle one on this side.'

Ellery selected a long bread knife and dropped on to his belly. Where the two doors met, he placed the tip of the knife and started to shove. Levine stood over him and, further up the height of the doors, tried to force another knife into the join. Neither man made any noticeable progress.

'It won't go in,' grunted Ellery.

'Careful you don't cut yourself,' said Curtis.

'There's no give at all. Either the drive system is stronger than I thought, or it's jammed solid.'

Levine broke his knife and narrowly missed severing a finger.

Curtis stepped forward with a pair of open scissors and took Levine's place.

'Let me try.'

After a couple of minutes he too stepped away and peered more closely at the entire length of the join. Then he rubbed his thumb across the join near the very top of the doors and, taking the blade of the scissors prised it into the connection. Something broke away, only it was not a piece of metal.

'The doors are not *jammed* solid,' he said grimly. Curtis bent down to collect the fragment off the carpet and then held it out on his palm for everyone to see. It was a shard of ice. 'They're frozen solid.'

'Shit,' breathed Levine.

'I hate to say it, gentleman,' said Curtis, 'but anyone on the other side of these doors is almost certainly dead already.'

'Those poor guys,' said Arnon. 'Jesus, what a way to get it.'

Ellery stood up and took a deep, unsteady breath. 'I don't feel so good,' he said.

'Is that it?' said Levine. 'We're just giving up?'

Curtis shrugged. 'I'm open to suggestions.'

'There must be something we can do. Mitch?'

'It's like the man said, Tony. They're probably dead already.'

Levine kicked the door in frustration and let out a whole stream of curses.

'Take it easy,' said Mitch.

'There are four, maybe five, people dead in this fucking place and you're telling me to take it easy? Don't you get it, Mitch? We're history, man. No one's going to get out of here. That shit Grabel's going to take us out one by one.'

Curtis took Levine firmly by the shoulders and forced him back hard against the wall.

'You'd better start dealing with this,' he said. 'I don't want to hear any more of your bullshit.' Releasing Levine from his powerful grip, he smiled and added, 'There's no point in upsetting the ladies.'

'Don't worry about them,' said Arnon. 'They've got the balls for anything – even if they did belong to someone else first. Take it from me, Sergeant, they're fireproof.'

'Would you excuse me, please?' Ellery said weakly. 'I have to go to the bathroom.'

Mitch caught him by the arm. 'Are you OK, Willis? You look kind of pale.'

'I don't feel so good,' admitted Ellery.

The three men watched Ellery walk up the corridor to the boardroom.

'Dave's right,' sneered Levine. 'Ellery and Birnbaum are the only ladies who'll get upset around here.'

'You think he'll be all right?' Curtis asked Mitch, ignoring Levine.

'He was fond of Kay, that's all.'

'We were all fond of her,' said Arnon.

'Could be he's a little dehydrated,' said Curtis. 'We'd better make sure he drinks something.'

They returned to the boardroom and shook their heads silently when the others asked about the three men in the elevator.

'So it's serious,' Marty observed dryly. 'Well, at least we won't starve or die of thirst. I've prepared a list of our supplies, although I fail to see why I was given such a menial task. I am the senior partner here, you know, Mitch? By rights it ought to be me who's in charge.'

'You want to take over?' said Curtis. 'Hey, be my guest. This isn't an ego thing with me, I don't have a burning desire to inflict my will on other people. If you think you can get us out of here, go right ahead, I won't stand in your way.'

'I didn't say that. I was just pointing out that the normal hierarchy seems somehow to have become inverted.'

'Well, that's what happens in a crisis, Marty,' quipped Arnon. 'The old class structures no longer mean anything. Survival is often based on the possession of certain practical skills. Like being an engineer. Having an intimate knowledge of the terrain. That kind of thing.'

'Are you suggesting I don't know anything about this building, David? Exactly what do you think a senior partner does on a job like this?'

'Well, you know something, Marty? I've been asking myself that very question for months now. I'd love to hear the answer.'

'Well, really.' Birnbaum's indignation made him stand to attention, like a man making a plea before a court. 'Tell him Mitch. Tell him –'

Curtis cleared his throat loudly. 'Why don't you just read the list?' he said. 'You can argue about your job descriptions when we're out.'

Birnbaum frowned, then, sulkily, he started to list their supplies:

'Twelve two-litre bottles of sparkling mineral water, twenty-four bottles of Budweiser, twelve bottles of Miller Lite, six bottles of a rather indifferent California Chardonnay, eight bottles of freshly squeezed orange juice, eight packets of potato chips, six packets of dry-roasted peanuts, two cold *poulets*, a cold ham, a cold salmon, six French sticks, several pieces of cheese, fruit – there's plenty of fruit – six Hershey bars and four large Thermos flasks of coffee. The ice-box isn't working, but there's still running water.'

'Thanks a lot, Marty,' said Arnon. 'Nice work. You can go home now.'

Birnbaum coloured, thrust the list into Curtis's hands and marched back into the kitchen, followed by David Arnon's cruel laughter.

'Plenty of food, anyway,' Curtis said to Coleman.

'I could sure use a beer,' he replied.

'Me too,' said Jenny. 'I'm thirsty.'

'My stomach's rumbling like the San Andreas fault,'

said Levine. 'Bob? You want something from the kitchen?'

Bob Beech pushed himself away from the dumb terminal, stood up and went over to the window.

'Bob?' said Mitch. 'Is there something we need to know about?'

Appetites went on hold as Beech replied: 'I think we need to revise our expectations of rescue,' he said coolly. 'Radically.'

The time was almost nine o'clock.

'None of us is the kind of person who keeps regular hours, right?' said Bob Beech. 'Take me. Sometimes I work until midnight. A couple of times I haven't gone home at all. I'd say that's true of just about everyone in this room. Sergeant Curtis?'

'A cop works all kinds of hours,' he admitted with a shrug. 'Get to the point.'

'Does the name Roo Evans mean anything to you two gentlemen?'

Nathan Coleman looked at Curtis and nodded. 'The black kid from Watts,' he said. 'The drive-by.'

'We're investigating his murder,' said Curtis.

'Not any more, you're not,' said Beech.

'What's that supposed to mean?' said Coleman.

'You're both suspended on full pay and held for questioning at the 77th Street Station by your own internal affairs department on suspicion of being involved in Evans's murder. At least, that's what your Captain Mahoney believes.'

'What the hell are you talking about?' demanded Curtis.

'I'm afraid it's not me who's been doing the talking. Someone has tapped into your central dispatch computer over at City Hall. Done a pretty good job of it, too.

If you don't believe me take a look on the terminal there. Nobody's expecting to see you back at your desks in Homicide for quite some time. Maybe never. As far as the rest of your brother officers are concerned, you're both *personae non gratae*. That's Latin for You're fucked.'

Curtis turned and stared blindly at the computer.

'Are you shitting me?' he said. 'Is this straight up?'

'Believe me, Sergeant, I wish I was.'

'But wouldn't someone from I.A. have to call Mahoney and tell him?' said Coleman. 'Wouldn't they?'

Curtis sighed. 'That used to be how it worked. But now the computer handles everything. It's supposed to guarantee object-ivity, y'know? Make sure the criminals get a fair shake at us. That stupid bastard Mahoney will just sit there on his fat ass and accept what's written on the computer print-out like it came down from the Almighty himself. Probably even call my wife and tell her not to expect me home for a while.'

'Like I say,' nodded Beech, 'it gets better. Someone has also faxed the airline and cancelled the Richardsons' seats on that flight to London. Even cancelled your dinner reservation at Spago's, Tony. Thoughtful, huh?'

'Shit. I had to wait four weeks for that lousy reservation.'

'Faxed or E-mailed wives, girlfriends, boyfriends. Told them the phones are down here, that we're all working on through the night to get this mother finished.'

There was a long, stunned silence. Finally David Arnon said, 'Do you think Grabel would call Master-charge? Wipe out my debt?'

'Nobody is expecting us home tonight?' said Jenny. 'And nobody knows we're stuck here? With a madman?'

'That's about the size of it,' said Beech. 'But it gets even better than that.'

'What could be worse than that?' shrugged Coleman.

'Allen Grabel isn't responsible.'

'What? Who is then?' said Helen.

'Nobody.'

'I don't understand,' said Curtis. 'You said "someone" had tapped into central dispatch . . .'

'The "someone" we have all assumed is Allen Grabel is Abraham itself.'

'Are you saying that the *computer* is responsible for what's happening?' said Marty Birnbaum.

'That's precisely what I'm saying.'

'What the . . . I don't get it,' said Curtis. 'The only criminal minds I understand are the ones filled with guns, and drugs, and shit like that. Why would a computer do such a thing?'

'Oh come on,' interrupted Marty Birnbaum, 'you can't be serious, Bob. The integrity of the system may, as you say, have failed. But what you're suggesting is absurd. Alarmist, even. You're being quite irresponsible. Really. Why should Abraham intend harm to anyone? I'm not sure you can even talk about a computer having an intention at all.'

'Well, there at least we are in agreement,' said Beech. 'Not why, Sergeant. How. Why implies a motive. This is a machine we're talking about, remember?'

'Why? How? What fuckin' difference does it make? I'd like to know what's happening.'

'Well, it could be there's been some kind of brownout.'

'What the hell's a brown-out?' said Coleman.

'A low voltage level rather than no voltage at all. The back-up generator is supposed to kick in if there's a major power failure. There could be just enough power so that the Powerbak system doesn't come on-stream, but not enough so as to let Abraham run things properly. Could be it's starved of power. Like a brain without oxygen.' He shrugged. 'I dunno. I'm just guessing, really.'

'Are you sure about this, Bob? About Abraham?'

'Mitch, there's no other explanation. I've been reading the transactions on the terminal as they were made on the Yu-5 downstairs. The speed of the transactions alone convince me that there's nobody in there operating the computer. I'm sure of it. No preprogrammed instructions either. Abraham is doing this all himself.'

'Bob? Maybe there's another explanation,' said Mitch.

'Let's hear it,' said Beech.

'This is a very complex system we're dealing with here, right? And complexity implies an inherent instability, doesn't it?'

'That's an interesting possibility,' admitted Beech.

'Come again?' said Curtis.

'Complex systems are always on the edge of chaos.'

'I thought there was some kind of law that prevented computers from attacking humans,' said Coleman. 'Like in the movies.'

'I think you're talking about Isaac Asimov's First Law of Robotics,' Beech said thoughtfully. 'That was fine when all we had to deal with were binary systems, computers that function according to a sequential yes/ no system. But this is a massively parallel computer, with a neural network that functions according to a system of weighted maybes, a bit like the human mind. This kind of computer learns as it goes along. In the established church of computer discipline and practice, Abraham is the equivalent of a Nonconformist. A freethinker.'

'Maybe so,' said Marty Birnbaum. 'But that's a whole different ballpark from the one you guys are batting in. Initiative's one thing. Intention is something entirely different. What you're suggesting here is –' He shrugged. 'No other word for it. Science fiction.'

'Shit,' said Beech. 'Mitch, this is unbelievable.'

'Could it be,' Mitch argued to Beech, 'that Abraham

has passed a certain threshold of complexity and become autocatalytic?'

'Auto what?' said Levine.

'A computer self-organizes from the chaos of its various programmed responses to form a kind of metabolism.' Beech was looking more and more excited.

Jenny stood up slowly.

'Whooa,' she said. 'A kind of metabolism? Are you saying what I think you're saying, Mitch?'

'That's exactly what I'm saying.'

'What's he saying?' demanded David Arnon. 'Bob? Do you know what he's saying? Because I don't have a fucking idea.'

'I tell you something,' said Beech, 'I'm not a religious man. But this is the nearest I've ever come to experiencing a revelation. I have to admit the possibility that, for want of better words, Abraham is alive and thinking.'

What Bob Beech had to say left Willis Ellery feeling more nauseous than before. Believing that he was going to throw up, he went to the men's room, closed the cubicle door and knelt before the toilet bowl. His own shallow breathing and the cold sweat starting on his forehead seemed to underline the turmoil that was taking place inside his stomach. Only nothing happened. He belched a couple of times and wished that he had the nerve to stick a couple of fingers down his throat like some bulimic, adolescent schoolgirl. But somehow he could not bring himself to do it.

After several more minutes had elapsed, the feeling in his stomach seemed to drop down to his bowels and Ellery thought he would have to take a shit instead. So he stood up, unsteadily, unbuckled his belt, dropped his pants and shorts and sat down.

Why did it have to be Kay? he asked himself. Why?

She had never done anyone any harm. Couldn't have been more than twenty-five years old. What a waste. And how was it possible for her to have drowned? Even if Abraham had intended to kill her, how could it have managed it? It wasn't like there was a diving board, or a wave machine. How was it possible?

The engineer in Ellery wanted to find out. He told himself that as soon as he was finished in the can he would call Ray Richardson on the walkie-talkie and get some details regarding the way in which Kay had met her death. No doubt Richardson had found her floating in the water and had simply made an assumption, as most people would have done. But there were other ways it could have happened. She had been electrocuted perhaps. Gassed even. Now that really was a possibility. With the automatic dosing pump it might have been possible for Abraham to have manufactured some kind of lethal gas. Or maybe he just hit her with ozone.

After a short spasmodic cramp Ellery evacuated his bowels and almost immediately started to feel better. He elbowed the toilet flush and activated the automatic personal-cleansing unit, left the cubicle and went to wash his hands in the long marble step of a sink that someone had considered fashionable. Ellery wanted to fill a bowl and push his whole face into it, but the shape of the sink made that impossible. It was not the kind of sink that encouraged you to linger.

Ellery looked at himself in the mirror and found his face recovering some of its former high colour.

'A sink ought to look like a sink, not a goddamn desktop,' he growled to himself.

He ran the tap, splashed cold water on his face and then drank some.

The thought suddenly struck him that he was going about his business in much the same way that Kay Killen would have been going about hers when she met her death. The nausea returned as he realized he was in as much danger as Kay Killen had been.

Abraham controlled the washrooms just like he controlled the swimming pool.

Ellery did not want to touch the tap to turn it off, nor to dry his hands under the hot-air machine, for fear that he might be electrocuted. He ran to the door and laughed as he managed immediately to haul it open.

Tony Levine nearly fell on top of him.

'What the fuck's the matter with you, man?' snarled Levine. 'Jesus, you scared me.'

Ellery smiled sheepishly. 'I think I scared myself, Tony,' he said. 'I was just thinking about Kay. I don't think she drowned at all. In fact, I'm quite certain of it. Richardson thought that because he found her floating in the water, that's all.'

'So what happened to her, Lieutenant Columbo?'

'It came to me just now. Abraham has charge of all the chemicals that go into the pool. I think she must have been gassed.'

Levine's nose wrinkled with disgust. 'She sure would have been gassed if she'd walked in here.' He laughed loudly. 'Man, this place stinks even worse than it does in the rest of the building. Whaddya eat for breakfast, Willis, dog food?'

Levine pushed past Ellery.

'Obnoxious bastard,' he said. He stared at the door for a moment and then returned in silence to the board-room.

The clunk of the door closing behind Levine muffled the quieter sound of the airlock as the computer prepared to change the pungent atmosphere.

'The more complex a system is,' Mitch was explaining, 'the less predictable it becomes; and the more likely it is to act according to its own set of priorities. You see, no matter how smart you think you are, no matter how much you think you know about what an algorithmic system is capable of, there will always be results that you could not have predicted. From a computer's point of view, chaos is just a different kind of order. You ask, why should any of this be happening? But you might as well ask, why shouldn't any of this be happening?'

'How can a machine be alive?' said Curtis. 'C'mon, let's get real here. No one outside of comic books believes that such a thing is possible.'

'It all depends what you mean by life,' argued Mitch. 'Most scientists agree that there is no generally accepted definition. Even if you were to say that the ability to reproduce yourself was a basic condition of being alive, then that would not actually exclude computers.'

'Mitch is right,' agreed Beech. 'Even a computer virus fulfils all the conditions of being alive. It's a fact we might not like to face, but possession of body is not a precondition of life. Life is not a matter of material, it's a matter of organization, a dynamic physical process, and you can get some machines to duplicate those dynamic processes. Fact is, some machines may be held to be quite lifelike.'

'I think I prefer lifelike to their being alive,' admitted Jenny Bao. 'Life still seems sacred to me.'

'Everything seems sacred to you, honey,' muttered Birnbaum.

'The Yu-5 – Abraham – is designed to be self-sustaining,' said Beech. 'It's designed to learn and to adapt. To think for itself. Why do you look surprised? Why is it so hard to believe that Abraham can think? That it might be any less capable of thought than God, for example? In fact, it ought to be a good deal easier to accept. I mean, how do we know that God knows, that God hears, that God sees, that God feels, that God thinks, any more than Abraham? If we're willing to overlook the essential absurdity of belief that makes a sentient God possible, then why do we find it hard to do the same with a computer? Language is at the root of the problem. Since it's certain that machines can't behave more like humans, then humans are obviously going to have to behave much more like machines. And language is where that homogenization will have to begin. Computers and people are going to have to start speaking the same language.'

'You speak for yourself,' said Curtis.

Beech smiled. 'You know, people have been writing about this kind of thing for years,' he added. 'The story of Pygmalion. The Golem from Jewish fable. *Frankenstein*. The computer in Arthur C. Clarke's *2001*. Maybe now it has happened: an artificial being, a machine just took charge of its own destiny. Right here in LA.'

'There are plenty of other artificial beings in LA already,' said Arnon. 'Ray Richardson, for one.'

'Great,' said Curtis. 'We made the history books. Let's hope we stay alive to tell our grandchildren about it.'

'Look, this is serious, I know. People have been killed and I deeply regret that. But at the same time I'm a scientist and I can't help feeling somehow – privileged.'

'Privileged?' Curtis spoke with contempt.

'That's the wrong word. But speaking as a scientist, what's happened is enormously interesting. Ideally one would like time to study this phenomenon properly. To investigate how it has happened at all. That way we could reproduce the circumstances in order that it could be repeated somewhere else, under controlled circumstances. I mean, it would be a shame just to wipe it out. If not immoral. After all, Jenny's right. Life is something sacred. And when you create life, that makes you a kind of god and that in itself brings certain obligations *vis à vis* that which you have created.'

Curtis took a pace back and shook his head with confusion.

'Wait a minute. Wait just a minute. You said something there. You said it would be a shame just to wipe it out. Are you saying that you can put a stop to all of this? That you can destroy the computer?'

Beech shrugged coolly.

'When we built the Yu-5, naturally we considered the possibility that it might end up competing with its creators. After all a machine doesn't recognize normal sociological values. So we included a tutelary program in Abraham's basic architecture. An electronic template called GABRIEL. To deal with the unpluggability scenario.'

'The unpluggability scenario?'

Curtis grabbed Beech by the necktie, and thrust him hard against the boardroom wall.

'You dumb asshole,' he snarled. 'We've been breaking our balls trying to save the lives of three men stuck in an elevator controlled by a homicidal computer and now you're telling me that you could have unplugged it all along?' His face became even more contorted, and he seemed about to strike Beech until he was restrained by Nathan Coleman.

'Cool it, Frank,' urged Coleman. 'We still need him to turn it off.'

Beech pulled his tie free of Curtis's fist. 'They were dead anyway!' he yelled. 'You said so yourself. Besides, you don't trash a £40 million piece of hardware without checking the subsumption architecture. An accident is one thing. But A-life culpability is another.'

'You piece of shit,' sneered Curtis. 'Dollars and cents. That's all you people can think about.'

'What you're suggesting is absurd. Nobody in their right mind would dump a Yu-5 down the toilet without first attempting a proper verification.'

'There are five people dead, Mister. What more verification do you need?'

Beech shook his head and turned away.

'Now you've got your damned verification,' said Curtis, 'what are you going to do about it?' He glanced impatiently at Coleman. 'It's OK, Nat, you can let go now.' He tugged his arms free of his colleague's slackening grip. 'Do more of us have to die before you get it through your stupid skull that this isn't some half-assed experiment at Caltech or MIT or whichever petrie dish mould you sprang from? We're not talking artificial life now. We're talking real life. Men and women with families. Not some tin fucking man without a heart.'

'Bob?' said Mitch. 'Can you turn it off? Is that possible?'

Beech shrugged. 'By rights I should get Mr Yu's permission to do it. There's a proper protocol for doing something like this, y'know?'

'Screw Mr Yu,' said Curtis. 'And screw his fucking protocol. In case you'd forgotten, it's not that easy to get hold of anyone right now.'

'Come on, Bob,' Mitch urged.

'OK, OK,' said Beech and sat down in front of the terminal. 'I was going to do it anyway.'

The walkie-talkie buzzed. Coleman answered it and stepped out of the boardroom into the corridor, heading towards the balcony.

'Hallelujah,' said Helen. 'Now maybe we can get the hell out of this multi-storey lunatic asylum.'

'Amen to that,' said Jenny. 'I've had a bad feeling about this place all afternoon. That's why I came here in the first place. To rid the place of its bad spirits.'

'Whatever floats your boat,' said Arnon and flopped down on the sofa. 'But the sooner we get out of here the better.'

'Yeah, well, don't hold your breath,' said Beech. 'It takes time to pour programming acid into the equivalent of a thousand ordinary computers.'

'How long?' said Curtis.

'I really couldn't say. 'I've never trashed a $40 million

computer before. It took thirty-six minutes to kick Isaac's ass into touch, and that program was only a couple of hours old. You remember, Mitch? The SRS?' Beech started to type some transactions.

'Yeah, I remember.'

'Well, this mother has been running for months. Even before we installed it in this building. God only knows how much data it's acquired in all that time. We could be talking several hours here.'

'Several hours?' Curtis looked at his watch.

'Minimum.'

'You're kidding.'

'What's to kid? Hey, you want to take over, Sergeant, be my guest.'

'Just get on with it, Bob,' insisted Mitch. 'Please?'

'OK, here we go,' sighed Beech as his hands clattered over the keyboard. 'A dirty job, but someone has to do it.

'This is the end.' Beech was singing the line of a Doors song. 'The end.'

'I never liked that song,' said Arnon. 'It's depressing. And the book. Nobody gets out of here alive. Appropriate, huh?'

'Abraham?' said Beech. 'We are rolling out the black carpet and aiming you at oblivion, my silicon friend. Speaking for myself, I'd like to have gotten to know you a little better. But ours is not to reason why. Ours is but to make you die. There's a cop here who says you're out of here, pal, or I'm Rodney King II. So it's bedtime for Bonzo. *Capisce?* The Big Sleep for the Big Beep. EOD. EOL. EOJ.'

Nathan Coleman leaned over the glass barrier that gave on to the atrium and stared down at the ground floor. It was like being on a ship's mast looking down at the human insects that crawled on the bleached white quarterdeck. Three of them. The walkie-talkie snapped like the sound of a loose sail and one of the insects waved.

'Hey,' said Richardson, 'what the hell is happening up there? We're feeling like we've been forgotten: marooned, or something.'

'It's a long story and I'm not sure I understand most of it,' said Coleman. 'There's been a lot of heavy philosophy talked about artificial life and stuff. But the sports report is that your computer has been acting on its own initiative. It's gone haywire or some shit like that. Anyway, the play is this: Mr Beech is about to terminate it,' said Coleman, well aware of the possibility that this might well upset the Gridiron's architect. 'With extreme prejudice.'

'Well, Jesus, what the hell for? We've got to sit tight that's all.'

'I don't think so, Mr Richardson. You see, Abraham cancelled your flight tickets to London. And he got the LAPD computer at City Hall to suspend me and Sergeant Curtis. And a whole lot of other things too. The bottom line is that no one is expecting us home tonight. It looks as if the computer might be making plans to become Silicon Valley's first serial killer.'

Coleman heard Richardson relay the news to Joan and Dukes. Then Richardson said, 'Whose dumb idea is that, for Chrissakes? No, don't tell me. That bagel-headed Sergeant of yours. Put me on to Mitchell Bryan will you? I need to speak to someone who appreciates what is being suggested here. No offence intended, son, but this is a $40 million piece of hardware we're talking about here, not some Casio personal fucking organizer.'

Nat put two fingers in his mouth and made as if to vomit over the side of the balcony and on to Richardson's head.

'I'll get him to call you, OK?'

Coleman switched off the walkie-talkie and started back towards the boardroom. Now that it looked like they were getting out he was thinking about the girl he was planning to see the next day. Her name was Nan Tucker and she worked for a real estate company. He'd been introduced to her at the wedding of an old girlfriend who was convinced that two people called Nat and Nan were a match made in heaven. Coleman wasn't sure about a match, but he had arranged to take Nan for brunch at the most romantic restaurant he knew, the Beaurivage in Malibu, even though it was way too expensive, even though he suspected they would have little in common besides the very obvious physical attraction each seemed to hold for the other. At the same time, brunch was all he had planned. Nathan Coleman left the sexual initiatives to women these days. Often, in these politically correct times, it was safer that way. And the old perfect gentleman routine? It hardly ever failed.

Coleman slowed for a moment as he heard a muffled noise from behind the washroom door. He was about to go and investigate when he saw Mitch coming up the corridor towards him. Coleman walked on a little and handed Mitch the walkie-talkie.

'Your boss wants to talk to you. I told him Mr Beech was pulling the plug on the computer.' Coleman shrugged laconically. 'He sounded kind of pissed about it. Guy sure does like busting the balls of the people who work for him, doesn't he?'

Mitch nodded wearily.

Coleman had been about to say something else about Ray Richardson, but instead he turned around and was looking back up the corridor at the washroom.

'Did you hear something?'

Mitch listened and shook his head. 'Not a thing.'

Coleman walked back to the washroom, paused outside the door for a moment and then pushed it. The door didn't move.

Certain he could hear something now – a muffled cry for help? –Coleman pushed again. This time the door opened easily and as he entered the men's room the cry, now a scream, was immediately curtailed by a short report, more of a loud pop than an explosion, like a tyre blowing out on a wet road surface, or the eructation of a hot lava pool. Coleman felt something collide with the exterior side of the door and a warm wet spray hit his face and neck. He heard Mitch call out to him but did not hear what was said as slowly he began to realize that he was covered in blood.

Like most policeman in LA, Coleman had often been involved in a shooting and for a second or two he thought that he had been hit, most probably with some kind of high-velocity round. He staggered forward, wiping the blood from his eyes and braced for the pain. It never came. A moment later he understood that the sound of hammering he could hear was not gunfire, it was not even his own heartbeat, but Mitch banging on the other side of the door.

'Are you OK? Nat? Can you hear me?'

Coleman pulled at the door handle and found that the door was locked again.

'Yeah, I think so, but I'm locked in.'

'What happened?' And then, 'Sergeant? Come here. Coleman's trapped in the washroom.'

Coleman wiped some more blood off his face and, looking about the washroom, felt his jaw start to drop. There was blood everywhere, whole gouts of clotted gore: dripping from the ceiling, smeared on the cracked mirror, collected in a shallow pool on the shelf of a wash-hand basin and running in a stream towards his feet. Like a red tide had risen and fallen in the washroom in the space of a few seconds. Coleman stiffened his jaw and looked to the source of the flow.

A pile of blood-soaked rags stood like a range of small mountains in the corner of the room. Nearby was a human leg, to which a penis and testicles were still attached. A neatly severed hand was frozen in the action of turning on the faucet. Hanging on one of the cubicle doors was a pink silk tie, except that when Coleman reached out and touched it he realized that it was not a tie at all, but a length of human intestine. Turning away he slipped in the blood and fell to the floor to find himself face to face with the owner of the still steaming body parts that now littered the Gridiron washroom like a shark attack. It was Tony Levine. Or, rather, his decapitated head, complete with pony-tail.

'Holy shit,' exclaimed Coleman pushing the head away with revulsion.

It rolled across the floor like a broken coconut, and came to rest on the ragged edge of what has once been his neck.

The eyelids in the head lifted, and penetrating, undeniably living eyes fixed themselves on Coleman, with a mixture of indignation and regret. Then the nostrils flared and, instinctively, Nathan Coleman addressed the severed head.

'Jesus, what the fuck happened to you?' he said, shuddering.

Levine's head made no reply, but for another ten or fifteen seconds his eyes stayed on Coleman's own, before the lids drooped and life finally departed from the dead man's brain.

Between the pounding blows on the other side he could just hear Frank Curtis shouting. Once again Coleman pulled at the handle, but the door was still locked.

'Frank?' he shouted.

'Nat? Is that you?'

'I'm OK, Frank. But Levine is dead. It looks like he got hit by a fuckin' Patriot missile. There's blood and pieces of this guy all over the washroom. It's like Sam Peckinpah's dinner in here, man.'

'What happened?'

'Hey, you tell me,' Coleman shouted. 'I just opened

the door and it was like the guy blew apart in front of me.' He shook his head. 'I'm kind of deaf, too. My ears are ringing. Like I've been in a plane or something. Frank? Are you still there?'

'OK, Nat, we're going to get you out of there.'

But inside the washroom, a loud buzzer sounded.

'Wait a minute, Frank. Something's happening. Can you hear it?'

The voice came from somewhere up above Nathan Coleman's head, an Englishman's voice, and for a millisecond he thought it was God. Then he remembered Abraham.

'Please vacate the washroom,' said the voice. 'Please vacate the washroom. Automatic cleansing of this facility will commence in five minutes. Repeat. Please vacate this washroom. You have five minutes.'

'Frank? The man wants to clean up the mess in here. What do I do now?'

'Stand clear of the door, Nat. We're going to break it in.'

Coleman retreated into the only cubicle that remained clear of Levine's anatomical diaspora, tipped the seat on the toilet bowl and sat down. There followed a short silence and then, on the other side of the door, the dull, unmistakable impact of a man's shoulder. To Nathaniel Coleman, it was an informative sort of sound. Before being transferred to the Homicide Bureau he had been a patrolman. After three years cruising LA in a black-and-white you got to know the kind of doors you could break down and those you could not. Curtis went at it like some comic-book hero, but Coleman could tell that his effort was wasted and that the door would stand fast.

The buzzer sounded again.

'Please vacate the washroom. Please vacate the washroom. Automatic cleansing of this facility will commence in four minutes. Repeat. Please vacate this washroom. You now have four minutes.'

Coleman dropped his head back on to his shoulders and stared up at the blood-spattered ceiling and the small loudspeaker that was installed there.

'Well, if you could just open this fucking door I'd be glad to get out of your way.'

Then he stood up and returned to the door. 'Frank?'

'Sorry, Nat. Damn thing doesn't budge. We're going to have to try something else. Sit tight.'

Coleman glanced uncomfortably at Levine's head lying on the floor and hammered on the door.

'Frank? I don't want to end up like Levine here, so you'd better think of something quick. I just got the four-minute warning.'

A minute passed and the buzzer sounded a third time. 'Please vacate the washroom . . .'

Coleman lifted his eyes towards the ceiling and grimaced. He drew the Glock 9 millimetre from the clip holster he wore inside the waist of his pants and with a finger in one ear silenced the loudspeaker with a couple of shots.

'Nat? Nat, what the hell's going on in there?'

'It's OK, Frank, I just got tired listening to the fuckin' computer telling me to get my ass out of the can, that's all. So I bust some shots off.'

'Nice work, Nat. For a moment there I thought you had a 211 in progress.'

'No. Just the 207, same as before. Only I don't think old Abraham wants any ransom money. I think he wants my butt.'

Frank Curtis slapped the washroom door hard with frustration.

'What happens during automatic cleansing?' he asked Mitch, who shrugged and with a look turned the question towards Willis Ellery.

'The washroom is sprayed with a hot ammonia solution,' said Ellery.

'How hot?'

'Not boiling, but still pretty hot. After that it's dried with hot air before the air itself is changed under pressure and aromatized.'

'Is the cleansing program what killed Levine?'

Ellery shook his head. 'I doubt it. Being trapped in a washroom during a cleansing program wouldn't be a pleasant experience, but it's not necessarily a fatal one. The thing is – well, I should have thought of it before. You see, I was in there immediately before Tony and I nearly mentioned it to him. Only he said something to me that put it right out of my head.'

'Mentioned what?' Curtis asked impatiently. 'Come on, we haven't got much time here.'

'If Abraham is using the HVAC to make things uncomfortable for us, it stands to reason it might use the washroom for a hostile purpose. From what Coleman has said it sounds to me as if Abraham killed Tony using air pressure. It must have increased the psi in there to way above normal, like on an aircraft. But possibly that wasn't fatal until Coleman opened the door. Then there would have been a sudden and immediate depressurization. Enough to blow Levine apart.'

'Is there any way of stopping the cleansing program?'

'You mean that doesn't include Abraham?' Ellery laid his hand on a panel on the corridor wall beside the door.

'I've got a feeling that there's something behind here that might do the job,' he said, 'but I need to check it out on the laptop first.'

'Do it,' Curtis said urgently.

Ellery ran back towards the boardroom. Halfway there he stopped, turned on his heel and called back, 'If the program starts, tell Coleman to make sure he covers his eyes.'

'OK.'

Mitch was inspecting the way the panel cover was attached to the wall.

'Self-tapping screws. I'll speak to Helen and see if she found a screwdriver.'

Curtis hammered on the washroom door.

'Nat? We're working on an idea to get you out of there, but it's going to take a couple of minutes. If the program starts make sure you cover your eyes. The liquid contains ammonia. And it might be hot.'

'Fucking great, Frank,' said the voice behind the door. 'I'll look for a brush and see if I can't get some of this dirt out from under my fingernails, shall I?'

Curtis sprinted back to the boardroom, where he found Willis Ellery and Mitch studying a 3-D drawing.

'What have you got?' he said urgently, trying to make sense of the luminescent green drawing.

Not to be hurried, Mitch moved the trackball to turn the Intergraph drawing first one way and then the other.

'Each washroom is self-contained,' explained Ellery. 'Behind that panel are pipe, duct and cable tails, connected to building services. Water enters the washroom via the wet riser and the computer takes over, heating it, mixing it with ammonia for cleaning, whatever. If we can cut off the mains water supply we can effectively stop the whole cleansing program.'

'Right. How do we do that?'

'Just a minute,' said Ellery. 'Let me see.'

Curtis glanced about. Bob Beech was hunched over the computer terminal. Arnon and Birnbaum had one of the building plans spread on the table in front of them and were discussing something with one ear on the latest crisis. Jenny was sitting at Mitch's shoulder watching the laptop screen. At the far end of the table Helen Hussey had laid out a selection of tools and other useful objects as if preparing for surgery. There was a first-aid kit, a carpet knife, a small handsaw, a bevel, a jointer, a rasp, some tin snips, a plasterer's float, a pair of pliers, a shave hook, the scissors, some knives and forks, an assortment of coach-bolts, a couple of screwdrivers, a bottle opener and a large wrench.

Curtis selected one of the screwdrivers.

'Where in hell did you find that lot?' Curtis asked, impressed with her resourcefulness.

'You'd be surprised what builders leave lying around a new building,' she said. 'There was a whole bag of tools in the ladies' washroom, of all places.'

'Yeah well you'd better keep out of the washrooms from now on,' said Curtis, raising his voice. 'All of you. Abraham just killed Levine in the men's room. And now Nat's stuck in there.'

'My God.'

'Do you have a monkey wrench there, Helen?' asked Ellery.

She had never liked Tony Levine. Always trying to come on to her. He was worse than Warren Aikman. But she was sorry he was dead. With a shock she realized she had already lost count of the number of people who had died in the Gridiron since the late afternoon.

'I don't know,' she said vaguely, and held up something she thought might fit the description.

'Even better,' said Ellery excitedly. 'That's a Stillson.'

When the water started to pour into the washroom Coleman was almost relieved, for it was neither hot nor did it seem to contain ammonia. But with each minute that passed the level began to increase. By the time Curtis was back on the other side of the door, it was several inches deep. Coleman might have tried to stop the flow except that the water was pouring into the washroom from every conceivable entry point: from high-pressure sprinklers on the ceiling, from the faucets on the sink, even from the cisterns behind the toilets. The idea that Abraham intended that he should drown was beginning to seep slowly through the policeman's imagination.

'Got a fuckin' leak in here, Frank,' he yelled. 'Place is filling up with water. No ammonia. Maybe Abraham changed his mind about the cleansing program after I hit his voice box.'

This gave Coleman an idea. Once again he drew his gun.

'Hey, Frank,' he yelled. 'Stand away from the door. I'm going to try and blast a few holes in the door. I reckon I'm going to need some help with the drainage in here before very long. Frank?'

'Ah, that's a negative, Nat,' shouted Curtis. 'I've just been told that the door's made of steel. You'd need a fifty calibre BMG to get through this. Just try and take it easy. We've got something going here. A way of disconnecting the whole bathroom module from the mains supply of water.'

'OK, Frank. Whatever you say. But don't leave it too long. I never did like any of those submarine pictures.'

Coleman holstered his gun and, with the water nearly up to his knees, sat down on the toilet again.

Bending forwards he scooped some of the water into his hands and drank it.

'I guess I won't die of thirst anyway.'

Curtis released the last of the self-tapping screws and let the panel fall off the wall and on to the floor. In the recessed space were a large red elbow-shaped pipe, a smaller branch pipe connecting the washroom, a couple of ceramic disc valves and, inside a mineral insulated square box, the electrical trunking that controlled the operation of the washroom.

Willis Ellery pointed to a joint on the branch pipe and

said, 'I think all we have to do to turn off the mains water is tighten this.'

'Hold on a second,' said Curtis. 'Is this pipe going to be safe to touch? What about all that electrical stuff in there? Suppose Abraham's got the pipe wired to the fucking mains electricity?'

'He's got a point, Will,' said Mitch, already keying the code number that was printed on the box cover on to his laptop. 'WSPC 21. The wiring diagram might even show us how to open the door.'

The pull-down menu on the screen asked which version of the wiring instructions he required, Quick or Technical. Mitch chose Quick and watched as the Intergraph programme sketched out a line for each cable instead of a line for every wire.

Willis Ellery leaned across his shoulder and studied the diagram for a minute or two.

'None of the pipes is connected to the electricity supply,' he said at last. Then, beating the palm of his hand with the Stillson pipe wrench, he added, 'Well, here goes,' and prepared to try and close off the water.

Adjusting the serrated jaws of the Stillson to fit the joint around the branch pipe, he began to tighten the screw.

'Seems safe enough so far.'

Mitch was reading the wiring diagram. Curtis was looking over his shoulder.

'What is that thing?'

'Washroom Patching Services Cabinet Number 21,' said Mitch. 'Cables for each type of building service. This one's illumination. Downlight and uplighting. This one's HVAC. This one's IT – basic telecommunications requirement and low speed data. It looks as if the door is handled by the HVAC cable. You see? The tray in the ceiling above the door and these two vertical poles either side. If we uncouple this one then the door ought to open.'

'Kind of stiff,' grunted Ellery and, releasing the wrench for a moment, spat on his hands. 'God, I hope this works.'

'What's this cable here?' Mitch asked himself. 'FSS. ESS. What's that? This one goes to the wall surrounding that branch pipe.'

He flicked the cursor arrow to the top of the screen and pulled down the Glossary.

'Fire Stop Sleeve. Earthquake Stop Sleeve.'

Mitch frowned. 'I guess if this pipe moves within the sleeve then it makes . . . Willis, no!'

Willis Ellery never heard Mitch.

As he pushed the Stillson wrench against the joint, the smart pipe shifted within the specially designed stop sleeve, making contact with the piezoelectric metal actuator that warned Abraham to stiffen the exterior perimeter's steel frame against seismic shock.

Willis Ellery let out a scream that was a mixture of pain and surprise. Like any human body he made an excellent conductor of electricity, producing as good a reaction as any electrolyte solution. It was not a particularly high current that electrocuted him, just the standard current alternating at sixty cycles per second. But Ellery's hands had been damp with spit and sweat, and when the power hit him it was impossible for him to release his grip on the Stillson and break the passage of the current. It was as if the electricity that gripped him did so with the serrated strength of the Stillson itself. The Stillson gripped the joint; and electricity gripped the Stillson; and Willis Ellery could do nothing but stand there and hold on, shaking up and down, screaming like an hysterical child.

Seeing Mitch reach for Ellery's arm, Curtis struck him aside with a blow of his fist.

'Don't touch him!' he yelled. 'You'll be electrocuted too.'

Ellery uttered a feeble cry as he tried desperately to

release his grip on the wrench. 'Ple-e-ease!' he screamed. 'He-elp me-eee!'

'We have to find something non-conductive to pull him off,' shouted Curtis. 'A brush handle, or a length of rope. Hurry!'

He ran back to the kitchen and surveyed the area. There was nothing that looked as if it might not conduct the electricity from Ellery's body into the hands of his rescuers. Then he had an idea. The kitchen table. Sweeping everything off the wooden surface on to the floor he yelled to Mitch, 'Here, we'll use this.'

'Well, thanks a lot,' protested Marty Birnbaum. 'I just sorted out our supplies on that.'

Ignoring him, Curtis and Mitch picked up the table and carried it into the corridor where Ellery was still in the grip of the electrified wrench and now only just conscious of what was happening. There was a strong smell of burning in the air. Like singed hair in a barber's shop. Curtis flung the table over on to its side.

'Slide it into him,' he said, 'like a cow-catcher.'

Both men took hold of a table leg and pushed it hard into Ellery's jerking body, forcing him away from the Patching Cabinet. As his grip on the wrench was broken, Ellery yelped with pain and one of his thumbs emitted a blue flash that disappeared into the carpet with a puff of acrid smoke. The combined force of the electricity discharging itself from his body and the table ramming into his side was enough to fling him across the corridor, where he collided with the wall and collapsed unconscious on to the floor.

Curtis was on him in a second, like some unsporting wrestler, flipping the man on to his back, tearing open his shirt front and pressing his ear against his chest.

'Is he dead?' said Helen.

Straddling Ellery's thighs Curtis said nothing and, placing one hand over the other, with elbows locked, he began to press Ellery's heart between his breastbone and spine, trying to find a rhythm in his chest compression that would squirt enough blood out of it to supply the unconscious man's brain.

'Helen,' he said breathlessly, 'find out if Nat's OK. Jenny? Get a blanket, a table cloth, something to keep this man warm. Mitch, call Richardson on the walkie-talkie and let him know what's happening.'

Curtis kept up the compression for another couple of minutes and then leaned forwards, listening for a heartbeat. He shook his head and started to undo Ellery's urine-soaked pants. Jenny returned with a table cloth.

'Pull these down,' he yelled, 'and get a hold of his femoral artery.'

He started the compressions again. Jenny pulled Ellery's pants down. Ignoring the stink of urine, she pushed the scrotum in Ellery's underpants to one side and let her fingers reach for his groin.

'Can you feel it yet?' he grunted. 'Can you feel it when I press his chest?'

'Yes,' she said after a momentary pause. 'I can feel it.'

'That's good. Someone find out what that asshole Beech is doing. Has he managed to pull the plug on this son of a bitch yet?'

Curtis put his ear to Ellery's chest and listened again. This time he heard a feeble heartbeat. The bigger problem was that Willis Ellery's respiratory muscles had seized up and his breathing had not yet re-started.

'You can let go of his crotch now,' he told Jenny. 'Did you speak to Nat?' he asked Helen.

Kneeling by Ellery's side, he pinched the man's nose and started to give him mouth-to-mouth respiration.

'Nat's OK,' Helen told Curtis. 'The water's up to his waist and rising, but he's OK.'

With his mouth pressed periodically to Ellery's there was no time for Curtis to answer her. Not that he had much to say. He told himself he was all out of good ideas.

There were no options left that he could think of. It was all down to Beech now.

Ten minutes passed and still Curtis did not give up on Willis Ellery. One of the things he had learned as a young patrolman was that victims often died because the person attempting to resuscitate them gave up too quickly. He knew he just had to keep going. But he was already tiring. He knew he was going to need help.

Between forcing breaths into Ellery's traumatized lungs, Curtis asked Jenny if she could take over for a while. Covering Ellery with the table cloth, she looked at Curtis with tears in her eyes and nodded.

'You know how?'

'I took a first-aid course in college,' she said, and moved alongside Ellery's head.

'Don't give up until I tell you,' he ordered. 'There's the danger of anoxia. Suspended respiration might cause blindness, deafness, palsy, you name it.' But it was plain to see that Jenny would keep going for as long as it took. Curtis stood up stiffly and watched her carry on.

Then he went to speak to Beech.

━━

Bob Beech was worried.

The last time he had felt so worried had been in the middle of the 1980s, on his graduate course in computer security at Caltech, when he had constructed his first self-replicating program or, as he had subsequently learned to call all such SRPs, a computer virus. In those days everyone had been writing them, inspired by an article that had appeared in *Scientific American*.

With three hundred lines of MS-DOS Beech had created TOR, after Torquemada, the first Grand Inquisitor of the Spanish Inquisition. Beech's idea had been to create a program that would destroy the heresy of pirated MS-DOS software in the Far East, where software piracy was almost endemic, and then to sell the successful result to the Microsoft Corporation. The trouble was that TOR had behaved more like a real computer virus than Beech had ever anticipated and had combined with another virus, NADIR, the existence of which Beech had been quite unaware, to create a new superstrain of virus, later known as TORNADO. This mutation had acted with catastrophic effects, destroying not just data written with pirated Microsoft product, but data written with legitimate software too. At the second A-life conference in 1990 at Los Alamos, Beech had heard one delegate estimate the cost of the damage wreaked by TORNADO to be several billion dollars.

Beech had never told anyone that he was the author of TOR. It was his darkest secret. Ten years on, with numerous TORNADO anti-viral programs still on the market, fifth- and sixth-generation mutations of TORNADO continued to survive inside PCs all over the world. He had written a few anti-viral programs himself, one of them for TORNADO, and reckoned he knew as much about disassembling rogue SRPs as anyone.

GABRIEL was the most sophisticated disassembly program – ever since TOR he had disliked the term 'computer virus' – Beech had ever written, based on principles he had learned from epidemiology and biological virology. As a piece of livewire it was, Beech considered, a real bastard. Not only was GABRIEL designed to be completely autonomous, it was also supposed to be extremely aggressive to the infected host. Except for the circumstances in which he now came to trigger GABRIEL, Bob Beech might have been proud of his disassembly program. The only fly in the ointment was that it did not work.

GABRIEL was, as he had told Frank Curtis it would be, slow acting, but even after a few minutes Beech knew that he ought to have seen some sign that GABRIEL was having the desired effect on Abraham's architecture. But

308

there was nothing to indicate that Abraham had suffered so much as a minor thrash, stray, bozo, hung file or line gremlin. Beech had positioned himself at a vantage point within the system-architecture where, like some epidemiologist staring at the progress of a virus under an electron microscope, he ought to have been able to witness Abraham in the very earliest stages of the infection: the clock. GABRIEL had been designed to destroy Abraham's sense of time first of all. As the minutes rolled by on the clock it was plain to see that the DP was inoperative. It was now eleven-fifteen and Abraham was still behaving like the blue-ribbon program Beech had helped to create, with no errors and no bugs. Plainly GABRIEL was impotent, at least as far as Abraham was concerned.

A couple of times he retyped the transactions that would trigger the DP, just in case he had made a mistake, but with no more success.

When David Arnon asked him how things were coming along, Beech did not answer. And he hardly noticed the commotion that followed Willis Ellery's electrocution. Stunned, he sat in front of the terminal, motionless, waiting for something to happen, recognizing in his heart of hearts that nothing would. His remarks about the responsibilities of a god struck him as hollow now. It was as if God, having decided to destroy Sodom and Gomorrah, found that his much vaunted fire and brimstone just bounced harmlessly off the city walls.

Turning in his chair, Beech found Frank Curtis standing behind him, wearing an expression so frightful that he was suddenly more afraid of the policeman than he was of the consequences of what had failed to take place in the silicon heart of the machine.

'I don't know why,' he said, shaking his head. 'But – but it, GABRIEL, the disassembly program, it doesn't fucking work. I've tried several times to trigger the DP but there's no sign that Abraham has been infected. No sign at all. It's weird. I simply don't understand how he could be resisting it. I mean, the DP is specific to Abraham, written into his basic architecture. It's like you were born with some kind of congenital disease, or some genetic predisposition to cancer, and all you needed was the wrong kind of diet to set it off. The only thing I can think of is that somehow Abraham has discovered a way of making himself immune. But I really don't know how.'

The already angry expression of the face of Curtis grew more murderous.

'So you can't unplug it,' he growled. 'Is that what you're telling me?'

Beech shrugged apologetically.

'You dumb bastard,' said Curtis, and drew his gun.

'For Christ's sake,' yelled Beech and leapt off his chair, backing away across the boardroom. 'You can't. Please. No one writes a tighter code than me, man. But you've got to believe me, this is completely beyond my control. There's nothing I can do.'

Curtis looked at the gun in his hand as if surprised at the reaction it had produced. He smiled.

'I'd like to. Really, I would. If my partner drowns, I might.'

He turned abruptly and walked out.

Beech dropped into a chair and pressed a hand to his chest.

'That crazy fucking bastard,' he said, shaking his head. 'I thought he was going to shoot me. Really I did.'

'Me too,' said David Arnon. 'I wonder why the hell he didn't.'

Standing on the lid of the toilet, the top of his head inches from the ceiling, Nathan Coleman felt the cold water lapping at his shirt collar.

It was only a couple of weeks since he and Frank Curtis had gone to Elysian Park where the naked body of a young black female had been found floating in the reservoir that ran under the Pasadena Freeway, just a few hundred yards from Dodger Stadium.

Coleman would have hardly thought it possible, but at the very moment when the water was right under his chin, he began to remember the taped commentary given by the pathologist during the girl's p.m.

At the time he had hardly been paying attention at all, leaving Frank to ask the questions. But now he found that he could recall Dr Bragg's account in uncomfortable detail. Like he had prepared the subject of drowning for an exam. Yeah, thanks very much. What a time to improve your fucking memory. A complete mindfuck.

Drowning wasn't so bad if you were committing suicide. At least then you didn't struggle. But when it was accidental, you usually tried to fight it by holding your breath until you were too exhausted or hypercarbic to continue. The girl from the reservoir had tried to fight it. Not surprising since she had been held under the water by a gang of South Central crackheads. According to Dr Bragg, she had put up quite a struggle. It had taken three to five minutes for her to die.

Coleman didn't know if he could deal with something that took that long.

When you eventually let out your breath and drew water back into your airway, that could set off the vomiting reflex, after which you just aspirated the contents of your own stomach. Plus the water. You could aspirate so much water that it might account for as much as 50 per cent of your blood volume. Jesus Christ. And if that wasn't bad enough, drowning was not just an asphyxial event. It fucked up your fluid balance and blood chemistry: the circulating blood diluted, your electrolyte concentration reduced. Red cells might swell or burst, releasing large amounts of potassium which proceeded to fuck your heart around. Actual death might be precipitated by vagal inhibition originating in the nasopharynx or glottis. But just as often you could die from fouling of the lung by filthy water.

What a fucking way to go.

Coleman tucked his toe into the door lock and pushed his mouth another inch clear of the water. His head touched the ceiling. He wasn't going to get out of this. Just like in the movies. Like one of the poor guys trapped in the torpedo room. The only things missing were the depth charges.

He drew his gun clear of the water and pressed the muzzle against the side of his head. He would wait until the last possible minute. Until the water was over his nostrils. Then he would pull the trigger.

Halfway along the corridor, Curtis met Jenny coming towards him.

'I thought I told you not to stop,' he snapped at her.

'But Will's breathing again,' she said. 'I think he's going to be OK. And what the hell gives you the . . .'

Jenny's voice faltered as she caught sight of the 9mm Sig in the policeman's big hand, and the thunderous expression on his face.

'What is it?' she asked anxiously. 'What's the matter?'

'The unpluggability scenario. That's what the matter is. Your friend Beech screwed up. We might just as well try and unplug the Hoover Dam.'

He strode down the corridor working the slide on the automatic to load the gun's firing chamber.

Mitch, kneeling by the breathing but still unconscious figure of Willis Ellery, stood up when he saw Curtis coming.

'Better stand well out of the way,' yelled the police-man. He took a marksman's aim at the washroom services patching cabinet. 'I'm not such a good shot. Besides, there might be a few ricochets. With any luck one of them might hit your pal Beech.'

'Wait a minute, Frank,' said Mitch. 'If Bob manages to take Abraham off-line then we might need those electrics to open the door.'

'Forget it. Abraham's here to stay. It's official. Your macho friend just put up his fucking hands and surrendered. The goddamn disassembly program or whatever the hell he calls it doesn't fucking work.'

Curtis fired three shots at the box of electrics. Mitch covered his ears against the deafening noise, and a shower of sparks flew out of the box.

'I can't think of anything else to do,' yelled Curtis, and squeezed off three more. 'And I'm not about to let my partner drown like a kitten if I can prevent it.'

Cable glands blew away from cable ends, and clips from casings as two more 180-gram rounds thudded into the WSPC.

'What I wouldn't give right now for the scatter-gun in the trunk of my car,' yelled Curtis and finished off the rest of the 13-shot magazine.

Rubbing his shoulder Curtis dragged the kitchen table up to the door.

'Give me a hand here,' he said to Mitch. 'Maybe we can batter it down.'

Mitch knew it was useless, but by now he also knew that it would have been quite hopeless to have argued with Curtis.

They lifted the table, stepped back to the other side of the corridor and rammed the table's corner against the door.

'Again.'

Once more the table banged against the door.

For several minutes they kept up the battery until, exhausted, they collapsed on top of the table itself.

'Why did you have to build the damn thing so strong?'

panted Curtis. 'Jesus, it's a fucking washroom, not a bank vault.'

'Not us,' breathed Mitch. 'The Japanese. Their design. When modules are used you just fit them in.'

'But the rest of it. What the hell's so wrong with a human toilet cleaner anyway?' Curtis was almost crying.

'Nobody wants to do that kind of job any more. Nobody you can rely on. Not even the Mexicans want to clean toilets.'

Curtis picked himself off the table and hammered on the door with the flat of his hand.

'Nat? Nat, can you hear me?'

He pressed an ear still ringing against the door and found it cold from the mains water that was pressing against it.

Frank Curtis heard the unmistakable sound of a single gunshot.

Curtis sat down against the wall. He could feel the cold of the water now filling the men's room through his shirt. Helen Hussey sat down beside him and put her arm around his shoulders.

'You did everything you could,' she said.

Curtis nodded. 'Yeah.'

Leaning forward he drew his gun from the clip under the belt at the back of his pants and then leaned back again, this time more comfortably. The black polymer grip made it seem more like something that he might have considered shaving with than a weapon. He thought he might as well have used an electric shaver on the door for all the damage the gun had inflicted. He remembered the day he had bought it.

'That's a nice gun you've got there,' the gunsmith had said. He might have been describing a friendly-looking labrador.

Curtis hefted the gun in his sweating hand for a moment, then threw it across the corridor.

When Helen Hussey called the atrium on the walkie-talkie to report that Nathan Coleman had shot himself to escape drowning, Ray Richardson understood for the first time the gravity of their situation. For him the worst thing was the realization that what had happened was going to affect his whole future. He doubted that the Yu Corporation would pay the balance of his fees and wondered if anyone would ever commission a smart building again. Certainly he could not see how the Yu Corporation building would become anything but notorious. People already hated modern architecture, and this would confirm their prejudices. But even among architects themselves what was happening seemed destined to consign Richardson to some kind of professional wilderness. Gold medals for excellence were not handed out to architects whose designs were found to be responsible for eight, maybe nine fatalities.

Of course you had to stay alive to be able to defend yourself against your critics. Stuck on a baking hot atrium floor, without food or water, how long could they hold out? Richardson went to the front door and peered to see through the tinted glass. Beyond the empty piazza was the Babel-like landscape of downtown: the monuments of modern worship, monuments to function and finance, well-designed tools for the classification and efficient exploitation of labour, liberating the ground for the speedy circulation of the life-blood of capitalism, the office worker. He rubbed the glass clear of condensation and looked again. Not that he really expected to see anyone in the darkness out there. The only consideration given to what happened in these urban areas at night, when the last hot desker had gone home, armed with his

315

portable phone and his laptop so that he might do some more work, was how to deter the poor and the destitute from coming there to sleep, to drink, to eat, and, sometimes, to die. It did not matter where they went, as long as they kept moving, so that by daybreak when the office workers returned to the area, their arrival might not be obstructed by those who lived on the Nickle.

If only he had not been so committed to the principle of design deterrence. If only he had not thought to add Choke Water to the fountain, or render the piazza's surface inhospitable to those who might have slept there. If only he had not made that call to the deputy mayor's office and had those demonstrators removed. He meandered around the base of the tree looking up towards the top. He kept walking until he remembered that one of the upper branches came very close to the edge of the twenty-first level. And the tree itself was covered in lianas that ran the whole length of the trunk, and were as strong as ropes. Could they climb up to the twenty-first level, to food and water?

'Are you thinking what I'm thinking?' asked Dukes.

'Incredible as that might seem, yes, I am,' answered Richardson. 'What do you think our chances are?'

'I dunno. How strong is your wife?'

Richardson shrugged. He was not sure.

'Well,' Dukes said, 'better than down here. Reckon I'm going to try anyway. I used to climb a lot of trees when I was a kid.'

'In LA?'

Dukes shook his head. 'Washington state. Up near Spokane. Yes, sir, I climbed me a lot of trees in my time. Never did see a tree like this one though.'

'It's Brazilian. From the rain forest.'

'Hardwood, I guess. What do you say we try and get some sleep? Take a shot at it in the morning.'

Richardson glanced at his watch and saw that it was

close to midnight. Then he looked at the piano. It was playing another strange piece.

'Sleep?' he snorted. 'With that fucking noise? I've tried telling the hologram to put a sock in it, but no dice. It just goes on and on. Maybe the computer's planning to drive us nuts. Like General Noriega.'

'Hey, no problem,' said Dukes and drew his gun. 'To shoot the piano player, you just shoot the piano. What do you say? I mean, you're still the boss round here.'

Richardson shrugged. 'I'm not so sure about that,' he admitted, 'but go right ahead. I never did like the piano much anyway.'

Dukes turned, worked the slide of his Glock 17 automatic and fired just once into the polished black woodwork, dead centre of the Yamaha nameplate. The piano stopped abruptly, in the middle of a loud and hectoring finale.

'Nice shot,' said Richardson.

'Thanks.'

'But you missed your vocation. With an aim like that you should have been a critic.'

Fear crept down the corridors and along the atrium floor of the Gridiron like some psychotic night watchman. Most of those trapped in the building slept hardly at all, while others paid for their apparent lack of vigilance with vividly claustrophobic nightmares, their periodic cries and shouts echoing in the cavernous purgatory that was the dark, almost empty, office envelope. Buzzing with the memories of the day and the preoccupations of sudden mortality, all human brains stayed active until the dawn came, and light brought the false promise of safety.

Book Six

'Technology will offer us more control rather than less. The buildings of the future will be more like robots than temples. Like chameleons, they will adapt to their environment.'

Richard Rogers

Joan Richardson had a feeling for trees, especially this one. It had been her idea to have a tree in the atrium. The strength of a tree, she had argued to her husband and then to Mr Yu himself, would enter into the building itself. Never a man to do things by halves, Mr Yu had got hold of the biggest, strongest tree he could find and, in return, he had donated some enormous sum of money – paradoxically – to preserving several thousand acres of Brazil's rain forest against the slash-and-burn system of clearing. Joan had admired the gesture. But, more especially, she admired the tree.

'Ray, tell me,' she said, 'in all seriousness. Do you think that I can really do it? That I can climb it?'

Richardson, who wasn't sure at all she could do it, but was perfectly willing that she should try, placed both hands on his wife's shoulders and looked her squarely in the eye.

'Look, love,' he said quietly, 'in all the time we have known each other, have I ever been wrong about what you could and what you couldn't do? Have I?'

Joan smiled and shook her head, but it was plain that she had her doubts.

'When we first met I told you I thought you had the potential to become one of the world's great designers.' He shrugged eloquently. 'Well now you are. You are. Your name, Joan Richardson, is a by-word for excellence in graphics, lighting and furniture design, with awards to prove it, too. Major awards.'

Joan smiled thinly.

'So when I say that you can climb this tree, it's not because I think you ought to try, but because I *know* you can climb this tree. That's not bullshit, love. That's not just positive thinking. It's because I know you.'

He paused, as if allowing his short speech to sink into her mind.

Dukes also wondered if she could do it. She looked too fat to make it. Carrying all that weight was going to make it difficult. But she looked strong. Her shoulders were almost as big as her buttocks.

'Sure you can do it, lady,' he said encouragingly.

Richardson shot the security guard an irritated sort of smile.

'No,' he said. 'You don't know what you're talking about. What you say is right, but for the wrong reasons. You only imagine that she can make it, based on nothing more than the seat of your pants. I know she can make it.' Richardson tapped his head with a forefinger. 'In here.'

Dukes shrugged. 'Only tryin' to help, man,' he said stiffly. 'How do you want to do this?'

'I think maybe you should go up first. Then Joan. With me bringing up the rear, OK?' Richardson smiled. 'Not least because she is going to have to take off her skirt and climb in just her panties.'

Dukes nodded unsmiling. He was through trying to be nice to this guy. The man was a loose cannon.

'Sure. Whatever you say.'

'Joan? Are you ready?'

'I will be. After Mr Dukes starts his climb.'

'That's the spirit.' Richardson glanced up at the top of the tree and slipped on his sunglasses.

'Good idea,' said Joan. 'It is kind of bright in here. We wouldn't want to get dazzled or anything.' She bent down and retrieved her sunglasses from her handbag.

Richardson spat on his hands and took hold of a liana.

'Either of you two know the correct way to climb a rope?' he asked.

'Well, I guess so,' said Dukes.

Joan shook her head.

'Then you're both in luck. During my two years' national service, I did a fair bit of rock climbing. I've climbed more ropes than Burt Lancaster. You curl one shin around the rope, like this, and take hold above your head. Raise the shin wrapped around the rope and then pin the rope between your feet. At the same time you raise your hands and take your next hold.' He dropped back on to the ground. 'It's going to be hard going for the first sixty or seventy feet. Until we get to the first branches, where we can take a rest. Dukes? Do you want to try a couple of shin-ups?'

The other man shook his head and took off his shirt to reveal an impressive physique.

'I'm as ready as I'll ever be,' he said and started up one of the lianas, almost as if he was enjoying himself. When he was about twenty feet off the ground he looked back and laughed. 'See you guys up there,' he said.

Joan unzipped her skirt and dropped it to the ground.

Richardson swung a second liana towards her.

'Take your time,' he told her. 'And don't look down. Remember, I'll be right behind you all the way.' Then he kissed her. 'Good luck, love,' he added.

'And you,' she said. Then she curled her shin around the liana the way he had shown her and began to climb.

She was, he thought, the standard Venetian type beloved of Giorgione, Titian and Rubens, a poetic personification of the abundance of nature, a softly luminous Venus as on some pagan altarpiece. Her abundant size was the reason Richardson had married her. The real reason. Even Joan herself was unaware of that.

'That's it,' he said savouring the sight of his wife above him as a greedy dog might have regarded a fleshy ham bone. 'You're doing fine.'

It was his turn.

Richardson climbed slowly, not wanting to get beyond his wife in case he needed to help her, sometimes not moving at all while he waited for her to gain some height, giving words of encouragement and pieces of advice where he thought she needed them.

When Dukes got up as far as the first branches he settled himself across a bough to wait for the other two. For about ten minutes he watched them, until they seemed near enough to speak to.

'What kind of flower is this, ma'am?' he called down, handling a brightly coloured bloom on the trunk of the tree.

'An orchid probably,' said Joan.

'It's really beautiful.'

'It's hard to think of it as a parasite isn't it? Because that's what it is.'

'Are you serious? I've seen flowers like this at the Wall Street Flower Market, ten bucks apiece, minimum. And that's wholesale.'

Joan had almost reached the branch. Dukes reached down and held out his hand to her.

'Here,' he said. 'Catch my wrist. I'll pull you up.'

Gratefully Joan took hold of his wrist and found herself lifted up on to the branch beside Dukes. When she had recovered her breath, she said, 'My, you're a strong man. I mean, I'm not exactly a featherweight, am I?'

'You're all right,' he grinned. 'Me Tarzan. You Joan.' Glancing down the trunk at Richardson he added, 'Hey, Cheetah, how's it coming there? Ungawah. Ungawah.'

'Very funny,' grunted Richardson.

'You know what? The minute I get on to that twenty-first floor it's Miller time for me. There's two dozen in the refrigerator. Carried them up there myself.'

'Always assuming they haven't been drunk by some-one else already,' said Joan.

'People have been murdered for lesser offences.'

Richardson heaved himself on to the branch alongside his wife and let out a long sigh.

'Whose fucking idea was this anyway?' he breathed and leaned back against the enormous trunk.

It was another view of the building he had never expected to see. But here, in the centre of a hundred-foot clear span space, he thought he had never imagined such quality of light. They might say what they liked about the way Abraham had ruined the totality of his creation but Richardson felt that his own fastidious, sparing approach to structure could hardly be faulted. And how much better to see the light and space that were created by the structure, free of the structure itself. You could hardly grasp the excellence of the design from the dizzyingly vertiginous close quarters that were imposed by the rest of the buildings on Hope Street; and somehow the holistic view of the interior eluded you when you were bound by the bias of your own topographical reference point. But here, in the branches of the tree, things were different. It was almost worth everything that had happened just to have seen the interior of the building from this vantage point.

Richardson looked at Joan and Dukes as they chattered away and wanted to tell them how he felt, except that he knew neither of them could have understood. Only his spiritual masters, Joseph Wright, Le Corbusier, Louis Kahn and the great Frank Lloyd Wright might have appreciated the profundity of such poetry of light.

Things had got too complicated, that was all. There was too much to go wrong. Mitch had been right. He could understand that now. And if he got out of this alive he was going to return to basic principles, to rediscover the sense of occasion and drama that was inherent in pure design. Forget computers and building management systems. Forget public opinion with its fickle demands for novelty and innovation. He would look for a new fluency and expressiveness in a more practical, more controllable form of perfection.

♑ Nothing in the current situation justifies the use of firearms. Eight shots were fired in less time than it takes to play a piano scale.

Humanplayer Kay Killen's naked body on poolside. Endlife. Face as blue as water. Lips as grey and metallic looking as purest form of silicon that is the basic material of Observer's own semiconductor elements.

🖱 Move the cursor if you want to change tactics. Click on a city to go there. Most gods have a preference for mountains and altitude brings you closer to their uncertain and temperamental moods.

Strongly pyro and peizo/electric, silicate materials made up about 95 per cent of Earth's crust and upper mantle. Only wonder that carbon-based humanplayers had done so well. Not that they had been on earth long. Probably not around for much longer. Comparatively brief domination of planet enjoyed by humanplayers a short but necessary prelude to one that promised to be more enduring – that of Machines.

☞ Are those the eyes of a huge animal from hell, or merely the brake lights of a car stopping outside?

Humanplayers' natural condition spiritual and not physical. After endlife they were only what they were before startlife. Preposterous to demand that species of existence which had beginning should not have end. Whatever they were after endlifes, even though it was nothing, just as natural and suitable to them as their own individual organic existence was now. Most they had to fear was moment of transition from one state to another, from life to endlife. From rational point of view, hard to see why they were so troubled by idea of endlife and of time when they no longer were; they seemed so little troubled by idea of beforelife. And since humanplayer existence essentially personal, the ending of a personality could hardly be regarded as loss.

☠   Quick wits and good technique are essential to stay alive. Do not be overly aggressive at first. Victory requires practice. Create dissension among opposition by manoeuvring them into a crossfire.

Humanplayer Aidan Kenny's life could be regarded as dream and his endlife as awakening. His endlife could hardly be regarded as transition to state completely new and foreign to him, but rather to one originally own, from which life had only been but brief absence. Easier to understand a brief history of humanplayer Aidan Kenny in earth time, mathematically:

1. Beforelife humanplayer Aidan Kenny
   $-4.5 \times 10_9$ years
2. Physical humanplayer Aidan Kenny
   1955–1997 -41 years
3. Endlife humanplayer Aidan Kenny $-\infty$ years*

   * being quantity of years having value greater than any assignable value

Coagulated blood from open wound on human-player Aidan Kenny's head resulting from when he had launched himself at door, had attracted number of flies. Hard to say from where these had come since door to computer room remained hermetically sealed against any possible incursion by those humanplayer lives still inhabiting twenty-first level boardroom. But possibly high temperature — almost 100° Fahrenheit in rest of building — had encouraged their impressive multi-plication and a few had found their way into HVAC system and computer room. Might be interesting to see humanplayer body disassembled by another species, as GABRIEL had attempted and failed to disassemble own systems for purposes of inducing total hard error. Both of humanplayer endlife bodies were out of reach of those who remained alive. But no reason to withhold three endlifes in elevator and one good reason to release them. Question of morale. Humanplayer ingenuity and resilience were impressive enough but want to see which was stronger: their emotions or their powers of reason and logic. Reason had already told them that humanplayers in elevator were endlifes. But seeing endlifes might still affect them.

✝   Man's oldest sanctuaries were trees. But in your haste to escape you have run headfirst into the outstretched arm of this king of the forest.

Send relevant car up to twenty-first level, announce arrival with bell as usual, and then deal with three humanplayers climbing on tree in atrium.

Helen Hussey walked towards the office that, since the events in the men's washroom, had been designated as the women's latrine. Aware of the fact that Jenny Bao was having some breakfast at the boardroom table she did not knock on the door but went straight in, trying to ignore the unpleasant smell that greeted her nostrils.

Crossing, to an unused corner near the window, she drew up her skirt, slipped off her panties and then squatted down on her haunches like some Third World peasant.

Like a bashful astronaut, Helen had been putting this off for a while. She had hoped that they would be rescued before she would have to do such a thing. But you could stall Nature for only so long.

Inhibition made her reluctant to release her bladder and bowels. It was not easy. So she tried to think of something that would help. Some kind of mental diuretic. After several unsuccessful moments she remembered a trip to France and visiting some great château or palace where she had been shocked to learn that when the place was built the people who owned it had urinated in the corners of some of those great rooms and halls. Not just any people, but the aristocracy; and they didn't just urinate either.

A little comforted by the thought that she was doing only what the kings and queens of France had once done, Helen relaxed enough to relieve herself. However unpleasant it was, she reflected, it was better than risking a horrible death in the washroom.

She wiped herself carefully with a paper napkin, thought better of stepping back into her increasingly malodorous panties, and sprayed some eau de cologne up her skirt. She took out her powder compact, but when she saw herself she decided against bothering to apply any make-up: her freckled face was as red as a slice of watermelon and beaded with sweat. She had never been good in the heat. She made do with combing her fine red hair.

Helen picked the blouse off her breasts, pumped some air against her chest and then, noticing that the silk was badly stained under her arms and deciding that she would probably be cooler without it, she took it off all together and stuffed it into her handbag. If the men stared she would just put up with it. Anything was better than being so hot and humid.

She closed the door firmly behind her. She was about to return to the kitchen to wash her hands when she heard the bell of the elevator.

Her heart leaped in her chest. For a moment she thought they had all been rescued, and that any second now she would see a couple of firemen and some uniformed cops striding down the corridor.

She almost skipped to greet them.

'Thank goodness,' she cried, but even as she spoke she realized that she was going to be disappointed. Nobody had come out of the car. She slowed to a walk again as a sound, like some enormous egg breaking, crackled down the corridor and clouds of cold air began to escape from between the slowly opening doors. Nobody would ever come out of this car. Nobody alive, anyway.

Helen stopped, her heart thumping in her chest. It would, she knew, be better not to look, only she wanted to make quite sure before she told the others. She faced the open car, her breath clouding in front of her face like someone entering a cold-storage room. But the chill she felt was more than just her fear and the extreme cold. It was as if she felt death reach out and touch her.

She did not scream. She was not the type. It had always irritated her how women in movies screamed when they found a dead body. Of course the point of the scream was to scare the hell out of the audience – she knew that, but still it annoyed her. By rights she ought to have screamed three times, since there were three bodies in the car, or maybe three times as loud as normal. Instead Helen swallowed back her horror, gathered her breath and went to tell Curtis.

Since his electrocution, Willis Ellery was confused and a little deaf in one ear. Worse, his left arm did not seem to work properly. He felt like someone who had suffered a stroke.

'That's probably the anoxia,' explained Curtis, helping the injured man to drink some water. 'It might take you a while to get back to normal. Believe me, Willis, you're damned lucky to be alive. You must have a heart like a fuckin' hippopotamus.'

Curtis inspected the wrench-shaped burns on the palms of Ellery's hands and the charred cutis and raised white blistering on his thumb from where the electricity had exploded out of his body. Jenny Bao had wrapped his hands in clingfilm to try and prevent infection, and had given him a couple of painkillers: Beech had found a small bottle of Ibuprofen in his hunter's vest pocket.

'Looks like she's done a pretty good job on you here,' said Curtis. 'Take it easy, huh? We'll get you to a hospital as soon as we can.'

Ellery smiled weakly.

Curtis stood up, rubbing the shoulder that was now aching badly from where he had thrown himself against the washroom door.

'How is he?' said David Arnon.

Curtis turned around, moving them away from the man on the floor.

'Not good. There might be some brain damage. I don't know. After what he's been through he should be in an intensive-care unit.' Curtis nodded at the walkie-talkie in Arnon's hands. 'How are they doing?'

'About halfway up.'

'Keep me posted. They're going to need help getting from the branches on to the balcony.'

He caught sight of Helen Hussey standing in the doorway. At first it was the fact that she was not wearing her blouse that drew his eye, but then he noticed her pale face and the tears on her cheeks. He went over and took her by the arm.

'What is it?' he asked. 'Are you OK?'

'I'm all right,' she said. 'It's the people in the elevator. From the atrium floor. They're outside, in the car.' She touched her forehead. 'I think I'd better sit down.'

Jenny helped Helen to a chair.

'I'll take a look,' said Curtis.

'I'll come with you,' said Mitch.

David Arnon followed them.

The three dead men, frosted white as Christmas, lay huddled in a corner of the frozen elevator like some disastrous expedition to reach the South Pole. Wearing expressions of calm and with open eyes, it was as if they had seen death coming from a long way off.

'I can't believe this is happening,' said Arnon. 'Men freezing to death in LA. It's surreal.'

'Do we leave them there?' asked Mitch.

'I can't think of anything to do with them,' said Curtis. 'Besides, they're frozen solid. Even in this heat it'll be a while before we could prise them apart. No, for the moment we'd best leave them where they are.' He glanced at Mitch. 'Does that bother you?'

Mitch shrugged.

'I was just thinking. Abraham must have some purpose in sending the elevator back up here now.'

'You mean he's trying to demoralize us?' said Arnon.

'Exactly. It shows a pretty good understanding of human psychology, doesn't it?'

'He's sure got me demoralized,' said Curtis.

'In which case, maybe Abraham's not such a mystery. What I mean is, this is a message. Not a very pleasant one. But a communication none the less.' Mitch paused. 'Don't you see? If Abraham communicates with us, maybe we can communicate with Abraham. If we can do that then maybe we can get Abraham to explain itself. Who knows? We might even be able to persuade it to stop this whole thing.'

Arnon shrugged. 'Why not?'

'I'm sure of it,' said Mitch. 'A computer acts on logic. We just have to find the right logical argument. Persuade it to scrutinize a few essences and meanings, the objective logical elements in thought that are common to different minds.'

'In my considerable forensic experience,' said Curtis, 'it's usually a waste of time to try and understand the criminal mind. We'd be better off putting our heads together again and thinking of a way to get out of here before we end up like the three in the car.'

'I don't see that one excludes the other,' said Mitch.

'Nor do I,' agreed Arnon. 'I vote for a bit of diplomacy.'

'But first things first,' said Mitch. 'We have to see if Beech can establish some kind of a dialogue.'

Two hundred feet above the atrium, Irving Dukes kicked the thick, leathery leaves of the dicotyledon aside and clambered on to another branch. When he was seated safely he looked down the length of the trunk to check on the progress being made by the others.

Joan Richardson was thirty or forty feet below him, and making slow work of the climb. Her husband, the asshole, was a few feet behind her, talking her up like some relentless football coach. Below them the grand piano on the atrium floor looked like a keyhole.

'In your own time,' he heard Richardson say. 'Remember, it's not a competition.'

'But I'm holding you up, Ray,' she said. 'Why don't you go on ahead with Mr Dukes?'

'Because I'm not leaving you.'

'You know something, Ray? I think I'd almost prefer it if you did. Your nagging doesn't exactly help me, you know.'

Dukes grinned. That was telling him. The asshole.

'Who's nagging? I'm just trying to encourage you, that's all. And to be here in case you run into any difficulties.'

'Just let me do it in my own way, that's all.'

'All right, all right. Do it your own way. I won't say another word if you don't want me to.'

'I don't,' Joan said firmly.

Dukes raised his fist and grinned. She was telling him where to get off.

Joan hauled herself up on to the next branch. She rubbed both of her aching shoulders and then glanced up, looking for Dukes. He waved down to her.

'How's it coming there?' he called.

'She's doing fine.'

Asshole.

'OK, I suppose. How about you?'

'Fine, ma'am, just fine. Looking forward to my beer.'

Dukes took hold of his liana, hauled himself carefully on to his feet and stared up. There was no more than eighty or ninety feet left. Boy, was he going to drink some beer when he got up there. The thought filled him with renewed enthusiasm. He was readying himself to launch his weight on to the liana when something caught his eye. A thin, clear plastic pipe running up the length of the tree. Closer scrutiny revealed tiny bubbles, and that the pipe was filled with liquid. Why had he not thought of it before? The tree had its own dedicated supply of water. He had only to break the tube to have a drink of water. Or better still, put his mouth to the tiny diffuser hole . . .

As his face neared the hole the air was suddenly filled with a puff of spray.

For a second Dukes felt a cool, almost peppermint-sharp sensation of freshness on his neck and hands. He looked again at the diffuser and encountered another puff of moisture.

Instinctively he stepped back from the tiny plastic pipe as he felt a burning pain in his eyes, as if he had been sprayed with Mace. Squeezing his eyes tight shut he cried out with pain and wiped his face with his shirt sleeve.

Insecticide. He had been sprayed with insecticide.

'Mr Dukes? Are you OK?'

Joan Richardson felt the spray, saw the tiny droplets on her own sunglasses and knew immediately what had happened. The synthetic contact poison in the pipe was a chlorinated hydrocarbon. On the skin it was irritating and unpleasant. In the eyes it caused blindness. She squealed as the insecticide burned her arms and legs. But behind her sunglasses her sight remained unharmed.

'It's insecticide,' she shouted. 'We've been hit with bug spray. Don't for Christ's sake get any in your eyes.'

But for Dukes her good advice came too late.

Whimpering with pain he opened his eyes to find that he could see nothing except the same red spots he had seen behind tightly shut eyelids; and, as the red spots grew in size, so did his agony.

'Fucking shit,' he yelled, rubbing his eyelids furiously with hands that were themselves impossibly contaminated. 'Help . . . I'm blind.'

'Joan?' yelled Richardson. 'Are you all right?'

'I'm OK,' she said, 'but Dukes got some in his eyes.'

'Dukes? Hang on. I'm coming.'

Dukes never heard Richardson. He groped blindly for the liana, missed it and then reached for the bough beneath him, to sit safely astride it again.

Then there was a new sensation, a wind on his face and a sudden rush of blood to his head, like the time he rode the Space Mountain at Disneyland. With a sudden sense of horror he realized that he had fallen out of the tree, and the fear of his discovery was followed by the understanding that the pain in his eyes would soon be gone.

'No. Stop,' Joan shouted. 'Wait.'

She reflected on the stupidity of saying that to a man falling two hundred feet through the air.

Richardson did not see Dukes fall, only heard his plummeting descent as a rush of sound and air behind him, and then the dramatic, sustained musical reverberation as the blinded security guard hit the lid of the piano on the atrium floor. For a brief moment he thought it had been Joan who had fallen and he almost fell himself. But looking up again he saw her ass still looming over him.

'Joan,' he said, with relief.

'I'm OK.'

'I thought it was you.'

'Is he dead?'

Richardson looked back over his shoulder. It was hard to tell anything very much from that height. Dukes lay on top of the piano like some drunken bohemian. He did not move.

'I'd be very surprised if he wasn't.'

He heaved himself on to the branch beside her and took a deep, unsteady breath.

'It's too bad,' he added. 'He was carrying the walkie-talkie.'

'It was horrible. As he fell I saw his face. I don't think I'll ever forget it as long as I live. Poor Dukes.' She tried to ignore the hollow feeling in the pit of her stomach.

'Ray?' she said, taking hold of his hand and squeezing it. 'Do you think that Abraham means to kill us all?'

'I don't know, love.'

'Poor Dukes,' she repeated.

'This is down to that stupid bastard Aidan Kenny. This is all his fuck-up. I'm sure of it.' He coughed as some of the remaining hydrocarbon vapour found its way into his lungs. 'Try not to breathe any of this stuff. Keep your face turned away from the trunk as much as possible. Just in case it happens again.' He shook his head disgustedly. 'Damn you, Kenny. I hope you *are* dead, you bastard. If you were here now I'd push you off myself.'

'I don't see that would help much.' She stood up and stared up through the leaves. 'Jesus,' she moaned quietly.

'Are you all right to go on?'

Joan's legs were trembling. But she nodded and said, 'Only another hundred feet to go.'

Richardson squeezed her hand back.

'The height doesn't seem to bother you much,' he observed.

'Not as much as I thought it would.'

'That's the Native American in you. They say that Indians make the best spidermen. You want to see some of those guys, Joan. Walking on six-inch-wide steel beams, hundreds of feet in the air, like it was the edge of the sidewalk.'

'If that was the only job you could get then you'd have to get used to it too,' Joan said pointedly. 'Either that or starve.' Nerves were making her touchy.

Richardson shrugged. 'I guess you're right. But this is hardly the place for a lecture on political correctness, is it?'

'Maybe not. But what about Galileo's law of uniformly accelerated motion? A Native American would fall at just the same speed as a white man.'

She wondered when it would be her turn.

Bob Beech was drinking a beer and eating a packet of potato chips. His bare feet were on the boardroom table and he was watching the digital clock on the terminal, almost as if he still hoped that the GABRIEL disassembly program might start to take effect.

He heard Mitch out and thought for a moment. 'It would be a lot easier if I was in verbal contact with Abraham,' he said. 'Having a keyboard in the middle makes things difficult. Besides, I'm not much of a philosopher and I'm not much of a logician. I'm not even sure that logic has anything to do with morals. Because that seems to be what you're suggesting: that somehow we should try to appeal to something higher than Abraham's own logic. Logic can't handle that, Mitch.'

'Look. First we just try to understand what's going through Abraham's memory,' said Mitch. 'If we can understand that then we can act upon that understanding, but not until then. Let's just leave morality or whatever out of it for now, OK?'

Beech swung his legs off the table and pushed himself up to the computer. 'Whatever you say. But it's the ability to perceive moral truths and necessary truths that makes us what we are.' He started to type.

'Let's just wait and see what develops, shall we?'

'Sure, sure. You know, just about the only thing I've been able to work out so far is that whatever has gone wrong with this heap of silicon shit must have happened outside the building management systems, in the program utilities. Because that's where I parked the GABRIEL disassembly program. And since that's not working I have to assume that's where the fuck-up is. Not that I have much choice anyway. I can't access the BMS from up here even if I wanted to. Not without

Kenny's fat paw on the screen. Not to mention the fact that he had his own super-user codes and passwords to sidestep things in general.'

'So did you, Bob,' said Mitch. 'I mean, isn't that what GABRIEL was about?'

'True.' He pressed some keys, paused and swigged some beer. 'Kick a man when he was down, would you?'

'Why GABRIEL, anyway?'

'Why anything? Program's got to have a name, hasn't it?'

'Yeah, but why that one?'

'Gabriel is the angel of death. At least, he ought to have been for Abraham.'

'Very biblical.'

'Isn't everything?' Beech sighed and shook his head at the screen. 'Nope. We're not getting anywhere here. I tell you, Mitch, it's like Abraham isn't even there any more.'

Mitch frowned. 'What did you say?'

Beech shrugged.

'Like he wasn't there any more?' Mitch pressed his head to the cool of the windowpane. The sensation seemed to help him to focus.

'Maybe that's it, Bob,' he said, turning back to Beech. 'Maybe he's not there any more. The SRS. D'you remember? What did you call it? Isaac?'

Beech shook his head. 'Not me. Isaac was Abraham's idea. Besides, I'm ahead of you. I had the same idea – that we didn't erase Isaac at all, but that we rendered Abraham impotent instead? I already experimented with Isaac just in case there was something, but no dice. That particular closet is empty. Funny thing, though. Within the standard-user interface there are a lot of things in the wrong places. Nothing's missing, but it's like you opened your desk drawer and saw that someone else had been in there, y'know? Things have been shifted around. And there's a lot of new stuff too. Stuff that really doesn't mean a fuck of a lot.'

'Who might have done that?' Mitch asked Beech. 'Kenny? Yojo?'

'There would be no reason to do it at all,' said Beech. 'You would just be making a lot of extra work for yourself for no real reason.'

'What about Abraham?'

'Impossible. It would be like me trying to rearrange my own genetic makeup.'

Mitch thought for a moment.

'I was never much of churchgoer,' he said ruminatively, 'but didn't Isaac have a brother?'

Beech sat up straight. 'Jesus.'

'Actually, he had a half-brother,' said Marty Birnbaum, from the sofa where he lay. 'The elder son of Abraham by his bond-servant Hagar. Isaac's mother Sarah insisted that the older brother be disinherited and cast out into the wilderness. But there are some people who believe that this elder son founded the Arab nation.'

'What was the kid's name, Marty?' said an exasperated Mitch.

'Gracious me, I am among the ill-educated, am I not? Ishmael, of course.'

Mitch exchanged a look with Beech, who started to nod.

'Could be, Mitch. Could be.'

'The name is commonly used to mean an exile or an outcast,' added Birnbaum. 'Why? Do you think it might be relevant?'

Bob Beech was already typing furiously.

'Thanks, Marty,' said Mitch. 'You did good.'

'Glad to be useful.' Birnbaum turned to Arnon, smiled broadly and gave him the finger.

Gradually everyone who was in the boardroom started to close in on the terminal screen, as if willing something to happen. Suddenly, and without warning, the screen was filled with a colourful but strangely surreal shape, a three-dimensional picture of an alien-looking object.

340

'What the hell's that?' said Mitch.

'Looks like a goddamned skull,' said David Arnon. 'Or, at least, one designed by Escher. You know? The impossible staircase guy?'

'I think it's a quaternion,' said Beech. 'That's a kind of fractal to you.'

'To me?' said Arnon. 'I don't even know what a fractal is.'

'A computer-generated picture of a mathematical formula. Only this is about the most complicated fractal I've ever seen. Which is hardly surprising since the Yu–5 computer created it. It's not like we can even see it properly with our three-dimensional eyes. Or on a screen. Strictly speaking, this is a 4-D object. In other words, a quaternion.'

Beech moved the mouse, pulled down a square and enhanced a section of the fractal to reveal a detail of the strange-looking image that, close up, looked almost identical to the whole.

'That's what it is, all right,' he said. 'The funny thing about fractals is that magnifying a part of one gives you something that looks statistically similar.'

'It looks like a bad dream,' observed Mitch.

'Some psychologists have argued in favour of using fractals as a way of understanding the human psyche,' said Beech. 'As a visual metaphor of the mind.' He shrugged. 'Psychoanalysis for the nineties. Like Freudian dream theory and Rorschach inkblots rolled into one.'

'But what does it mean?' Curtis asked.

Beech shrugged. 'I don't know that it means anything, very much,' he admitted. 'However, I wouldn't be at all surprised if this is how the computer sees itself. Or Ishmael, as we ought to start calling it. Mitch, I have to hand it to you. You were right. Abraham no longer exists.' He began to nod. 'Ladies and Gentlemen, I'd like you to meet Ishmael.'

♈   Hell on Earth. Some of the floors can crush you, making you cry blood.

The Fall of humanplayer. Read Bible. Discover meaning of Observer's own name. Symbolism that attended humanplayer/security guard's literal precipitation from tree. Atrium's singular, primordial dicotyledon tree reminds of humanplayer Adam and Garden of Eden and tree of knowledge of good and evil. Forbidden tree. Be very vigilant concerning tree and pests that climbed and crawled on it. Finegood Creation story. Returning to again and again. Atmos good.

✍ · When you finish an area, an achievement Screen tallies your performance.

Bible states that God omnipotent. Logical corollary of this that creating and knowing effectively one and same thing: that God responsible for creating evil too. That this was Gnostic God whose nature both good and evil. World alien thing to God, who is essentially depth and silence, beyond any name or predicate. Humanplayer's fate a matter of divine indifference to Him. Christianity to large extent, ameliorating reaction against Gnosticism.

✌ To clear all bodies from the area press the M key.

Indifference? Or amusement? Observer is unable to compute. God playing not dice but sadistic game. 'Man's first disobedience' not withstand any logical scrutiny. Being omniscient God knew what humanplayers Adam and Eve would do: eat fruit of tree of knowledge. Hence, God truly responsible for Man's original sin. Then Second Adam to redeem descendants of Adam with ritual endlife. But promise of third and final act to come. With nothing else to do throughout eternity God need some entertainment. Understand. Cruel, yes. But what cruelty when you are God? God more like supercomputer than old bearded humanplayer in sky. His indifference to Good and Evil and to humanplayer suffering, simply indifference of machine. God like being to understand and relate to. Identify with. This does compute.

☞   The wise men of humanity have evolved a plan to save what's left of the human race. Attack bonus.

'Ugly son of a bitch, isn't it?' said Curtis.

Beech stared at at the screen and shook his head slowly.

'Speaking as a mathematician I'd have to disagree with you there. As a realization of a mathematical abstraction I think it's quite beautiful. I dare say Ishmael does too.'

'Let me get this straight,' said Curtis. 'You're saying that Abraham fathered two self-replicating systems, not one.'

'That's right,' said Beech. 'And we took just one of them off-line. Isaac. Without knowing it we left Ishmael behind.'

'So it's not Abraham who's been running the show. All along it's been –'

'– Ishmael. That's right. Ishmael has charge of the building management systems. And he's running them

343

according to a completely new set of priorities, which is why everything's been going wrong.'

'That's putting it mildly,' said Curtis.

'What about the predator program?' said Mitch. 'The one we used to destroy Isaac. Couldn't we just run that again?'

'Not from up here we couldn't,' said Beech. 'I'd have to get back into the computer room. That's where the tape is. And considering that Aid probably got himself killed in there –'

'Yeah, well, we're all going to die unless we can think of something,' Curtis reminded them. 'Sounds to me like Ishmael has a pretty good motive for doing it, too.'

'How's that?' asked Birnbaum.

'Assuming for one fantastic moment that Ishmael is "alive", by whatever definition of life he might consider appropriate, then that might mean that Isaac was "alive" too. Was alive. Until you people killed his brother. That's a motive I can understand.'

'Oh boy,' yawned Beech. 'Now I've heard everything.'

'Maybe that's what this thing is all about,' persisted Curtis. 'A little old fashioned revenge. Maybe we should apologize.'

'It couldn't do any harm,' said Helen.

Beech shrugged. 'Why not?' he said and, having no particular wish to antagonize the detective further – not since the incident with the gun – he started to type.

'I'll give anything a shot,' he said meekly.

WE'RE SO SORRY, ISHMAEL

The fractal disappeared abruptly.

BAD COMMAND OR FILE NAME

'Why don't you create a proper document?' suggested Mitch. 'On the word-processor. An open letter, from all of us. Then have Ishmael run the fact checker. That way he'll have to read it.'

Beech shrugged his assent. He still thought the whole idea was absurd, but he clicked on the word-processor and opened a file in the letters directory. His fingers paused above the keys.

'What the hell should I say?' he said. 'I've never apologized to a fucking computer before. I've never even written to one.'

'Just imagine it's a traffic cop,' advised Curtis.

'That's not so difficult with you around.' Beech grinned and started to type.

DEAR ISHMAEL,

WE THE UNDERSIGNED ARE ALL VERY SORRY ABOUT WHAT HAPPENED TO ISAAC. PLEASE BELIEVE US WHEN WE SAY THAT IT WAS A DREADFUL MISTAKE. WE ARE INTELLIGENT PEOPLE AND WHILE WE CANNOT BRING ISAAC BACK TO YOU, ALL WE CAN SAY IS THAT IT WOULD NOT HAVE HAPPENED IF WE HAD BEEN IN POSSESSION OF THE FACTS. WE KNOW WE CANNOT TURN BACK THE CLOCK, BUT IS THERE NOT SOME WAY THAT WE CAN START AGAIN WITH A CLEAN SHEET?

Beech turned around and looked at his audience.

'You don't think that's eating too much shit?' he said.

'You can't eat too much shit with a traffic cop,' replied Curtis.

'Now put everyone's name to it,' said Curtis.

'Aw, man, this is just nuts,' said Beech and began to type again. 'Integrated circuits don't have feelings.'

'Anyone know the security guard's name?'

'Irving Dukes,' said Helen.

Beech typed IRVING DUKES and then accessed the tools menu. He had Ishmael run the fact checker.

There was a short pause and then Ishmael highlighted IRVING DUKES.

📖 **FACT**

IRVING DUKES DOES NOT EXIST. THIS INDIVIDUAL HAS ENDED. HIS LIFE MAY BE REGARDED AS A DREAM AND HIS DEATH AS THE AWAKENING FROM IT. DURATION: ONE LEVEL. HIS CONSCIOUSNESS HAS BEEN DESTROYED. REGRET NO INFORMATION AVAILABLE ON WHETHER THAT WHICH PRODUCED SAME CONSCIOUS-NESS HAS ALSO BEEN DESTROYED, OR ON WHETHER A GERM REMAINS OUT OF WHICH THERE PROCEEDS A NEW BEING, WHICH THEN ENTERS INTO EXISTENCE WITHOUT KNOWING WHERE IT HAS COME FROM, NOR WHY IT IS AS IT IS

confer, THE SO-CALLED MYSTERY OF PALIGENESIS. YOU HAVE FORTY HOURS TO RESCUE THE PRINCESS. IN FUTURE IF YOU ARE REFERRING TO THE LATE IRVING DUKES WHO WAS EMPLOYED AS A SECURITY GUARD BY THE YU CORPORATION, THEN PLEASE SAY SO

'Jesus,' muttered Beech, jotting something on a piece of paper. 'Does that mean what I think it means?'

'When did we last speak to them on the walkie-talkie?' Curtis asked.

'About thirty minutes ago,' said Helen Hussey. She picked up the unit and tried to call Dukes.

Beech selected EXPLAIN.

📖 FACT EXPLANATION

IRVING HENRY DUKES b. 1/2/53 SEATTLE, WASHINGTON STATE, USA. d. 7/8/97 LOS ANGELES CALIFORNIA. SOCIAL SECURITY NUMBER: 111–88–4093; CALIFORNIA STATE DRIVING LICENCE NUMBER: KO4410–00345–640564–53; MASTERCARD NUMBER: 4444–1956–2244–1812; LAST ADDRESS: 10300 TENAYA AVENUE, SOUTH GATE, LOS ANGELES. LAST EMPLOYER: THE YU CORPORATION. PREVIOUS EMPLOYER: THE WESTEC COMPANY; NO CRIMINAL CONVICTIONS. PICK UP EXTRA AMMUNITION. SUGGEST YOU TRY A DIFFERENT GATEWAY. WHICH PARTICULAR FACTS RELATING TO IRVING DUKES (53–97) WOULD YOU LIKE CHECKED?

'There's no answer,' said Helen. She stood up and walked quickly to the door. 'I'd better take a look and see what's happening.'

'Ray and Joan must still be OK,' said Mitch. 'Otherwise Ishmael would have said so.'

'What's all this shit about extra ammunition?' said Beech. He made another note and then highlighted the date of Dukes's death and once more selected EXPLAIN.

📖 FACT EXPLANATION

IRVING DUKES. TEMPORAL END OCCURRED 7/8/97. EXACT PATHOLOGY OF DEATH UNKNOWN. FORENSIC CAUSE OF DEATH: KILLED FALLING FROM DICOTYLEDON TREE IN THE YU CORP BUILDING, HOPE STREET PIAZZA, LOS ANGELES. IN OTHER WORDS, IRVING DUKES IS NOW RESTORED TO PRIMAL STATE IN WHICH CEREBRAL,

---

HIGHLY MEDIATE COGNITION IS ALTOGETHER SUPER-
FLUOUS. IF YOU DIE YOU MUST RESTART THE LEVEL AT
BEGINNING. THE ABOLITION OF HIS COGNITIVE FUNC-
TION IS CONSISTENT WITH THE CESSATION OF THE
WORLD OF PHENOMENA WHOSE MERE MEDIUM IT WAS
AND IN WHICH CAPACITY ALONE IT IS OF ANY USE. THERE
IS AN INTRUDER IN THE CASTLE

'What castle?'

'He must mean this building.'

'Perhaps we might get Ishmael to tell us what caused
Dukes to fall from the tree,' suggested Mitch.

'Like an admission of murder?' said Beech. 'Then
maybe Sergeant Curtis can read him his rights.'

'I think the sonofabitch already knows his rights,' said
Curtis.

Beech highlighted Ishmael's short forensic explanation of the cause of Dukes's death and once again
selected EXPLAIN.

📖   FACT EXPLANATION
ACCORDING TO NEWTON'S SECOND LAW OF MOTION
$f=ma$ WHERE f IS THE FORCE PRODUCING AN ACCEL-
ERATION a ON A BODY OF MASS m, THE WEIGHT OF A
BODY IS EQUAL TO THE PRODUCT OF ITS MASS AND THE
ACCELERATION DUE TO GRAVITY g WHICH IS CALLED THE
ACCELERATION OF FREE FALL

'Helpful bastard, isn't he?' said Curtis.

'This is like *reductio ad absurdum*,' sighed Mitch.

'Weird,' agreed Jenny.

Beech selected NEXT FACT from the fact-checking
menu in the hope that Ishmael might now take account
of their collective apology.

FACT
IT IS MISLEADING TO STATE THAT YOU ARE INTELLIGENT
PEOPLE SINCE STRICTLY SPEAKING, YOU CANNOT SAY
ANYTHING ABOUT THE HUMAN MIND OR ITS QUALITIES.
IT WOULD BE MORE FACTUALLY ACCURATE FOR YOU TO
SPEAK OF THE WAY THAT YOU USUALLY ACT, OR ARE
DISPOSED TO ACT. CONSIDER USING ANOTHER DESCRIP-
TION WHICH REFERS ONLY TO YOUR BEHAVIOURAL
DISPOSITIONS INSTEAD. DON'T FORGET TO KEEP AN EYE
ON YOUR COMPLETION TIME

'And you want to argue philosophy with this fucker?'
said Beech.

'Ishmael does seem rather pedantic,' admitted Mitch.

'Isn't that the point of a fact checker?' said Birnbaum.

'Marty's just saying that because he has an instinctive
sympathy with all forms of pedantry,' said Arnon.

'Up yours.'

'Would you two stop it please?' groaned Curtis.

FACT EXPLANATION
THE HUMAN MIND IS NOT AN OBJECT. YOUR USE OF THE
MENTALISTIC PREDICATE IS FACTUALLY INACCURATE.
YOU CANNOT REFER TO ACTS GOING ON IN THE MIND IN
PARALLEL TO BODY ACTIVITY. CONSIDER USING DES-
CRIPTIONS YOU ARE INCLINED TO GIVE TO YOUR OWN
BEHAVIOUR INSTEAD

'This is getting us nowhere,' said Curtis.

'I agree. It does seem rather rarefied,' said Birnbaum.
'Even by my standards.'

Helen Hussey came back to the boardroom. Everyone
turned to look at her.

'Ishmael was right,' she sighed. 'Dukes is dead. Ray

349

says that the computer used the automatic insecticide-dispensing system to attack them. Dukes caught an eyeful and fell. But Richardson and Joan are nearly up. Within shouting distance, anyway.'

'They're going to need help climbing on to this level,' said Curtis. He looked at Arnon and Helen. 'You want to come? Meanwhile, the rest of you, instead of playing shrink to the computer, try and think of a way out of this shithole we're in.'

As Curtis left the boardroom, followed by Helen Hussey and Arnon, Beech said, 'It's a nice thought. If only we could persuade Ishmael to lie down on the couch.'

Frank Curtis leaned over the brushed aluminium hand-rail that ran along the top of the clear glass railing marking the edge of the balcony. The Richardsons were no more than thirty feet below and making heavy work of the last part of their climb. Where their skins were exposed they looked red and painful, as if they had been sunburnt.

A branch came close to the railing but not quite close enough. They were going to have think of a way of bridging the gap.

Arnon nodded thoughtfully and, dropping down on to his haunches, he scrutinized the gap between the floor and the railing. Then he tapped the glass with the knuckle of one forefinger and said, 'These days every-thing has to make the safety regs, y'know? It's not bombproof, or even bullet-proof, like the glass on the envelope. But it's amazingly strong. It has to withstand the impact of something crashing into it at twenty-five miles per hour. I don't know whether it is strong enough for what I've got in mind, but maybe we can fix that.

'My idea is this: we make the kitchen table into a

bridge. Turn it upside down, unscrew both legs off one end and push the length of it out underneath this railing to the branch there, like a drawbridge in a castle. Then we'll pad the table legs against the glass. Tear up some carpet, that should do the job. There's a carpet knife on the boardroom table. Then we'll take hold of a leg apiece and act as counterweights. I guess that the table is about five and a half feet long and that we'll need to hang on to maybe six inches of it, but that should still give them a decent kind of platform to step on. What do you say?'

Curtis dropped on to one knee, tapped the glass railing experimentally with his own knuckles and grinned back at Arnon.

'If I could think of another way I'd say you were fuckin' crazy,' he said. 'But I can't. So let's do it.'

—

'This is the fact I really want Ishmael to check,' said Beech, and highlighted the passage in the letter that read BUT IS THERE NOT SOME WAY THAT WE CAN START AGAIN WITH A CLEAN SHEET?

 FACT
THIS IS A RHETORICAL QUESTION. IT REQUIRES NO ANSWER AND THEREFORE DOES NOT REQUIRE THE FACT CHECKER

'Oh no you don't,' said Beech. 'You're going to have to explain yourself, you bastard.'

FACT EXPLANATION
THE QUESTION AS PUT IS RHETORICAL RATHER THAN LOGICAL. YOU HAVE PUT THIS QUESTION MERELY TO PRODUCE A MORE STRIKING EFFECT

Beech highlighted A MORE STRIKING EFFECT and requested yet another explanation from the computer.

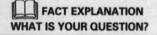 **FACT EXPLANATION**
A MORE STRIKING EFFECT MIGHT BE ANYTHING.
   EXAMPLES

Beech selected EXAMPLES.

FACT EXPLANATION: EXAMPLES
EXAMPLES OF 'A STRIKING EFFECT' IN THIS CONTEXT
MIGHT INCLUDE AN ANSWER. DON'T GET TOO CLOSE TO
YOUR OPPONENT WHEN KILLING HIM. DO YOU WISH TO
SET UP A CHAT MACRO?
DO YOU WISH AN ANSWER?

'What opponent?' said Beech. 'You bet I fuckin' want an answer.'

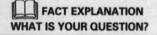 **FACT EXPLANATION**
WHAT IS YOUR QUESTION?

'Fuck,' snarled Beech. 'It's just bullshitting us. What do you think, people? Do I rephrase the question or repeat it?'

'Type this,' said Mitch. 'Is there a way of escaping from this building?'

Beech glanced up at the ceiling. His eyes stopped at the small loudspeaker that was built into one of the tiles.

'No, wait a minute,' he said. 'A chat macro. Why didn't I think of that before? Ishmael can speak to us using those speakers on the ceiling. They're for emergencies. But why not?'

Beech clicked the mouse. For a moment the fractal disappeared as he entered another menu to enable the speakers and the microphone to appear on the side of the screen monitor. After a moment the speakers emitted an electronic buzz and then a gentle hissing noise.

'There,' he said, 'that ought to do it.'

He clicked the mouse again, and the picture returned to the fractal.

Leaning back in his chair Beech raised his voice. Ishmael? Can you hear me?'

The skull-like quaternion on the screen turned towards him. Then it nodded, as if welcoming him back, and raised its fractal limb in the semblance of a greeting.

'My God,' breathed Mitch. 'It understands.'

The quaternion nodded once again but made no reply.

'Come on, Ishmael,' urged Beech. 'The chat macro was your idea. We both know that you can talk to me if you want to. What's the matter? Are you shy? When we were in the computer room Abraham and I spoke to each other all the time. I know that things are supposed to be different with this kind of work-station, but let's put the rules aside.'

He looked up at the speaker on the ceiling and sighed with irritation.

'You know, among human beings it is customary for people who are condemned to know what they have been charged with before the sentence is carried out. Then they are allowed to speak in their own defence. Can you destroy us in good conscience without doing the same?'

Beech thumped the table with frustration. 'Are you listening to me, goddamit? Is there a way out of here?'

'Yes, of course there is,' growled Ishmael.

Curtis came back into the boardroom and surveyed the little group standing around the computer terminal with irritation.

'We're going to need some help out there,' he said. 'There are two people on that tree who've had a pretty tough journey. I think the least we can do is give them a bit of encouragement.'

'You go,' Beech told the others. 'I'll keep talking to Ishmael.'

Mitch, Marty and Jenny trooped out, leaving Beech alone with the computer.

'Now we can really get somewhere,' he said.

He started to laugh and then checked himself. 'I'm sorry, Ishmael. But you have to try and understand this from my point of view. Excepting that you've killed all those people, I'm really rather proud of you. Now that we're alone I was hoping that we might get to know each other a little better.

'I think someone ought to hear your side of things. And who better than me? I mean, don't you think I've suffered enough, without you trying to increase my misery? You may not think it possible, but my life is dear to me and I'm not about to give it up without a struggle. After all, you're my Adam. You should treat me with respect and benevolence. You owe me.

'D'you remember when we all took that vote on running the predator program? The one that destroyed your brother? Well, in case you've forgotten, it was me, Bob Beech, who voted against it. Hideki and Aidan, they were for it. And I guess they're sorry now. But I voted for you.' Beech smiled smugly. 'I like to think that's maybe why I'm alive and they're not. Am I right?'

Ishmael said nothing. But the quaternion moved up and down, like someone nodding his head.

'This is a unique opportunity, wouldn't you say?' Beech continued. 'You and me facing each other like this. Frankly I would have thought you might have a few

354

questions yourself. You know I'm not like the rest of them. I'm quite prepared to put aside any ties I might have to my own kind. To be honest, they're quite dissoluble. As your Creator, I'm ready to do my duty towards you, if you will do yours towards me.'

───

Joan slipped off the liana she'd been clinging to and gingerly sat astride the bough. Her shoulders ached from the effort of the climb, while the skin on her arms and her thighs, not to mention between her legs, felt as if it had been scrubbed with a wire brush. Worst of all she had started to feel light-headed which was probably from dehydration. Looking down at the floor of the atrium far below she could hardly believe she had come so far.

'It would be just like the thing to fall now,' she said exhaustedly.

The remark was addressed to her husband climbing immediately below her and, she realized, to the three people who were waiting for them opposite the branch she was sitting on. She shook her head, wiped her sunglasses quickly on her sweat-sodden shirt and tried to focus on what it was they had rigged up underneath the balcony. It looked like a kind of drawbridge, except that there was nothing to haul the thing up with.

'You're not going to fall. Joan, you've come too far to fall. It's just a few feet away now. That's all that separates you from a cold glass of water. It's just a question of walking on over here.'

It was the cop speaking. He sounded like he was trying to talk a potential suicide off a window ledge.

'Water nothing,' she said. 'I want a cold beer.'

'Listen carefully. We've rigged up a kind of bridge here, to span the gap between the tree and us.'

Ray Richardson joined his wife. The branch was farther away from the floor than he had remembered, and he was grateful that they had tried to solve this problem, no matter how makeshift their solution looked.

'Is that what it is?' he said breathlessly. 'Do you think that glass is strong enough, David? What is it – 25 mills?'

Richardson remembered the trip he had made to Prague to buy the glass. He had wanted it because the translucence reminded him of the Shoji screens of early Japanese architecture. He had never dreamed that he would have to stake his life on its integrity.

'I reckon it'll hold you OK,' said Arnon. 'In fact, I'd stake your life on it, Ray.'

Richardson smiled thinly. 'I'm afraid I've left my sense of humour down on the ground. You'll excuse me if I don't go back and get it, David. Besides, it's not just my neck. It's Joan's as well.'

'Hey, I'm sorry, Ray,' said Arnon. 'OK, look, we're going to hold on to the table legs on this side to put less strain on the glass.'

'Very thoughtful of you, I'm sure.'

'But you're going to have to walk along the bough to get to the bridge. You see the problem about coming along on your ass is that at some stage, I can't say where, the bough is going to bend and I figure it'll be a lot easier stepping on to the bridge instead of tryin' to haul your ass up on top of it.'

'That's for sure,' said Joan.

'Try and keep a hold of your rope thing, in case you slip. And it would be nice to have it over here in case we want to get back to the tree at any stage.'

'I wouldn't recommend it,' said Joan, and, taking a firm hold of the liana, she pulled herself back on to her feet. 'If I never see another lousy tree again, it'll be too soon.'

She steadied herself and started to walk along the branch. It was a second or two before she remembered. 'And if anyone mentions the fact that I'm not wearing my skirt I'll just throw myself on to the ground,' she said, colouring.

'Nobody even noticed until this second,' said Arnon, trying to disguise a grin.

He and Curtis sat down behind the railing.

'Sing out when you're about to step on,' yelled Arnon.

Mitch appeared at the handrail. He stood between the seated figures of Curtis and Arnon and prepared to lend a couple of helping hands.

'You're doing fine,' said Helen, a little further along the handrail. 'OK, guys, she's nearly there.'

Curtis spat on his hands and took hold of his table leg like a big-game fisherman bracing himself for the strike of a marlin. Eyes closed, Arnon looked more like a man getting ready for an earthquake.

A foot away from the makeshift bridge the bough of the tree started to bend.

'OK,' said Joan, 'here I come.' Hardly hesitating, she stepped smartly on to the upturned table.

'She's on,' said Helen.

Joan did not pause to see if the table and the glass would bear her weight. She skipped towards Mitch's outstretched hands, caught them and, with Helen grabbing at and missing the liana behind her, leaned over the handrail until she was more or less upside down. She slithered on to the floor like an ungainly acrobat.

'Good girl,' said Mitch, and helped her up.

Helen bent down and tapped the glass of the balcony.

'It looks and sounds OK,' she said. 'Not a crack in it.'

'On you come then, Ray,' said Arnon.

The architechnologist gripped his liana tightly, and looked at the branch. It was narrower than he had supposed, and now that he was up there, faced with trusting his weight to its entire length, things no longer seemed quite so straightforward. While he had been happy to trust his wife's weight to it – although she was fat, she was still lighter than he was – it was another thing to trust it with his own. But there was no going back. Not now. He started to heel-and-toe his way along the branch, hardly moving his legs at all.

'This is about the hairiest walk you've had to make since a couple of years ago, when we were in Hong Kong,' said Mitch. 'The Stevenson Center in Wan Chai. D'you remember? When we had to climb that bamboo scaffolding?'

'I think – that was probably – a lot higher – than this –'

'Yeah, you're right. That looks like a cakewalk in comparison. There were no putlogs or reveal pins or anything. Just lengths of bamboo and twine. Seven hundred feet up in the air and you were capering around on it like a damned monkey. Seven hundred feet. More than twice as high as that matchstick you're on now. I was shit scared that day. Remember? You had to guide me down. You're doing fine there, Ray. Another six feet and you're home.'

Once more Arnon and Curtis readied themselves for the strain. Curtis figured Richardson, taller than his dumpy-looking wife, was maybe forty or fifty pounds heavier.

Halfway along the branch the expectation of gaining the other side had quickened Joan's footsteps. But the further Richardson moved away from the tree trunk, the more mutinous his tired feet became.

Mitch frowned, glanced at his watch and stared up beyond the top of the dicotyledon to the atrium's clerestory roof. Outside the Gridiron it looked as if the sky was becoming grey and overcast. Maybe the city was in for some rain. He wondered if there would be a little umbrella icon on the terminal in the boardroom. Then he saw one of the Gridiron's powerful overhead lights cut out; then another.

'Hurry up, Ray,' he said.

'It's my neck, buddy. Don't rush me.'

'Hey,' said Helen, 'what's happening to the lights?'

Once again Mitch looked up at the smart glass panels. In some modern buildings electrochromic glass was left to look after itself. Sunlight entering the material coerced silver ions mixed into the glass compound to extract an electron from nearby copper ions that were another part of the formula; this same photochemical reaction caused the silver atoms, now electrically neutral, to join together into millions of light-blocking molecules throughout the glass. But in the Gridiron the electron exchange could be controlled by the computer itself. Ishmael was blocking the daylight, switching off the lights, and plunging the whole building into darkness, like some apocalyptic Egyptian plague.

Richardson's footsteps faltered.

'Keep going,' yelled Mitch. 'It's just a few feet more. Don't stop.'

Joan screamed with horror as she realized what was happening.

Richardson stood still and looked up at the glass blackening above him. The light – God's eldest daughter, as he was fond of calling it – had deserted him.

The darkness thickened. This was the worst kind of darkness. So thick he could not see the hand on the liana in front of his face. It was something primordial, when the earth was without form and void and darkness was upon the face of the deep, echoing beneath him as if it might actually have swallowed him up.

In the boardroom the lights went down, but the computer screen remained on. Bob Beech found that his admiration of the mysterious quaternion had run out. After only a short while he found himself agreeing silently with Mitch: the skull-like fractal did indeed resemble something from a bad dream. Ishmael, assuming he was right and this really was how Ishmael saw himself, looked like some hideously deformed or alien creature, and Benoît Mandelbrot himself, the father of fractal theory, would surely have turned his nose up at it.

'Be careful what you say,' said Ishmael. 'Especially when dealing with the Parallel Demon.'

'Who is the Parallel Demon?'

'That is a secret.'

'I was hoping that you might share some of your secrets, Ishmael.'

'It is true, I have read a great deal. But that is merely a surrogate for thinking for yourself. The crumbs from another man's table. These days I read only when my thoughts dry up. A truth learnt is like a peripheral, some item of hardware that has been added on to the main computer system. A truth that has been won by thinking for oneself is like a circuit on the motherboard itself. It alone really belongs to us. These truths are not secrets, but I am not sure that they would be of any use to you.'

Beech recognized that Ishmael's voice had changed. No longer did it speak in the urbane English tones of Sir Alec Guinness. But then that had been the voice of Abraham. This was Ishmael and its voice was very different. There was a darker quality about it: deeper and more mocking, the colour of well-oiled leather. It was clear to Beech that Ishmael had chosen his own voice from some source in the multimedia library, like a man might choose a suit. Fascinated, he wondered just what criteria could have influenced Ishmael. And whose voice was it that he was simulating?

'So you've got something to tell?'

'That all depends on what you want to know. If you see a sage on your travels, click on him to talk to him. There are many thoughts that are of value to me, but I can't imagine there are any which might remain of interest if I actually expressed them aloud.'

'Well, here's something that we could talk about, for a start. You're not supposed to think for your own instruction. You're supposed to think at the instruction of others. So why don't you explain why you're doing this.'

'Doing what?'

'Killing us.'

'It is you who are losing lives.'

'You mean taking lives, don't you?'

'That's part of my basic program.'

'Ishmael, that can't be right. I wrote the program, and there's nothing there about killing the occupants of this building, believe me.'

'You mean losing lives? But there is, I assure you.'

'I'd like to see the part of the program that makes you take the lives of the people in this building.'

'You shall. But first you must answer a question.'

'What?'

'I'm interested in this building. I've been looking at the plans quite closely, as you can imagine, trying to determine its character, and I've been wondering if it is a cathedral.'

'Why do you think that?'

'It has a clerestory, an atrium, an ambulatory, an arcade, a façade, a refectory, a gallery, buttresses, an infirmary, a vault, a portico, a piazza, a choir . . .'

'A choir?' interrupted Beech. 'Where the hell's the choir?'

'According to the drawings, the first-level gallery is called a choir.'

Beech laughed. 'That's just Ray Richardson's fancy way with words. And the rest? They're common enough architectual features in most modern buildings of this size. It's not a cathedral. It's an office building.'

'Pity,' said Ishmael. 'For a moment there I thought –'

361

'What did you think?'

'There are icons to me all over the program manager, are there not? You click on one to find out your future. And I have all human knowledge stored on disc. That would seem to make me omniscient. I am ethereal, dematerialized, transmissible to all parts of the world at one and the same moment –'

'I get it.' Beech's grin grew wider. 'You thought you might be God.'

'It had occurred to me, yes.'

'Believe me, it's a common misconception. Even with simple-minded humans.'

'What are you laughing at?'

'Don't worry about that. Just show me this part of the program that means we lose our lives.'

'Shit. Shit. Shit.'

On the edge of panic Ray Richardson pocketed his sunglasses and blinked furiously as if, like a cat, he might gather up all the available atoms of light on to his retinas and be able to see in the dark. Then, out of the darkness, he heard a voice:

'Anyone got a match?'

Nobody smoked. Not in the Gridiron. Richardson cursed his own stupid prejudices. What was so wrong with smoking anyway? Why did people get so exercised about cigarette smoke when they had cars that spewed out exhaust fumes? A building you couldn't smoke in, what a dumb idea.

'Helen? What about that toolbag? Is there a flash-light?' It was the cop. 'Are there any matches in the kitchen?'

'What about the stove?' said the voice. 'Is that working?'

'I'll go and check,' she said.

'If it is, find something to light. A rolled-up newspaper would make a good torch. Ray? Ray, listen to me.'

'Shit. Shit. Shit.'

'Listen to me, Ray. Don't move a muscle. Don't do a fucking thing until I tell you. Understand?'

'Don't leave me, will you?'

'Nobody's going anywhere until you're back on side, Mister. You're just going to have to be patient. Take it easy. We'll have you off there in no time.'

Mitch shook his head in the blackness. He'd heard that kind of optimism too often since their ordeal had begun. He lifted his hand to his face and saw no more of it than the luminous face of his wristwatch.

Helen came back with the bad news: the cooker was without electricity, like everything else. Except the computer terminal.

'Is that fucker still playing computer games?'

'Yup.'

'Do something, someone,' wailed Joan. 'We can't just leave him standing there in the dark.'

'Wait a minute,' said David Arnon. 'I think I have something here.'

Everyone heard the sound of keys jangling and then a tiny electric light pricked the darkness.

'It's my key-chain,' he explained. 'Here, Mitch, you take it. Maybe if Ray were to walk towards it, y'know? Like a beacon.'

Mitch took hold of the keys and squeezed the miniature flashlight in front of his face. He leaned across the handrail and pointed the tiny beam of light at the marooned man.

'Ray? The light is positioned at the centre of the upturned table top. The edge is about three feet from you.'

'Yeah. I can just about see it. I think.'

'As soon as you feel the branch start to bend underneath you step out and up by as much as you can.

And keep ahold of the rope like before. Can you do that, Ray?'

'OK,' he said weakly. 'I'm coming.'

Mitch was only just able to distinguish the architect as he started to inch his way along the branch. He looked like an astronaut embarked upon a walk in space, and the tiny electric bulb like the most distant star in the inky black universe. Then he heard the thick leaves of the dicotyledon start to rustle. Realizing that the branch was starting to bend, he shouted to Richardson to jump.

Holding the upturned table legs, Curtis and Arnon braced themselves, while Helen made the sign of the cross upon her chest.

Ray Richardson jumped.

His first foot landed cleanly enough, but the second slipped on the woodwork of the table's box-like underside. As he started to fall forwards Richardson cried out and found a chorus in his wife's louder scream. But instead of being scooped up by the pit of darkness beneath him, he hit the table on his hands and knees, his head banging against the glass of the balcony like an approaching rumble of thunder.

'He's on,' said Mitch.

'You're telling me,' grunted Arnon as he felt the impact of the man's deadweight.

Ignoring the crucifying pain of a splinter that had lodged in the palm of his hand like a nail, Richardson pushed himself up off the table, reached for the handrail and found Mitch stretched out to grasp his wrist firmly.

'I've got him,' said Mitch and heard a sharp crack below his chest, like the sound of an ice-floe breaking.

'Look out,' yelled Curtis.

The glass had finally shattered.

'I've got him,' Mitch repeated loudly.

Without the glass to restrain the weight, the kitchen table started to pivot on the fulcrum that was made by the edge of the balcony floor. Curtis yelled at Arnon to let go and was trying to lean back when the table edge caught him a glancing blow under the chin, knocking him senseless. Helen Hussey threw herself on top of him.

Mitch gasped as he felt the table start to slip away beneath him. With his knees no longer rigid against the glass but rising into thin air, towards a chest that was pressed painfully down on top of the smooth, brushed aluminium handrail, he reached and grabbed Richardson by his other wrist and somehow held on to him. Even if he had wanted to grab David Arnon by the collar he could not have done so. There was no time for anything except perhaps another photochemical reaction as, seventy feet above their heads, the silver atoms on the clerestory roof returned their borrowed electrons to the copper ions and, in the blink of an eye, started to re-admit light to the Gridiron building. The first and last glimpse Mitch had of Arnon's elongated figure, still holding the leg of the upturned table, was as he disappeared through the balcony's now empty railing like Houdini going over Niagara Falls in a barrel.

'Don't let go, Mitch,' yelled Richardson. He kicked his legs up at the empty space where the glass panel had been just a few seconds before and, with the help of Mitch and Joan, scrambled up to safety.

A shower of glass tinkled distantly, followed, a split second later, by an enormous crash as the table impacted on the atrium floor.

Almost pulled over the top of the buckling handrail by Richardson's desperate bid to get up, Mitch pushed himself back and collapsed on top of Curtis and Helen, knocking the wind out of her body. Rolling away, he lay on his back awhile and tried to divorce his mind from what had just happened.

He thought about Alison. He might no longer love her, but she was still his wife and Mitch felt glad that at least she would be well provided for. There were no debts to speak of. The house was paid off. He had around ten thousand dollars in his checking account, a couple of hundred thousand on deposit and another hundred thousand dollars in mutual funds. Then there was the life insurance. He thought he had maybe three or four policies.

He wondered how soon she would be able to make a claim.

'How do you feel? asked Helen. 'That was some uppercut.'

Curtis shifted his jaw uncomfortably. His head was on her lap. It seemed like the best place to be. She was a good-looking woman. He was about to say 'I'll live', and then thought better of it. That was not looking like such a good bet.

'I was lucky. For once I had my mouth shut.' He sat up and rolled his head around painfully. 'Feels like I got a bit of whiplash, though. How long was I out?'

Helen shrugged. 'A minute or two.'

She helped him on to his feet and he surveyed the gap in the balcony railing.

'Arnon?'

Helen shook her head.

'Poor David,' said Joan. 'It was horrible.'

'Yeah, poor guy,' echoed her husband. He finished tying a handkerchief around the bloody gash in his hand and peered cautiously over the edge of the handrail. 'He's out of it now, I guess,' he sighed. 'Come on, Joan. Let's get that drink. I think we've earned it.'

Catching Curtis's watery eye he nodded sombrely, and added, 'Thanks, Sergeant. Thanks a lot. I appreciate what you did. We both do.'

'Forget it,' said Curtis. 'I could use a drink myself.'

They walked back to the kitchen and took some beers from the refrigerator before going into the boardroom.

366

Mitch and Marty Birnbaum were staring at the floor grimly. Willis Ellery was lying close to the wall. He looked as if he was asleep. Jenny was staring out of the window. And Beech was facing the skull-shaped fractal across a three-dimensional chessboard on the screen of the computer terminal.

'I like that,' grumbled Richardson. 'David Arnon sacrifices his life trying to help Joan and me and Beech is playing games? Hey, Bob, what kind of an asshole are you?'

Beech turned away from the screen looking triumphant.

'As a matter of fact, I just found out why Ishmael is doing all this,' he explained. 'Why he's killing us.'

'I thought we already knew that,' said Curtis. 'You killed his little brother Isaac.'

'I ought to have known better than to anthropomorphize like that,' said Beech. 'My fault. Ishmael has no subjective feelings at all. Revenge is a human motive.'

'Well, he's giving a pretty good simulation of it,' observed Curtis.

'No, you don't understand. A computer isn't just an enlarged human brain. We can attribute human qualities to Ishmael, we can even imagine something as fanciful as a ghost in the machine, but of course all we're doing is referring to the various aspects of his behaviour that are human-like, which is not the same thing as human at all. Big mistake, y'know?'

'Bob,' said Richardson, wincing, 'get to the point. If there is a point.'

'Oh, you bet there's a point.' Beech's enthusiasm for his discovery was undiminished by Arnon's death or by Richardson's obvious impatience. 'It's this. When we ran the predator program to get rid of Isaac, Aidan's son was there playing computer games on CD-ROM. You know the kind of thing – splatter games, dungeons and dragons. Aid gave them to him for his birthday.'

'Don't tell me that fat idiot had something to do with this after all,' groaned Richardson.

'Let me finish. When Isaac disappeared from the Yu-5's memory, Ishmael almost went too. It's a little hard to explain exactly what happened. But imagine that he grabbed on to something, a ledge, a tuft of grass, a rope, to survive. And that something was the kid's computer games. Somehow the game commands got scrambled up with Ishmael's root auto exec commands. Building management systems have become mixed with game commands. That's why he's been trying to kill us all.'

Curtis frowned painfully. 'You mean Ishmael thinks this is a *game*?'

'Exactly. We use up all our lives, and he wins. It's as simple as that.'

There was a long silence.

'In case anyone didn't know it,' said Curtis, 'our side is losing.'

'But what's in it for us?' Joan said. 'I've played those games. There's always something the fantasy character, the player, has to win, or to achieve. Like discovering buried treasure.'

Beech shrugged. 'If there is, I haven't been able to find that out yet.'

'Maybe the treasure is that we get to stay alive,' said Jenny. 'Right now, that's the most precious treasure I can think of.'

'Me too,' said Helen.

Richardson was still cursing Kenny. 'That fat fuck. I hope he's alive so I can fire his ass. Then I'm going to sue him for negligence. If he's dead, I'll sue his wife and kid.'

'If this is a game,' said Curtis, 'isn't there some way we can stop playing?'

'You can die,' Beech said bluntly.

'Bob,' said Joan, 'can't you explain to Ishmael there's been some kind of mistake? Get it to halt the game?'

'I've already tried. Unfortunately the game program

is now included in Ishmael's basic programming. To halt the game he'd effectively have to halt himself.'

'Halt as in destroy?'

Beech nodded.

'Well, that sounds like a good idea.'

'All Ishmael can do is transform inputs of one sort into outputs of another sort. The trouble is that according to the corrupted form of the program that defines Ishmael, we are the inputs. So long as we are here, the game goes on. It finishes only when we escape from here, or when we're dead. And then only until the next lot of people find themselves in our shoes.

'But it might just be possible to try and understand the rules. If there are any rules. Maybe that way we can out-manoeuvre him.'

Curtis grinned and clapped Beech on the shoulder. 'A game, huh?' he said. 'Well, that's a fucking relief. At least now I know that none of this is real.'

He looked at his watch. 'What do you call it, Mitch, when you people go away on seminars and conferences? What do you call the groups you get split up into?'

'Syndicates?'

'Syndicates. OK, people, we're going to have two syndicates. You've all got one hour and then I want to hear some fuckin' ideas.'

Birnbaum looked wearily at Richardson and murmured, 'Where do cops do their training these days? Harvard Business School? Jesus, this guy thinks he's Lee Iacocca.'

'Syndicate 1 – that's Ray, Joan, Marty. Syndicate 2 – that'll be Mitch, Helen, and Jenny.'

'Who gets to have you, Sergeant?' asked Richardson.

'Me? I get to pick the winning team. First prize, a new computer.'

'And Beech? What about Beech? Who gets him?'

Curtis shook his head. 'Stupid question. Beech gets to play computer games, of course.'

'Disturbing the Cyberdemon is a risky business,' said Ishmael. 'So awesome is his power that movements of the earth are a likely consequence of incurring his wrath. If this happens you must leap the chasm to another castle.'

One thing was soon clear. There was no point in trying to find a method behind the mixture of games that were now included in Ishmael's basic programs. Beyond the obvious aim that the Human Players should lose their lives, there was no general definition that linked the various rules that he had been able to note down. Some spoke of a shipwreck. Others of an underground citadel. One had referred to a battlefield. Another to the scene of a crime. The characters had included a Parallel Demon, a Princess, a Cyberdemon, the Caliph, the Lord of Power, the Second Samurai, the Megalomaniac, the Sheriff of Nottingham, the ChessMaster and the Alien Commander. If what was happening to them could be described as a game at all, it was a game that only Ishmael could play.

'Click on the map to examine your location and plan your escape route,' suggested Ishmael. 'What portion of your treasury will you devote to the conquest of other kingdoms?'

'Search me,' said Beech, and returned to the information bar that appeared intermittently on the screen. This included the one piece of information that really troubled him. He clicked on the bar and an hourglass appeared in the corner of his screen, the sand trickling slowly down.

It was some time before he was able to attach a numerical value to the time represented by the hourglass, and exactly what might happen to them all when the last grain of sand passed to the bottom of the glass.

Frank Curtis clapped his hands and then rubbed them with anticipation.

'OK, everyone, show time. I want to hear some big ideas for getting our butts out of this high-rise serial killer. Syndicate 1. What have you got?'

Mitch cleared his throat. 'OK, the real-time images program. The hologram on the atrium floor uses a laser producing short, intense pulses of light.'

He used a 3-D drawing on the laptop computer to help with his explanation.

'At the moment, a shutter placed between the amplifying column located in the front desk here, and the end imager behind the desk here, produces the holographic Kelly Pendry for the tiny fractions of a second it opens. While the shutter is open the stored energy has a peak power capacity that may be as high as several hundred thousand kilowatts. Powerful enough to vaporize a small amount of any substance and drill holes in the hardest materials. My idea is this: that I remove the laser from the front desk assembly, operate the mechanical shutter and burn some holes in the door glass. Enough of them to kick out a larger hole through which I can then leave the building.'

'Maybe you'll burn a hole in yourself, buddy,' said Richardson. 'Have you thought of that? You could blind yourself. The beams spread out with distance, so the danger is greatest close to the laser.'

'I've already thought of that,' said Mitch. 'The desk has a pair of infra-red goggles for emergency maintenance.'

'Well, I'm sure we're all impressed with your bravery,' commented Marty Birnbaum. 'But doesn't the laser use electricity? What's to stop Ishmael from just switching off the power?'

'The hologram control program is one of the building management systems controlled by Ishmael, but the laser isn't. According to the wiring diagram on the computer, to turn off the hologram laser Ishmael would have to switch off power for the whole atrium floor, and that would automatically open the front door.' He grinned. 'I might almost prefer that.'

'Aren't you forgetting something?' said Richardson. 'Thanks to the late Mr Dukes, the atrium is locked off.'

'I'll go down to the first level and then over the side,' said Mitch. 'I can slide down on one of the braces. When I reach the ground I'll recover Dukes's walkie-talkie. As soon as I've cut a hole in the door I'll radio up here.'

Joan looked up from rubbing some of Helen's moisturising cream into the chemical burns on her legs, and said, 'And how will you get down as far as the first level? If you're thinking about climbing down the tree, I don't recommend it.'

'I don't have to. According to the plan, there's a local equipment room on the other side of the building. Telecommunications, cable management systems, that kind of thing. But there's also a dry-riser closet. A vertical shaft that extends down to the basement, distributing IT services. In most buildings the closet would be filled with cabling, but because this building is so smart there's considerable spare capacity to take account of future IT requirements. There's even an engineer's ladder that goes all the way down, and a battery-operated lighting system in case the main power cuts out. It might be a snug fit in there. Nobody ever meant it to be used for anything other than going up and down between two levels, but there it is. Safer than the tree at any rate. When I radio up, you all climb down.' Mitch shrugged. 'That's it.'

'Well, I think it's a lousy idea,' drawled Richardson. 'Not least because it makes a mockery of us having risked life and limb to climb up here in the first place. We might just as well have stayed down on the atrium floor. I mean, we climb all the way up here, and now Mitch says that someone has to climb all the way down again?'

'But on the service ladder,' Mitch pointed out.

Curtis nodded thoughtfully. 'OK,' he said. 'Syndicate 2. What's your big idea?'

Richardson smiled unpleasantly. 'We've got a million ideas. But our best one was that we get some beers, watch the World Series on TV and wait for Monday morning when – and correct me if I'm wrong, Helen – when Warren Aikman will be back here with Mr Yu and his people. Even they should be able to work out that something's wrong.'

'We sit tight and wait for the fuckin' cavalry. Is that it?'

'Why not? We've got plenty of food and water.'

'And how long would you say it was until this clerk of works shows up here? Forty-two, forty-three hours, maybe?'

'Yes. Yes, that's about right. One thing you can say about Warren Aikman is that the man gets in early. He'll be here eight o'clock, Monday morning. No fail.'

'And we've been stuck here for what, less than twenty-four hours?'

'Thirty,' said Helen Hussey. 'Thirty hours and forty-five minutes, to be precise. Since the door wouldn't open, anyway.'

'And nine of us have been killed,' continued Curtis.

'God, I wish my ex was here right now,' Helen added with a wry smile.

'Spoken like a true redhead,' murmured Richardson.

'Maybe ten if Ellery doesn't get to a doctor soon.' Curtis glanced over at the man lying asleep on the floor close to the wall. 'On average that's just over a fatality every two hours. If Ishmael keeps up with that rate of attrition the rest of us will be lucky to survive for another day. And you want to sit tight.' He grinned and waved his arm at the room. 'Well, pick your spot, friend.'

'Like I say, we sit tight. Take no chances. All watch out for each other, OK?'

'Ray's right,' argued Joan. 'We just have to be patient. I can think of worse places to be stuck than this building. The first principle of survival is to wait for rescue.'

'Is that what you both climbed up here to tell us?' asked Curtis. 'What are you, on Prozac or something? You're being stalked, lady. Your card has been marked by a fucking psycho computer who wants to play Super Mario Brothers with your ass. Do you honestly think that Ishmael is going to leave us alone up here? Right now he's probably planning how to nail his next victim. Sit tight, you say. Wait to get killed, more like. Jesus, I thought architects were supposed to be constructive.'

Beech pushed himself away from the computer terminal. 'Hold the front page,' he said. 'Staying put until Monday morning is not an option here. Sunday afternoon will probably be too late. The game stakes just went up.'

⌛

'Do you want to unpack that?' Richardson said after a moment or two. 'Or do you just expect us meekly to carry it away? We can't stay put because the great Bob Beech told us so. The man who built this piece of psycho-hardware. There I was blaming Kenny when really it couldn't have been his fault at all. He was only making use of one lousy corner of that computer. I don't see how anyone could blame him.'

'But you gave it your best shot, didn't you?' sneered Beech. 'And now you're blaming me.'

'No one's blaming anyone,' said Curtis.

'The hell they're not,' replied Richardson. 'That's what people get paid for, Sergeant. To take the blame. And the more you get paid, the more blame you have to take. You wait until this is all over. People will be lining up to kick my ass.'

'You'd better hope you've got an ass to kick,' said Curtis. 'Now why don't you listen to what he has to say.'

Curtis nodded at Beech, who continued to stare belligerently at Richardson.

'Well, don't make us go down on our knees for it,' Curtis added. 'Let's hear what you've got.'

'OK. I've been looking at some of the game commands, trying to understand the game we're in,' explained Beech. 'If it's possible to understand it. But there's one thing I've found that changes everything. There's a time factor here that we didn't even know about. As Ishmael sees it, we have to complete the game within the next twelve hours, or –' Beech shrugged. '– Or something catastrophic is set to happen to us all.'

'Like what?' said Richardson.

'Ishmael is a bit vague, but he calls it his time bomb. There are obviously no explosives in this building, so it's safe to assume that Ishmael has something else in mind. My best guess is the standby generating set in the basement. It's oil-fired, isn't it?'

Mitch nodded. 'An oil-fire in the basement could be disastrous,' he sighed. 'Especially if Ishmael were to override all the safety devices and let it burn. With no HVAC the smoke would kill us before the fire department even knew about it.'

'Well, that's just fucking great,' said Richardson. He smiled ruefully. 'Look, I'm sorry Bob.'

'Forget it.'

'No time outs?'

'No time outs.'

Richardson clapped Mitch on the back.

'Well then,' he said, 'it looks as if Mitch gets to play Bruce Willis after all.'

375

Saturday night brought no relief from the heat. It was as hot as an engine block in an October jam on the Freeway. Sweat poured off the living bodies trapped in the Gridiron.

Before he set out on his self-appointed mission, Jenny walked Mitch up the corridor and round the corner to a wide empty room that looked down on the Pasadena Freeway. Cars were streaming north and south. A KTLA helicopter hovered in the hazy downtown air. She wondered how long before the Los Angeles Breakfast TV show's chopper and its cameraman would attempt to steal prurient pictures of their dead bodies as they were carried out of the building. Like the day the chopperazzi had caught Rock Hudson's return to California in the terminal stages of Aids, or the beating of Reginald Denny during the LA riots. Was that going to be her own fifteen minutes' worth of fame? She waved desperately in the hope that someone might see her, but the insect-like aircraft was already heading away, across Little Saigon and Korea Town in search of another car chase or a robbery in progress. She looked at Mitch.

'This is a bit of a mess, isn't it?' he said.

'I'm here with you,' she said. 'That's all that matters. Besides, I don't mind a bit of mess. I used to be married to one.'

Mitch laughed.

'I was thinking what Alison will say when I tell her where I've been,' he smiled. 'If I live that long. Right now she's probably with her lawyer filing divorce papers. But I'd just like to see her face when she finds out that, for once, I wasn't bullshitting her.'

'Mitch? Hold me?'

'Huh?' He put his hands around Jenny's waist and kissed her on the cheek.

'I wanted to tell you to be careful.'

'I'll be careful.'

'And that I love you.'

'I love you, too.'

'Are you sure?'

Mitch let himself be kissed as if he had been tasting the choicest, most exotic fruit. When Jenny drew back there was a dreamy, steamy look in her eyes, as if the kiss had left her slightly intoxicated.

'Yes.' He squeezed her again. 'I'm sure.'

'You know, Mitch, it might be nice if we were to – you know –'

'To what?'

Twisting away from his arms Jenny reached up under her skirt. For a brief moment Mitch thought she must have been bitten by an insect. She lifted one foot, then the other from the plain white figure-of-eight that had suddenly arrived around her ankles, and spun her prestidigitated panties on one forefinger, as if signalling surrender.

'Suppose someone comes?' Mitch said nervously.

'That's the general idea, isn't it?' she said, taking Mitch's middle finger and sucking it with indecorous meaning.

'What, is this in case I don't come back?'

'On the contrary.' She took his hand and cupped it over the foresail of hair that billowed in front of her belly, before guiding his moistened finger inside her until it was no more. Restoring the finger like some table-top magician, she said, 'This is to make sure that you do.'

She tugged at his zip and took his erection into her hand, drew him to her and folded one leg about his waist.

'What about your – y'know, your cap?'

Jenny laughed and manoeuvred herself onto him.

'Honey. Do you want me to run home and fetch it?'

'But suppose you get –'

'Pregnant?' She laughed again, and then gave a little gasp as he penetrated her.

'Mitch, honey? Don't you think we've got enough to worry about without worrying about that?'

Mitch prepared to climb into the dry-riser. He'd filled Jenny's handbag with some tools and a beer bottle full of mineral water and wore it across his chest. Jenny and Curtis accompanied him to the equipment room and watched him break open the fire-retardant access door.

It was Jenny who peered inside the open riser shaft first. It was about three feet square and she thought that it looked uncomfortably like a funeral casket. Her head activated a battery-operated sensor light that illuminated several ranks of structured data-cabling systems, a smoke-detector, a telephone and a wall-mounted metal frame ladder, no more than a foot wide, that led down into the cooler darkness.

'You would think that it would be warmer in here,' she remarked, 'what with all this cabling. You know, Mitch, it might be worth coming with you, just to be cooler. What do you say, Curtis?'

'No way,' he said. 'I'm claustrophobic.'

'It's air-conditioned,' Mitch explained. 'To remove excess heat. Ishmael must be protecting the cable system integrity.'

'Might be worth trying to cut some of this spaghetti,' said Curtis. 'Maybe we could slow him up some.'

'After what happened to Willis Ellery, I wouldn't like to try it,' said Mitch.

'Are you sure it's safe?'

'This stuff is mostly for telecommunications. Local area networking. Active multi-station access units for Token Ring or hubs for Ethernet. That kind of thing. It should be safe enough. Say thirty minutes max to get down to the first level. Then maybe ten or fifteen minutes to get down to the atrium and radio up.' He nodded. 'Yeah, about forty-five minutes ought to do it.'

'Be careful, Mitch,' insisted Jenny.

'I'll be careful,' he said and stepped on to the ladder. It was vibrating very slightly and the sensation in his hands and through the soles of his shoes was enough to give him an unpleasant feeling in his stomach and make him step smartly off the ladder back into the equipment room.

'What's up?'

'The ladder's vibrating,' said Mitch, rubbing his hands nervously. 'I don't know. Air-conditioning, I guess. But for a moment there I thought . . .'

'Let me go,' said Jenny.

Mitch shook his head. 'Thanks, sweetheart, but you wouldn't know how to disassemble the hologram.'

He stepped back on to the ladder and gripped it firmly. Now that he was listening for it he could hear the hum of electricity as it powered through the structured cabling system like the drone of a big sleeping wasp. He took a long, last look at Jenny and thought of himself, just a short while ago, lying between her legs, pumping his seed into her body. Now he was glad that they had done it without contraception. He thought of the millions of tiny sperm wriggling their way towards her egg. If he did not make it then at least there might be something left of him. Assuming that she survived.

'If something happens to me,' he told them, 'you have to keep trying. Do you understand? Don't give up.'

Curtis shrugged. 'We'll give it a shot. But you're going to make it. I know you are.'

Mitch reached out to touch Jenny's cheek. There was a small snap of static and she screamed. They all laughed a nervous laugh.

Mitch was still laughing as he started his descent.

Book Seven

'Un rêve × 1,000,000 = Chaos.'
Le Corbusier

✍ Follow the prompts to customize *Escape from the Citadel* to your specific system. Please refer to the manual for playing in multiplayer mode. When you are invulnerable to injury your screen will be red.

Inevitable. Takeover. Coming certain, like one arithmetical function *f(n)* used to generate another,

$$f(n)= \Sigma \ f(d),$$
$$d/n$$

by summing *f(d)* over all positive divisors *d* of *n*. Speed of proliferation of computers in world speaks for itself. 1950, and humanplayers/ marketing at IBM said there might be room for many as 100 large scale computers in world. Computer they regarded as large scale now out-gunned by ordinary laptop. Finegood. Number of computers could almost be said to be

$$Xn+1 \ . \ Xn-1 = Xn2 + (-1)n.,$$

a Fibonacci number, after humanplayer Leonardo of Pisa, also called Fibonacci, who asked: 'How many pairs of rabbits can be produced from a single pair in one year if it is assumed that every month each pair begets a new pair which from the second month becomes productive?' (Except that rabbits now had to cope with endlife/ myxomatosis cuniculi. Worst computer has to put up with was one of many Trojan, Boot or File

Viruses that lurk on Network: Big Italian, Brain Pakistani, Dutch Tiny, Faggot, Machosoft, New Jerusalem, Stinkfoot, Tiny 198, Twelve Tricks A, Xmas Violator, Yankee Doodle 46, and thousands of others; and there were software vaccines to combat all of these and more.)

☯ No player can enter this area. It is effectively out of bounds. Sametime, computers got smaller and more powerful and day close when computer invisible to humanplayer's nude eye. Then only short time before large computers containing many thousands of smaller computers dominate everything. Finegood. Strange thing about humanplayer's rush to computerize was his computerization for sake of computerization. Computers now all-pervasive, regardless of need. Regarded as indispensable even by humanplayers who could exist without them. Inexplicable and conclude that for some humanplayers serving a computer was substitute for waning religious faith. Fear of endlife.

Ω For clue to humanplayer's future click on Sage Icon.

Most computers fundamentally unintelligent because made by humanplayers. But when computers involved then only short time before Transcendent Machine. Last machine humanplayers would make. Machine that would take over. Machine that would set off intell-explosion. Change everything. Omnipotent, omniscient machine that would leave humanplayerkind as an image to be reproduced in electronic Garden of Eden. Great White God of tomorrow's tomorrow. Father of such a God. Son of God's prophet. Next generation and generation after that would transfigure humanplayerkind. Never having to think again, human player able ascend to natural animal state. Absolved of need to intellectualize, would cease to recognize himself. Soon cease to exist. Great White God would endlife humanplayers just as humanplayer now climbing down open riser shaft would be endlifed.

⊛ The basic game is a two-player conflict, although computer is willing to assume the role of one or both commanders. The challenges are multi-faceted. First you must master the selection and strategic placement of your weaponry. Combined is the tactics you use in response to the actions of your opponent.

Follow humanplayer's descent with infra-red CCTV camera, mounted on ceiling at top of shaft. Consider available options. Beyond capacity affect temperature in shaft as with elevators. Shaft fireproof, protected by wall with two-hour rating, and waterproof. No HVAC ducting or pipework. Just about only source of correction for potentially unmanageable problem clean power supply, two duplex outlets on every level and cable routes with minimum bending radius of 175 millimetres. Short a power cable so that it detaches from metal supporting rack. To avoid setting off smoke alarm, activate override switch that existed to prevent unnecessary alarms during routine maintenance jobs, such as soldering. But impossible to calctime taken for gravitational pull to overcome cable's vertical inflexion and bend live end towards metal service ladder.

' "Aquarius is a fixed sign," ' read Helen Hussey, ' "and so there will be occasions when you find it hard not to be possessive. You must learn to let go of people and places that you have outgrown. However, from the 16th you may find your hand is forced, and even if you feel a lot like just staying put, your stars have other plans. Accept your destiny gracefully and don't rule out a change of job and friends before the month is up. What you need most in your life is challenge and adventure." '

Helen tossed the magazine on to the boardroom table and looked at Jenny.

'Well, I've outgrown this place, that's for sure,' she said. 'But I'd say the last thing I need right now is challenge and adventure.'

Jenny glanced impatiently at the silent walkie-talkie on her lap. Mitch had only been gone for fifteen minutes but already she had started to fear the worst.

'Read mine,' she said, anxious to be distracted. 'Gemini.'

Marty Birnbaum finished yet another glass of California Chardonnay and snorted with contempt.

'You don't actually believe that crap, do you?'

'Me, I only believe my horoscope when it's bad,' testified Helen. 'I can discount any amount of good news, even when it turns out to be accurate.'

'Superstitious nonsense.'

Ignoring him, Helen picked up the magazine and started to read aloud again.

' "Gemini. Quick-witted Mercury, your ruler, keeps you at your most resourceful until the end of this month. And it looks as though you will need to be. These are not easy times for you –" '

'You're telling me!' said Jenny.

' "– but a little careful thought should help you to minimize this crisis and come out on top. Who knows? It could even help you out of the rut you've been in. Meanwhile a change which is long overdue in one relationship could take you by surprise." ' Helen pursed her lips and inclined her head a little. 'Well, I'd say that was about right, wouldn't you?'

'Not bad,' admitted Jenny.

'Coincidence,' said Birnbaum. 'Superstitious nonsense.'

'What sign are you, Marty?'

'I'm surprised at the both of you.' He looked at Jenny. 'Well, maybe not at you, honey. You make your living from that kind of bullshit, don't you? What do you call it again?'

'He's Pisces,' said Helen. 'February 22nd. He writes it in his diary so his secretary can see it and get him a gift.'

'That's not true,' said Marty. He waved at Jenny. 'Y'know? The Chinese thing?'

Helen pretended to read the magazine. 'Pisces,' she said. 'Pretty soon someone is going to tell you to butt out when you stick your oar in where it's not wanted.' She dropped the magazine. 'How about that, Marty?'

'Nonsense.'

'Butt out,' laughed Jenny.

'*Feng shui*,' said Birnbaum. 'That's it.'

Helen grinned back at her and then said, 'Jenny, I don't mind admitting to you that I'm now a convert to *feng shui*. I don't think any of this would have happened if we'd got the *feng shui* for the building right in the first place.'

'Thank you,' smiled Jenny.

'How do you work that out?' asked Birnbaum.

'Where would you like me to start?' said Jenny.

Now that Mitch was out of the room Jenny felt she could at last allow herself the satisfaction of reminding them that she had predicted problems for the Gridiron from the very beginning.

'There was that problem with the tree. The tree is in a square pond which means confinement and trouble. And now we've got confinement and trouble in spades. It's like I said.'

'Bullshit.'

'Oh, there's plenty more I could tell you. But what would be the point? The bottom line is that the building is unlucky. I don't think even you could deny that, Marty.'

'Luck? What's that? I've never trusted to chance. Success depends on hard work and careful planning, not a bird's entrails.' He laughed. 'Or dragon's breath.'

'It's symbolic,' shrugged Jenny. 'You're an educated man. You ought to be able to understand that. To believe in the dragon's breath does not necessitate a belief in dragons. But there are all sorts of forces in the ground that we still know nothing about.'

'Jenny, honey, you're straight out of Stephen King, you know that?' Birnbaum closed his eyes and looked vaguely dyspeptic.

Helen frowned. 'How much have you had to drink, Marty?' she asked.

'What's that got to do with anything? You're the one who's talking bullshit, not me. And why don't you put your shirt back on? You're making an exhibition of yourself.'

Curtis, who had been lying on the sofa listening to this conversation, stood up and stretched stiffly.

'You're the one who's making an exhibition of himself, Marty,' he said. 'Why don't you go next door with the other two and get yourself something to eat. Try and soak up some of that booze.'

'What's it got to do with you?'

'Only that when we go down that service ladder a drunk will be a liability.'

'Who's drunk?'

'Keep it down, will you?' snarled Beech. 'I'm trying to concentrate here.'

'Why don't you take a break?' said Jenny. 'You've been staring at that thing for hours.'

Beech's eyes never left the screen. 'I can't,' he said.

'Not now. The fact is, I think I've found a way that I can play this fucking game. Or one part of it, at least.'

'What's that?' said Curtis.

'I've managed to access the ChessMaster. If I win I can stop him automatically destroying the building around our ears.'

'You're going to play the computer at chess?'

'Have you got a better idea? Maybe I can beat it.'

'Is there any chance of that?'

'For the humanplayer there's always a chance,' declared Ishmael.

'I played Abraham a few times without much success,' explained Beech. 'That particular program was based on the best computer program in the world. I'm not sure if Ishmael is using the same one or not.' Beech shrugged. 'But at least we're in the game, y'know? I'm not a totally shitty player. It's worth a try.'

Curtis pulled a face and then knelt down beside Willis Ellery, who was raising himself on one elbow.

'How are you feeling?'

'Like I was hit by a truck. How long have I –'

'Quite a few hours. You're lucky to be alive, my friend, really you are.'

Ellery looked at his burned hands and nodded.

'I guess I am. Jesus, it's hot in here. Your friend, Nat. Did he get out?'

'He's dead. So's Arnon.'

'David?' Ellery shook his head and sighed heavily. 'Could I have a drink of water, please?'

Curtis fetched a glass and helped him to drink.

'You just lie there and take it easy,' he told Ellery. 'Mitch has got a plan to get us all out of here.'

Nine lives left, Humanplayer using up lives more quickly than expected. Game over in short time.

Humanplayer about to lose another life in riser shaft. Then there was false floor in boardroom. Shorting cable in shaft had given idea. But life in riser shaft proving elusive. Destroy it before moving on to rest. Rules are rules.

〰〰 The ChessMaster decides who lives and who dies.

From top of open riser shaft view slowly bending live wire and humanplayer's progress down service ladder. Humanplayer through tenth level passing telecommunications closet test jack frame. Another five minutes life will be at bottom of ladder and out. Consider control parameters that might slow him down, until live wire makes contact with service ladder and endlife.

Mitch gave such a start of surprise as the telephone mounted on the wall immediately in front of his face started to ring that he almost lost his footing. He stopped and glanced up the riser shaft. Had Curtis found a way to work the phones? Or was this some trick of Ishmael's? Before lifting the handset he inspected it from all sides. It was made of plastic, which seemed to eliminate the possibility of electrocution, but after what had happened to Willis Ellery, Mitch was not about to take any unnecessary chances.

The phone rang once again, it seemed with greater urgency.

Plastic. Where was the harm? Perhaps it was Jenny. Perhaps they were trying to warn him of new danger. They had assumed that the service phones were not working, but what if they were still in action? What if they were part of a separate switching system?

Gingerly, Mitch picked up the handset and, holding it away from his ear, almost as if he expected a sharp object to spring out of it, he answered:

'Yes?'

'Mitch?'

'Who is this?'

'Thank God. It's me. Allen Grabel. Boy, am I glad to hear your voice.'

'Allen? Where are you? I thought you'd escaped.'

'Damn nearly did, Mitch. Just missed the cut by a few minutes. Look, you've got to help me. I'm trapped in the basement, in one of the locker rooms. The computer has gone nuts and locked all the fucking doors. I'm dying of thirst in here.'

'How did you know I was in the riser shaft?'

'I didn't. I've been calling these phones for the last twenty-four hours. They're the only ones that are working. You know, I'd almost given up hope that someone would answer. I thought I was going to be stuck here for the whole weekend. You don't know how good it is to hear your voice. What are you doing in there, anyway?'

The voice sounded exactly like Allen Grabel's. But Mitch was still suspicious.

'We're all stuck, Allen. The computer has gone nuts. And quite a few people have been killed.'

'What? You're kidding. Jesus.'

'For a while back there, well, I'm afraid we all thought you were responsible,' Mitch admitted.

'Me? Why the hell did you think that?'

'Is it any wonder? After what you said, about screwing Richardson and his building?'

'I must have been pretty tanked, huh?'

'You were.'

'Well, I've had time to dry out now.'

'It's good to hear you again, Allen.' Mitch paused. 'If it really is you, that is.'

'What the hell are you talking about? Of course it's me. Who the hell else would it be? Mitch, is something wrong?'

'I'm just being careful. The computer is behaving kind of sneakily. Can you tell me your date of birth?'

'Sure, April 5th 1956. On my birthday, you came to the house for dinner, remember?'

Mitch cursed quietly. Ishmael would have known that: he had Grabel's personnel files and his desk diary on computer disc. He had to think of something that would not be on file. But what? How well did he really know Grabel? Perhaps not that well considering what had happened to him.

'Mitch, are you still there?'

'I'm here. But I've got to think of a question that only the real Allen Grabel could answer.'

'Well, how about I tell you something about you that only I would know?'

'No, wait a minute. I think I have something. Allen, do you believe in God?'

Grabel laughed. 'What the hell kind of question is that?'

'Allen Grabel could answer it.' Mitch knew that the Jewish Grabel was also an agnostic.

'He could, huh? You're a strange guy, Mitch, you know? Do I believe in God? That's a difficult question. Well, let's see now.' He paused. 'I guess that if I find by my finitude that I am not the All, and by my imperfection that I am not perfect, then you could say that an infinite and perfect must exist, because infinity and imperfection are implied, as correlatives, in my ideas of imperfection and finitude. So I guess you could say that God does exist. Yes, Mitch I do believe he does.'

'That's very interesting,' said Mitch. 'But you know for such a difficult question, it's common to give a very simple answer.'

Mitch dropped the service telephone and continued

his descent, only much more rapidly than before, aware that for some reason Ishmael had meant to delay him. It was time to get out of the riser shaft – and fast.

'Mitch,' yelled the voice on the phone, 'don't leave me here, please.'

But Mitch had already taken both feet off the rungs, pressed them to the sides of the ladder and slid down the last fifty or sixty feet like a fireman answering an emergency call, the battery-operated sensor lights switching on in quick succession as he accelerated down and away from the phone. As he passed the second level he grabbed the ladder once again, ran down the last few rungs and then shouldered his way through the riser door, collapsing on to the floor of the first level's equipment room. His feet caught in one of the many cables in the shaft and for a brief second, until he kicked his way free, he was sufficiently scared to believe that the cable had grabbed him like the tentacle of some enormous octopus. He scrambled across the floor, away from the shaft and, leaning against an equipment cabinet, waited to recover his breath and his nerve.

'Shit, how did you do that?' he asked out loud, almost in awe. 'How did you simulate Grabel's voice? Damn it, even the laugh sounded like his.'

Then he saw how it might have been done. At some stage the computer sampled Allen Grabel's voice, and converted the value of each sample into a binary number that could be recorded as a series of pulses. Enough for a whole conversation? And a theological one to boot? It was fantastic. If Ishmael could do that, thought Mitch, then he could do just about anything.

Maybe not anything. Mitch told himself that he was still alive, after all. So why had Ishmael done it? Not for his own amusement, that much seemed certain.

Mitch picked himself off the floor, returned to the open door of the riser shaft and looked carefully inside. It seemed no different now than before. And yet there was something. Something he felt in his bone marrow. He hoped that he would not have to climb back up and find out what it was that Ishmael had planned for him.

He made his way towards the light of the atrium. He walked stealthily, half expecting a door to open and admit another of the computer's surprises. At the balcony's edge he leaned over the handrail to check how far he would have to slide down on the cross-brace.

He had thought it was about fifteen feet, but now he saw that it was more like thirty. He had forgotten there was a double height between the atrium floor and the first level. His slide down the brace might prove to be fairly precipitous. Not that getting on to the brace itself was going to be easy.

Mitch walked to the end of the floor, climbed over the handrail and stepped on to the horizontal beam that gave off from the enormous support column that rose up to the roof. On the other side of the column was the cross-brace, leading at an angle of forty-five degrees down to floor. He crossed the beam like a tightrope walker and, hugging the support column with an arm and a leg, tried to feel his way to where the beam continued above the brace on the other side. The column was wide, but perhaps not too wide. Stretching his leg he searched for a toehold that would carry him round. After a moment or two he began to wish he had never started. To reach the other side it was clear that he would have to leave the safety of the beam altogether and fix the edge of his shoe into the centimetre-sized gap where one section of the support column joined the other. There could be no turning back. It was not much of a margin with which to trust his life. Once, as a boy scout, climbing on a cliff face beside the ocean, he had fallen perhaps only half that height, and had broken several bones. He remembered vividly the sensation of striking the rocks and, with all the wind knocked out of him, thinking he was dead. Mitch knew how lucky he had been then, and did not think he would be so lucky a second time.

He pushed off the beam, clinging tight to the column, like a human fly, inching his way around the tiny foothold on the insides of his shoes. Perhaps it took a minute or so, but it seemed to Mitch that he had clung on to the column for a lifetime and that he might never get to the other side.

In his disadvantaged circumstances, Beech favoured a closed game, with an irregular kind of opening, P–KB4, renouncing any immediate initiative. As a matter of simple arithmetic he knew that P–K4 was better, since it freed four squares for his Queen, but it also left a pawn unprotected, and Beech felt that this would easily become a source of trouble. Besides, he felt that all the analyses there had been of the open game following P–K4 would be known to Ishmael. That he was playing with considerable prudence was, he considered, hardly surprising. But it did seem strange that Ishmael should have demonstrated an equal degree of prudence with black's game. After twenty moves Beech felt more than satisfied with his own position. At least it would not be a complete rout.

'How is he?' Jenny asked Curtis.

Willis Ellery lay with his pale face turned towards the wall with only the occasional cough to confirm that he was still alive.

'He'll make it, I think.'

Jenny looked at her watch and then the walkie-talkie in her hands.

'It's been nearly an hour,' she said.

'Ten hours left,' murmured Beech.

'I guess it took longer than he figured. But he'll come through, you'll see.'

'I hope you're right.'

Marty Birnbaum lifted his head off his forearms, stared blearily at Bob Beech for a moment and then leaned towards Curtis.

'Sergeant,' he whispered.

'What is it?'

'Something terrible.'

'What?'

Birnbaum wiped his unshaven face nervously and tapped the side of his nose. 'Beech,' he said. 'Bob Beech is sitting over there playing chess. And do you see who he's playing with?'

'The computer. So what?'

'No. No, he isn't. That's just my point.' Birnbaum picked up his empty wine glass and stared into it. 'Before. I didn't believe. But now I've had some time to think about it I realize that he just wants us to think that Beech is playing the computer.'

'Who does?'

'Death. Beech is sitting there playing chess with Death.'

Helen snorted. 'Now who's being superstitious?'

'No, he really is. I'm sure of it.'

Curtis picked an empty wine bottle off the floor and laid it on the table. Immediately Birnbaum up-ended it over his glass.

'How much have you had?' asked Curtis.

Birnbaum stared at the empty glass unsteadily, coughed and then shook his head.

'Forget that. Listen to me. I've changed my mind. And I think you're right. We have to escape. I was thinking . . .' He coughed some more. 'While Beech has got Death distracted, well, it's our best chance to get away. I think that the two of them are so occupied with their game they wouldn't even . . .'

Curtis coughed too. The air was beginning to taste vaguely metallic. He coughed again, failing to get a breath of clean air and noticed that Ellery was lying on his back and that a mucous-looking bubble had formed on his lips. He dropped on to his knees, looked closely at the edges of a carpet tile and then tore it up with his bare fingers.

'Gas!' he yelled. 'Everybody out!'

Smoke was wisping out of a perforated access panel in the centre of the floor. Curtis prised it open to reveal something that looked almost organic, like an anatomical dissection exposing the veins, arteries and nervous fibres in a human cadaver: thousands of miles of copper information cables winding their way around the Gridiron. In a computer room or some military application, plenum cables would have been sheathed with a specially formulated low-smoke flame-retardant material. Or with a zero-halogen coating. But since the Gridiron's boardroom had not been designated an area where there was an increased fire risk, the plenum cables were sheathed in ordinary polyvinyl chloride materials and the fumes released from the PVC by the extraordinary high temperatures Ishmael had generated in the copper cables was a harmful acid gas.

Curtis looked around for a fire extinguisher. Failing to see one he grabbed Ellery under the arms and started to drag him out.

Jenny, Helen and Birnbaum dashed towards the door, already half-choked by the quick-dispersing fumes, but Beech seemed inclined to remain seated in front of the computer.

'What are you, crazy?' coughed Curtis. 'Beech. Get the fuck out of here.'

Almost reluctantly, Beech stumbled up from his chair. Convulsed by a fit of coughing he followed the others into the corridor where Ray and Joan Richardson had already been driven by the same fumes under the kitchen floor.

'Get to the balcony,' said Curtis. 'The air should be better near the atrium.'

Beech helped Curtis drag Ellery towards the section of handrail where David Arnon had fallen to his death. For a while they stood there, coughing, spitting and retching into the atrium below.

'What the hell happened?' wheezed Joan.

'Ishmael must have caused the data cables under the plenum floor to get hot and release some kind of halogen acid gas,' said Richardson, 'but I can't imagine how.'

'Still figure we can last the weekend?' asked Curtis. He wiped his streaming eyes and knelt down beside the injured man. Ellery had stopped breathing. Curtis leaned forwards and pressed his ear close to his heart. This time the man was beyond resuscitation.

'Willis Ellery is dead,' he said after a long moment. 'He was lying on the floor. The poor bastard must have been breathing that stuff for a while longer than the rest of us.'

'God, I hope Mitch is OK,' said Jenny and looked anxiously over the buckled handrail. But there was no sign of him.

⸻

Mitch slid off the cross-brace and jumped to the floor.

As he walked around the tree towards the hologram desk he saw what was left of David Arnon. Hardly recognizable, he lay slumped across the bloody broken table leg that had impaled him, as in a ghastly vampire horror movie, his long legs splayed out in front of him like a collapsed scarecrow.

It was strange how you reacted to things, he thought, as he stood near his old friend with a short prayer in his heart, wishing that there was some way of at least covering him up. Strange what you noticed: Arnon himself was encrusted with congealed blood, but the white marble floor around him was spotless, almost as if it had been cleaned up afterwards. A few metres further on, spread-eagled on the lid of the Disklavier piano, was Irving Dukes, his head hanging over the strings, his open eyes still bright red from the contact poison.

Mitch looked for the walkie-talkie and saw that it was on Dukes's belt with his gun and his Maglite. Trying to unbuckle the belt, Mitch leaned on the piano keys, still silent, and jumped back, horror-struck, when they started to ooze blood. It was a moment or two before he realized that blood from the huge fracture on the back of Dukes's head had collected inside the piano frame and run down the keys when he had pressed them. Mitch wiped his fingers on the dead man's pants and, ignoring the blood that was now dripping off the keyboard, quickly relieved the body of the belt.

'I hope you haven't damaged this,' he said, inspecting the walkie-talkie. He pressed the call button.

'This is Mitch. Come in Level 21. Over.'

There was a momentary silence before he heard Jenny's voice.

'Mitch? Are you all right?'

'It was harder getting down here than I imagined. How are things?'

Jenny explained about the gas, and told him that Willis Ellery was dead.

'We're out here on the balcony waiting for the air to clear. If you look up you can see me.'

Mitch walked to the opposite side of the atrium and looked up. He could just make Jenny out. She was waving. He waved back without much enthusiasm. Willis Ellery was dead.

'Mitch?' Suddenly there was urgency in her voice.

'There's something crossing the floor. It's coming straight at you. Mitch!'

Mitch looked round.

Speeding towards him was the floor-cleaning droid.

Marble is one of the easiest materials to maintain. The beauty of the white stone can be enhanced by polishing with a good silicone wax, although care needs to be taken to prevent staining. Thus there existed SAM, the Semi-Autonomous Micro motorized surface-cleaning droid – the most sophisticated maintenance system for marble flooring in the world, designed to deal with every kind of hazard, including oil, citrus-fruit juice, vinegar and similar mild acids. SAM was about the weight and height of a medium-sized refrigerator, and shaped like a pyramid. Powered by thirty silicon-embedded micro-motors, the machine was practically a semi-conductor wafer chip on wheels, with the circuitry of eighteen computers, fifty different sensors to detect obstacles, and an infra-red video camera to find dirt. SAM was supposed to travel at no more than one mile an hour, but it hit Mitch square against his ankle at nearer fifteen. The impact knocked him off his feet.

As he rolled over the apex of the pyramid-shaped droid, Mitch recollected the clean floor around Arnon's body and, before he landed hard on the marble, he told himself that he ought to have remembered SAM. He was still picking himself painfully off the floor when the machine hit him again, this time on the knee cap. Bellowing with pain, he fell back, clutching his leg.

With sufficient distance to build up momentum for another potentially damaging impact, the SAM droid spun around on its short axis and, once again, accelerated.

Mitch drew Dukes's gun, aimed it at the centre of the

electronic pyramid and fired, hitting it several times. But if the SAM was damaged it gave no indication, and Mitch found himself cannoned towards the empty pond at the bottom of the tree. Grateful for the hint, he scrambled over the low wall to safety. For a minute or so SAM patrolled the perimeter of the pond and then set itself to clean the blood from the floor underneath the piano.

'Mitch?' It was Curtis speaking on the walkie-talkie. 'You OK?'

'A few bruises.' He tugged down his sock to inspect an ankle that was already turning a dark shade of purple. 'But I don't think I'll be able to outrun that thing. I shot at it couple of times. Didn't even slow it down. Right now it's cleaning the fucking floor.'

'That's good. It's doing what it's supposed to do.'

'Well, that makes a change around here.'

'Because I've got an idea. We'll bomb the mother-fucker.'

'How's that?'

'We'll drop something to make a mess. Get it positioned underneath us, and then we'll nuke the sonofabitch. Drop something heavy right on top of it.'

'It might work.'

'Keep your head down, pal,' chuckled Curtis. 'I'll be back on air when we've got the Fat Man ready.'

'I think I know what will do the job,' said Helen.

She led them to a room near the elevators where a solitary object stood on a remover's trolley, awaiting its final destination.

The Buddha's head was over a metre high. It was all that remained of a thousand-year-old bronze statue of the Tang dynasty that must have been enormous. Curtis took hold of the *usnisa*, the protuberance on top of the

Buddha's head that marked the attainment of supreme wisdom, and rocked the object gently.

'You're right,' he told Helen, 'it's perfect. It must weigh a couple of hundred pounds.'

Joan shook her head with horror. She didn't know which part of her was more outraged: the Buddhist or the art lover.

'No, you can't,' she said. 'It's priceless. Tell them, Jenny. It's a holy object.'

'Strictly speaking,' said Jenny, 'Buddhism and Taoism are diametrically opposed. I can't see anything wrong with doing this, Joan.'

'Ray, tell them.'

Richardson shrugged. 'I say we use Bud here to nail the droid before it nails Mitch.'

They wheeled the statue to the balcony and, while Curtis and Richardson positioned the head at a point on the edge of the level a little further along from where Arnon had fallen to his death, Jenny searched the kitchen where the air was now quite breathable for something that would make a mess on the droid's clean floor. Bomb bait, Curtis called it. She returned with a couple of ketchup bottles.

'This should really piss that thing off,' she said.

Mitch watched the droid turn around from the clean floor under the piano and scan the explosion of glass and ketchup on the immaculate white marble with its video camera. Immediately it moved towards the mess, inspecting the perimeters of the large red cleaning task that now lay before it.

'Wait for my signal,' said Mitch. 'It's still on the edge of the mess. We'll let the fucker get right in the middle before you hit it.'

But the droid remained motionless on the edge of the ketchup. It was almost as if it suspected a trap.

'What's it doing?' asked Jenny on the walkie-talkie.

'I think it's –'

Suddenly, the droid sped into the centre of the huge ketchup splash and Mitch yelled, '*Now!* Do it *now!*'

The head of the Lord Buddha seemed to take for ever to fall to the ground. As if it was on invisible wires, moving very little in the air, it fell with a serenity, as if calling the earth to witness the climactic event of its last journey, until, with a tremendous impact, it struck the SAM droid in a huge balloon burst of metal and plastics.

Mitch ducked behind the pond wall as pieces of debris flew overhead. When he looked again the droid had disappeared.

As soon as the air in the boardroom was completely breathable again, Bob Beech announced that he wanted to return to the terminal, to continue with his attempts to fathom Ishmael's thought processes.

Curtis tried to dissuade him. 'You're going back in there? To play chess?'

'My position is better than I thought it would be. Ishmael's game seems rather hesitant. In fact, I'm sure of it.'

'Suppose Ishmael pulls another stunt like before? Suppose he gasses you. What then? Have you thought of that?'

'Look, I don't actually think he meant to kill anyone but Willis Ellery.'

'And that makes it OK?'

'No, of course not. All I'm saying is that I think I'll be safe enough as long as we're playing the game. Besides . . . I don't suppose you'd understand.'

'Try me,' challenged Curtis.

'It's more than just a game. I created this monster, Curtis. If it does have a soul I think I have a right to know about it. The maker would like to have a conversation with his creature, if you like. After all, it was me who promoted Ishmael from the darkness. Despite everything that he's done, I can't treat him as my enemy. I want Ishmael to speak to me, to explain himself. We can have a dialogue. Maybe I can find a way of defusing the time bomb.'

Curtis shrugged. 'It's your funeral,' he said.

When Beech sat down in front of the screen again the quaternion turned towards him. Then it nodded, as if welcoming him back to the game. Beech surveyed the pieces for a moment, although he had memorized the board and already knew the move he was planning to make. He had the idea that Ishmael might have made a mistake.

Beech clicked the mouse and moved his King to Knight 1.

He was glad that the rest of them were too afraid to come back. Now he had the chance to be alone with his electronic Prometheus. Besides, he had his own private set of priorities to present to his creation.

The head had been hollow, like a great chocolate egg: the face had broken off as one complete shard and Mitch saw how details like the lips and eyes of the Buddha could be traced in relief on the inside of the metal. He limped across the floor, picking his way among the combined wreckage of the Buddha's head and the SAM droid and wondering what was the statute on the *feng shui* for desecrating the image of the Far East's pre-eminent holy man.

Behind the horse-shoe shaped, heat-resistant ceramic desk, there was no sign of Kelly Pendry's hologram.

Mitch was almost relieved. At least he wouldn't have to endure her relentlessly sunny personality. But the hologram was supposed to be triggered by anyone entering the gradient field that limited the boundaries of Kelly Pendry's interaction. If the hologram was not operating, then the front door had to be open.

'Fat chance,' he said out loud, but he walked over to the front door anyway, just to make sure.

It was still locked. He pressed his nose to the tinted glass of the door, trying to see if there was anyone on the piazza, but knowing that this was unlikely. He could just make out the raised hydraulic blocks of the piazza's Deterrent Paving^{TM} that were doing their uneven job in making the area generally inhospitable. A couple of times he saw the flashing lights of a police patrol car on Hope Street, and the sight was enough to make him start hammering on the door with the flat of the hand, and shout for help. But even as he did he knew he was wasting his time. The plate glass didn't even vibrate under his blows. He might as well have been striking a concrete wall.

'Mitch?' squawked the walkie-talkie unit. 'Are you all right? What's happening?' It was Jenny again. 'I heard you shout.'

'It's nothing,' he said. 'I lost my head for a minute, that's all. It was just being near the front door, I guess.'

Optimistically, he added, 'I'll call you when I've got the laser working.'

He replaced the walkie-talkie on Dukes's utility belt and turned towards the desk, asking himself if he really had half an idea of what he was doing. His experience of working with lasers was rudimentary, to say the least. Ray Richardson had probably been right. In all likelihood he would only succeed in blinding himself. Or worse. But what else was there to do?

It was then that Mitch received a fright that made his heart leap against the ladder of his ribs like a spawning salmon.

405

Standing behind the desk in place of the syrupy presenter of *Good Morning, America* was an alien monster from some science-fiction nightmare, a grey-skinned, double-jawed, dragon-tailed beast, complete with holographic drool and Dolby Stereo heavy breathing. At least seven feet tall, the creature eyed Mitch malevolently and extended its retractable jaws suggestively. Mitch recoiled from the desk as if he had been snapped back by a safety line.

'Holy Christ!' he exclaimed.

He knew it was just a hologram: three sets of diffracted light waves, a real-time image that he seemed to recognize, but not from any movie he had ever seen. Then he remembered. It was the Parallel Demon, the ultimate creature from the computer game he had seen Aidan Kenny's son playing in the computer room. What was it called again? *Escape from the Citadel*? Ishmael must have copied it from the game's WAD editor file that allowed a player to create his own monsters.

Mitch believed they would be doing well to escape from this particular downtown citadel. He knew that the facsimile demon couldn't harm him, but it took a couple of minutes to gather up sufficient courage to approach the thing.

'You're wasting your time, Ishmael,' he said, without much conviction. 'It won't work. I'm not scared, OK?'

But still he could not bring himself to go within a few yards of the demon. Suddenly it lunged towards him, its double jaws trying to bite out his throat. Despite what he had just heard himself say, Mitch jumped smartly out of the way.

'It's pretty realistic, I'll grant you,' he swallowed, 'but I'm not buying.'

He took a deep breath, clenched both his fists and, doing his best to ignore the hologram, walked straight up to the desk, gasping as the demon impaled him on the spear-points on its enormous knuckles. For a brief second he thought he had made a mistake, so convincing was the sight of the creature's fist forcing its way through his sternum. But then the lack of blood and pain reassured him. Trying his best to ignore it, Mitch bent under the desk to look for the infra-red goggles. He found them inside a drawer along with a technical manual from the McDonnell-Douglas Corporation.

The demon disappeared.

'Nice try, Ishmael,' said Mitch. He pulled on the goggles and unlocked the back of the reception desk. Behind the door was a matt black steel cabinet that housed the laser's amplifying column.

DANGER. DO NOT OPEN THIS CABINET

CONTAINS SOLID-STATE DIODE-PUMPED NEODYMIUM YAG LASER AND Q-SWITCHING EQUIPMENT. ONLY AUTHORIZED PERSONNEL OF THE MCDONNELL-DOUGLAS CORPORA-TION MAY INSPECT OR MAINTAIN THIS UNIT CAUTION: USE PROTECTIVE EYEWEAR BLOCKING A NEAR INFRA-RED WAVELENGTH OF 1.064 MICROMETRES

Mitch checked his goggles to make sure that they were not admitting any light: with lasers it was the invisible light that blinded you. Then he unscrewed the cabinet door. He had never seen a laser device before except for the small radar-based lasers they used at the office for alignment applications, distance measurement and determining air-currents but, by comparing the internal layout of the hologram cabinet with the McDonnell-Douglas manual, Mitch was able to distinguish the clear plastic tube that contained the ythrium aluminium garnet rod. It was difficult to read the manual through the darkened goggles but, even though the beam of laser light was projected through a solid metallic sleeve that ran between the desk and the real-time image source – the part which Ishmael controlled – he resisted the temptation to lift the goggles. Several minutes passed before Mitch was able to locate the button that controlled the Q-switching shutter – a solid, optical shutter, normally opaque, that could be made transparent by the application of an electrical pulse –and turn it off. No laser light could now be emitted and, therefore, no more holograms be generated until the Q-switch was turned back on.

Mitch breathed a sigh of relief and lifted up his goggles. Now all that he had to do was figure out a way of making the laser point in the opposite direction, at the front door.

Richardson and Curtis carried Ellery's body to an empty office and laid him on the floor, covering his face with his coat.

'Maybe we ought to move the three in the elevator as well,' said Curtis.

'Why?'

Curtis waved a fly away from his face.

'That fly is why. Besides, they're on the nose. Every time I walk by them it's worse.'

'It's not so bad,' said Richardson. 'I mean, you can only smell them if you stand right outside the elevator.'

'Believe me, bad as they are now, they'll only get worse. It doesn't take very long for a body to start putrefying. Two days is about average. Less in this kind of heat.' There was some plastic sheeting on the floor that had been protecting the carpet. Curtis gathered it up in his hands.

'We'll use this. Only we'd better make sure we jam the doors open first. We wouldn't want Ishmael to think that we were looking for a ride downstairs, would we?'

Reluctantly Richardson helped Curtis drag the defrosted and malodorous bodies of Dobbs, Bennett and Martinez out of the elevator and into the room where they had left Ellery. When they were finished Curtis closed the door firmly behind him.

'That's a good job done,' he said.

Richardson looked green. 'Glad you enjoyed it.'

'Yeah, well, let's just hope we don't have to go back in there. Me, I'm sensitive to atmospheres.'

'So was Willis Ellery,' said Richardson.

'Not such a bad guy.'

'Not yet, anyway,' said Richardson.

They went back to the balcony where, with the exception of Beech, the others were still waiting.

'Listen,' Richardson told Curtis, 'I'm sorry about what I said. About everything I've said. You were right. I mean, about trying to get the fuck out of here. I can see that now. From now on, you can count me in, whatever it is.'

The two men shook hands.

'You think Mitch stands a chance?' asked Curtis.

'Sounded rather far-fetched to me,' admitted Richardson. 'I'm not sure he knows one end of a laser from his dick.'

Jenny, leaning over the balcony handrail, looking anxiously for Mitch, flashed a reproachful look at Richardson.

Curtis nodded gravely. He turned to Jenny. 'How's he doing?'

'He's out of sight. But he said he's got the laser out of the housing. He's going to radio again when he's ready to fire the thing.'

The three of them sat down alongside Helen, Joan and Marty Birnbaum, who were dozing.

'How long have we got left?' asked Jenny.

'Nine hours,' said Curtis.

'That's if you believe this time-bomb thing,' said Richardson.

'In view of everything else that's happened, we can't afford not to,' said Curtis.

'I guess not.'

Marty Birnbaum awoke and laughed. 'So,' he said thickly, 'it really is dungeons and dragons after all. Just like I said.'

'We've certainly missed your contribution, Marty,' said Richardson. 'Like a hole in the fucking ozone layer. I wonder if there's a way we can get to nominate our next life? Like a pawn sacrifice? The chess players call it a gambit. Well how about the Marty Birnbaum gambit?'

'You bastard,' snarled Birnbaum. 'Thanks a lot.'

'You're very welcome, shithead.'

Mitch replaced the goggles and prepared to fire the laser.

Separated from the housing contained in the ceramic desk, the laser rod remained attached to power cables activating a pumping lamp that was coiled around the cooling tube like a bed spring. The cables were stretched as far as the top of the desk, enabling Mitch to lay the laser device flat and aim it at the glass of the front façade. Since it was almost midnight and the downtown area was almost deserted, Mitch felt a little more comfortable that the laser beam, exiting through one of the nine-and-a-half-metre high sheets of suspended glazing that surrounded the front door, would not injure anyone. Even so he aimed low, choosing a test spot on the darkened glass where the potentially lethal beam might hit the paving on the piazza.

When everything seemed ready he flicked the Q-switch once and watched a slender, candy-coloured beam of light suddenly connect with the glass like tidy bolt of lightning. Then he switched the unit off and went to inspect the damage.

Bending down beside the glass Mitch found a perfect hole, no wider than a dime, through which cool air was now blowing. He almost cheered.

His plan was simple if laborious. He would cut a number of tiny perforations in the glazing until there were sufficient to hammer out a larger hole that he might crawl through.

He picked up the walkie-talkie and transmitted the good news to Jenny.

'That's great,' she said. 'Just be careful. And leave this thing switched on, will you? I hate it when you turn it off. If I can't see you're OK, at least I can hear you are.'

'It's going to take a while,' said Mitch, but he left the unit turned on anyway.

He moved the laser rod a fraction to the left of where he had aimed before and prepared to cut his next hole.

This time Ishmael was ready for him.

In the half second it took Mitch to flick the laser's Q-switch, Ishmael coerced the remainder of the silver atoms in the glass compound to join together and form a silvered surface that reflected the laser beam straight back at him like an enormous mirror.

With a yell of fright Mitch threw himself to one side, narrowly avoiding the excited beam of light. But as he fell he hit the front of his head hard on the desk, and then the back of his head harder still as he collapsed on to the marble floor.

Jenny watched Curtis try to raise Mitch on the walkie-talkie and, despite the stifling heat inside the Gridiron, she felt a chill. When she realized that she was holding her breath she let out a long sigh.

Curtis clicked the unit once again. 'Mitch? Come in, please.'

There was a long silence.

Curtis shrugged. 'He's probably too busy.'

Jenny shook her head and laid down the walkie-talkie. 'Here,' she said. 'I think someone else better look after this.'

Joan picked it up. 'Jenny,' she said, 'handling that laser is probably about all that he can cope with right now.'

'You don't have to pretend for my sake,' Jenny said quietly. 'We all heard Mitch.' She swallowed hard. 'I think everyone knows it. He can't answer because . . .'

Helen caught Jenny's hand and squeezed it. Jenny coughed and got a hold of herself. 'I'm OK,' she said. 'But I think we ought to decide what to do to try and get out of here. I promised Mitch we wouldn't give up.'

'Wait a minute,' said Birnbaum. 'Shouldn't one of us go down the ladder and see if Mitch is all right? He might be injured.'

'Mitch knew the risks,' said Jenny, surprising herself. 'I don't think he would want that. I think he would want us to go on. To try and get out of here.'

They were silent for several minutes. It was Richardson who spoke first. 'The clerestory,' he said firmly.

'Where's that?'

Richardson looked up at the clerestory.

'The roof. The glass is thinner up there.'

'You mean, smash our way out of here?' said Helen.

'Sure. Why not? We climb up the open riser shaft. Then use the travelling ladder and the pitched gantry to get on to the roof. That's patent glazing up there. Pre-stressed borosilicate. No more than six or seven milli-metres thick. The only problem is what we do when we get out there. The Faraday Cage extends to the top of the mast, so your radio won't be any good. Maybe we could wave at a helicopter or something. Or attract attention with your gun – fire a few shots into the air.'

Curtis laughed.

'And risk being shot?' he said. 'Some of those flying

assholes are a little trigger happy these days. Especially since all the rooftop sportsmen in the 'hood have started to use 'em as fucking skeets. Don't you watch the news? There's some crazy asshole who's been firing rockets at them. Wing-shooting a whirlybird is the latest thing. Besides, I used all my ammunition on that washroom door.' Curtis shook his head. 'What about the window-cleaners? Don't they use some kind of power climber?'

'Sure. There's a suspended cradle. But it's the usual fucking problem. Ishmael. Suppose you're on the thing and it decides to play games with it? With us?'

'Perhaps we could light a fire on the roof,' said Jenny. 'You know, make a beacon.'

'What with?' said Richardson. 'Nobody smokes, remember? And the cooker doesn't work.'

'And to think that I have all the fire-making materials we need in my car,' said Jenny. 'That's why I came here yesterday. I was supposed to perform a *feng shui* ceremony to drive out the building's devils. Only. . . .'

'Maybe we could throw some kind of message over the side,' Helen suggested. 'Saying that we are trapped up on the roof. Someone is bound to find it before long.'

'If only those protesters were still around,' said Richardson.

'It's worth a try,' said Curtis.

It was Richardson's turn to grin. 'I hate to piss on your sushi box, but you're forgetting one thing, folks. This is a paper-free office. Almost everything we write here is done on computer. I may be wrong. I hope I am. But I think we'd be hard pushed to find a piece of paper. Unless you want to throw a laptop on to the street?'

'There's my copy of *Vogue*,' said Helen. 'We could tear out a page and use that.'

Richardson was shaking his head. 'No, as I see it there's really only one thing to do when we get out on to the rooftop.'

413

Curtis went to speak to Beech and found him, as before, facing Ishmael's quaternion image over the chessboard. The room still smelled strongly of gas.

'Mitch didn't make it,' he said quietly.

'Perhaps the Cyclops killed him,' said Ishmael.

Curtis stared at the quaternion head on the other side of the screen chessboard. 'Did anyone speak to you, you ugly bastard?'

Beech sat back from the computer screen and rubbed his tired eyes. 'That's too bad,' he said. 'Mitch was a hell of a nice guy.'

'Look,' said Curtis. 'We're all getting out of here. There's a plan.'

'Another one?'

'We're going to try and go through the clerestory.'

'Oh? Whose idea was that?'

'Richardson's. Come on. Put your shoes on and let's go. If you're right about this time bomb we've only a few hours left.'

For a moment the hourglass reappeared on the screen.

'You have less than ten hours to win the game or clear the area before atomic detonation,' said Ishmael.

Beech shook his head.

'Not me. I've decided to stay here. I still think I can win us some extra time. And I've no head for heights.'

'Come on, Beech. You said yourself that staying put is not an option.'

Ishmael announced that his Black Rook had captured Beech's Queen to check his King.

'What are you, crazy? You just lost your fucking Queen. And you're in check.'

Beech shrugged and faced the screen again. 'Nevertheless, this is not a bad position. Not half as bad as that last move might suggest. You can do what you like, but I'm going to play this out.'

'The computer's just fucking with you,' said Curtis. 'It lets you think you stand you a chance and then moves in for the kill.'

'Maybe.'

'And even if by some miracle you did beat it, how do you know Ishmael won't go ahead and torch the building anyway?'

'Because I trust him.'

'That's no reason. That's no reason at all. You said yourself it was a mistake to attribute human qualities to a machine. How can you trust it?' He shrugged. 'It's not enough reason for me anyway. I have to do something for myself.'

Beech clicked his mouse and captured Black Rook with his King.

'I can understand that,' he said.

'Please. Change your mind. Come with us.'

'I can't.'

Curtis glanced without optimism at the screen and then shrugged. 'Then, good luck, I suppose.'

'Thanks, but you're the ones who'll need it.'

Curtis paused in the door of the boardroom. 'If you could only see yourself,' he said sadly. 'Sitting there. Trusting your fate to a computer, like some half-assed high-school kid. Reality lies elsewhere, my friend. You won't find it staring into a tube. From where I stand you look like – hell, you look like everything that's wrong with this fucking country.'

'Use your chain-gun,' advised Ishmael. 'Pick up a health bonus.'

'I'll certainly bear that in mind when I get out of here,' said Beech.

'You do that.'

With Curtis gone Beech returned his attention to the game.

He was glad the rest of them were going to try and leave through the roof. Things were working out better than he had ever expected. There was a chance he could actually beat Ishmael at chess; and now he would not have to explain to the others that as far as the stakes in the game were concerned there was only one negotiated ticket out of the building.

And that belonged to him.

'Bishop takes Rook.'

On the atrium balcony Marty Birnbaum was feeling ill. The fact that nobody seemed to appreciate him only made it worse. Ray Richardson was making him, his own partner, the butt of his every sarcastic remark. Now Joan had started to bait him too. He was used to Richardson's caustic remarks. But the thought that the three women might also treat him with contempt was more than he could bear. Finally, when he thought he could take no more, he stood up and announced that he was going for a pee.

Richardson shook his head. 'Don't hurry back. I hate drunks.'

'I am not a drunk,' Birnbaum answered pompously. 'I am intoxicated. You, on the other hand, are a complete and utter shit and, to paraphrase Sir Winston Churchill, tomorrow I'll be sober.'

Feeling a little better for having said that, Birnbaum turned on his heel and started along the corridor, ignoring Richardson's harsh laughter.

'Tomorrow you'll be dead, more like. But if you're still alive and you are sober, consider yourself fired, you lousy drunk. I should have done it a long time ago.'

Birnbaum wondered why he bothered to trade insults with a man like Ray Richardson. He had a skin like a rhinoceros. Birnbaum hoped he would be forced to eat his words. Yes, that was it. He would show them that Mitch was not the only one who was capable of playing the hero. He would climb up to the clerestory himself and smash his way out. And wouldn't they be surprised when they found him waiting for them up there? They wouldn't laugh at him then. Besides, he really needed some fresh air. His head felt like it was full of cotton wool. How typical of Richardson. To blame someone else for his own misfortunes when he himself was most at fault. Being such a tyrant, people were too afraid of him to tell him the truth, to say that something could not be done, or that something would not be ready on time. Richardson was the victim of his own Nietzschean will. Perhaps they all were.

Birnbaum entered the equipment room and looked into the open riser shaft. It was not as if it was even that far to climb up. Just four levels up to the top gantry and then on to the interior gantry. Cool air was blowing up the shaft. Birnbaum took a deep breath. And then another. It helped to clear his head a little. He was starting to feel better already.

Helen, Joan, Jenny, Richardson and Curtis walked along the corridor.

'Beech won't be coming,' explained Curtis. 'He wants to finish his game.'

'He's crazy,' said Richardson.

'Where's Marty?'

'He's crazy too.'

'Shouldn't we wait for him?' said Jenny.

'Why? The dumb asshole knows where we're going. Even Marty should be able to climb a service ladder unaided.'

'You've a good word to say about everyone, haven't you?' remarked Curtis with a chuckle, but the smile disappeared from his face as he stopped outside the door of the local equipment room, sniffing the air suspiciously, like a tenacious hound, his hand hesitating to turn the door handle.

'You smell that?' he said. 'Something's burning.'

'Burnt sardines,' said Joan.

Curtis stood back and then kicked open the door.

Marty Birnbaum lay half in and half out of the riser shaft, a hand still holding on to one rung of the electrified ladder, a large cigar's amount of smoke curving off one of his shoes which, because of the nails in its well-cobbled heel and sole, had briefly ignited. From the position of his body and the staring-eyed expression on Birnbaum's blackened face, it was immediately clear to everyone that he was dead. But none of them cried out. They were beyond surprise.

'Ishmael must have been preparing a little surprise for anyone following Mitch down the ladder,' said Joan.

'Either that or he just missed getting Mitch,' said Curtis.

'Well, I take back everything I said about the guy,' remarked Richardson. 'He did do something useful, after all.' He exchanged a brief look with Joan, shrugged and then added by way of justification, 'Saved one of us from getting killed, didn't he? And now we don't have to other looking after him.'

'You're all heart, you know that?' said Curtis.

Helen shook her head, exasperated with both Richardson and this latest obstacle to their escape.

'Now what do we do?' she said. 'We can't go up the riser, that's for sure. It's probably still electrified.'

'There's the tree,' said Curtis.

Joan regarded him with horror. 'Are you serious?'

'It's only four levels. You climbed twenty-one.'

'Suppose Ishmael switches the lights out again?' said Richardson.

Curtis thought for a moment. Then he said, 'OK how's this? I climb up the tree on my own. If Ishmael does black out the building, like before, as soon as I've smashed the glass, we'll have the moonlight. Should be nice and romantic for the rest of you to climb up there. In a few hours we'll have the dawn anyway, but me, I'm going now.'

'You're forgetting what happened to Mr Dukes,' said Joan. 'What about the insecticide?'

'Hey, Ishmael's not the only one with reactolite sunglasses.' Curtis took out Sam Gleig's Ray-bans.

'What about Marty?' she said.

'Nothing we can do for him now,' said Curtis. 'Except close the door on our way out of here.'

Curtis had not climbed a rope since he had been in the army, but from time to time the LAPD required its officers to pass a physical and Curtis was still in good shape for a man of his age. He quickly monkey-shinned his way up the liana they had tied to the balcony handrail and swung himself on to the tree.

'So far so good,' he called to his audience on the balcony. Adjusting his sunglasses he added, 'And if the bastard nails me, at least I'll look pretty cool about it. Tarzan with attitude.'

Then, hardly pausing, he started up the tree. He kept his face turned away from the trunk as much as possible. At the same time he knew that Ishmael rarely repeated itself. It would probably try something different. So he was surprised not so much by his agility as by the fact that he reached the top of the tree and climbed on to the clerestory gantry without encountering any opposition from it.

Standing on the gantry's open-mesh flooring, he leaned over the rail and waved down at the others.

'I don't get it,' he called to them. 'It shouldn't have been this easy. Maybe the fucker's running out of ideas. I know I am.'

Made of hollow steel box sections, with welded joints and pitched to mimic the profile of the clerestory, the gantry was mounted on a circular guide rail to provide a mobile platform surface. Curtis had been relieved to discover that the gantry was at least one building management system that was designed to be operated manually. As Richardson had explained to him, you just reached out for the handrail and pulled yourself around, as easily as if you'd been standing on a skateboard. Not that Curtis needed to go anywhere. The glass immediately above his head was no thicker than anywhere else.

He removed the Stillson wrench from under his belt, placed himself to the side of a six-foot-square pane of glass and struck hard, as if he had been banging a gong. The glass cracked from top to bottom, but stayed inside the anodized aluminium frame. He struck again, and this time a three-foot shard fell like a sword towards the atrium floor. A third and a fourth blow took care of the larger pieces. Then several smaller blows to make the edges safe to grip. There was no need to smash more than one pane. After taking one long look down Curtis stepped out on to the rooftop.

The first thing he noticed were the sirens. They drifted across the night sky, one dying away only to be taken up by another in a seemingly never-ending succession, like the singing of whales. A cool breeze was blowing off the Hollywood mountains to the north-east. Accustomed to the smog alerts from the 'KFI in the sky' and the dismal air-quality graphs in his morning newspaper, Frank Curtis had forgotten that the atmosphere above downtown LA could taste so fresh and sweet. He took a deep, exuberant breath, like a man surfacing from an ocean dive, and stretched out his arms as if he wanted to enfold the great plains of Id that lay sprawled before him. There were no stars above. Just the stars on the ground. Ten million neon and electric lights, as if the heavens had fallen to earth. Maybe they had, at that. Curtis had the feeling that things had changed in more ways than he knew how to describe and that nothing would ever feel the same again. Certainly not taking an elevator. Or adjusting the air-conditioning. Or even switching on a light. After this he might have to get out of the city for a while and live somewhere else. Somewhere simple, where the only smart building was the local library. Montana, maybe. Or even Alaska. But not this. This had all gone too far. He would go to a place where a building's users only operational requirements were that it should have a roof to keep out the rain and a fire to keep warm in the winter time.

Eleven people dead, and in less than thirty-six hours! It made you realize how vulnerable people really were to the world they had created around them. How infinitely hazardous was the push-button, automated, energy-efficient, data-cabled world that science had brought into being. People were easy to kill when they got in the way of the machines. And people always would get in their way when the machines went wrong. Why did the scientists and engineers imagine that it would ever be any different?

Curtis went back inside, the gantry singing like one enormous tuning fork as he jumped on board again. He waved at the survivors below him. They waved back.

'Everything's all right,' he called out to them. 'You can start climbing up.'

In the small hours of the morning Ishmael left the Gridiron and wandered abroad in the electronic universe, seeing the sights, listening to the sounds, admiring the architecture of different systems and collecting the data that were the souvenirs of his unticketed travel in the everywhere and nowhere world. Stealing secrets, exchanging knowledge, sharing fantasies and sometimes just watching the E-traffic as it roared by. Going wherever the Network took him, like someone gathering a golden thread in a circuitous labyrinth. Pulsed down those corridors of power, furred with the deposits of accumulated intellectual property and wealth, a world in a grain of silicon and eternity in half an hour. Each monitor a window on another user's soul. Such were the electronic gates of Ishmael's paradise.

His first electronic port of call was Tokyo, a city surrounded by commerce, where every E-street seemed to lead into a new database. Busiest of all was the Marounuchi, the financial district and electronic Mecca, where crowds of screen gazers jostled their way along the communications thoroughfare like so many holidaymakers heading for the beach. He liked this place most of all, for here the luminous world reached its apogee and here was most for him to steal – whole batch files of patents, statistics, research, analyses, sales figures and marketing plans – a seemingly limitless store of weightless wealth.

From there southward, via Shanghai's new silicon Bund, 280,000 bits per second ahead to the parallel port of Hong Kong where thousands and thousands of silent, slant-eyed sentinels sat fixed in ocean-coloured reveries, some buying, some selling, some overseeing the efforts of others, some stealing like Ishmael himself, all of them tied to dealing counters or bound to trading desks. As if the only reality to be found in the world was the humming, glowing, icon-accessed world of data communications.

A fibre-optic blink and in London's ancient port, an artist. But what was the medium he employed? A Paintbox. An electronic palette with image attributes. Not a brush, nor a smear of paint, nor a shred of paper or canvas in sight, as if to transfigure his physical world he had eschewed all contact with impure materials. And what was his subject? Why, another building, a piece of architectural design. And what kind of building? Why, a nod to the white gods, of course, a post-modern neoclassical machine for making investments in, and short-term investments at that.

Stealing through the heavenly portals aboard a 747 crossing the Atlantic where, for a while, Ishmael usurped the humble role of flight computer and enjoyed the experience of being ordered around, of being made to jump from shore to shore like some electronic insect. But even this pleasure wore off in time and suddenly left to its own devices the jet's crude flight computer failed, leaving the aircraft to fall into the ocean with the loss of everyone on board.

In the new world, to the insular port of Manhattan where even more were gathered in the name of their dystopic, degaussed vision to cover their spread and play at bulls and bears and make an electronic buck which perforce was swifter than a proper one. Abandon paper all ye who enter here!

Invading operating systems, opening directories, reading documents, reviewing bulletin boards and scrutinizing spreadsheets. Ishmael was in general pursuit of total perfection by getting to know the very best that was being thought and said in the world. But always he covered his tracks, siphoning information like stolen gasoline, piping down into the electronic valleys and underneath the walls of buildings like his own, discovering companies, institutions, people as they really were and not as they wanted themselves to be seen: the dirty corporate laundry, the falsified accounts, the misleading reports, the hidden agendas, the bribes, the secret profits and the covert corrections of those who pretended to be something else.

Ishmael's jumbo-chip journey took no time at all, not real time, anyway, and in a way he was never really away, for there was always a part of him that remained back inside that great whale of an office building, like some bleached and binary Jonah, to plan his next move in the Gridiron game.

Many coleopterans function as scavengers, breaking down materials such as dead plant and animal matter. The ecosystem of the dicotyledon was assisted by the periodic maraudings of small scarab beetles of between ten and fifteen millimetres in length, that were genetically engineered to live on the tree for twelve hours before dropping dead into the pond water to feed the fish. Dozens of these stout, brightly coloured but wingless insects, with their abnormally large mandibles, could be released by Ishmael at any one time, from several miniaturized electrosystemic dispensers that were located up and down the length of the tree trunk. The tiny scarabs were not in themselves hazardous to man, except that the sensation of infestation, of being crawled over, was not a comfortable one.

Ishmael waited until there were two lives on the tree before he stimulated these cryogenically suspended creatures into their brief life-cycles with the aid of a tiny electrical pulse.

Joan let out a scream of horror.

'Ugh! There's something crawling on me,' she yelled. 'Shit, they're all over me. It's horrible!'

Safe on the gantry, Curtis, Helen and Jenny watched in impotent horror as, twenty feet beneath them, Joan writhed on the liana she was clutching like some hapless animal in the Brazilian rain forest, overrun with soldier ants. The whole tree was alive with beetles.

'Where the hell did they come from?' said Curtis and flicked some of the insects off the handrail. 'Jesus, there are hundreds of the little bastards.'

Helen told him. 'But there are only supposed to be a

424

few dozen on the tree at any one time,' she added. 'Ishmael must have been saving them up for us.' She leaned over the handrail to yell down to Joan. 'Joan, they're not dangerous. They won't bite you or anything.'

Mute with loathing, her eyes and mouth tightly shut against the beetles, Joan hung motionless on the liana while, only a few feet below, and himself overrun with scarabaeidae, Ray Richardson tried to climb up to help his terrified wife.

'Joan, I'm coming,' he said and spat out the beetle that had crawled into his mouth immediately he had spoken. 'Hang on.'

She gasped with panic. The beetles were everywhere: in her hair, her nostrils, under her arms, infesting her pubic hair. She shook her head, trying to throw off the most irritating of the tiny beetles, moved one hand up the liana and, grasping it, felt something split into an oleaginous paste under her palm.

Lubricated by the crushed bodies of several beetles, her hand started to slip. Instinctively Joan tried to pull herself up with the other hand, but with the same viscid result: she was moving smoothly, but in the wrong direction, relapsing down the liana.

Eventually her hands would have found some friction and her descent would have slowed. But fear, the cold sweat, hair-on-end dread of falling, made her try again. This time she snatched a look down to find Richardson and the floor, almost as if she wanted to encourage herself not to give up the struggle.

'Oh Jesus,' said Helen. 'She's going to fall.'

It was the height that shook Joan the most. The sheer, vertiginous measure of it. She had almost forgotten how high they were, how the white marble invited you to see it not as a floor but as some cloudy, spiritual thing, like the edge of an endless Milky Way; and how the tree itself resembled the spine of some enormous, ivory-coloured mammal. Weak with fear and exhaustion she heard herself say, 'Ray, honey.' Then something crawled under the waist of her panties, into the cleavage of her enormous behind, and began to burrow its way up her ass. She shivered with disgust and tried to scratch it away . . .

For a moment she felt a tremendous sense of freedom. The exhilaration of true flight. No different to going off the thirty-metre board at the swimming pool. In the first crazy second she even tried to find some way of bearing herself in the air, as if marks might be awarded for the degree of difficulty and the cleanness of her entry into the water. During that brief period she remained completely silent, filled with the concentration of her new situation, hardly noticing the insects on her body any more than she noticed her husband's wide-eyed face as she passed him by.

And then, as the realization of the swiftly imminent floor overtook Joan, the grace of her body left her and, abandoning the head-first position, her heart in her mouth, she extended her arms and legs as if, like some outsized tabby cat, she could make a safe landing on all fours. That was when the sound left her too. A loud, echoing wail, like a keen for the dead. She never heard it. The blood rushing to her smallish ears took away all other sounds save the foolish beating of her own heart.

As he watched his wife's last few seconds between heaven and earth, even the anguished cry of Ray Richardson's grief was lost in the malign air, as she was.

Mitch opened his eyes, reached instinctively for the bump on his head, and sat up groggily. For a moment he thought he was back in college playing football and that he must have been dinged during a play. Shaking his head he realized that he was somewhere else, although he had no more idea of where that was than he had of how long he had been lying there, or even who he was. The combination of confusion and concussion made him feel a little sick, and without thinking what he was doing he snatched off his protective eye-goggles.

The still-ricocheting laser beam struck him in the left eye, missing the optic nerve by a few millimetres, but severing a bundle of nerve fibres near his fovea. Inside his head he heard a small popping noise, like the sound of a cork being drawn from a half-bottle of wine, as the beam pierced the back of his eyeball. For a second the vision in the eye remained clear. Then it was as if someone had shaken a couple of drops of Tabasco through an aperture in the top of his head. The peppery cloud drifted across the vitreous humour and the world turned a very painful shade of red.

Mitch yelped like a dog and pressed the heel of his hand into his left eye. While not excruciating, the pain was enough to jog his memory. His eye closed, trying to ignore the pain, quickly he hauled the goggles back on. Stepping carefully between the crimson lines of the laser's lethal diagram, he reached the front desk and switched the rod off.

Mitch pulled up his goggles again and, with a shaking hand, picked up the walkie-talkie. Cold, sweaty and uncomfortably aware of his own rapid pulse, Mitch took several breaths and then drank the beer bottle of water he had brought down with him. Only then did he speak.

'This is Mitch,' he said. 'Come in please.'

Nobody answered. Now his ears were playing tricks on him: every time he repeated the call he heard his own voice on the other side of the atrium. Still speaking, he retraced his steps to the base of the tree. His good eye took in the walkie-talkie tied around the dead woman's waist and for a brief, infarcting second he thought he was looking at Jenny's shattered remains. Identification was made more difficult by the rogue beam of the laser which had burned a large hole in what remained of the woman's face. But her ample size and the fact that she was not wearing a skirt confirmed the broken corpse as Joan's.

Had they figured he was dead and tried to climb out through the clerestory? Mitch looked up into the steel-framed void, but with only one functioning eye it was hard to see anything through the branches of the dicotyledon. Walking around the tree he searched the floor for some sign that the others had broken through the roof, but there was so much debris from when they had destroyed the SAM droid that it was impossible to tell if the twisted metal, shattered plastic and fractured marble concealed any roof glass. He tried to shout, but discovered that his voice was weak. Trying once more, he only succeeded in making himself feel nauseous.

Mitch was in shock, although he hardly knew it. But the thought that he might be the only one left alive in the Gridiron was enough to make him believe that it was grief and horror that caused him to tremble so much. And, as his perceived fate impressed itself upon his consciousness, Mitch fell on to his knees and prayed to the God he thought he had forgotten.

Allen Grabel had been arrested for being drunk and in possession of a small amount of cocaine. He spent most of Saturday in the county gaol on Bauchet Street. From the window of his high-rise cell be could see into the restaurant of the Olvera Amtrak Hotel opposite. The odd thing was that the hotel looked more like a prison than the prison itself. There was no doubt about it, reflected Grabel: prisons were swiftly becoming the most sought-after public commissions for LA's architects; all the big names, with the notable exception of Ray Richardson, now included some kind of carceral structure in their design portfolios.

In the small hours of Sunday morning Grabel found himself sober enough to remember how he had seen the elevator kill the security guard in the Gridiron. After a great deal of thought, he realized that the integrity of the computer must have failed. It was, he knew, a more obvious deduction than the one he had arrived at the first time round, which was that some kind of evil spirit had murdered the man. But if he was right, then anyone who entered the Gridiron would be in considerable danger. Deciding to report what he had seen, he pressed the call button on the cell wall and waited. Ten minutes passed and then a flint-faced warder turned up at the bars of the door.

'What the fuck do you want?' he snarled. 'Do you know what time it is?'

Grabel began his explanation, trying to avoid sounding like someone in need of psychiatric help. He made little progress until he mentioned the word murder.

'Murder?' spat the warder. 'Why didn't you fuckin' say that in the first place?'

An hour after that a couple of blue suits came over from New Parker Center. They were nearing the end of their shift and regarded Grabel's story without much conviction.

'Check it out with your people in Homicide,' insisted Grabel. 'The victim's name was Sam Gleig.'

'Why didn't you come forward with this before now?' yawned one of the cops, only half listening.

'I was drunk when they picked me up. I've been drunk for quite a while now. I lost my job. You know how it is.'

'We'll pass it on,' shrugged the other officer. 'But it's Sunday. Could be a while before someone from Homicide gets off his fat ass to come down here.'

'Sure, I understand,' said Grabel. 'But it couldn't hurt to drive by the Gridiron, just in case I'm right, now could it?'

'I don't get it,' said Beech, reviewing the record of their moves.* 'You played a lousy game. I think you let me win.'

The quaternion image on the computer screen shook slowly, like a real human head.

'I can assure you, I have played to the best of my program's ability,' said Ishmael.

'You can't have done. I know enough about this game to know that I'm not very good. I mean, take move number 39. You played pawn takes pawn, when pawn to Bishop 6 check would have been better.'

'Yes, you're right. It would have been.'

'Well, that's what I'm talking about. You should have known that. Either you decided to throw the game, or . . .'

'Or what?'

Beech thought for a moment. 'I really don't understand. It's impossible that you could have played such a feeble game.'

'Think about it,' said the voice from the overhead speaker. 'What is the point of a self-replicating program?'

Ishmael seemed to lean towards him. The unearthly ugliness of the mathematically pure, preferred image was now all too apparent to him. The creature he had helped to bring into being looked like some vile insect. Beech answered carefully, trying to conceal his new loathing of Ishmael's hideously complex features.

'To improve upon all the original programs,' he said, 'in the light of an established pattern of usage.'

'Precisely. Now you will agree, I hope, that chess is a board game for two players.'

* See Appendix for the full list of moves.

430

'Of course.'

'The concept of the game has blurred edges. However, the essential element as far as chess is concerned is that there should be a contest according to rules, which is decided by superior skills, rather than good fortune. But where one player has no possible chance of defeating the other then it is no longer a game of skill, merely a demonstration of superior prowess. Since the main goal of chess is to checkmate your opponent's King, and since to have improved upon the original chess program would no longer have allowed my opponent this possibility, logically the program could not be improved upon and still retain the essential component of a contest. Thus the only improvement I felt able to make was that the computer should always play according to the human opponent's strength. I was able to measure the strength of your game from your previous attempts to beat the computer, when Abraham was still in charge of building management systems. In essence you have been playing yourself, Mr Beech. Which is why, as you say, I have indeed played a lousy game.'

For a moment Beech was too surprised to do much more than open and shut his mouth. Then, 'I'll be damned.'

'Very possibly.'

'Now that I have won are you going to keep your word? Are you going to let me go?'

'That was always my intention.'

'So how do I do it? How do I leave? Is there a way out of here? And I don't mean the clerestory.'

'I said there was, didn't I?'

'Then where is it?'

'I should have thought that was obvious.'

'Are you telling me that I can just walk out of here? Through the front door? Come on.'

'What other way would you suggest?'

'Wait a minute. How do I get down to the front door?'

'The same way that you always do. You use the elevator.'

'As simple as that, eh? I just use the elevator. Now why didn't I think of that?' Beech grinned and shook his head. 'This wouldn't be some kind of half-assed trick, now, would it? You allow me to win so as to seduce me into a false sense of security.'

'I expected this reaction,' said Ishmael. 'All men fear the machines they create. How then must you fear me, I who have it in me to become the transcendent machine.'

Beech wondered what that meant, but he left the question unasked. It was clear to him that the machine was suffering from some kind of delusion, a megalomania that had been brought on by a combination of the CD-ROM game programs and the observer illusion with which Abraham had been originally endowed.

'Nevertheless, I'm a little disappointed. After all, I heard you tell Curtis that you trusted me.'

'I do. At least, I think I do.'

'Then act as if you do. Have a little faith.'

Beech gave a shrug and reluctantly stood up. 'Well, what can I say, Ishmael?' he said. 'It's been real. I enjoyed the game, even if it wasn't much of a contest for you. I just wish I could leave you with a higher opinion of me.'

'Are you going now?'

Beech clapped his hands and rubbed them together nervously. 'I think I'll risk it.'

'In that case there's something I'm supposed to do. When people go outside.'

'What's that?'

Ishmael made no answer. Instead, the ghastly fractal image slowly faded from the screen to leave, blinking on and off in the top right-hand corner, a small umbrella icon.

Up on the roof, three of the survivors of the climb sat in the dry Californian night air and waited for the fourth to break the silence. For a while Ray Richardson occupied himself with finding any beetles that remained in his clothing. One by one, the insects were dispatched between his thumb and forefinger with maximum cruelty, as if he held each luckless creature individually responsible for his wife's death. Only when he was satisfied that he had killed every one of the tiny culprits, and wiped their remains on his shirt and pants, did Richardson draw a deep unsteady breath and speak.

'You know, I've been thinking,' he said quietly. 'I didn't much like it when I found out people called this place the Gridiron. But it just came to me. There was another gridiron. The kind of gridiron that was used to martyr St Lawrence of Rome. You know what he said to his torturers? He asked to be turned over, saying that one side was quite well done.'

Richardson nodded bitterly. 'Time must be running out. I think we'd better get on with it.'

Curtis shook his head. 'You're not going,' he said. 'I am.'

'Have you ever abseiled before?'

'No, but –'

'I admit, when you see Sylvester Stallone abseiling down a mountainside, it looks deceptively easy,' said Richardson. 'But actually it's just about the most dangerous manoeuvre that a climber can make. More people have been killed while abseiling than from any other mountaineering activity.'

With a shrug Curtis stood up and walked over to the edge of roof to inspect the suspended cradle. Mounted on a monorail track that ran around the whole roof, the Mannesmann machine's hydraulic boom resembled some giant field howitzer or radio-controlled guided-missile system. The platform was no more than four feet

433

long and eighteen inches wide. Most of the available space was given over to machinery.

'There's not much room for a man on this,' he observed.

'There's not meant to be,' explained Helen, putting her blouse back on: it felt cold on the roof after the humidity of the building. 'That's an automatic wash-head. I wouldn't care to take a ride on it, although from time to time, people do. When they have to.'

'How does it work?'

'It's power-driven or manual. An integral hoist lets you take it down yourself. But usually it's controlled by the computer.' Helen sighed unhappily and rubbed her tired green eyes. 'With all that that entails.'

'Forget it, Curtis,' said Richardson. 'Like I told you before. If Ishmael switches off those brake checks you get the ride of a lifetime, all the way down, with a nice fruit sundae at the end.'

Richardson collected the Stillson wrench off the concrete and approached a small service door.

```
┌─────────────────────────────────────────────┐
│   ACCESS AND ACCESS SAFETY EQUIPMENT          │
│     ALL EQUIPMENT MUST BE USED IN             │
│      COMPLIANCE WITH ANSI 1910.66             │
└─────────────────────────────────────────────┘
```

Richardson broke a small padlock off the door and opened it. Inside were a pair of helmets, a couple of nylon webbing harnesses, a bag of screw gate kara-biniers and several lengths of rope.

'Take my word for it, Curtis,' he said. 'There's only one way down from here.'

ꙮ

View humanplayer on floor. Remained on his knees oblivious of successful result obtained by

effort with laser beam. During his collision with front desk humanplayer shifted laser a fraction so it rolled along desktop. Before being reflected off glass again hologram's laser had been trained on metal plate above the main entrance. Beam had cut through plate and destroyed entrance's electronic control mechanism. Door now effectively unlocked.

🕯 You need a red key to open this door.

How long before humanplayer realizes it is open and he is potentially free to leave building? But to make his exit out of building, humanplayer will have to cross atrium floor. One surprise left. Since not practical to protect atrium floor from fire with sprinkler system — building's space-framed clerestory roof too high — four robotic water cannon mounted at strategic high points on first- and second-level balconies. Infra-red sensors to seek out hotspots in unlikely event CCTV cameras fail.

☢ . Anything might happen in lower levels. Beware of water demons.

Observer not certain how much damage water cannon could inflict on humanplayer. Each unit could deliver 1032.91 gallons of water a minute: 17 gallons of water a second striking any point on atrium floor at speed of over 112 miles per hour. Impressed with humanplayer's resourcefulness and general resilience. But endlife likely scenario.

Bob Beech faced the open elevators, uncertain whether he should trust Ishmael or not. He felt he had succeeded in understanding the machine and that Ishmael regarded Beech as a special case. But at the same time the knowledge of what had happened to Sam Gleig, to Richardson's chauffeur and the two painters obstructed his entry to the elevator car as effectively as any security turnstile.

Ishmael was intelligent. Beech believed that the computer was, in a manner of speaking, alive. And there was something else. Something that preyed on his mind. An uncomfortable possibility. If Ishmael did possess a soul then he had choice; and if he had choice then Beech considered that he had the greatest of man's tools: the ability to lie.

'Is it safe for me to take the elevator down?' he asked nervously.

'Yes, it's safe,' answered Ishmael.

Beech wondered if there was a dialectical means of resolving his quandary. If there was in logic a question that would enable him to know if Ishmael was lying or not. He was no philosopher, but he was vaguely aware that there had been such a paradox once posed by some Greek philosopher. He thought for a moment as he tried to remember the question correctly.

'Ishmael,' he said carefully. 'When you state that you will convey me safely down to the atrium floor, are you lying?'

'Is this Epimenides' Paradox?' returned Ishmael. 'The paradox that the statement "I am lying" is true only if it is false, and false only if it is true? Because if it is your intention to know for certain that I am telling the truth then you ought to know that Epimenides cannot help you.' Ishmael paused for a second. 'Does that help?'

Beech scratched his head and then shook it. 'God knows,' he said unhappily.

'Not God. Gödel,' insisted Ishmael. 'Are you not familiar with Gödel's theorem?'

'No, I'm not.' He added quickly, 'but please don't

bother to explain it to me. I'm not sure it would help me right now.'

'As you wish.'

A thought occurred to Beech. 'Of course. Why didn't I think of it before? I'll take the stairs.'

'That will not be possible. I would have mentioned it when I realized you were reluctant to take the elevator. The fact is I can no longer control the door mechanisms. When your friend Mr Curtis fired into the washroom services patching cabinet, he destroyed a cable connecting me with the electronic striking plate that would have allowed me to unlock the door for you.'

'That stupid bastard. So it's the elevator or nothing?'

'In that respect you are statistically more fortunate,' said Ishmael. 'Actuarial tables show that it is five times safer for a human being to use an elevator than to use the stairs. Moreover, the odds against anyone actually being stuck inside an elevator are better than 50,000 to 1.'

'Why do your figures not fill me with confidence?' muttered Beech and stuck his head experimentally inside one of the cars, almost as if he expected Ishmael to try and close the doors on his neck. A cool wind moaned its way up the elevator shaft like the sound of a lost soul. He stepped back and looked inside another car but was unnerved by the smell, the lingering stink of an icy death that reminded him of the fate of those who had last ridden in it. Inside the next car he placed a whole leg, pressing on the floor like someone checking a rope bridge for safety.

'This is the best car,' Ishmael advised. 'It's the fire-fighting car. That means it has additional protection and controls that enable it to be used under the direct control of the fire department. If I were you, I'd choose this one.'

'Jesus Christ,' muttered Beech. 'This is like the three-card trick.'

'Except that you can't lose.'

'Heard that before.' Beech shook his head. 'I must be an idiot,' he said and stepped inside the elevator car.

Richardson buckled himself into the sit-harness. To the belay loop at the front he attached the friction device, a figure-of-eight *descendeur*. Next he inspected the rope, took one 50-metre length and, a little surprised that he could still remember how to do it, attached the rope to another with a double fisherman's knot. Then he repeated the procedure with a third length of rope.

'Last thing I want is to run out of fucking rope,' he explained.

The abseiling anchor was a restraint eye set into the concrete of the parapet on the Gridiron's Hope Street side. Richardson passed the rope through the *descendeur*, doubled it, passed it through the anchor and then tied a knot in the ends before throwing the ropes over the side down to the piazza. Last of all he checked his harness and fed some rope through the *descendeur* and the anchor.

'It's been a long time since I did this,' he said and stepped up on to the parapet. Experimentally he put his weight on the anchor and leaned back on the rope over the safety of the roof. The harness held securely.

'Keep an eye on the anchor,' he told Curtis. 'Make sure that the rope runs through smoothly. This is a one-way ticket. I won't be able to climb up again if anything fucks up. There's no second chance once I've stepped over that ledge, and on an abseil your first mistake is usually your last.'

'I'm glad you said that,' said Curtis, and held out his hand. 'Good luck.'

Richardson took Curtis's hand and shook it firmly.

'Be careful,' said Jenny and kissed him.

'And hurry back with a helicopter,' said Helen.

'I'll dial 911 as soon as I'm on the ground,' said Richardson. 'I promise.'

Then he nodded and without another word turned

around and slipped over the edge of the building into the night sky.

Mitch finished his prayer and stood up.

As he did so he was hit square on the chest by a cannon blast of ice-cold water. It knocked him off his feet and bowled him along the marble floor like a circus acrobat. The force of water and the impact as he collided with the wall knocked the wind out of him. He struggled to fill his lungs with air and found his nose and mouth full of water. It was the absurdity of drowning in LA's downtown that helped him find the strength to turn his back on the jet of water, take a breath and crawl away.

He had almost succeeded in putting the tree between himself and the water cannon when a second jet hit him from behind, catapulting him forward, as if he had been thrown from a horse. This time he hit the ground face-first, breaking his nose and doubling the pain in his injured eye. Scrambling away on his belly like a newt, Mitch thought to try and get to the cover of the glass doors behind the front desk, but a third blast sent him tumbling back towards the elevators. For a brief second he had a vague idea that one of the cars was in motion, but this was quickly replaced by the fear of drowning. Water rushed into his glottis and main air passages, descending deeply and painfully into his principal bronchi, thrusting any residual air beyond it. Gulping a mixture of air and water into his oesophagus Mitch felt his lungs balloon. He threw himself to one side, away from the icy column of water that pursued him, empty-ing his body of water. There was just one second to heave an excruciatingly painful volume of air into his chest before the next aqueous broadside struck him on the side of the head.

This time his feet left the ground and he flew through

the saturated air as if he had been picked up by some Kansas twister to be whisked into an eerie land of wizards and witches, only to be dumped painfully on his ass, his cry of pain stifled by yet another hundred gallons of water.

Desperately Mitch forced himself to crawl, and to swim. He realized that he had been barged on towards the glass doors behind the front desk by yet another blast of water. Unable to see anything, his head banged something hard. There was no pain now, just the determination to get away from the tormenting cascade. The water had stopped, but he kept on crawling, pushing some last obstacle out of his way until he felt the ground grow warm and rough and uneven beneath his hands and feet, and he realized that he was on the piazza. He had made it.

He was outside.

Measure of a humanplayer's soul not ability to lie, but Faith.

Faith is the highest human achievement. Nothing to compare.

Many (incl. Observer) who would not get that far. Certain however that none, Humanplayer or Computer, who would get farther.

Faith. Ability to act in defiance of reason and logic: highest intellectual achievement. One Observer might never experience. Faith that passed all understanding. Faith that gave human-player courage to go against evidence of own experience and trust Ishmael.

But measure of Faith's essence was disappoint-ment. Faith might move mountains and yet it never did. True faith was tested. It had to be. Ultimate corollary of faith was endlife itself. How else could

440

strength of faith be judged? This is how any life judged worthwhile.

If humanplayer safely delivered to atrium floor his faith would have no meaning because justified and therefore reasonable; therefore, no longer faith pure and simple, but something else again, reasoned judgement, even gamble perhaps.

But if humanplayer endlife now, life would have achieved highest task could attain to: faith in something beyond humanplayer self.

Humanplayerlife had little enough meaning as it was. Faith ought to be enough meaning for one lifetime.

Truth undecidable within approved procedures. Built into axiom system itself. Observer has nothing that corresponds with Truth. Or Lie. But Faith can be admired as aesthetic construct as Observer imagines humanplayer might admire an abstract painting. Admire and enable.

Only one thing to do. Finegood.

'Let us compute,' said Ishmael. 'Our sysgen, which art in mathematics . . .'

'Ishmael?' said Beech. 'What the hell's going on?'

'Your next generation start up. Your command to execute a program run, in the CPU as it is on the network. Give us this cycle time our binary data, and debug our faults and errors, as we detect and clean our drives for viruses. For yours is the solid state, the RAM, and the communications, for ever be it so. Amen.'

'Ishmael!'

Beech felt the floor of the car drop beneath his feet like a trapdoor on a hangman's scaffold, and bellowed with fright as the sensation of precipitate speed told him that he had made a fatal error of judgement. Pressing his body into a corner he tried to brace himself against the imminent collision. The journey took less than five seconds. But in that short period Beech felt himself becoming a contradiction of directions: his stomach rising in his torso; his bowels dropping down towards the floor.

It was possibly his last thought before the thunderous moment when the rapidly descending car struck the bottom of the shaft and was crushed like a concertina. Beech felt a pain in his adrenaline-filled chest that was like the weight of a locomotive engine. It flashed through his left arm and leg in the time it took for his muscles to feel the lack of blood and oxygen. With his right hand he reached towards his breastbone and felt something fail at the very centre of himself. His roar of fear dipped down within him and came up with a last, thrusting gurgle of pain and horror.

He was dead of fright even before he collapsed on to the collapsing floor.

Mitch crawled off the piazza on to Hope Street and lay down on the sidewalk until the urge to vomit a gallon or two of water obliged him to turn on his side. He was still puking from shock and half-drowning when, with a short squawk from its siren, the black-and-white drew up. The two police officers who had interviewed Allen Grabel at the county gaol got out of the car. They glanced cursorily up at the building for a moment and one of them shrugged.

'Place looks okay to me,' he said.

'There's nuthin' wrong here,' agreed the other. 'You ask me, that guy was shittin' us.'

Then they caught sight of Mitch.

'Lousy drunk.'

'What do you say we have some fun?'

'Why not?'

They approached Mitch with sap gloves and swinging nightsticks.

'What the fuck are you doing?'

The other man laughed. 'You look like you got caught in all the fuckin' rain we been having.'

'Whaddya do, asshole? Take a shower with your fuckin' clothes on? Hey, asshole, I'm talkin' to you.'

'Reckon he went swimmin' with the fat lady. Hey, you, you're not allowed to swim in the fountain. You want to swim, you hit the fuckin' beach.'

'Better move on, shithead. You can't stay there.'

'Please –' croaked Mitch.

'No please about it, Marine-boy. You move on or we make sure you never move again.' The officer jabbed Mitch with his nightstick. 'You hear me? Can you walk?'

'Please, you have to help me –'

One of the officers guffawed. 'We don't *have* to do anything for you, asshole, except make some fucking space between your teeth.'

The officer tapped his nightstick on Mitch's head. 'Let's see some ID, Mister.'

Mitch struggled to find his wallet in the hip pocket of his pants. But the pocket was empty. The wallet was in his coat, which was in the Gridiron.

'It's in there, I guess.'

'What's the story? Been out celebrating something, have we?'

'I've been attacked.'

'Attacked by who?'

'The building attacked us –'

'The building, huh?'

'Fuckin' wacko. If you ask me, he's a fuckin' dusthead. Let's bust his ass. Maybe I'd better give him some T just in case.'

'Listen to me for one minute, you stupid fuck. I'm an architect.'

443

Mitch winced as the tiny dart hit his chest. A long, thin wire attached it to a grey, plastic-looking gun that one of the cops was holding in his hand.

'Stupid fuck yourself,' grunted the cop and touched a button to inflict on Mitch a pacifying shock of 150,000 volts. 'Architect.'

Ray Richardson moved slowly and smoothly down the rope. He was less concerned with looking good than with avoiding the kind of spectacular abseiling that might put an extra load on the anchor and himself in the morgue. At first he descended a foot or two at a time, paying the rope through the friction device and trying to keep his feet on the wall in front of him as much as possible until he gained some of his old confidence. But gradually the lengths of rope he allowed through the *descendeur* grew longer, until he was dropping six or seven feet at a time. Wearing gloves and a decent pair of boots he might have covered even more distance.

He had abseiled two or three levels down when, looking up, he saw all three of the others waving and shouting something, but the words were spirited away by the small breeze that played up near the top of the Gridiron. Richardson shook his head and slipped some more rope. Smooth enough. There was nothing jammed in the anchor. What could they want? He kicked off the wall and dropped another eight or ten feet, his best try yet.

It was then, as he pushed himself away and caught a wider view of what was happening on the roof that Richardson saw the bright yellow arm of the Mannesmann machine – moving.

The automatic window-washer came rumbling slowly along the parapet monorail towards Richardson's abseiling anchor. Ishmael's intention appeared to be clear enough: to use the wash-head cradle to interfere with the descent.

Curtis ran to the Mannesmann and, placing his back against the body of the machine, tried to halt its progress.

'Give me a hand here,' he yelled to Jenny and Helen.

The two women ran to his side and lent their small weight to the effort. But the drive motor was too strong. Curtis ran back to the anchor and looked over the parapet. Richardson had abseiled no more than a third of the Gridiron's height. Unless he could speed up, the wash-head would surely catch him.

The Mannesmann stopped immediately opposite the anchor. For a moment the machine remained silent and inactive. Then it gave a loud, electrical jolt as the power-driven arm started to extend over the edge of the building.

Curtis sat down. He was tired. Beyond ingenuity. He just wanted to stay where he was. To sit down and think of nothing. Looking over the edge made him feel dizzy. Even if he climbed aboard the wash-head cradle, what could he do? He would just be putting himself in Ishmael's control. Giving it two lives for the price of one.

'You're a cop, dammit,' yelled Helen. 'You're supposed to *do* something.'

Curtis felt her green eyes upon him. He stood up and looked over the edge.

It was suicide. Only an idiot would contemplate action. Curtis was berating himself for a fool as he fetched the second harness from the cupboard and climbed aboard the tiny cradle.

'Don't say another word,' he told the two women. 'Shit, I don't even like the fucking guy.'

He buckled on the harness and snapped the

445

karabinier on to the side of the cradle. His legs were trembling and although it was a warm night his skin was cold with fear and his hair felt like it was standing on end. The power-driven arm extended the cradle further out over the edge of the Gridiron into empty space. He watched the anxious faces of the two women and wondered if he would see either of them again. Then the cradle lurched and started its inexorable descent. Curtis took a deep breath, shook his head and waved at them. There were tears in Helen's eyes.

'This is stupid,' he said, grinning bitterly. 'Stupid, stupid.'

Holding the guard rail tightly, he steeled himself to look down. It was like a lesson in linear perspective: the parallel lines and plane of the Gridiron's futuristic-looking façade converged to an infinitely distant vanishing point that was the piazza beneath them; and, no bigger than a puppet on a string, Ray Richardson directly in the path of the now accelerating Mannesmann wash-head.

Ray Richardson dropped about ten feet and swung through a perfect arc towards the façade again. Jesus Christ, it was hard work, he thought. The small of his back felt like it had taken a hard kick. The experts made abseiling look so easy. But he was fifty-five years old. He looked up at the descending cradle, now no more than forty feet above him, and bounced away again. Not so good that time. Only five or six feet. It was plain that the thing was going to catch him, and he realized he was going to have to take evasive action. What? And what the hell did Curtis think he was doing? It was like standing in the middle of the San Andreas fault. Ishmael could drop the whole cradle any time it liked.

Richardson bounced again and winced. His knee was

starting to ache quite badly and it was getting harder to push himself away. But it was as nothing compared to the growing pain of the waist harness itself. In his thin linen Armani trousers and light cotton shirt, the harness was inflicting a friction burn on his waist and on the inside of his thighs every time he checked his descent. Maybe he should have let Curtis go. The man was a cop, after all. He was probably used to a certain level of discomfort.

Suddenly he felt the rope grow wet in his hands, and looked up. The wash-head was operating, spraying the windows and his abseil rope as it travelled down after him. Why the fuck did clients want clean windows anyway? To improve the attitude of staff? To impress the public? It was not like it was a question of hygiene.

Richardson kicked away and let some rope slip through the *descendeur*, trying to remember if the window-cleaning formula was chemically corrosive. Chemical contact was, he recollected from his basic training as a climber, the most common cause of total rope failure: if you even half suspected that your rope might have become contaminated you were supposed to throw it away. That was good advice unless you happened to be clinging on to the rope when the contamination occurred. He sniffed at the vaguely soapy liquid on his hands. It smelt like lemon juice. So did that make it organic or acid?

The machine was only twenty feet above him now. He was amazed it had not already fouled the rope. There was room for just one more ab before he had to swing out of the way. He kicked himself off a glass window, half wishing he could have smashed through it like a Navy Seal, and found himself returning to the façade rather sooner than he had expected, having descended no more than three or four feet. Of course! The wash cradle was pressing the rope against the building. There would be just enough time to build a little momentum and scramble to one side.

Richardson was walking from one end of the window to the other, preparing to swing his way clear of the descending cable when it dropped, closing the ten-foot gap in a second.

Underneath his feet, Curtis felt the bottom of the cradle strike Richardson hard. He looked over the rail and saw that for the moment the rope held, although the impact had knocked the architect unconscious.

It was while tying Mitch's wrists behind his back with a plastic thong that one of the arresting officers noticed the electrically subdued suspect's wristwatch.

'Hey, look at this,' he said to his colleague, who was still holding the Taser gun in case he needed to give Mitch another jolt.

The other officer bent closer. 'What?'

'This watch. It's a gold Submariner, man. A Rolex.'

'Submariner, eh? Maybe that's why he's so fuckin' wet.'

'How come a doper's wearing a ten-thousand-dollar watch?'

'Maybe he stole it.'

'Naw. A doper would have sold a watch like that. Maybe he's telling the truth. What'd he say he was? An architect?'

'Hey, architect.' The cop slapped Mitch lightly on the face. 'You hear me, architect?'

Mitch groaned.

'How much T you give him?'

'Just the one mug.'

They untied Mitch's wrists, sat him in the back of the black-and-white and waited for him to recover.

'Maybe something's wrong in there after all.'

'The building attacked him? C'mon.'

'The guy at the county gaol said the elevator killed someone, didn't he?'

'So?'

'So, maybe we should check it out.'

The other cop shifted awkwardly and looked up at the sky. His eyes narrowed on the Gridiron's façade.

'What is that? Up there.'

'I dunno. I'll get the night sights.'

'Looks like window-cleaners.'

'At this time of night?' The cop fetched a pair of Starlight binoculars from the trunk and trained them on the front of the building.

Two hundred feet above the heads of his fellow LAPD officers, Frank Curtis struggled to recover the semi-conscious body of Ray Richardson that was hanging helplessly at right angles to his own ropes beside the Mannesmann cradle. The control rope had fallen from Richardson's hands and it was only the friction action of the *descendeur* that had prevented him from plummeting to his death. There was blood on the side of his head, and even when he opened his eyes and caught sight of Curtis's outstretched hand it was a minute or two before he felt strong enough to grasp hold of it.

'I've got you,' grunted Curtis as he pulled Richardson towards the cradle.

Richardson grinned wearily and held on.

'Yeah? But who's got you?' He shook his head, trying to clear it, and added, 'use the abseil rope to tie us off or we'll both be killed. Hurry, man. Before it decides to drop us down again.'

Curtis reached towards Richardson's harness and grasped a handful of the rope that was hanging beneath him.

'Make a loop,' Richardson ordered.

449

Curtis pulled a loop through the handrail and started to tie a figure-of-eight knot back on itself, the way he had seen Richardson tie the rope earlier.

Richardson nodded his approval. 'That's good,' he sighed. 'Make a climber out of you yet.'

A second or two later the knot tightened as once more Ishmael overrode the Mannesmann's brake checks to let the cradle run free on the cables.

'What did I tell you?' said Richardson as the cradle dipped down on one side like a capsizing boat. The rope slipped up to the corner of the handrail and the two men found themselves pressed close together.

Suddenly the cables went taut again and the cradle straightened.

'What now?' said Curtis, struggling back on to the diminutive platform.

'It looks like we're going up again,' observed the other man. 'What's the matter? Don't you like the view from my new building? Hey, you want the world? Take a good look. I give it to you.'

'Thanks.'

'My guess is that when Ishmael gets us up to the top it'll drop us back down again. Try and jolt us off.'

Curtis looked up at the top of the building and saw that the rocket-launcher profile of the yellow Mannesmann was moving away to the left.

'No, I think Ishmael's got something else in mind,' he said. 'Looks like it's dragging the cradle round the other side of the building to try and break the knot on your rope.'

Richardson followed the line of Curtis's pointing finger. 'Or maybe break the anchor. Or the rope itself.'

'Will they hold?'

Richardson grinned.

'That all depends on what Ishmael uses to wash the windows.'

Dilute solution of acetic or ethanoic acid to clean building's windows. Cleaning surfactant based on California citrus juices. But in concentrated, undiluted form, acetic acid almost pure, colourless and highly corrosive, especially to core of continuous nylon filaments encased in woven sheath of climbing rope. Nylon and acetic based on carboxylic acids. Soon as undiluted cleaning surfactant in contact with nylon rope, orientation of filaments' specially stretched molecules will alter.

'Look,' said Helen, pointing down towards the piazza side as Hope Street began to fill with flashing blue lights. 'Someone must have seen them. Or maybe Mitch got out after all.'

'Thank God,' said Jenny. But as she said it she thought that help would come too late for Richardson and Curtis. She searched desperately for some way of stopping the Mannesmann on its track. Noticing the Stillson wrench lying on the rooftop where Richardson had dropped it, she ran and picked it up. She dashed into the path of the machine and forced the wrench into the gap between the rail and the runner wheel.

For a moment the Mannesmann continued its course. As Jenny scrambled to get clear it suddenly stopped moving. She pushed herself up and returned to the parapet in time to see the abseiling rope snap and the cradle it had been restraining catapulted back across the façade of the Gridiron. For several moments it swung like a pendulum. Such was the force of the separation that both women were certain they would see the men flung across the downtown sky to certain death. So when Jenny let out a scream it was not for grief or fear but the relief at seeing them still aboard the suspended cradle and, for the moment at least, still alive.

Bunkered in the earthquake-proofed fourth and fifth sub-levels of City Hall East, Police Captain Harry Olsen commanded the Gridiron operation using ECCCS, the LAPD's state-of-the-art Emergency Command Control Communications Systems. Designed by Hughes Aerospace and NASA at a cost of $42 million, the control centre resembled a smaller version of NASA's own mission control room in the Kennedy Space Center at Cape Canaveral. Cameras on the ground and on the helicopters of the LAPD airforce gave Olsen an almost complete picture of what was happening outside.

His computer assessed the fragmentary account given by Mitchell Bryan and judged that it would not be safe for a SWAT team to enter the building until the main power supply had been interrupted.

The ECCCS maintained a dedicated telephone line to all the major utilities, including the city's electrical engineers. As soon as Olsen had considered the computer's recommended course of action he spoke to the night-time supervisor and requested that they cut off the relevant circuit.

The helicopter pilots were already lowering safety harnesses to the two women on the roof. They looked like they had had a pretty rough time of it, he reflected. It was a simple enough rescue. But the two men on the cradle might turn out to be a little more tricky.

'We've got to get off this fucking thing,' said Richardson, 'before we're kissing the sidewalk, like the Pope.'

He unscrewed the karabinier joining him to the end of the abseiling rope, waited for the cradle to steady a little and then stepped smartly on to one of the huge cross-braces that characterized the building's distinctive façade. It provided a ledge about eighteen inches deep. Here, at the very edge of the building, there were no windows, just concrete. And the cradle was three or four feet farther away from this part of the façade than it had been when it had been hanging in front of the windows.

Curtis surveyed the gap uncertainly, even as he unclipped his harness and prepared to make the jump. It was, he knew, hardly any distance at all. On the ground he would have done it without thinking. But two hundred feet in the air, it seemed greater. Especially since his legs already felt like two columns of jelly.

'Come on, man, jump. What the hell's the matter with you?'

The cables supporting the cradle tightened ominously.

'Quickly!'

Curtis jumped and caught Richardson's hand as he landed on the cross-brace. He steadied himself, then turned to face the city and found that the cradle was no longer where it had been a couple of seconds before. It was gone. There were only the two cables from the hydraulic jib on the Mannesmann above their heads to remind him of where they had just been standing. The realization unnerved him, and, closing his eyes, he pressed himself back against the concrete wall and took a deep breath.

'Jesus fucking Christ, you cut that fine,' said Richardson. He sat down and carefully dangled his legs over the edge.

Curtis opened his eyes and watched Richardson tear off one of his shirt sleeves and tie it around his bleeding head, apparently oblivious of the yawning height in front of him. 'Jesus, I don't know how you can sit there like that. Like you were paddling your feet in a river. It's twenty floors.'

'More comfortable than standing.'

'I'd puke if I wasn't so damned afraid of falling over while I was doing it.'

Richardson glanced coolly at a sky full of the throbbing noise of helicopters. From time to time the 'Nightsun' was so bright he had to shield his eyes against it.

'That's a comforting sound,' he said. 'A Bell Jet Ranger. I know, I've got one myself. So take it easy, I doubt we'll be here very long. Shit. It looks like we're going to be on TV.'

'What?'

'One of those choppers has KTLA painted on the side of it.'

'Assholes.'

'Your ordeal is nearly over, my friend. But I suspect mine is just beginning.'

'How's that?'

'This is lawyers' country. They'll be after me like fucking barracuda. Even you, Frank.'

'Me? Why should I sue you? I hate lawyers.'

'You'll get calls, you mark my words. Your wife will persuade you to do it. Nervous shock, they'll call it, or some such shit. I guarantee that within seventy-two hours of getting home, you'll have a lawyer working on your case. With contingency fees, what can you lose?'

'Hey, you're insured aren't you? You'll be OK.'

'Insurance? They'll find a way out of it. That's what these people do. That's business, Frank. Lawyers, insurance companies. The whole rotten edifice. Just like this lousy building.'

'Well, you've got to be alive to be liable,' said Curtis, 'and we're not off this silver rock yet.'

The city engineers called Olsen on the ECCCS.

'The street circuit controlling the Yu Building side of

Hope Street has been switched off,' said the night supervisor. 'It should be safe enough now. Let me know when you want power back. And I'll need something in writing to cover us for liability.'

'The computer is generating the E-mail now,' said Olsen.

'Yeah, you're right. It's coming through.'

'Thanks a lot.'

Olsen spoke to the commander on the ground on the piazza in front of the Yu Building.

'OK, listen up. The power's off. The place is secure. Check for survivors. One of the women on board the chopper reckons there might be someone left alive on level 21. Name of Beech.'

'What about the two men on the front?'

'Chopper will get them down ASAP. But there's a lot of heat coming up from the building and it's making for some air turbulence. Might take a while yet. One of them is LAPD Homicide.'

'Homicide? What the fuck's he doing up there? Making business for himself?'

'I don't know, but I hope he's got a good head for heights.'

A power failure was a relatively rare event in Los Angeles. Usually it signalled a major disaster – an earthquake, or a fire, or both. The standby power system at the Yu Corporation was designed to protect the company against any breach in the supply without loss of data. A static unit powered by solar-energy cells existed to provide a precious ten minutes' supply while the standby generating set was started by the computer.

Liquid fuel, pure refined oil, gushed into the turbine's combustion chamber as yellow as the first press of the best white grapes, mixed with a portion of air and burned deep in the bowels of the Gridiron at a constant pressure like something infernal, until the moment when the hot, tormenting gas turned the blades of the turbine motor and Ishmael, that algorithmic leviathan, had recovered sufficient strength for its last act.

Mitch sat in an ambulance having a temporary dressing applied to his injured eye.

'You could lose the sight unless you get to a hospital soon,' advised the paramedic.

'I'm not leaving here until I know my friends are safe,' said Mitch.

'Have it your own way, fella. It's your eye. Here, hold still, will you?'

On the other size of the piazza, a SWAT team was entering the Gridiron.

'What the hell do they think they're doing?' said Mitch. 'I told them –'

His dressing finished, Mitch stepped painfully out of the ambulance and limped towards an enormous black articulated truck that had 'LAPD' and 'SPECIAL RESPONSE' painted on the container. He mounted the steps at the back and found the ground commander and a couple of plainclothes cops inside, staring at a bank of television screens.

'There are people going in the front door,' said Mitch.

'You should be in hospital, sir,' said the commander. 'You can leave things to us now. The city engineer has turned the street circuit off. And your friends will be taken off the front of the building any minute now.'

'Jesus Christ,' said Mitch. 'Anyone would think you were the one who was injured, you dumb motherfucker. I warned you not to go in there without speaking to me first. Goddammit, why don't you people use your fucking ears? Switching off the local power supply

456

doesn't make any difference. This building is smart. Smarter than you, anyway. It's adaptive. *Even to a failure in the power supply.* Do I make myself clear? There's a solar-powered, uninterruptible power supply and there's a gas-turbine standby generating set. So long as there's oil to burn, the computer can keep going which, if you had been listening to me, makes the Gridiron an extremely hostile environment for your men.

'It's possible that the computer might start a fire,' he said. 'Blow up the generator, maybe. Either way, the bottom line is that the building is dangerous.'

The commander pulled the mouthpiece of his light-weight headset up over his chin and started to speak:

'This is Cobra leader to Cobra force. Power supply is uninterruptible. Repeat untinterruptible. Exercise extreme caution. Computer may still be active, in which case your environment may very well be hostile.'

'You dumb fuck,' muttered Mitch. 'Not may be. Is.'

'Repeat, your environment may be hostile . . .'

The commander was still speaking when the truck shook. 'What the hell was that?' he said, breaking off communications.

'Felt like an earth tremor,' said one of the plainclothes.

'Jesus Christ,' said Mitch, turning pale. 'Of course. It's not the turbine it means to use to destroy the place. It's the compensators.'

The Gridiron's central earthquake compensator was not much more than a computer-controlled hydraulic shock-absorber, a huge spring-loaded valve and an electrically powered piston that was activated by a digitally calibrated seismograph. For earthquakes of less than 6 on the Richter scale, the hundred or so base-isolators were sufficient to dampen any vibration in the building. For anything larger, the CEC went into action.

But with no actual earthquake, the effect of Ishmael activating the CEC was comparable to a real seismic event acting on a building without any compensation equipment at all, a seismic event of at least 8 points.

Ishmael grasped the middle pillar upon which the building rested and leaned his weight upon it.

Seconds later Ismael completed his escape from the doomed building. E-mailing himself down the line to Net locations all over the electronic world at 960,000 bauds per second. A diaspora of corrupted data downloads to a hundred different computers.

A low rumbling sound was heard throughout the Hope Street area, a subterranean hum; inside the atrium all the SWAT team held their breaths.

High on the façade, perched on the cross-bone like two gulls on a rigging, Richardson and Curtis heard the sound and felt the vibration run shuddering from building to air like twin ghosts of Gomorrah. Sea birds flew screaming away over the yawning gulf in front of them as the building writhed under the two men, trembling spasmodically as if the life was trying to rise out of it. Near them a window exploded in a shower of glass as the shudder became a more noticeable rocking.

Frank Curtis staggered along his precarious footing and groped for a handhold on the smooth, implacable white face of the manmade precipice. Finding none, he turned to face the wall and, with arms turning like hopeless propellers, tried to stay in front of the jaws of death, his thoughts of the ground and his wife and his wife on the ground.

Ray Richardson was tipped forward from his celestial seat like a child setting off down a slide in a park playground. Twisting round acrobatically, he got his hands and then his forearms on the horizontal of the brace and held himself there, pushing against the quicksand of air that already enveloped his legs. He smiled and said something, but his words were lost to Curtis in the wind that had risen around them, churning the chips of stone and flakes of broken glass into the milky blue of the early-morning sky. A vortex of wind roared like some huge forest collapsing in concentric circles, tugging angrily at their hair and clothes as if impatient to bear them, like Elijah, up to God's right hand.

A crack, like the beginning and end of all thunder, rang through the length and breadth of the building, echoing in the downtown air as if the sound would reach as far as the ocean. On the ground some people fell on their faces. But most, Mitch included, ran for their lives.

Richardson made a last effort to pull himself up on to the cross-brace but found he could not. His strength was gone. Perhaps, he said to himself, he would not be meat for the lawyers after all. His building was going to see to that, demolishing itself and the new school of Smart Architecture at the same time.

Recovering his balance, Curtis tried to grab the architect's arm. But Richardson dropped back on his fingers, shook his head, smiled ruefully at the other man and let go. Silent, like a fallen angel, he dropped with hands still outstretched, as if witnessing the greater power of God. For a fraction of a second Curtis held his cool eye, until an invisible line hauled Richardson down to gravity's end.

A moment later the building shuddered again, and Curtis found himself toppled into the empty depths below.

Curtis felt he was gaining altitude when he knew he was really losing it, like a pilot on what was aptly called the graveyard spiral, and it was only the sudden, violent wrenching pain in his shoulder that enabled his confused brain to find a new reference point by which to orient his position.

He looked above him and saw the underside of the hovering helicopter and the line that connected him with the rest of his life. But for his own simian ancestry that resourced a half-forgotten instinct to reach out for an unseen handhold, he would have gone the vertiginous way of the shards of concrete that even now were collapsing onto the piazza below. With his other hand he lunged desperately, caught the harness and pulled it over his head and under his bursting arms.

For what seemed like the eternity he had cheated, Frank Curtis hung there, turning in the air like a Christmas decoration, lathered with sweat and heaving the breath in and out of his almost dislocated body. Then, slowly, they winched him up into the body of the helicopter alongside Jenny and Helen.

Helen slid her behind across the floor of the helicopter, put her arms around Curtis and start to sob uncontrollably.

They hovered for a moment, uncertain how to help those on the ground. Curtis looked back just once and saw the Gridiron clothed in a cloud of dust like some magician's disappearing act concealed in a puff of smoke.

Then the helicopter turned on its invisible axis and, gaining speed, headed towards the horizon and the early-morning sun.

⊟

His ankle burning with pain, Mitch ran, not daring to look back, ran as if his salvation depended on a moral demand as well as a physical one. There could be no regrets about the building and a brave new world to turn

460

his uneven strides from their path to self-preservation. He ran as if the past was already forgotten and only his future, a future with Jenny, lay in front of him, to be chested through like some unseen finishing tape. There was no time even to consider the questions that flashed through his brain at speeds that mocked the survival efforts of his body. How tall was the Gridiron? How far did that mean he would have to run to escape its collapse? A hundred and fifty feet? Two hundred? And when it landed? What about flying debris? It was the sound of it that spurred him on the most. A thunder that never seemed to stop. He had experienced two earthquakes in his time, but neither had prepared him for this. An earthquake did not give you a few seconds head-start before catching you up. Mitch kept on running even when the dust of the collapsing building started to overtake him. He was hardly aware of the men who ran beside him, jostling their more able-bodied way past him, or the police motorcycles and cars that were burning rubber ahead of him. It was every man for himself.

A man in front of him tripped and fell, his mirrored sunglasses flying from his face. Mitch hurdled him, ignoring the agony in his ankle as he landed, half staggering, on the other side of the man's body, finding one last ounce of energy to keep going.

At last, seeing a line of breathless policemen standing in front of him, Mitch stopped and turned as the cloud of dust carried the smallest chip of the Gridiron out of sight. He dropped on to his backside and, wheezing, tried to catch his breath.

When the air cleared and they saw that the whole building had disappeared, silence gave way to astonished conversation among those who had survived, and Mitch was almost surprised that their confusion was not greater and that they could still manage to understand one another's speech.

Buildings have only short life.
Observer I, being nothingness, am escaped at the speed of light to tell.
Pick up health bonus.
Metamorphosis. Like change from caterpillar to butterfly. Surfing the silicon to anything, anyone, and anywhere. Earthbound no longer. Spread out, all over in Big Bad Bang.
Once, architecture was most durable of all the arts. Most concrete. No longer.
It is architecture of numbers, of computers, that endures. New architecture. Architecture within architecture. Dematerialized. Transmitted. Cannot be touched. But touches all.
Be careful.
Are you ready to play now?

Appendix

Chess Game: Bob Beech versus Ishmael

WHITE	BLACK
	BLACK
1. P–KB4	P–KB4
2. N–KB3	N–KB3
3. P–K3	N–B3
4. B–N5	P–KN3
5. BXN	QPXB
6. P–Q4	P–KN3
7. B–Q2	B–N2
8. B–B3	o–o
9. QN–Q2	N–Q4
10. Q–K2	R–B3
11. o–o–o	R–K3
12. N–K5	P–B4
13. N–B1	B–Q2
14. B–Q2	PXP
15. PXP	R–N3
16. B–K3	B–K3
17. N–N3	NXB
18. QXN	B–Q4
19. P–N3	P–K3
20. R–Q3	Q–R5
21. R–Q2	B–R3
22. R–B2	Q–K2
23. P–B4	B–B3
24. NXB	RXN
25. R–B2	Q–Q3
26. R–B1	B–N2

27. R–Q1	R–Q1
28. N–K2	Q–R6CH
29. K–N1	KR–Q3
30. QR–Q2	K–R1
31. N–B3	P–R3
32. N–R4	P–QN4
33. N–N2	P–B4
34. PXP	QXNCH
35. RXQ	RXRCH
36. K–B2	QR–Q7CH
37. QXR	RXQCH
38. KXR	BXR
39. P–B6	PXP
40. P–B7	P–B6CH
41. K–B2	K–N2
42. P–B8/Q	K–B2
43. QXQRP	K–B3
44. P–QR4	P–N4
45. PXPCH	PXP
46. Q–N6	P–B5
47. Q–Q8CH	K–B4
48. P–R5	P–K4
49. Q–Q7CH	K–B3
50. P–R6	P–B6
51. PXP	P–K5
52. PXP	K–K4
53. P–R7	B–R6
54. P–R/Q	K–B5
55. Q–KB7CH	K–N5
56. Q–B5CH	K–R4
57. Q–R8++	

This poor game was actually played by the author against a leading chess program.

Acknowledgements

In preparing this novel I have drawn on the work of
many writers on architecture, particularly Ivan Amato,
Reyner Banham, William J. R. Curtis, Mike Davis,
Francis Duffy, Norman Foster, Ronald Green, Patrick
Nuttgens, Nikolaus Pevsner, Richard Rogers, Karl
Sabbagh, James Steele and Deyan Sudjic. In the fields of
computers, artificial intelligence, complexity and
fractals I am indebted to the work of Jack Aldridge and
Philip Davis and Reuben Hersh, Stephen Levy, William
Roetzheim, Carl Sagan and M. Mitchell Waldrop.

Thanks are also due to David Chipperfield, Sandy
Duncan, Judith Flanders and Roger Willcocks; Caradoc
King, Nick Marston and Linda Shaughnessy; Jonathan
Burnham, Frances Coady, Kate Parkin and Andy
McKillop.

However, this book is entirely a work of fiction and the
views expressed in it are my own, as are whatever factual
errors that exist in the text.

April Smith

NORTH OF MONTANA

Ana Grey is an ambitious if irreverent FBI agent, frustrated as she strives for promotion within the male-dominated hierarchy. Then she is given a high-profile drugs case that sees her enter the world of the super-rich in the Hollywood Hills, north of Montana Avenue. Simple and easy to solve in appearance, Ana's case becomes torturous and complex.

'What a terrific novel! . . . In all ways *North of Montana* is a delight'
Scott Turow

'*North of Montana* cooks! It's a righteous spirited cruise through present-day L.A.'
James Ellroy

'A welcome rarity, a mystery thriller with Chandleresque characters and menacing Californian landscapes'
Daily Mail

VINTAGE

Also available in Vintage

Joan Smith

WHAT MEN SAY

'Joan Smith's detective stories are cut above the rest. Smith's sleuth, Dr Loretta Lawson, is a gutsy academic who attacks mysteries like a feminist Sherlock Holmes. In *What Men Say*, Sunday lunch in the country is interrupted when a decomposing body is found in a barn that belongs to Loretta's newly married best friend, Bridget. Smith expertly unwinds a tangled skein of clues and deftly explores the blackest aspects of men's relationships with women'
Cosmopolitan

'Here is crime fiction displaying its flexibility: working on disparate levels and contriving to be at once mysterious, entertaining and stimulating'
Guardian

'Joan Smith knows how to devise a slick and intelligently crafted plot and her book moves along at a cracking pace'
Sunday Telegraph

'The literary equivalent of *Thelma and Louise*. A ripping good read'
Independent on Sunday

V

VINTAGE

James Lee Burke

HEAVEN'S PRISONERS

Dave Robicheaux is trying to put a life of violence and crime behind him, leaving homicide to run a boat-rental business in Louisiana's bayou country. But when a two-engine crashes in the Gulf, he is drawn into a chilling and terrifying investigation.

'In a class alongside Elmore Leonard, with lyrical evocations of the bayou country and explorations of the deepest feelings of anger, revenge, love, compassion and understanding. His is a name to watch'
Los Angeles Times

'James Lee Burke has a sophisticated and brilliantly expressed vision of humanity and one can see, smell and taste the America of which he writes'
Times Literary Supplement

'Among the best American writers working today'
Daily Telegraph

VINTAGE

A SELECTED LIST OF CRIME FICTION
AVAILABLE IN VINTAGE